{42}

*selected
fiction, poetry
and drama*

RABINDRANATH
TAGORE
FOR THE 21ST CENTURY READER

Preface by Satyajit Ray

Translated by Arunava Sinha

ALEPH BOOK COMPANY
An independent publishing firm
promoted by *Rupa Publications India*

Published in 2014 by
Aleph Book Company
7/16 Ansari Road, Daryaganj
New Delhi 110 002

This translation copyright © Arunava Sinha 2014
Preface copyright © The Estate of Satyajit Ray 1961

Bengali handwriting courtesy Maitreyi Shome

All rights reserved

No part of this publication may be
reproduced, transmitted, or stored in a
retrieval system, in any
form or by any means, without
permission in writing from Aleph
Book Company.

ISBN: 978-93-82277-27-9

5 7 9 10 8 6 4

Printed in India

This book is sold subject to the condition that it shall not,
by way of trade or otherwise, be lent, resold, hired out, or
otherwise circulated without the publisher's prior consent
in any form of binding or cover other than that in which it
is published and without a similar condition including this
condition being imposed on the subsequent purchaser.

RABINDRANATH
TAGORE
FOR THE 21ST CENTURY READER

Translator's Dedication

To the memory of my mother-in-law
Roma Chakraborty

Contents

Preface by Satyajit Ray	ix
Translator's Note	xxi
THE HOME AND THE WORLD (A *Novel*)	3
POEMS	183
Camellia	185
An Ordinary Girl	190
An Unexpected Meeting	195
Deprived	197
The Other Side	200
Writing a Letter	202
THE MONK-KING (A *Novella*)	207
STORIES	327
Just One Night	329
The Gift of Vision	336
Misplaced Hope	356
Dead or Alive	370
A Letter from a Wife	382
The Laboratory	396
CHANDALIKA (A *Play*)	441

Preface

On the seventh of August 1941, in the city of Calcutta, a man died. His mortal remains perished, but he left behind him a heritage which no fire could consume. It is a heritage of words and music and poetry, of ideas and of ideals. And it has the power to move us, to inspire us, today and in the days to come.

Founded in the year 1690 by an Englishman named Job Charnock, Calcutta, in 1861, was a thriving metropolis. Queen Victoria was proclaimed Empress of India in 1877. As the capital of India, Calcutta was the seat of the Queen's Government. In the northern part of the sprawling city, in the area known as Jorasanko in Chitpore, was the family residence of the Tagores. The Tagores had an impressive lineage. It dated back to the first group of learned Brahmins that came from Kanauj and settled in Bengal in the eighth century. One thousand years later, Panchanan, a descendant, came to the new city of Calcutta and found a lucrative position with a British shipping company. His grandson Nilmoni added to the family fortune and built the house at Jorasanko. The peak was reached with Nilmoni's grandson. One of the most brilliant and colourful figures of the nineteenth century, Dwarakanath Tagore combined cultured sophistication with a largeness of heart and a rare degree of business acumen. Gold, sugar, indigo, exports, banking, newspapers—there was no end to his enterprises, and he succeeded in all. If his earnings were fabulous, so were his spendings.

Although a Hindu and a Vaishnav, Dwarakanath defied the ban of Brahmin orthodoxy and twice went to England. There he had an audience with Queen Victoria, discussions with Gladstone, and dinner with men like Dickens, Thackeray and Max Mueller.

Shortly before his death in England, Dwarkanath had written to his eldest son in Calcutta, reproving him for neglecting the family's business affairs. For some years past, young Devendranath had been developing tendencies which might well have distressed his father. It began in a burning ghat. The last rites were being administered to Devendranath's grandmother. Not far away on the river bank sat Devendranath. Like many a rich man's son he had been leading a wayward life, but tonight, he was overcome by a strange feeling. Worldly possessions seemed to lose their meaning for him. This led to a period of profound disquiet followed by a ceaseless quest for the meaning of existence in the great sourcebooks of the East and West. He read the materialist philosophers of modern Europe—Locke, Hume, Bentham and others, whose ideas were so much in vogue among the students of the time. Then he learnt Sanskrit and read the Mahabharata. But peace of mind would not come until one day he chanced upon a torn page of a Sanskrit book. There was a sloka in it, which said: 'God is supreme and all pervading. Enjoy by renunciation. Covet not another's wealth.' This was a page of the Ishopanishad, edited by Raja Rammohan Roy. Rammohan had been a close friend of Dwarakanath's. As a boy, Devendranath had a deep and silent admiration for the man. But the greatness of the Raja's vision and the magnitude and nobility of the tasks he had set before himself were beyond the boy's comprehension. Rammohan lived in times when India's spiritual heritage was being submerged in ritual and superstition while in the west a whole new concept of humanity was emerging.

Rammohan advocated western education for Indians, because he wanted the new ideas of the west to spread in the country. He also wanted that we should respect what was old and true in our own heritage. Like the Upanishads, for instance, which revealed to him the monotheistic basis of Hinduism. Rammohan's work was left unfinished by his death in England. But Devendranath, inspired by two lines of Sanskrit text, went on to prove himself to be the Raja's true spiritual son and heir. Devendranath suffered social ostracism for preaching the monotheistic faith that he called Brahmoism. But to his followers—and there were many—he was Maharshi, the great sage. When Rabindranath was born,

Maharshi was forty-five years old; his wife Saradamoni was thirty-three. Rabindranath was the fourteenth child. The eldest was Dwijendranath—poet, philosopher, mathematician. Second son Satyendranath translated the Gita and *Meghdoot* in Bengali verse and became the first Indian Member of the Indian Civil Service. The fifth son Jyotirindranath was a born musician, translated Moliére and Sanskrit drama into Bengali and wrote and staged some of the most popular Bengali plays of his time. Among the daughters was Swarnakumari, the first woman novelist and the first woman to edit a journal in India. Indeed, it was a household which hummed with artistic activity.

For Rabi the time hadn't yet come to participate in the activities of the elders. Going out in the street was forbidden too. And this was indeed a pity, for nothing seemed more fascinating to the boy than the world outside. At the age of seven Rabi was sent to school. Rabi went to four schools and hated them all. But to say that he lacked an education would be wrong. For his third brother Hemendranath saw to his studies at home and it was all done by the clock.

When Rabi was twelve, Devendranath went on a trip to North India and took the boy with him. The last stop on a lone tour was the resthouse on Bakrota, the highest hill in the hill station of Dalhousie in the Punjab. Rabi was told by his father to roam about on his own. He was also taught to rise before the sun. And to handle money and keep accounts. The days often ended with the boy singing devotional songs to his father.

Rabi was thirteen when his first book of verse, *Kabi Kahini*, came out. When Rabi was sixteen, Dwijendranath brought out a literary magazine called *Bharati*, and Rabi found an admirable platform for his literary activities. The essays included pieces on European poets like Dante and Petrarch, whose acquaintance Rabi had made in Ahmedabad in the library of his elder brother Satyendranath. Satyendranath's wife Jnanadanandini, who was staying in England with her two children, was a remarkable woman who had been persuaded by her husband to come out of orthodox seclusion. Rabi set out for England in the summer of 1878 and joined Jnanadanandini in Brighton. If the plan was to provide the boy with a proper education, it came to nought, for

Rabi returned without completing his course of studies at the London University.

While in England Rabindranath had become acquainted with western music. Some of the tunes he had learnt found their way into his enchanting opera *Valmiki Pratibha*. There were other tunes, however, which came from classical Indian ragas used for the first time in an operatic context. *Valmiki Pratibha* was staged in the Tagore residence with Rabindranath in the role of the bandit-turned-poet. The rest of the cast too was composed of members of the Tagore family, all gifted with degrees of talent for acting and music. Among those who saw and praised this performance was the greatest literary figure of the time, Bankimchandra Chatterjee. A year later, when Rabindranath's *Sandhya Sangeet* was published, Bankimchandra personally congratulated the poet and acknowledged his pre-eminence among the rising writers of the day. Of all the members of Rabi's family, two were closest to his mind and heart. They were Jyotirindranath and his wife. Kadambari Debi was two years older than Rabi. She was his friend and severest critic. Rabi lived with these two for a time in a house in Sudder Street in South Calcutta.

One morning a strange experience befell the poet. In his words:

> One day, while I stood watching at early dawn the sun sending out its rays from behind the trees, I suddenly felt as if some ancient mist had in a moment lifted from my sight and the morning light on the face of the world revealed an inner radiance. The poem I wrote on the first day of my surprise was named The Awakening of the Waterfall.

At the age of twenty-two Rabindranath married Bhabatarini Debi. The old-fashioned name later changed to Mrinalini. Two months before the wedding, Rabindranath had received a letter from his father in which he was asked to prepare himself to look after the family estate. After a period of initial training in the estate's offices in Calcutta, Rabindranath found himself in the very heart of rural Bengal in the region around the river Padma. With a worldly wisdom unusual in a poet, but characteristic of the Tagores,

Rabindranath in later life set about in a practical way to improve the lot of poor peasants of his estates, and his varied work in this field is on record. But his own gain from this intimate contact with the fundamental aspects of life and nature and the influence of this contact on his life and work are beyond measure. Living mostly in his boat and watching life through the window, a whole new world of sights and sounds and feelings opened up before him.

It was a world in which the people and moods of nature were inextricably interwoven. People found room in a succession of great short stories, and nature in an outpouring of exquisite songs and poems. Dominant was the mood of the rains—exultant and terrible.

In 1901 Rabindranath was forty years old. His already enormous output of poems and plays had been gathered in one big volume. It comprised twenty-one books and included 'Sonar Tori', his first masterpiece. The same year, 1901, marked an event of a somewhat different nature. In Bolpur in the district of Birbhum in West Bengal, Devendranath had acquired some property in 1862, one year after Rabindranath was born. The property was made over to a board of trustees and the deed specified that the place was to be used for meditation on the supreme formless being. According to Maharshi's wishes, a seat of prayer and a temple of worship had been built. And close to the temple, a residential house, which was called Santiniketan, the abode of peace. Rabindranath had been worrying about the education of his children, and he decided to start an experimental educational institution in Santiniketan. It was to be a school, but not like the schools that had been the nightmare of his own childhood. It was to be like the forest hermitages of classical India. But to bring it into being was not an easy task. For one thing, it cost money. He was obliged to sell, among other things, the copyright of his books. His wife added her bit by selling her wedding ornaments. Two months after the school was opened, she was taken ill. Three months later, at the age of twenty-nine, she died. For Rabindranath it was the beginning of a series of personal tragedies. Nine months after his wife's death, his second daughter Renuka passed away. The hardest blow of all came four years later.

His youngest son Samindra took after his father in many ways. He was only thirteen when he fell victim to cholera. It was in the midst of these bereavements that Rabindranath participated in one of the greatest political upheavals in the history of India. In December 1903 was published the decision of India's Governor-General Lord Curzon to split Bengal into two provinces. The idea was to create a separate province with a Muslim majority, which would induce a rift between the two main religious groups and avert the possible growth of a united front against the government. But in proposing the partition, Curzon merely fanned the flame of patriotism that had been smouldering in the minds of certain visionaries all through the period of the Renaissance in Bengal. These men now came to the fore and led millions to rise in protest.

The series of stirring patriotic songs which Rabindranath composed for the occasion were sung in procession in the streets of Calcutta with the poet himself in the lead. On 16 October 1905, the partition became an accomplished fact. In a form of protest that only a poet could conceive, Rabindranath turned a black day into a mass festival of Rakhibandhan, the tying of the band of friendship. But this swadeshi movement was fated to grow and assume a character which was not possible to foresee in its early stages. While admitting the bravery and patriotism of those who killed or were killed in a reckless bid for freedom, Rabindranath could not condone terrorism. He stated his credo in clear terms: the path of violence was not for India. Good could come only out of constructive work carried out in a spirit of tolerance. He had himself followed up his retirement from the political scene by devoting himself to the work of rural welfare in his estates. And there were other activities too. He was teaching at his school, editing journals and engaging himself in every conceivable form of literary activity. That his own countrymen now regarded him as their leading man of letters was proved by his fiftieth birthday celebration in Calcutta. Sponsored by the Bengal Academy of Letters and attended by thousands, it was a unique occasion and the first time that such an ovation had been given to a literary man in India. But to the outside world, Rabindranath was still an unknown name.

The object of Rabindranath's visit to England in 1912 was to study the educational methods of the West and also to acquaint the West with his own work in Santiniketan. He happened to carry with him on this occasion a notebook containing his own English translations of some of his songs, mainly from *Gitanjali*. He showed these translations to the English painter William Rothenstein, who had met him on an earlier visit to India. Rothenstein was so impressed that he sent a copy of the translation to the well-known Irish poet Yeats. In introducing the poems to a gathering of English writers and intellectuals, Yeats said, 'I know of no man in my time who has done anything in the English language to equal these lyrics. Even as I read them in these literal prose translations, they are exquisite in style and thought.' *Gitanjali* was published in England in the same year. There has rarely been another instance of a poet gaining world fame in like manner. The Nobel Prize came in 1913 and the knighthood in 1915, while war was raging in Europe.

Touring the United States and Japan in 1916, Rabindranath made eloquent appeals for peace through intellectual co-operation between nations. He said, 'The call has come to every individual in the present age to prepare himself and his surroundings for the dawn of a new era, when man shall discover his soul, the spiritual unity of all human beings.' Pursuing this noble idea of international co-operation, Rabindranath gave the school at Santiniketan a new status and a new name: yatra visvam bhavaty eka-nidam, (where the world becomes a single nest). This was the motto of Visva-Bharati. It was inaugurated on 24 December 1918, with philosopher Brajendranath Seal presiding. Rabindranath made over the entire Nobel Prize money towards the building of this university.

While peace had been restored in Europe, in India there was unrest. The Rowlatt Bill, designed to suppress all political movements, dashed India's hopes of gaining self-government, which the British rulers had kept promising through the war years. Dominating the Indian political scene at this time was Mohandas Karamchand Gandhi, who as a barrister in South Africa, had fought for the rights of the Indians living in that country. As a protest against the Rowlatt Act, Gandhi launched a movement of passive resistance, but the masses misinterpreted the movement. And, following a rumour of Gandhi's arrest, violence broke out in many parts of the country. As a result of this, the government started taking repressive measures out of all proportions to the magnitude of the violence. In the Punjab, martial law was declared. In charge of the troops at Amritsar was Brigadier-General Dyer. On the first day of the month of Baisakh, a crowd gathered in Jallianwala Bagh as it had done every other year. It was a peaceful crowd, but Dyer was taking no chances.

News of the Amritsar incident was suppressed by the government, but details filtered through to other parts of the country and even to 'the abode of peace'.

Rabindranath rushed to Calcutta. But the Defence of India Act was still in force and no leaders would support him in a plea for a meeting of protest. At four o'clock on the morning of 30 May, Rabindranath finished writing a letter. It was addressed to the Viceroy. Condemning the government for the killing in the Punjab, Rabindranath ended by saying, '... and I for my part, wish to stand shorn of all special distinctions, by the side of my countrymen who, for their so called insignificance are liable to suffer degradation not fit for human beings. And these are the reasons which have painfully compelled me to ask Your Excellency to relieve me of my knighthood ...'

The next ten years of Rabindranath's life were filled with ceaseless activity. The urge to travel and the necessity to collect funds for his university took him to all parts of the weld. And the West as much as the East welcomed him with open arms.

Wherever he went, he spread the message of peace and stressed the importance of intellectual cooperation between nations. He said, 'We ought to know that isolation of life and culture is not a thing of which a nation can be proud. In the human world giving is exchanging, it is not one-sided.' He also said, 'I do not put my faith in any new institutions, but in the individuals all over the world who think clearly, feel nobly and act rightly. They are the channels of moral truth.' His great Humanist ideas found an echo in the best minds of Europe, and some of them became his close friends.

In the meanwhile, the institution at Santiniketan had come a long way from its modest beginnings. Its scope for studies had greatly increased. There was Kala Bhavan for the study of painting, under masters like Nandalal Bose who was himself a pupil of Abanindranath, the poet's nephew. The Sangeet Bhavan, which neglected no branch of Indian music, had also grown under Dinendranath, another nephew of the poet. Special provisions were made for conducting Oriental Studies as scholars came from all over the world to lecture, to research, to exchange ideas.

Such men were Levi, Winternitz, Lesni, Sten Konow, and there were some Europeans who did even more than that. Charles Freer Andrews, a missionary who was present at Yeats's reading of *Gitanjali*, and William Winstanley Pearson, who had also met the poet in England, came to the ashram in its early days and stayed on until their death, working with a selfless devotion to the poet and his cause, that few Indians could equal. Leonard Elmhirst was another Englishman whom Tagore met in America. Drawn by the poet's personality, he came over to Santiniketan and took charge of the school of rural handicrafts, another of Rabindranath's experiments at Surul, two miles from Santiniketan.

His last European tour began with a visit to Oxford, where he delivered the series of Hibbert Lectures, which were later published as *The Religion of Man*. It was also on this last trip that Rabindranath went to Soviet Russia for the first time. On the eve of his departure from Moscow, he told his hosts, 'You have recognised the truth that in extirpating all social evils, one has to go the root, and the only way to it is through education.' In Russia as well as in other countries that he visited on this tour, Rabindranath held exhibitions of his paintings. At the age of seventy, Rabindranath had found a new outlet for his creative urge. It was astonishing, the way it started.

In 1931, the leading citizens of Calcutta united in an appeal to observe the poet's seventieth birthday. It was celebrated in a manner that was truly worth of the occasion. The Golden Book of Tagore was a testimony to the love and reverence that the intellectuals of the world bore for Rabindranath. Its sponsors consisted of three Europeans and two Indians. There was Romain Rolland from France, Albert Einstein from Germany, the poet

Kostes Palamas from Greece. The Indians consisted of the scientist Jagadish Chandra Bose, who had been the poet's closest friend for forty years. The other Indian was Mahatma Gandhi. In physical appearance, in personal habits and in general outlook, the two differed considerably. At several moments of crisis in India's political history, the two had disagreed over the course of action. But these were on the surface. Their deeper affinity transcended all occasional barriers.

The last years of the poet's life were spent largely in his beloved Santiniketan. He had a choice of small houses built for him, for he never liked to stay in the same room for long. It was, in a way, symbolic of the refusal to get into a rut, which marked his whole life. In his writings he was now producing some of his most striking, original and mature works. And these included textbooks and nonsense rhymes for children. Not an unusual occupation for someone who had loved and understood children so well and done so much to mould them for a better future.

His health was failing, but calls of duty which he was ever ready to answer gave him little rest. On 7 May 1941, Rabindranath was eighty years old. Three months later he was to leave Santiniketan, never to return. He would be taken to his ancestral house in Calcutta, fatally ill. In this house, once upon a time, a boy roamed the corridors.

Rabindranath attended his eightieth birthday celebrations in Santiniketan in spite of his failing health. For the occasion he had composed a message—his last message to the world. It was called 'The Crisis in Civilization'. It concerned itself with the state of the so-called modern civilization, a civilization that was being shaken to its very roots by a barbaric war of aggression. In the course of this message Rabindranath said, 'I had at one time believed that springs of civilization would issue out of the heart of Europe, but today when I am about to leave the world, that faith has deserted me. I look around and see the crumbling ruins of a proud civilization strewn like a vast heap of futility. And yet, I shall not commit the grievous sin of losing faith in man. I shall look forward to a new dawn, to a new chapter in history when the holocaust will end and the air will be rendered clean with the spirit of service and sacrifice. Perhaps that dawn will come from this horizon, from the East where the sun rises. On that day will unvanquished man retrace the path of conquest, surmounting all barriers, to win back his lost human heritage.'

SATYAJIT RAY

Narration of the documentary *Rabindranath Tagore*, written and directed by Satyajit Ray, produced by The Films Division, Government of India, through Satyajit Ray, in 1961, to mark Tagore's birth centenary.

Translator's Note

Tagore was the most versatile artist with words known on earth. His work encompassed poems, drama, novels, novellas, short stories, essays, letters and even question papers. But, arguably, it is his stories that continue to affect, even haunt, us the most, capturing as they do the conflicts and concerns that still rule human existence. The representation here offers a journey through Tagore's story-telling as evident in not just his novels and short fiction, but also in some of his poetry, drama and lyrics.

In Bengali, almost all of Tagore's works—prose and verse—are informed with a lushness of image, metaphor, sound and rhythm. Despite this, in Tagore's hands, the Bengali language is also steeped in an incredible lightness of being. The depth of the content is often set off by a buoyancy of language.

In translating these works, I have attempted to retain this lightness of touch. Of course, fidelity to the original in word, phrase, sentence, paragraph, stanza, cadence is the undiluted mission of these translations. But what might have turned into unnecessary, even sensation-deadening flourishes and excesses have been presented instead in forms as close to the spare and the unadorned as possible. This is especially true of the lyrics and the drama.

Tagore started writing as a child, published as a teenager, and didn't stop publishing till he died. Since these works were written at different periods during a creative life spanning over seventy years, there is considerable diversity in language, vocabulary, voice and the presence—or lack of—different sentiments. For instance, the differences in tone and dialogue between *Home and the World* (*Ghare Baire*, published 1916) and 'The Laboratory' ('Laboratory', 1940) are stark.

The translations work on the premise that each piece was written in a language that was contemporary at the time of publishing, even if they clearly belong to a different era when looked at from 2014. So, the translation reads contemporary as well, although not trendy. The luminosity of Tagore's works, I believe, is brightest when the language is from our immediate life, and not from a perceived past.

And so to the next question: why this novel, these stories, this novella, these poems, these lyrics, this play? And why in this particular sequence? Any anthology is a statement of the curator's choice, possibly reflecting more personal preferences than they're willing to admit. Still, the objective here is to take the reader on a journey through Tagore Familiar as well as Tagore Unfamiliar; to offer the comfort of the home and the unpredictability of the world.

So, the journey begins with *The Home and the World*, perhaps the best-known of Tagore's novels, and shockingly relevant today in its delineation of the conflict between the forces of nationalism and humanism, placed within the context of personal relationships. Next stop: a small set of poems where Tagore uses a new idiom—modern, sparse, even ironic, reflecting on individuals and their insecurities rather than their relationship with the universe.

After the verses, it's time for yet another facet of his writing. *The Monk-King* is one of Tagore's lesser known novellas—at least outside of the Bengali language, that is. It is a reminder of many of his qualities as an artist: his philosophical outlook, his sense of history and, perhaps most interesting, his underrated ability to tell a story brimming with action and characters.

The penultimate stop on this journey is a selection of short stories, arguably the finest form of Tagore's fiction. In these stories people, society, and, above all, drama in human life, are merged seamlessly.

The last station is a piece of abstraction in the form of the play *Chandalika*. It is the story of a so-called lower-caste woman in love with a monk. *Chandalika* shows Tagore in close communion with his concerns about equality, expressed through a creative sensibility.

Enjoy the ride.

ARUNAVA SINHA

IF THEY DON'T COME WHEN YOU CALL

যদি তোর ডাক শুনে কেউ

If they don't come when you call
Just walk alone
If they don't speak up, misfortune's child,
If they all look away, if they're all afraid
Just bare your heart
Just speak your mind, just walk alone
If they all retreat, misfortune's child,
If they all turn away from the hardest road,
Even if your feet are bloodied
Just crush the thorns alone
If they don't light your way, misfortune's child,
If they bar their doors on the night of the tempest
Let the lightning set
Your heart cage on fire, just blaze alone

The Home and the World

ঘরে বাইরে

A NOVEL

BIMALA'S STORY

Mother mine, today I remember the vermilion in your hair, your sari with the broad red border, your eyes—serene, loving, limpid. In my heart you were like a sunbeam at daybreak. My life began its journey with this golden gift. And after that? Dark clouds swooped down on me like highwaymen, leaving me not even a single drop of that light. But no matter—the virginal dawn's gift might be eclipsed by a storm, but it can never be destroyed.

Fair is lovely in our land. But the sky that gives us light is blue. My mother was dark-skinned, her glow was of piety. Her beauty put the vanity of loveliness in the shade.

Everyone tells me I resemble my mother. In childhood I even vented my rage over this on the mirror. I used to feel my body was an injustice—my complexion was not my own but someone else's, a mistake through and though.

I'm not beautiful, but I sought the boon of the virtuous woman's halo from the gods—just like my mother. When my marriage was being arranged, an astrologer sent by the groom's family had read my palm and pronounced, all the signs about this girl are propitious, she will be the ideal devoted wife. All the women said, naturally, doesn't Bimala resemble her mother, after all?

I was married into a family of rajahs. Their title had been bestowed in some ancient age of badshahs. Ever since I heard all the stories of fairy-tale princes in my childhood, I had held a particular image of my groom in my mind. A son of kings, with a body made of jasmine petals and a face assembled one grain at a time from the intense desire of all the unmarried women who had worshipped Shiva over the generations. A nascent line of a moustache like the wings of a bee, as black as it was tender.

When I saw my husband, he didn't quite match the image. Even his complexion, I discovered, was just like mine. While my regret over my own lack of beauty was mitigated a little, I also sighed deeply. Perhaps I would have died of mortification at my own appearance, but why could I not have had a glimpse of the prince who had reigned in my heart?

But maybe it's best when beauty evades the scrutiny of the eyes and presents itself within. It does not have to put on a pretty face when it appears at the pinnacle of devotion. From infancy I had observed how everything is made beautiful by the natural beauty of this devoutness. Even as a child I realized that when my mother peeled fruits specially for my father and arranged them in a white marble bowl, when she wrapped the paan sprinkled with rosewater in individual pieces of cloth with great attention, when she gently waved away flies with a fan of palm leaves while he ate, the care from her loving hands, the flow of affection from her heart merged into an ocean of infinite beauty.

These notes of worship played in my heart, too. Beyond debate or analysis, they made for pure music. If it was true that an entire life could be fulfilled through a paean of praise to the lord of life in his own temple, the attempt had begun with this morning melody.

When I woke up in the morning and delicately touched my husband's feet in reverence, I remember the line of vermilion in my hair blazing like the evening star. Waking up suddenly one day, he said with a smile, what *are* you doing, Bimal? I could have died of shame. Perhaps he had imagined I was covertly establishing my piousness. But it wasn't that, it wasn't piety for me—it was my womanly heart, whose love naturally seeks to express itself through worship.

My husband's family was bound to traditional customs. Some of its rules belonged to the age of Mughals and Pathans, and some others, to the principles of Manu. But my husband was absolutely modern. He was the first in the family to actually study and get an MA degree. His two elder brothers drank themselves to death early in life—they had no children. My husband did not drink; his mind did not run to other pursuits. This made him such a misfit in this family that not everyone approved of him—they believed that only those who had no bountiful women at home deserved to lead such pure lives. The stars cannot display blemishes, only the moon does.

My father- and mother-in-law having died a long time ago, my husband's grandmother was my guardian. My husband was the apple of her eye, her dearest possession, which was why he dared to flout tradition. So when he engaged Miss Gilby as my companion and teacher, all the tongues inside and outside began to drip poison—but still he had his way.

That was when he was reading for his MA examinations after getting his BA degree. He used to write to me practically every day—the letters were short and the language, plain. His rounded script seemed to gaze at me amiably.

I used to store all his letters in a sandalwood box, picking flowers from the garden every day to cover them with. By then the prince of my dreams had disappeared like the moon in the light of the sun. My real-life prince had occupied the throne in my heart instead. I was his queen, I had been given a seat by his side; but my greater joy was in finding my rightful place at his feet.

Having acquired an education, I had become familiar with the contemporary age through a contemporary language. These words of mine now sound unnecessarily ornamental even to myself. Had I not been confronted with modernity, I would have considered my feelings then as simple prose. I knew in my heart that just as I had been naturally born a woman, so too was it natural for a woman to recast love as devotion—there was no need to consider this particularly poetic and beautiful.

But the times changed even before I had travelled from my youth to middle age. Now I was being advised to apply craft to what was once as easy as breathing. All the thinking men of the world began to assert in high voices the wonders of fidelity in a wife and of celibacy in a widow. It was clear that truth and beauty had parted ways in this aspect of life. Could truth be regained if only beauty were to be invoked?

I don't believe that every woman's mind is cast in the same mould. But I do know that I held in my heart something my mother also did—the eagerness to worship someone. When the world no longer made this easy, I realized that this was my natural propensity.

But such was my fate, my husband would not allow me the opportunity for devoutness. This was his greatness. The money-hungry attendant at the temple fights for clients because he is not worthy of being worshipped; only cowards demand that their wives worship them. This humiliates both the worshipper and the worshipped.

But why all this opulence for me? My husband's love seemed to overflow, taking the form of clothes and jewellery and maids and servants and all kinds of material possessions. When would I be able to push all these away and give myself? More than taking, I needed the opportunity to give. By nature love is apathetic about possessions—it makes its flowers bloom in the dust on the wayside, it cannot display its riches in the porcelain pot in the drawing room.

My husband could not ignore each and every one of the traditional customs in our inner chambers. I could not meet him freely at any time during the day. I knew exactly when he would come—so our union could not take place spontaneously or casually. Our meetings were like rhyming lines in a poem; they materialized through rhythm and caesuras. After my day's tasks were completed, I bathed, did my hair carefully, put a vermilion dot on my forehead, dressed in a crisp sari, retrieved the scattered fragments of my mind, body and heart from the world outside and presented myself to my husband at the appointed hour on a golden plate. Only for a short time, but infinite in its brevity.

My husband had always said that men and women have equal rights to each other—and that, therefore, their relationship is one of equal love. I had never argued with him about this. But my heart said that devoutness does not prevent people from being equal; devoutness wishes to lift people to the same level of equality. So the joy of being equals is always available in it—it is never depleted or neglected. Devotion is like the ritual lamp whose light falls equally on the worshipper and the worshipped. Today I learnt with certainty that the woman is worshipped for her love because she worships. Otherwise, this love is to be condemned. When the lamp of our love is lit its flame rises upwards—only the oil being burnt can drip down to the floor.

My beloved, it was worthy of you not to seek to be worshipped, but it would have been good for you if you had accepted my devoutness. You arrayed me with so many things in order to love me, you taught me to love, you loved me with what I wanted, you loved me with what I did not want, I observed your secret breath in my love. You loved my body as though it was the eternal amaranth of heaven, you loved my nature as though it was your fortune to do so. You made me proud. I felt that it was for this wealth that you had appeared at my door. That was when I sat on the throne of the queen, demanding honour; the demand kept swelling, never fulfilled. Is it a matter of happiness for the woman to know she has the power to control men—is this where her well-being lies? Only by letting this pride be swept away by her devotion can she be saved. Shiva came as a beggar to the goddess Annapurna's door, but could Annapurna have withstood his fire had her devoutness not turned her into an ascetic?

Today I remember that many people had burnt with jealousy at my fortune. The jealousy was natural—I had got everything without effort, with a lie. But a lie cannot be sustained forever. You have to pay the price. The creator won't have it any other way—the debt of every instance of good fortune has to be paid back over a long period of time. Only then does one's claim become irrefutable. God can always give us things, but we have to take them with our own qualities. Even the things we get do not really belong to us, such is our fate.

Many a daughter's father had sighed at my good fortune. People whispered—was I really beautiful enough to deserve this? Did I have the necessary qualities? Was I worthy of this family? My husband's grandmother and mother had both been reputed beauties. You couldn't find women as beautiful as my two sisters-in-law. But when both of them lost their husbands, my husband's grandmother vowed not to hunt for a beautiful woman for her other grandson. I was able to enter this house only on the strength of the propitious signs associated with me—I had no other claim.

Very few wives in this pleasure-loving family had received suitable respect. Apparently this was the custom here. Even though all their tears were swept away beneath the bubbles of wine and the anklets of the dancing girls, they clung to the pride of being married to aristocrats. And yet my husband neither touched alcohol, nor bankrupted his humanity at the doors of the merchant houses of sin out of a desire for women's flesh. But was it really because of me? What power had god given me to subjugate the distracted and maddened mind of the male, after all? It was fate, nothing more. And was it only in their case that the accursed lord had paid no attention, allowing their lives to go astray? Their celebration of the senses ended when evening had barely fallen—only the lamps of youth and beauty burned on unnecessarily all night. No music anywhere, only light.

My husband's sisters-in-law pretended to ignore his masculinity. Imagine steering the ship of such an illustrious family with nobody but one's wife by one's side! I had to swallow their jibes at every step. As though all I was doing was stealing my husband's love—with nothing but deceit, since everything about me was fake. The sheer brazenness of today's wives! My husband had dressed me in contemporary fashion—my array of colourful jackets and saris and chemises and petticoats made them burn with envy. No beauty, only glamour. You've turned yourself into a shop, aren't you ashamed of yourself?

My husband was aware of everything. But his heart dripped with compassion for women. Don't be angry, he would keep telling me. I remember saying to him once, women's minds are small and crooked. He had answered, Chinese women have feet that are as small as they are crooked. Society everywhere has closed in on women to keep their minds small and crooked. Fate gambles with their lives and everything depends on how the dice rolls; they have no rights of their own.

My sisters-in-law got whatever they wanted from my husband. He never considered whether their demands were fair or not. My heart would burn when I saw that they were not the least bit grateful for this. In fact, my elder sister-in-law, who was an extreme ascetic in all her prayers, vows and fasts, using up so much of her detachment through her speech that she had none of it left for her heart, told me repeatedly that her brother, a lawyer, had told her that if she chose to file a case in court, she would . . . and so on and so forth, none of which bears writing about. I had promised my husband that in no circumstances would I talk back to them, which made me suffer all the more. I used to think that there was a limit to goodness, that crossing it was a hindrance to being a man. My husband said that neither the law nor society was on the side of his sisters-in-law—it was extremely humiliating for them to have to beg or borrow from others in order to get what had once been rightfully theirs. Asking for gratitude over and above this was too much. Be beaten up and still pay a tip . . . Should I tell the truth? I had often thought that my husband should have had the spirit to be a little bad.

The younger of my sisters-in-law was of a different nature. At her age, she did not believe in the humbug of asceticism. The young maids she had engaged did not behave particularly well, but there was no one to object to this, since this was the custom in this family. I could tell that my luck of having an uncorrupted husband was unbearable to her. So she would lay all sorts of traps in her brother-in-law's path. What I am most ashamed of is to admit that I began to worry even about a husband like mine. The air here was so murky that even transparent things did not appear that way. Once in a while my sister-in-law would cook a meal herself for her brother-in-law and send him a loving invitation. I wanted him to say on some pretext or another, no, I cannot go . . . The bad deserve punishment, don't they? But when he accepted each and every invitation happily, I felt an ache in my heart. The fault was mine—but what could I do, my mind wouldn't listen. I felt he too had some male instincts. Even if I had a thousand other things to do at that time, I would find an excuse to be in my sister-in-law's room. She would say with a smile, oh my, you cannot escape Chhotorani's eye for a moment, such strict surveillance. We too had husbands once, you know, but we never learnt to be so protective.

My husband was only aware of their sorrows, not of their flaws. Very well, maybe it is all society's fault, I would say, but why must you be so kind to them? Even if they suffer a little, that doesn't mean . . . but I could not win against him. Instead of arguing, he would only smile. I think he knew of the small discomfort in my heart over this. The real object of my ire was neither society not anyone else, it was only . . . but I shan't say more.

One day my husband told me, if they had really thought that all these things they criticise you for are bad, they would not have been so angry.

Then why this unfair rage?

How can I call it unfair? Envy does hold one truth—that the sources of happiness should be equally available to everyone.

Then they should quarrel with god—why me?

Because god is not within reach.

Then why don't they take whatever they want? You have no wish to deprive them. Let them wear the saris and jackets and ornaments and stockings and shoes; if they want to study with an Englishwoman there's one right here. And if they want to remarry, you have the resources to cross the seven seas like Vidyasagar did.

That's the problem. Even if what the heart wants is handed over, it won't be accepted.

And so you have to put on an act, as though what you haven't got is evil—and yet if someone else gets it you burn with jealousy.'

This is how the deprived person tries to transcend his deprivation, that is his consolation.

Say what you like, women put on acts. They do not want to admit the truth, they resort to trickery instead.

Which means they are the most deprived of all.

I used to be angry when he dismissed all the meanness that the women at home displayed. There was no use talking about what could have happened had society been different, but all these annoyances, these sarcastic taunts, this divergence between thought and speech, could not be pitied.

When he heard me say this he said, must kindness be displayed only when you feel a pinch personally? Is there no room for kindness when society's arrows destroy their lives? Must the people who are made to starve also be beasts of burden?

It must have been I who was small-minded, then, while everyone else was perfect. Angrily I said, you don't have to live in this part of the house—you don't know everything that goes on. As soon as I tried to tell him some of the things that happened in the ladies' chambers, he rose to his feet, saying, Chandranath-babu has been waiting for a long time.

I began to weep. How was I to live now that I had been proven to be so petty in front of my husband? I had no way of proving that I would not have behaved like them even if fate had decreed the same kind of deprivation for me.

Look, sometimes I feel that if the lord were to give women the opportunity to be proud of their beauty, they would be spared the mortification of many other kinds of pride. I could have been proud of my gold and diamonds, but they had no meaning in this king's home. And so my pride was over my purity as a woman, with the thought that here even my husband would have to accept defeat. But whenever I went to him to discuss minor annoyances in the household, I was made to feel so small that it hurt. So I had wanted to retaliate by making him feel small in turn, telling myself, I shall not accept that all these things are good—this is mere naiveté. This isn't a case of giving yourself, only of being cheated by others.

My husband was extremely desirous of taking me out into the world. One day I asked him, what do I need with the world?

The world might need you, he answered.

I said, if it has done without me all this while, it can do without me today too—it won't kill itself.

Let it kill itself if it wants to, that's not what I'm worried about—I'm worried for myself.

Really? What have *you* got to worry about?

My husband smiled without a word. Knowing his ways, I said, no, you can't evade the question with silence, you must finish what you started.

Not everything that's said ends with the spoken word, he countered. So many things we say are never finished in our entire lives.

Stop talking in riddles, tell me.

I want that you should find me out there in the world, and that I should find you. We have accounts to settle there.

And are we getting any less of each other at home?

Here they use me to cover your eyes and ears, all your senses—you neither know whom you want, nor whom you've got.

I know very well indeed, my dear.

So you imagine, but you don't even know that you do not know.

Look, I can't bear to hear you talk this way.

Which is why I didn't want to say any of this.

I can bear your silence even less.

That is why I want neither to speak, nor to remain silent. You must come into the centre of the world outside and understand everything for yourself. You weren't born just to be a victim of this domestic deception and run the household, and nor was I. Only if our getting to know each other is cemented in truth will our love be a success.

You may still be getting to know me, but I have nothing left to learn about you.

Very well, if it is I who have fallen behind, why don't you complete my journey?

This kind of discussion had taken place often, in different forms. He would say, the glutton who loves fish curry slices and cooks the fish with spices according to his taste, but the man who really loves fish does not consign it to a brass pot and a china bowl. If he can overpower it while it's still free in the water, well and good—if not, he waits on the bank. When he returns home later, he consoles himself, saying, I may not have got what I wanted, but I did not cut it up and kill it for my own convenience or fancy. It's best to get something in its entirety—and if that's absolutely impossible, it's best to lose in its entirety too.

I did not care for all these statements, but it wasn't because of them that I did not go out into the world at once. My husband's grandmother was still alive. Going against her wishes, my husband had filled the house with almost everything that the twentieth century had to offer, and she had tolerated this. She must have known that this too would take place one day, but I wondered whether it was important enough to make her suffer for it. The books told us we were caged birds, but while I couldn't speak for others, there was so much in my cage that the entire world was not large enough for it. At least, so I thought at the time.

The primary reason my husband's grandmother loved me so much was that she believed I had been able to attract my husband's love—either on the strength of my own qualities, or by a conspiracy of the stars. For it is the nature of the male to sink into a quagmire. Her other grandson's wives had not been able to keep their husbands confined to the home even with all their beauty— they were burnt to cinders by the flames of sin without anyone being able to help. She was under the impression that I was the only one in this family who had succeeded in dousing the fire of death. So she protected me closely, quaking in fear when I happened to fall ill. The things that my husband bought for me at English shops were not to her taste. But she believed that men should have a few worthless fancies, which only amounted to squandering money. They must not be prevented, and yet the only hope was that they would not be led to ruination. If not his wife, my Nikhilesh would have tried to dress up someone else. Whenever my husband bought new clothes for me, she would send for him and exchange much banter and laughter. Eventually even her tastes began to change. She so converted to modern times that her evenings would not pass unless her grandson's wife told her stories from English books.

After her death, my husband had wanted to move to Calcutta. But I simply could not agree. This was my father-in-law's house after all—and his mother had nurtured it through so many sorrows and separations. I was constantly assailed by the thought that if I were to wash my hands of all responsibility and move to Calcutta, a curse would fall upon me. The empty spot she used to occupy stared at me. A true devotee, she had entered this house at the age of eight and died at eighty-nine. Hers had not been a happy life. Fate had hurled one thunderbolt after another at her, but every blow only brought out more sweetness from her. This sprawling family had been purified by her tears. How could I forsake it in favour of the filth of Calcutta?

My husband had assumed that handing over the stewardship of the household here would not only offer his sisters-in-law some comfort, but also give our life a chance to spread its branches in Calcutta.

That was where my objection lay. After tormenting me all this time, after being jealous of anything good that came my husband's way, were they now to be rewarded for it?

Besides, the world of the zamindar lay here. All our subjects and officers, all those who had taken shelter here, all our guests and relations, were centred around the house. In Calcutta I didn't know who we were—very few people did. The fullness of our status and honour and wealth were all located here. Hand over all this to them and go into exile like Sita, while they laugh behind my back? They neither understood the value of my husband's magnanimity nor were they worthy of it.

And then, when we returned here some day, would I get my position back? My husband would say, what need do you have of that position? There are plenty of other things in life, worth so much more.

Men don't understand all this, I told myself. They do not know exactly what a household is, for they only occupy the outer chambers. They should follow women's advice in this matter.

The most important thing was to show some spirit. To give up everything to those who had always been my enemies would amount to defeat. Even if my husband was willing to accept this, I was not. I told myself that this spirit would flow from my purity as a wife.

Why didn't my husband force me to go with him? I know why. He did not precisely because he could have. He had always told me, that you have to obey me all the time just because you are my wife is the kind of oppression even I myself cannot bear. I shall wait—if we are well-matched, excellent. If not, what can we do about it?

But there is such a thing as spirit—that day I felt that in this aspect my . . . but no, I must not even talk about such things.

Could the difference between day and night be eliminated gradually, according to calculations? But the sun rises, the darkness is dispelled, and infinite time elapses in an instant.

The era of swadeshi had dawned on Bengal once, but it was not clear how. There seemed to be no continuity with the earlier age. That was probably why the new era had swept away our fears and worries in a flash, like a flood breaking through a dam. There was no time to comprehend what had happened or what would happen.

If women throng the balconies and windows without caring to hide themeselves when the groom is on his way, when the music plays, when the lights can be seen, how could these same women occupy themselves with housework when the music signalling the advent of the groom of the entire nation was heard? With ululation and the blowing of conch shells, they peeped out from every crack in the doors and windows and walls.

My eyes and ears, hopes and wishes, had also been tinged with red at the time by the fervour of this frenzied new era. The boundaries of the world that I had considered my own all this time—the limits within which I had tried to maintain the calling of my life, my desires and missions, in a pleasing way every day—had not yet been demolished. Yet, poised as I was on the edge, the sudden call from a distant horizon may not have made its meaning clear to me yet, but it still made me wistful.

From the time my husband was a college student, he had been trying in different ways to manufacture locally the things people needed. Our estates had an abundance of date-palm trees. He spent a long time trying to create a system whereby the juice could be collected from several trees with a single pipe, thickened on the spot, and converted to sweeteners. I was told that an excellent system was created, but more money than juice dripped from it, making it impossible to sustain the business. His experiments with agriculture had led to extraordinary crops, but the money he spent on them was even more extraordinary. He decided that it was impossible to embark on big enterprises in our country because of the lack of banks. He began to teach me political economy at the same time. That would have done no harm but he felt that first and foremost the habit and desire to save money in banks had to be generated among the people. So he started a small bank. The villagers grew very enthusiastic about saving their money, for the interest rate was high. But the very reason that increased people's zeal to save made the bank sink through the gaping hole of the high rate of interest. His long-standing officers became extremely annoyed and perturbed at all this, while his detractors taunted him. One day my elder sister-in-law said for my benefit that her famous cousin, the lawyer, had told her that if a petition could be made to a judge, there was still a chance of saving the respect, wealth and property of this aristocratic family from this lunatic.

My husband's grandmother was the only one in the entire family not to be dismayed. She would often summon me to rebuke me, asking, why do all of you bother him? Are you worried about the property? I have seen this property go into the hands of the receiver thrice. Are men supposed to be like women? They are profligate, they only know how to spend money. You're fortunate, my dear, that he doesn't spend himself too. You haven't been hurt, which is why it hasn't occurred to you.

My husband's charity list was very long. He provided financial support to anyone trying to make a loom or a harvester or something similar all the way till the final failure. An Indian company was set up to run ships up to Puri in competition with a foreign line; not one of its ships floated, but my husband's shares sank.

My greatest annoyance came when Sandip-babu sucked money out of my hand on the pretext of working for the country. He would run a newspaper; he had to travel to spread the cause of home rule; he had been asked to spend some time in Ootacamund on the doctor's advice—my husband paid for all this indiscriminately. In addition he had a monthly allowance for his household expenses. Astonishingly, it was not as though his views matched those of my husband's. My husband would say, not extracting the commodities locked up in our mines meant poverty for the country, but not discovering and acknowledging the mine of power in the soul of the country meant even more serious poverty. One day I told him in anger, these people are all deceiving you. Smiling, he said, since I have no qualities of my own, I am buying myself a share of theirs—I'm the one who's deceiving them for my own benefit.

This brief account of the previous period will help explain what followed in the modern one.

When the storm of the times stirred my blood, the first thing I did was to tell my husband, I want to burn all my clothes made of English fabric.

Why must you burn them, he asked. Just don't use them as long as you like.

What do you mean 'as long as you like'! I will never in this life . . .

Very well, you will never use them in this life. But why burn them so ceremoniously?

Why are you stopping me?

I am telling you to put all your energies into building something. It's not worth wasting even a fraction of it on the excitement of destroying the redundant.

It's the excitement that helps build things.

In that case one has to say the house cannot be illuminated unless it's set on fire. I can go to a lot of trouble to light a lamp, but I am not willing to set fire to the house for convenience. It may look heroic, but, in truth, it is the spurious arithmetic of weakness.

My husband continued, look, I can see that what I'm saying doesn't appeal to you, but still I shall tell you—think it over. Just like the mother who dresses up each of her daughters with her own ornaments, the day has come when the earth is dressing up every country with its own ornaments. What we do, what we think, what we eat . . . today everything is connected to the entire world. That is why I consider this a fortunate age for every nation—there is nothing heroic about denying such fortune.

And then there was one more problem. There had been something of an uproar when Miss Gilby came into the inner chambers, lasting quite some time. Things quietened down once everyone got used to her. But now there was trouble brewing again. It had never mattered to me whether Miss Gilby was a Bengali or an Englishwoman, but now it did. I told my husband that he would have to ask her to leave. He was silent. I told him my thoughts without inhibition and, having listened, he left the room sadly. I wept copiously. When my heart had softened after crying my heart out, he told me that night, look, I can't think of Miss Gilby differently just because she's English. Will your long association with her not let you overcome the barrier of her name? She loves you, after all.

With some embarrassment, but without relinquishing my pride entirely I said, very well, let her stay, who's asking her to go?

Miss Gilby stayed on. One day, the son of a distant relative threw a stone at her as she was going to church. My husband had brought this boy up all these years but now he threw him out of the house. This led to great trouble. Everyone believed the boy when he claimed that it was Miss Gilby who had insulted him and was now making up stories. Even I thought it wasn't impossible. The boy's mother was dead; his uncle turned to me for help. I pleaded strongly on his behalf, but to no avail.

At that time nobody could forgive my husband for this—not

even I. In my mind I criticised him strongly. Then Miss Gilby left on her own. Tears streamed from her eyes as she was leaving but my heart did not melt. How she had lied to ruin the child's future! And such a good boy—so caught up in the swadeshi movement that he forgot to eat or sleep. My husband took Miss Gilby to the station in his own carriage, which I thought was excessive. When the newspapers castigated him for this, after adding colour to the incident, I thought he deserved the punishment.

I had often been worried for my husband in the past but never embarrassed. This time I was. I didn't know whether Naren had done anything wrong with Miss Gilby or not, but trying to be impartial about it at this time was utterly embarrassing. In no circumstances did I want to quell the spirit which had brought forth Naren's audacity with an Englishwoman. My husband's insistence on not understanding this appeared to me as a lack of manliness on his part. This caused me shame.

Not just that, what mortified me the most was the fact that I had to admit defeat. My aggressiveness burnt only me, without making my husband shine brighter. This was an insult to my purity as a wife.

And yet it wasn't as though my husband had no relationship with the freedom movement or that he was against it. But he had not accepted the incantation of 'Vande mataram' as the absolute truth. I am willing to serve the country, he said, but the object of my worship resides on a higher plane. If I worship my country I will destroy it.

That was when Sandip-babu arrived with his followers to spread the cause of swadeshi on our estate. There was to be a meeting in our temple courtyard in the evening. We women were seated on one side behind blinds. Roars of 'Vande mataram!' came ever closer, making my heart tremble. Suddenly a wave of young men and boys in turbans and saffron robes swept into the enormous courtyard like the first flood of monsoon in a dry river. The place was filled with people. Cutting a line through the crowd, eleven or twelve young men came in, bearing Sandip-babu aloft on a large seat. Vande mataram! Vande mataram! Vande mataram! I thought the sky would be rent into pieces.

I had seen a photograph of Sandip-babu's already. I cannot

claim to have been attracted to him. He was not ugly—quite handsome, in fact. But still, I don't know why, I had felt that while his appearance was striking, there was much about it that was base—there was something in his eyes and mouth not quite pure. That was why I did not approve of my husband's meeting every demand of his without demur. I did not object to my husband squandering his money, but I constantly felt that this man was deceiving him despite being his friend. His behaviour was not that of an ascetic's or a poor man's, but very much that of a dandy's. He harboured a desire for comfort, and yet . . . many such thoughts had occurred to me. Was I reminded of all this today because . . . but never mind.

However, when Sandip-babu began his speech that day, making the heart of this mammoth gathering swell and overflow its banks, I observed an extraordinary figure. Especially when the sun declined gradually below the level of the roof and suddenly threw its beams on his face, it seemed that the gods had declared to every man and woman present that he belonged to the land of the immortals. From start to finish, every word in his speech seemed to be a stormy gust of wind—infinitely courageous. I could not bear the cover of the blinds. I don't remember when, unknown to myself, I moved them aside to stare at him. There wasn't a person in the entire gathering who had the time to look at me. But I noticed that at one point Sandip-babu's bright eyes fell on my face like a star from the Orion constellation. I wasn't worried—I was hardly the wife of a royal family then; I was the only representative of all the women of Bengal and he, a hero of Bengal. Like the sunbeams on his brow, he had to be crowned by the women of the land from their hearts. How else was the auspiciousness of his journey to war to be fulfilled?

I sensed clearly that the fire in his speech blazed higher after he had glanced at my face. The steed of the king of the gods could no longer be reined in—one thunderbolt after another was hurled, one flash of lightning after another. My heart told me that it was a flame from my eyes that had ignited this fire. We women are goddesses not only of plenty, but also of knowledge.

I returned home that day with wondrous joy, glowing with pride. A fire was lit within me too, its irresistible force transporting me to a new place in an instant. I wished I could cut off my locks that were cascading below my waist, like the heroines of Greece for the hero to string his bow with. Had my heart been connected to the ornaments I was wearing, my choker, my necklace, my bracelets would all have showered down on the gathering like meteors. I felt as though I would have to injure myself to withstand the tumult of this happiness.

When my husband came to our room in the evening, I feared lest he say something out of tune with that day's speech, lest he express the slightest reluctance to suffer a blow to his love for truth—for I would easily have ignored him had he done so.

But he said nothing to me. I did not like this. I should have said, today Sandip's speech has woken me up, I have realized my errors of all these years. I felt he was obstinately silent, that he was forcing himself not to express any enthusiasm.

How much longer will Sandip-babu stay here, I asked.

He will leave for Rangpur tomorrow morning, answered my husband.

So soon?

Yes, he is supposed to deliver a speech there.

I was silent for a while before asking, can he not find a way to stay back one more day?

It isn't possible, but why?

I would like him to have a meal with us.

My husband was astonished. He had often requested me to come out of the ladies' chambers and meet his friends, but I had never agreed.

He gave me a long, steady look whose meaning I could not quite comprehend. Suddenly I felt a surge of embarrassment. No, I said, no need.

Why not, he said. I will tell Sandip—if it is possible, he will stay one more day.

It turned out to be possible.

I shall tell the truth. That day I wished the creator had made me incomparably beautiful. Not to capture anyone's heart—but beauty was a matter of glory. On this auspicious day, let the men of this nation see the goddess in the women. But their eyes were unable to see the goddess without the trappings of external beauty.

Would Sandip-babu see the rising force of the nation in me? Or would he consider me an ordinary woman, nothing more than his friend's wife?

That morning I had washed my long hair and tied it up perfectly with a red silk ribbon. The invitation was for lunch—so there was no time to put my wet hair up in a bun. I was dressed in a white sari from Madras and a sleeveless jacket, both with zari borders.

I had chosen this as a most restrained form of dressing, nothing could be plainer. My second sister-in-law appeared, running her eye over me from head to toe before smiling slyly. Why are you smiling, Didi, I asked.

I'm looking at how you've dressed up, she told me.

Annoyed, I said, nothing special about this.

Smiling slyly again, she said, not bad at all, Chhotorani, rather nice, in fact. I was just thinking that your low-necked English jacket would have completed your attire well.

She left, her entire body shaking with laughter. I was very angry, and had half a mind to change out of these clothes into a coarse, ordinary sari. I'm not sure why I didn't actually do it, but I told myself, if I met Sandip-babu without dressing up properly, my husband would be angry—women are the wealth of society, after all.

I had thought of appearing in Sandip-babu's presence only when he sat down to his lunch. The awkwardness of the first meeting would be dispelled behind the facade of serving the meal. But the cooks were late today, it was almost one o'clock. So my husband had sent for me to introduce us. When I entered, I was too embarrassed to look at him at first. Forcing myself to overcoming this shyness, I said, lunch is late today.

Taking a seat next to me without hesitation, he said, you know, I do get plenty of food every day, but the goddess of plenty remains behind the scenes. Today the goddess herself has appeared, let plentiful food remain elusive.

His behaviour was as forthright as his speeches. No indecisiveness—claiming his own place at once in any situation seemed to come naturally to him. He was not hindered by the possibility of anyone being offended. He seemed to have a natural right to a seat close to me—anyone who considered this wrong was wrong.

I was mortified by the thought that Sandip-babu might consider me old-fashioned and a slow thinker. I simply could not achieve the state of mind where my repartee would be sharp, where I wouldn't be stammering, where my responses would astonish him. I felt a deep anguish, cursing myself for appearing unprepared in his presence.

I was about to rush off once the meal had ended; but he went to the door just as unselfconsciously as before and blocked my way, saying, don't consider me a glutton, I didn't come here for your food. My attraction was your invitation. If you run away as soon as the meal is over you'll be evading your guest.

All this would have sounded extremely discordant had it not been said freely and with conviction. My husband was a close friend of his; I was like his sister-in-law, after all. As I was in conflict with myself, trying to achieve a state of mind suitable for such a close relationship with Sandip-babu, my husband observed my confusion and said, very well, why don't you join us after you've eaten?

But promise me you won't run away, said Sandip-babu.

Smiling, I said, I'll be back soon.

Let me tell you why I don't believe you, he told me. Nikhilesh has been married for nine years. And you have evaded me for nine years. If you go on this way for another nine, we'll never meet.

Adopting the same familiarity, I said softly, even if that were the case, why wouldn't we meet?

My horoscope predicts early death, he answered. Neither my father nor my grandfather lived beyond their thirties. I've just turned twenty-seven.

He knew this would strike home. It did. My soft voice may now have acquired a touch of tragedy. The blessings of the entire country will ensure that the risk is averted, I told him.

The blessings of the country can only come from its goddesses, he said. That is why I was pleading with you to come—the rituals for remitting my sins will begin at once.

Even when the currents are muddied, the water can still be used easily. Sandip-babu moved so quickly that what was intolerable in another person offered no scope for protest when coming from him. Laughing, he said, I'm keeping your husband as surety—if you don't come back he shan't be released either.

As I was leaving, he continued, there's something else too.

I stopped. Don't be afraid, he said, just a glass of water. You may have noticed I don't drink water with my meals—only later.

Now I had to ask anxiously, but why?

The history of how he had once been afflicted by severe dyspepsia came up. I also heard how unbearably he had suffered. Concluding his account of the failure of all sorts of allopathic and homeopathic doctors, followed by the miraculous success achieved by an ayurvedic doctor, he said with a smile, god has given me the kind of diseases that will not depart till they have been given home-made pills.

Finally my husband spoke. He said, the vials of Western medicine don't want to abandon your sanctuary for a moment either—aren't three of the shelves in your drawing-room completely . . .

Do you know what those are? They're like the punitive police. They're not there because they're needed—modern rule makes them breathe down our necks. All I do is to pay the penalty, not to mention swallowing the blows from their batons . . .

My husband couldn't stand exaggeration. But every figure of speech is an exaggeration—made not by god but by man. I had once told my husband on the pretext of justifying a lie, only trees and animals tell nothing but the truth for the poor things do not have the power to lie. This is where humans are superior to beasts and women are superior to men—exaggerations and lies befit women alone.

When I left the room, I found my sister-in-law in the veranda, peering through the slats in the window. What are you doing here, I asked. Eavesdropping, she whispered.

When I returned, Sandip-babu said sadly, you can't have eaten at all.

I was very embarrassed. I had returned too soon—without waiting long enough for a reasonable meal. A calculation of how long I had been away would have made it obvious I had eaten very little. But it had not occurred to me that someone might have been calculating this.

Sandip-babu probably discerned my embarrassment, which made it worse. He said, just like the doe in the forest you were predisposed towards escaping—that you still took the trouble to uphold the truth is no small reward for me.

I could not respond suitably. With a red face, and perspiring profusely, I sat down on a corner of a sofa. None of my plans for appearing in Sandip-babu's presence without reservation and in full glory as the personification of woman-power, in order to draw the mark of victory on his forehead, actually materialised.

Sandip-babu deliberately provoked a debate with my husband. He knew very well that his sharp wit shone brightly in an argument. Even later, I discovered repeatedly that in my presence he never let go of the slightest opportunity to launch into a debate.

Referring to my husband's view of the 'Vande mataram' slogan, of which he was aware, he asked, don't you accept that the imagination has a role to play in serving one's country, Nikhil?

I accept that it does in one or two places, but not everywhere. I want to understand the idea of my country as the truth and pass it on to others—I am both afraid and embarrassed to deploy a magic incantation and cast a hypnotic spell on people for such an important thing.

What you refer to as a hypnotic spell is what I call the truth. I really do consider my country a god. I worship the divine man—just as the true expression of god is in human beings, so it is in one's country.

If you really believe this, to you there is no difference between two people, and, therefore, between two countries.

That is true, but my power is limited. Therefore, it is only through the worship of my own country that I worship the country-as-god.

I'm not stopping you from your worship, but how will you accomplish your objective through your antagonism to the gods resident in other countries?

Antagonism is an element of worship. Arjuna received a boon by battling with Shiva disguised as Kirata. We must attack god from some aspects—that will make him happy one day.

In that case those who serve the country and those who harm it are both worshipping him—there is no need to advertise patriotism.

It's different when it comes to one's own country; the heart has explicit instructions to worship.

Then it's not just one's own country, there are even more explicit instructions about oneself. The incantation to the god residing within oneself rings loudest in one's ears, wherever one might be.

Your arguments are nothing but the dry logic of the intellect, Nikhil. Don't you accept that there is such a thing as a heart?

I am telling you honestly, Sandip, when you people pass off the country as a god in order to label injustice as duty and immorality as good deeds, I am upset because it is my heart that suffers. If I steal for my own benefit, do I not strike at the root of my true self-love? That is why I cannot steal. Is that because of one's intellect or one's self-respect?

I was seething. Unable to contain myself, I said, whether it is England or France or Germany or Russia, is there any civilized nation whose history is not one of theft for itself?

They have to justify these thefts—they're still doing it. History has not ended.

Very well, so shall we, declared Sandip-babu. Let us pile the stolen goods in our houses first—then we will take our time to justify our act. But let me ask you, where is this justification that you say they are still offering?

No one was watching when Rome justified its sins. Its wealth was unlimited then. It is impossible tell just when the greatest civilizations built on plunder have to justify their actions. But don't you see the bagfuls of lies in their politics, the deception, the betrayal, the espionage, the sacrifice of justice and truth at the altar of prestige . . . Do you think the weight of this burden of sin is insubstantial? Does it not suck the blood out of the heart of their civilization every single day? I say that those who do not honour righteousness ahead of their country do not honour their country either.

I had never heard my husband argue with anyone outside the family. He argued with me, but he was so compassionate where I was concerned that it pained him to defeat me. Today I saw him wielding his weapon.

I simply could not bring myself to agree with what my husband was saying. I was sure there was a suitable response—it just did not occur to me. The trouble was that one had to be quiet if the issue of righteousness was raised. It was difficult to assert that I was not willing to follow the path of righteousness quite so far. Resolving to write a fitting reply to this debate and give it to Sandip-babu, I noted down the conversation as soon as I returned to my room.

After a while Sandip-babu turned to me and asked, what do you think?

I said, I don't want to go into the subtleties—I shall speak broadly. I am human, I covet things, I want things for my country; I want things I can snatch, things I can gather. I have anger within me, I shall be angry on behalf of my country; I want someone whom I can carve and slice; someone on whom I can avenge my humiliation of all this time. I can be bewitched, I shall be bewitched by my country; I want a visible form of the country whom I can address as Ma, as goddess, as Durga—to whom I shall sacrifice beasts, making their blood flow everywhere. I am human, I am not a goddess.

Leaping up from his seat and brandishing his fist, Sandip-babu shouted, hurrah, hurrah! Correcting himself the very next moment, he exclaimed, Vande mataram, Vande mataram!

A deep-seated agony threw a momentary shadow on my husband's face. He said very softly, I am not a god either, I am a man. That is why I say, I shan't give my vices to my country—I shan't, shan't.

Look, Nikhil, said Sandip-babu, the truth is fused with women's hearts into a single entity. Our truth has no colour, no life, nothing to savour—it has only logic. A woman's heart is like a scarlet lotus—truth adopts its real form on it; it is not as intangible as our debates. That is why only women know how to be properly cruel, but men do not—their righteousness weakens them. Women can cause ruination easily, and so can men, but they are assailed by doubts that spring from thought. Women can be as unjust as a cyclone—such injustice is a terrible beauty—while the injustice that men do is ugly, for its insides are sick with righteousness. That is why I tell you that today it is the women who will save our country. This is not the time for righteousness and ritual. Today we have to be dispassionate, shun justice, and be ruthless. We have to transgress; today our women have to ceremoniously welcome sin and adorn it with sandalwood and blood. Don't you remember what the poet has said?

> Come, sin, come, beautiful woman, let
> The fire and wine of your kisses rouse my blood
> Let the trumpets of doom sound
> Put the taint of disgrace on my brow
> The shameless slime-black mark of guilt
> Give my heart the power to wreak havoc

Shame on the righteousness that cannot laugh as it destroys.

He stamped hard on the floor twice—a mass of sleeping dustballs rose into the air in consternation. Dismissing in an instant all that people around the world and over the generations had considered noble, he rose to his feet in such glory, his head held at a lofty angle, that I had goosepimples when I looked at him.

Suddenly he roared again, there is a fire that burns the home, that burns the world—I can see clearly that you are the beautiful goddess of this fire. Give all of us today the invincible power to ruin ourselves, make our sins gorgeous.

It wasn't clear whom he addressed the last words to. It could be assumed that they were for the one whom he showered his adoration on with the words 'Vande mataram', or for the woman who was present as the representative of the goddess-country. It could be assumed that just as the poet Valmiki suddenly uttered the first canto at the attack by compassion on a sinful mind, so too had Sandip-babu exclaimed these words at the attack on righteousness by ruthlessness—or perhaps he had only demonstrated the extraordinary acting prowess which he used to steal the hearts of the people.

He might have said more, but my husband rose, and touching him said softly, Chandranath-babu is here, Sandip.

Startled, I turned to discover a stately man of advanced years standing at the door and wondering whether to enter. His face glowed with a soft light like that of the evening sun about to set. Coming up to me, my husband said, this is my teacher. I have told you about him many times, touch his feet.

I did. May god protect you forever, he blessed me.

I needed the blessings at that moment.

NIKHILESH'S STORY

Once upon a time I had believed myself capable of accepting whatever god doled out to me. This belief had not been tested yet, but now it seemed to be time.

Weighing up my response in my head, I had imagined many miseries—from poverty to imprisonment, from disgrace to death. I had even tried to imagine Bimal dying. I probably hadn't been lying when I told myself that I would accept all of these with humility.

But there was just the one thing that I had never imagined. That is all I have been thinking of all day today—can I bear this too?

Something is pricking at my heart. I'm going about my work, but the agony refuses to be abated. Even when I am asleep I suspect the pain gnaws away at my ribs. The moment I wake up I realize that the grace of daylight has evaporated already. How? What is this? What's gone wrong? What is this darkness? From where has it arrived to cast a shadow on my full moon?

My peceptions have been so heightened suddenly that every lie uttered by the past unhappiness lurking in my heart in the guise of happiness is tearing away at my entrails. The more desperately shame tries to draw a veil over itself at the prospect of imminent misery, the more it stands revealed to my soul. My heart can see everything now and I am being forced to helplessly witness what I should not, what I do not want to.

If I had been allowed to forget how beggarly I was despite the mockery of wealth all this time, why did the misfortune of my deceived life have to be revealed now in excruciating detail through every moment, every word, every glance? The tax that I have paid to illusion during these past nine years will now be claimed by truth with principal and interest till the last moment of my life. The one who can no longer afford to pay back his debt always has to carry the heaviest burden of it on his shoulders. But still I can say with all my might, may the truth triumph.

My cousin Munu's husband Gopal came yesterday for help with his daughter's wedding. When he saw the furniture in my house, he concluded that no one in the world could be happier than I. Tell Munu I will visit her tomorrow for a meal, Gopal, I told him. Munu has used the elixir in her heart to turn her frugal home into a heaven. My entire being longs for a taste of the food made by this goddess with her own hands. She has turned the scarcities in her home into adornments. Let me visit her today. Whatever is sacred has not yet been obliterated from this earth.

What use is forced pride? I might as well hang my head and admit my deficiencies. Perhaps I lack the power that women seek most of all in men. But is power merely bluster or nothing but whimsy? Can power be trampled on without hesitation . . . but then why get into all this? You cannot argue your way to being worthy. Unworthy, unworthy, unworthy! So be it—but doesn't the value of love lie in making even the unworthy victorious? The world holds many rewards for the worthy, for the unworthy the almighty had only reserved love.

Once upon a time I had told Bimal, you must come out into the world. Bimal was confined to the home then—she was defined by the home, identified by a small space and the fixed rules of small responsibilities. Did the constant love I got from her come from the depths of her heart, or was it an allocated amount like the daily supply of running water provided by the steam-operated taps of the municipality?

Am I greedy? Did I aspire to much more than I received? No, I am not greedy, I am a lover. Which is why I did not desire what was locked up in a safe; I wanted only that which could not be mine unless it gave itself up on its own. I never wanted to decorate my home with flowers cut from the pages of the scriptures; I was so very keen to see Bimala blossom with all the knowledge and energy and love of the universe.

The one thing that I did not consider then is that if we want to see a person as their completely free, real selves, we have to give up all hope of making an unquestionable claim on them. Why had I not considered it? Was it because of the arrogance of a husband's constant possessiveness over his wife? No, it wasn't that. It was because I had a deep trust in love.

I had prided myself on having the strength to bear the truth in its absolute naked form. This strength is being tested now. Whether I survive or I die, I retain the confidence of passing the test.

Even today, there is one aspect of myself that Bimal simply hasn't understood. I have always considered coercion a weakness. The weak do not dare be fair; they reject uprightness for the sake of quick results from unjust methods. Bimal turns impatient when she sees patience. She loves seeing the turbulent, the enraged, even the wrong-doer, in a man. A desire for fear seems to mingle with respect within her.

I had expected her to be released from the attraction to tyranny when she saw the world from a larger vantage point. But today I realize that this is part of Bimal's nature. She loves the monstrous from the depths of her heart. She likes to use chilli pepper to whip all the simple, pure elements of life into a red-hot flavour that will scorch everything from the tip of the tongue to the extremeties of the digestive system; she more or less ignores all other seasoning.

Similarly, I have vowed not to drink the raw alcohol of a passing enthusiasm to join patriotic acts in a frenzy. I would tolerate poor work rather than beat up the servants—the prospect of saying or doing something in a fit of anger makes both my mind and body shrink. I know Bimal is contemptuous of this disinclination—she considers it a form of mildness; she is angry with me today for the same reason, for she sees I refuse to be tyrannical and justify it with a cry of 'Vande mataram' on my lips.

That I have not joined in the worship of the goddess nation with a glass of alcohol in my hand has angered everyone. The people of this country believe that I either seek a title or am afraid of the police, while the police believe that I have evil intentions, which is why I appear to be harmless. But still I walk this path of mistrust and humiliation.

For I say that those who do not feel motivated to serve their country when they think of their nation as nothing but their nation, and respect people as nothing but people who need to be hypnotized with shrieking invocations to a mother or a deity, do not love their country so much as they love passion. The attempt to maintain a stronger infatuation with something over and above the truth is a symptom of our instilled sense of slavery. We no longer feel strong once we set our minds free. Our inanimate consciousness refuses to budge until a fancy or an individual or an exaggeration of eulogies is planted on our backs. So long as we are not aroused by the simple truth, so long as we require such infatuations, we must conclude that we have not yet developed the strength to claim our country through independence. Till then, no matter what state we are in, either an imagined ghost or a real exorcist—or both—will keep tormenting us.

Sandip told me the other day, you may have many qualities, but you lack the power of imagination, which is why you cannot see this divine form of the motherland in its real self. I found Bimal agreeing. I did not respond. There would be no joy in winning this argument, for this was not so much a divergence of logic as it was a difference in principles. Such differences appear minor within the narrow precincts of the home; so they do not mar the harmony of voices. But in the larger world such differences surge higher—they not only roar louder, they crash harder, too.

No power of imagination? In other words, the lamp in me might be equipped with a wick and oil, but lacks a flame. But I say the deficiency is in all of you. You are as devoid of light as flintstones; that's why you need to be rubbed so much, with so much noise for a small spark to emerge and this isolated spark only heightens pride, not vision.

I have long observed the coarseness of greed within Sandip. It is this carnivorous desire that goads him to weave a spell around religion and drives him towards oppression when working for his country. Because his faculties are sharp while his nature is crude, he dresses his proclivities in fanciful names. Just like the satisfaction that physical pleasure provides, a quick culmination of antagonism is a violent requirement for him. Bimal had told me several times earlier of Sandip's avarice for money. It was not as though I had not realized this for myself, but I could not be miserly with Sandip when it came to money. Even the thought that he might have been deceiving me was embarrassing. I did not want an altercation on the subject, lest my helping him with money appeared distasteful. But today it will be difficult to explain to Bimal that Sandip's attitude towards his country is largely a facet of his crude avariciousness. Bimal worships him in her head, which is why I hesitate to say anything negative about Sandip to her—for all I know, my jealousy seeps in, perhaps I exaggerate. It is possible that the searing heat of my agony has distorted the lines of Sandip's image in my mind. And yet it is better to write all this down than to store everything in my memory.

I have seen my teacher Chandranath-babu for almost the entire thirty years of my life; he fears neither criticism nor personal loss nor death. Considering the family I was born into, no advice in this situation could have saved me; but this man had established himself at the centre of my life with his peace, his truth, his hallowed figure. That is why I have found compassion in its truest, most direct form.

The very same Chandranath-babu came up to me the other day and asked, is Sandip needed here anymore?

Whenever there's an ill wind it always strikes at his heart first; in some mysterious way, he always knows. He is not perturbed easily, but on that occasion he had sensed the long shadow of danger. I know how much he loves me.

Over tea I asked Sandip, aren't you going to Rangpur? They've written to me—they're under the impression I'm refusing to let you go.

Bimal was pouring. Her face paled at once. She threw a single sidelong glance at Sandip.

Sandip answered, I've thought it over. Travelling around the country to spread the word about swadeshi is a waste of energy. I think the impact would be far more long-lasting if we could concentrate our activities around specific locations.

Don't you agree, he added, looking at Bimal.

At first Bimal didn't know how to respond. A little later she said, both methods could prove useful. You have to choose between doing your work in different places or in one place, according to your preference or your nature. The choice that the heart makes is your chosen path.

Then let me tell you the truth, said Sandip. All this while I had believed that travelling around the country and arousing people's passions was my vocation. But I was wrong. One reason for my error was that in no one place did I find the source of the power that could keep me fulfilled perpetually. That is why I had to agitate ever new people in ever new lands in order to collect the power of life from their fires. Today you are the voice of the country to me. I have not seen this fire in any one person till now. Shame on me for being proud of my own power. I no longer revel in being a leader of the nation. But I do dare to state that I can set the entire nation on fire with the spirit that you possess. No, there is no need to squirm, for your place lies far above hesitation or diffidence or humility. You are the queen bee of our hive; we will cluster around you and perform our tasks, but the power shall flow from you—if we go away from you our work will lose its core and become joyless. You must accept our devotion without reservation.

Bimal turned red with embarrassment and glory, her hand shook as she poured the tea.

On another occasion, Chandranath-babu told me, why don't the two of you go to Darjeeling for some time; you look unwell. Aren't you sleeping well?

Would you like to go to Darjeeling for a holiday? I asked Bimal in the evening.

I knew she was very keen to visit Darjeeling for a glimpse of the Himalayas. Not now, she replied that evening.

The nation might suffer.

I shall not lose faith, I shall wait. The path from a constricted space to a wide open one is perilous; the arrangements within the four walls of the rooms that had ruled Bimal's life are no longer sufficient now that she has stepped outside. Only when she understands everything after attaining complete familiarity with the unknown world outside shall I find out where I stand. If I discover that I no longer fit into the arrangements for this larger life, I will conclude that what I had lived with all this time was a pack of lies. I shall not need those lies anywhere. If such a day does dawn, I shall not argue—I shall disappear slowly. Coercion? Whatever for? Force cannot be used against the truth.

SANDIP'S STORY

The impotent claim—and the weak believe—that only what has fallen to my lot is mine. But what the world teaches is that whatever I can seize is rightfully mine.

The country is not mine just because I have been born in it; it will be mine only when I can plunder it from its owners and seize it by force.

It is natural to be greedy because the right to profit is natural. There is no message in nature that says we must be deprived for any reason whatsoever. What the heart wants, we must get from this world—this is the true statement of nature, at home and in the world. The education that does not allow this truth to be acknowledged goes under the name of ethics, which is why man has never been able to accept it.

There is a set of half-dead people in this world who do not know how to seize and hold on, whose grips are loosened easily. Let them be consoled by ethics. But only those who can desire with all their heart, and consume with all their life, who have no doubts, no hesitation, are the blessed children of nature. It is for them that nature has laid out all that is beautiful, all that is priceless. They will swim across rivers, vault over walls, kick doors down, grab and snatch whatever is worth possessing. This is what brings real joy, what brings value to invaluable things. Nature will surrender, but only to the plunderer. For it savours the force of desire, the force of usurping, the force of possession. So it is reluctant to place its marital garland of spring blossoms around the gaunt neck of the half-dead ascetic with protruding bones. The music is playing in the wedding hall—the auspicious hour is about to pass, I am pensive. Who is the groom? I am. The groom's seat belongs to the one who appears with a flaming torch. Nature's bridegroom arrives uninvited.

Shame? No, I have none. What I need I take, with permission or without. Those who are too inhibited to take what should be taken give it a complex name in order to smother their regret. This world where we have arrived is the reality. Why were these people even born on this planet with its unyielding soil—these people who have abandoned this marketplace of commodities empty-handed and hungry, fooling themselves with long-winded phrases? Were they commissioned by a bunch of upright gentlemen to play those hoary old sweet melodies in imaginary orchards? I am not interested in those cliches, and those imaginary orchards won't feed me. What I want, I want intensely. I will squeeze it with both my hands, stomp on it with both my feet, smear it on my body, eat it to my heart's content. I have no shame in asking, no hesitation in getting. The faint admonitions of those who have withered away from starving on their principles to become emaciated, like bedbugs on long-abandoned cots, will not reach my ears.

I do not wish to play hide-and-seek, for that involves cowardice. But if I cannot do so when needed, that is cowardice too. You will raise walls around what you want; therefore, I will have to bore a hole through it to get what I want. You are greedy, so you erect walls. I am greedy, so I cut through them. If you use machines, I shall resort to tricks. These are the facts of nature. It is on these facts that the kingdoms and empires of the world have been built, that the large enterprises of the world are run. As for the embodiments of the gods who have descended from heaven to spout heavenly jargon, their statements are not real. That is why all their vehement declarations only find a place in a corner of the homes of the weak; those who are powerful enough to rule the world cannot afford to pay attention to them. For heeding them is a waste of energy. Because the assertions are not true. Only those who do not baulk at accepting this without shame are successful; and those hapless individuals who are caught between nature and oppressive embodiments of virtue, swinging hopelessly between the real and the unreal, are able to move neither forward nor backward.

Some people are born with the vow not to live. They are captivated by the beauty of dying, like the sky at sunset. Our Nikhilesh belongs to this tribe; he could well be termed inanimate. Four years ago we had a bitter argument over this. He tells me, I accept that you cannot seize anything except by force but the question is: what is force, and how must you seize things? My force is the force of renunciation.

In other words, you are desperate to lose, I said.

Yes, in the same way that the chick within the egg is desperate to lose the eggshell, said Nikhil. The shell may be a very real object, but in exchange for giving it up the bird gets air and light—perhaps that makes it a loser by your standards.

Nikhilesh speaks this way, in symbols; it is difficult to persuade him that these are nevertheless just words, not the truth. So be it.

If he's happy with his symbols, let him be happy. We are the carnivores of the world. We have teeth, we have nails; we can run, we can capture, we can tear things apart; we are incapable of grazing on grass in the morning and then chewing the cud all day. Therefore, if you symbol-makers insist on guarding the doors to the food that has been provided for us here on earth, we shall not accept it. We will either steal or rob. Otherwise we cannot survive. We are not ready to fall hopelessly in love with death and lie down on lotus leaves to pass away in the final stage of life no matter how saddened my abstemious friends are to hear this.

Everyone will tell me, this is just your opinion. That's because the real movers in this world all follow this rule, though they claim otherwise. They do not know that this rule is the only principle. I do. What I am saying is not mere opinion—it has been tested already by life. My ways do not make it difficult for me to win women's hearts. They are creatures of the real world, after all. They do not wander about in balloons of empty ideas like men do. They can see the strong desire in my eyes and face and body and heart and words. This desire has not wasted away under austerity; it does not look backward because of arguments. It is brimming over, it whistles past like the hunter's arrow, intent on taking, intent on consuming. Women know in their hearts that this irresistible desire is the life-force of the universe, victorious wherever it goes because it is not willing to bow to anyone but itself. I have repeatedly seen how women let themselves be swept away by this will without any concern for life or death. The power that enables one to get women belongs to the hero—with this he can grasp the real world. Let those who imagine there are other worlds to conquer divert the flow of their desires from the earth towards the sky; I shall see how high their fountains can spurt and how long they can last. Women were not created for these subtle, idea-bearing creatures.

Affinity! The creator has paired specific men and women and sent them to earth. The attraction between them is truer than the one sought to be created by marriage rituals. I have said this often and everywhere. Human beings want to follow nature, but they are not happy till they have obscured it with language. That is why the world has been filled with lies. Why should there be only one affinity? There are thousands. Nature has made no rules that say you have to dismiss all other affinities for the sake of one. I have found many of them in my life but that has not closed the doors to finding one more. I can see it clearly, and it can see my affinity too. After that? If I still cannot make a conquest, I am a coward.

BIMALA'S STORY

I wonder where my inhibitions had vanished. I had no time to regard myself—my days and nights simply whirled around me. And shame had no opportunity to penetrate my heart.

One day my sister-in-law told my husband in my presence, laughing, it's the women who have done all the weeping in this family, Thakurpo, but it's the men's turn now. From now on we will make you cry. What do you think, Chhotorani? Now that you're dressed in your battle-garb, warrior princess, fire away at the hearts of men.

She looked me up and down. There was a new colour in the way I was dressed and was behaving, none of which had escaped her attention. I am embarrassed to write this today, but I felt no embarrassment that day. For my instincts were at work within me—nothing I did was a considered decision.

I know I used to take special care when dressing those days—but absent-mindedly. It was clear to me which of my dresses appealed to Sandip-babu the most. And there was no need to guess, either, for Sandip-babu used to discuss his preference openly. One day he told my husband in my presence, the day I set sight on Queen Bee for the first time she was sitting quietly in her elaborately embroidered sari, her eyes gazing at the infinite like stars that had lost their way . . . as though she had been gazing the same way for thousands of years in search of something, waiting for someone, on the edge of a bottomless darkness . . . my heart trembled then . . . I felt as though the flames within her had emerged to wrap themselves around her in the form of her sari. This is the fire we need, these discernible flames. Heed my request, Queen Bee, show yourselves to us from time to time dressed like fire.

All this while I had been a tiny village stream with its own rhythm and language—but one day the ocean's tides swept me away without warning. My currents swelled, my banks overflowed, the beat of my torrents resonated to the thumping drums of the sea—and I could make no sense of the sounds in my blood. Where had the old me gone? Where did all these waves of beauty come rushing in from? Sandip-babu's unfulfilled eyes seemed to light up at my beauty like lamps placed in front of a god. Every one of his words and glances appeared to split the sky like pealing temple bells to declare that I was extraordinary in both beauty and power. The bells covered every other sound on earth.

Had the almighty created me afresh today? Had he compensated for his neglect of all these years? She who was once not beautiful grew beautiful. She who was once ordinary sensed the glory of the land within herself. Sandip-babu was not a single individual—he was the confluence of millions of minds in the country. When he called me the queen bee of the hive, I was crowned to the sound of every patriot's murmurs of admiration. After this, the silent contempt of my eldest sister-in-law and the loud mockery of the younger one could not affect me anymore. My relationship with the entire world had changed.

Sandip-babu explained to me that the country needed me greatly. I didn't hesitate to believe him that day. I could . . . I could do anything, I had been endowed with a divine power, something I had not experienced before, which had been beyond me. There was no questioning the nature of the surging emotion within me; it was mine, and yet it was not—it belonged outside me, to the entire world. It was like floodwater, which did not need the justification of a pond behind the house.

Sandip-babu would seek my advice on every single matter concerning the movement. I was hesitant at the outset, but it passed quickly. He would be amazed at whatever I said. He would keep saying, we men can only analyse, but you women understand, you don't have to analyse. It is women whom god has created from his imagination, while he has made men with a hammer. Hearing him, I began to believe that my intelligence and abilities were so natural that I had not spotted them initially.

Sandip-babu would get letters on different subjects from all over the country, all of which I would read. He never replied to any of them without seeking my opinion. There were times when he didn't agree with me. I wouldn't argue with him, but a couple of days later he seemed to see the light on waking up in the morning. Sending for me immediately, he would say, I have suffered as a result of not seeking your approval—can you explain the mystery behind this?

My conviction that Sandip-babu seemed to be at the root of every activity in the freedom movement strengthened, at the source of which was the natural intelligence of a woman. My heart was filled with the glory of a momentous responsibility.

My husband had no role in these consultations. Sandip-babu's attitude towards my husband was similar to that of the elder brother who loves his younger brother dearly but does not rely on his counsel on important matters. Sandip-babu would say, smiling with great affection, that my husband was extremely childish about these issues, and his point of view was completely different. There appeared to be a humorous aspect to these strange opinions and intellectual crises of my husband's, which made Sandip-babu all the fonder of him. So, out of unbounded love, he had released my husband from all responsibilities.

Nature's skills provide many medicines to numb pain. When the umbilical cord of a special relationship begins to be severed, this medicine is applied without our knowledge. Eventually we wake up one day to find that the separation has taken place. While a knife was being taken to the most important relationship of my life, my mind was so overpowered by the anaesthetic effect of a powerful emotion that I could not even sense how cruel an act was being enacted. Perhaps this is the nature of women; when the feelings in their heart become turbulent, they are not aware of any other sensation. This is why we are destructive—we wreak havoc with our blind nature, not just with reason. We are like rivers—as long as we flow between our banks we follow the rules with all our might, but once we overflow those banks, we destroy with all our might.

SANDIP'S STORY

I could tell that trouble was brewing. There was a taste of it the other day.

Since my arrival, Nikhilesh's drawing room had become a combination of the outdoor and indoor worlds, an amphibious substance. I had my rights there from the external world, while Bee put up no barriers within.

Had we claimed our rights selectively, keeping some of them in abeyance and enjoying them leisurely, people might have become used to it. But when the levee breaks for the first time, the current is very strong. Our meetings in the drawing room continued with such intensity that we did not care to think of anything else.

I can always make out from my room when Bee appears in the drawing room. Some of the sounds are from her jewellery, and some from other things. Possibly she opens the door with greater force than is necessary. Then, the glass door to the bookshelf is a little tight—opening it makes considerable noise. When I arrive in the drawing room, I find Bee with her back to the door, engrossed deeply in selecting books from the shelf. When I offer help in this difficult task she objects, startled, after which the conversation veers off in other directions.

The other Thursday, I had left my room on hearing just such sounds. I found a guard standing in my way in the middle of the veranda. As I proceeded without paying attention to him, he stopped me, saying, don't go that way, babu.

Why not!

Ranima is in the drawing room.

Very well, inform your ranima that Sandip-babu wishes to meet her.

I cannot do that. Not allowed to.

I was furious. Raising my voice, I said, I'm ordering you, go ask her.

The guard hesitated, sensing trouble. I pushed him aside and went towards the drawing room. When I was almost at the door, he ran up to me to perform his duty, grasping my arm and saying, don't go in, babu.

What! Stop me physically! Shaking his hand off, I slapped him resoundingly. Bee came out of the room at this moment to find the guard preparing to confront me.

I will never forget the figure she cut. That Bee is beautiful is my discovery. Most people in our country wouldn't give her a second glance. Tall and slender, what our connossieurs of beauty critically refer to as 'lanky'. I am entranced by her appearance that is like an exuberant spray spurting skyward from the fountain of life within the cave in the creator's heart. Her complexion is dark, but dark like a steel sword—sharp and brave. That same spirit sparkled on her face that day. Standing on the threshold, the queen raised her index finger and commanded, go away, Nanku.

Do not be angry, I said. Since I have been forbidden, I shall go.

No, do not go, come in, said Bee, her voice quavering.

This was not a request, it was an order. I went in, sitting down and fanning myself. Scribbling on a piece of paper with a pencil, Bee summoned a servant and said, give this to babu.

I said, forgive me, I could not control myself, I slapped the guard.

Good for you, said Bee.

But it's not the poor fellow's fault, he's just following orders.

Nikhil entered the room. I jumped up and stood at the window with my back to him.

Bee told Nikhil, Nanku has insulted Sandip-babu today.

Nikhil asked 'why' with such innocent surprise that I could not contain myself. Turning, I looked at him steadily; I told myself that the saint's boasts about the truth cannot pass muster with his wife if she's the right kind of wife.

Bee said, Sandip-babu was on his way to the drawing room when Nanku stopped him, saying he had been told not to let him through.

Told by whom, asked Nikhil.

How should I know, answered Bee.

She was about to burst into tears from rage and resentment.

Nikhil sent for the guard. He said, it's not my fault, huzoor, I was merely following orders.

Whose orders?

Baroranima and Mejoranima told me to.

We were all silent for a few moments.

When the guard had left, Bee said, Nanku has to be dismissed.

Nikhil did not respond. I realized that he was in an ethical dilemma. There's no end to his dilemmas.

But this was a serious problem! She wasn't a simple woman!

The Home and the World 43

She would use Nanku's dismissal to take revenge on her sisters-in-law.

Still Nikhil did not speak. Bee's eyes began to emit sparks. Her contempt for his decency seemed boundless.

Nikhil left without a word.

The guard was not to be seen anymore from the next day. I found out that Nikhil had sent him into the villages with some work—he had benefited rather than suffered as a result.

I could make out from clues how violent a storm must have blown in the background to this little incident. I keep thinking how strange a person Nikhil is, almost a freak.

The outcome of all this was that Bee began to frequent the drawing room every day, sending for me and conversing with me; she did not bother to maintain the pretext of needing my help or of an accidental encounter.

This is how hints and signals lend the mass of clarity to ambiguity. She is someone's wife—who might as well be an inhabitant of the stars as far as an outsider is concerned. There is no predetermined route here. In this uncharted outer space, the attraction, the discovery, the throwing back of the curtains of tradition, and then the arrival at the centre of absolutely naked nature is an extraordinary victory march of truth.

For what else is it but the truth! The attraction between man and woman because of their affinities is real; everything in the universe, from a speck of dust to the stars in the sky are in its favour. But human beings want to keep it hidden under homilies and proverbs, trying to tame it with home-made rules and regulations. Like a commission to melt the universe down in order to make a watch-chain. And then, when reality wakes up to the call of the tangible, slashing and burning the deception of words to take its rightful place, can anything stop it—be it righteousness or be it faith? There is so much condemnation then, so much chest-beating and disciplining. But can you combat a tornado with words? It does not respond to words, after all, it only shakes you up. It is reality.

So I am enjoying this open display of truth in front of my eyes. So much embarrassment, so much fear, so much doubt! But there's no richness to truth without any of this. This trembling of the knees, this frequent looking away—all of this is so sweet! And the deception is not just in others, but also in ourselves. When the real has to fight with the unreal, trickery is its primary weapon. Because the enemy tries to shame what is concrete by saying, you're so crass, it has to either conceal itself or clothe itself in illusion. Given the circumstances, it cannot say with authority that yes, I am crass, for I am real, I am flesh, I am proclivity, I am hunger, I am shameless and heartless—as shameless and heartless as the enormous rock that slips from the mountainside under the force of the rain to crash down on human habitation without caring who lives and who dies.

I can see everything. There, the curtains are flying away; there, I can see the preparation for the journey on the road to apocalypse. That red ribbon, so small, visible through the mass of clean hair—it is nothing but the ravenous tongue of the nor'wester, reddened by the secret passion of desire. That fall of the border of the sari, that hint of the jacket, I can clearly sense the heat they emanate. And yet the pattern is being created unknowingly, even the one drawing them does not know.

Why doesn't she know? Because, by constantly suppressing reality, man has destroyed the capacity for understanding and accepting it. Human beings are embarrassed by reality. So it has to perform its tasks covertly, beneath the layers in which it has been shrouded. That is why we are not aware of its movements and when it eventually breathes down our necks, we cannot ignore it anymore. Man has tried to drive it away with the accusation of being the devil—it enters the garden of Eden surreptitiously, in the form of a snake, and whispers into the ears of the beloved of man to make her see clearly and become a rebel. There can be no comfort after this, only death.

I am materialistic. Naked reality is breaking out of the jail of contemplation to emerge into the light and my happiness grows stronger with every step it takes. What I want is going to be within reach, I will get it in all its solidity, I will grasp it firmly, I will not let it go in any circumstances. Whatever comes in between will be smashed to smithereens and blown away in the dust and the wind, this joy, this is what joy is, this is the destructive dance of reality—and after this, death or life, good or bad, happiness or sorrows are all irrelevant! Irrelevant! Irrelevant!

My Queen Bee is in a trance, she does not know the path she is treading. It is not safe to wake her up prematurely. It is best to inform her that I have noticed nothing. While I was eating the other day, Queen Bee was gazing at me in rapt attention, completely forgetting what such a look could mean. When I suddenly raised my eyes to hers, she reddened and looked away. You are surprised by the way I eat, I said. I can conceal many things, but my greed is exposed at every step. But then, since I am not embarrassed for myself, you cannot be embarrassed on my behalf.

Cocking her head and growing redder, she began to reply, not at all, you . . .

I know women love greedy men, I said. Women conquer them with the help of that greed. I am greedy, which is why I've received so much love from women that I do not have an iota of shame anymore. Therefore you can go on staring at me while I eat. I don't care in the slightest. I can chew these marrows till they're absolutely devoid of juice, such is my nature.

I was reading a recent English book a few days ago, where the relationship between men and women is dealt with in clear, realistic terms. I had left the book in their drawing room. Entering the room for something one afternoon, I found Queen Bee reading it. As soon as she heard footsteps she quickly covered it with another one—a volume of Longfellow's poetry—and rose to her feet.

I said, look, I simply don't understand why you women are embarrassed to read poetry. It is men who should be embarrassed, since some of us are attorneys and some are engineers. If we must read poetry, it should be at the dead of night, behind closed doors. But you women rhyme verses all the way. The god who created you is a lyric poet—it was at his feet that Jaydeva perfected his poem on the Bengali woman.

As Queen Bee smiled without answering and made to leave, I said, you cannot do that, please go on reading. I had left a book here, I'll take it and run.

I picked my book up from the table, saying, it is fortunate you didn't get your hands on this one, or else you might have whipped me.

Why, asked Bee.

Because this isn't a volume of poetry, I said. What's in here are the broad strokes of human life, told directly, without any cleverness. I really wanted Nikhil to read this.

But why, said Queen, frowning.

He's a man, you see, I told her. One of us. He only wants to see this material world in indistinct terms, which is why we quarrel so much. As you've seen, that's why he considers our swadeshi movement like Longfellow's poetry, his objective seems to be the preservation of the sweetness of the rhythm at every step. But we move about with the hammer of prose—we break rhythms.

What's the connection between this book and swadeshi, asked Bee.

You'd know if you read it, I answered. Whether it is swadeshi or something else, Nikhil always wants to live by manufactured ideas, which is why he is in constant conflict with human nature at every step. And then he blames nature. He simply refuses to accept that our nature was created well before words were, and our nature will live well after words have fallen silent.

Bee was quiet for some time; then she asked without smiling, isn't it our nature to want to rise above our nature?

I smiled to myself. My dear Queen, this is not your own slogan, you have learnt it from Nikhilesh. You are a completely healthy, normal person, happily brimming with needs; as soon as you've heard the call of human nature your entire flesh and blood has begun to respond. How can they hold you back in the magic web of the incantations they have been pouring into your ears all this time? Do you think I don't know that you have been set on fire by the flames of life? How much longer can they keep you cooled by wrapping you in the wet towel of pious homilies?

The majority of people on earth are weak, I said. To save their own lives they mutter these incantations into the ears of the world to ruin everyone's hearing. Those who have been debilitated and deprived by their own natures are the same people who advise weakening the natures of other people too.

Bee said, we women are weak as well, we must also join the conspiracy of the weak.

Who said you are weak, I asked with a smile. Males have damned you with the faint praise of being helpless and kept you weak out of shame. I believe that it is you who are stronger. I will sign a declaration to the effect that you women will demolish the fortress of incantations erected by men and achieve your freedom through violence. Men make a lot of noise, but it's all superficial. You've seen their insides, haven't you? They are encaged creatures. They are the ones who have written the scriptures till now and bound themselves, creating golden chains out of women with their own breath and fire to tie themselves up both within and without. If men did not have the remarkable ability to capture themselves in their own traps, who could have held them back today? Self-created traps are the gods that men venerate the most. Males have adorned these traps in different colours and forms, and worshipped with different names. But women? You have always wanted the flesh and blood reality of the world with all your heart and soul, you have given birth to reality, you have obeyed reality.

Bee is an educated woman; she does not concede an argument easily. If that were true, she said, would men have been able to like women?

Women are aware of this danger, I told her. They know that males love deception by nature. That's why they borrow words from males to deceive them. They know that males are natural drunkards who prefer drink to food, which is why they use all sorts of tricks and gestures and signals to present themselves as drink to men; they try their utmost to conceal the fact that they are actually food. Women are the basis of materialism, they need no ingredients to enchant; it is men who need all kinds of spells. Women have become enchanters simply out of necessity.

Then why do you wish to break this spell, asked Bee.

Because I want freedom, I answered. Freedom for the country and freedom for relationships between people. The country is very real to me, I cannot view it behind a misty curtain of principles. I am very real to me, you are very real to me, which is why I do not at all care for the business of using a plethora of words to take humans beyond one another's reach and comprehension.

I know it isn't difficult to jolt someone who is sleepwalking through life. But I am unrestrained by nature, it is not my way to proceed with caution. What I said that day was rather bold in its tenor and manner; the first impact of such statements is unbearable, but for women, victory goes to the valorous. Men love vagueness but women love material objects, which is why men are desperate to worship the embodiments of their ideas, while women place all their offerings at the feet of the forceful.

Just as our discussion was about to become heated, Nikhil's childhood teacher Chandranath-babu appeared in the room. The earth is not a bad place to be in, all told, but the intrusion of all these teachers makes me want to abandon it sometimes. People like Nikhilesh want to keep this world a school until they die. They grow up, but still the school follows them; they enter married life, and the school moves in too. They should make their teacher die with them too on the funeral pyre when they die. That day this embodiment of the school appeared, unwanted, in the middle of our conversation. Villain that I am, even I had to stop suddenly. And our Bee, her expression changed as though she was the best student in the class who had solemnly sat down on the front bench. She had suddenly remembered that she had a responsibility to pass an examination in this world. Some people sit on the roadside like railway pointsmen, unnecessarily shunting trains of thought from one track to another.

As soon as Chandranath-babu entered he shrank back and tried to leave. But before he could say 'Excuse me' Bee bent down and touched his feet, saying, please don't leave, master-moshai, do sit down. As though she was out of her depth in the water and needed Master-moshai's support. Coward! Or perhaps I had misunderstood. Maybe this was a ruse, a desire to raise her price. Maybe Bee wanted to let me know elaborately that you may think you have overwhelmed me, but I respect Chandranath-babu far more than I do you. Go ahead. Teachers must be respected. I am not a teacher, I do not seek empty respect. I have already said that trickery will not feed me; I understand material objects.

Chandranath-babu brought up the subject of swadeshi. I had wanted to let him rave on without interruption. It is best to let old men talk, this gives them the impression they are the ones winding the spring of the world. The poor things do not realize that the world is actually running somewhere far away from their tongue. I was quiet at first, but Sandip-chandra cannot be accused even by his strongest enemies of being patient. When Chandranath-babu said, look, we have never tilled the land and now if we expect an instant harvest . . .

I could not restrain myself. We don't want a harvest, I said. We say, *ma phaleshu kadachana*—we are not entitled to the fruits of our action.

Then what do you want, asked Chandranath-babu in surprise.

Thistles, I said, cultivating which involves no expenses.

Master-moshai said, thistles not only block the way for others, they are weeds even in our own path.

That is a principle for teaching in schools, I told him. We are not writing homilies with chalk on blackboards. Our hearts are burning, and that is what matters. Right now we shall plant thorns to target the soles of other people's feet; when they prick our own feet afterwards we will have plenty of time to repent. Is that too much? It will be time to calm down when it is time to die. When it is time to burn, restlessness is more appropriate.

Smiling, Chandranath-babu said, be restless by all means, but don't mistake it for bravery or achievement and praise yourself. Those who protected their own were not restless, they performed their duties diligently. Only those who have always been terrified of hard work suddenly wake up from their sleep to imagine they can take the non-path of non-effort to come to the aid of the world in a hurry.

Just as I was girding my loins to deliver a suitably strong reply, Nikhil came in. Chandranath-babu rose to his feet, telling Bee, I'll go now, ma, I have things to do.

As soon as he left I showed the English book to Nikhil and told him, I was telling Queen Bee about this book.

Ninety-five per cent of people in this world have to be deceived with lies, but this eternal student of the schoolmaster is easy to deceive with the truth. Nikhil is cheated most comprehensively when you allow him to be cheated openly. That's why with him it's best to lay my cards on the table.

Nikhil was silent when he read the name of the book. I said, people have blurred this world with a variety of words. These writers have taken up a broom to sweep away the dust gathered over them and expose what lies beneath. That's why I was saying it would be useful for you to read this book.

I've read it, said Nikhil.

What do you think, I asked.

Nikhil said, it's good for those who want to think about such books, poison for those who want to avoid it.

Meaning?

Nikhil said, look, anyone who says today that no one has an exclusive claim to his own property is worthy of saying it only if he's devoid of greed. But if he is a thief by nature, the statement is a lie. When such proclivities are strong in a person, books like these will not be interpreted correctly.

I said, proclivities are the lamp posts of nature whose light guides us. Those who deny proclivities labour from the misplaced hope of gaining divine foresight by gouging out their own eyes.

I consider proclivity the truth only when I also consider renunciation of the truth, said Nikhil. If I try to see something by wedging it into my eye, I will not only damage my eye but also be unable to see it. Those who want to connect everything to proclivities distort these very proclivities without seeing the truth.

Look, Nikhil, viewing life through the gold-rimmed glasses of righteousness is a mental luxury of yours, I told him. This is why you see reality indistinctly when it's time for action, why you cannot accomplish anything with force.

I don't consider achieving anything by force an achievement, said Nikhil.

What do you consider it then?

Why argue? Fruitless arguments over such things mar their elegance.

I had wanted Bee to join our debate. She had sat quietly all this while without speaking a single word. Maybe I had shaken her a great deal today, planting doubts in her mind; perhaps she wanted the schoolmaster to explain things to her.

I don't know whether I overdid it today. But it is necessary to shake their composure. The first lesson is that what has always been considered unshakeable can actually be shaken.

To Nikhil I said, I'm glad we talked about this. I was about to give this book to Queen Bee to read.

What's wrong with that, asked Nikhil. When I have read it, why not Bimal too? I just have one thing to explain; these days Europe weighs everything from the perspective of science; all analyses suggest that this object called man is just physiology or biology or psychology or, at most, sociology. But don't forget, I beg of you, that man is not just doctrine, that along with all the philosophies, reaching beyond all the philosophies, man extends himself towards the infinite. You call me the schoolmaster's student; but I'm not, all of you are—you want to understand man through the science teacher, not from your soul deep within you.

Why are you so agitated these days, Nikhil, I asked.

He said, because I see clearly that you belittle man, humiliate him.

Where do you see this?

In the wind, in my pain. All of you want to kill the one who is greatest among men, the ascetic, the beautiful.

What madness is this?

Rising to his feet suddenly, Nikhil said, look, Sandip, I have the conviction that man will suffer the agony of death but will not die. So I am prepared to bear it all knowingly, willingly.

He left immediately. I was looking at him in astonishment when I heard a sudden noise, and discovered that two or three books had fallen to the floor from the table, while Queen Bee left the room apprehensively, making sure not to pass by close to me.

Nikhilesh is a strange man. He knows very well that his home is under imminent threat, but still he doesn't throw me out—why? I know he is waiting to see what Bimal does. If she tells him, you and I are not well-matched, he will lower his eyes and say softly, then I see I have made a mistake. He cannot understand that the biggest mistake of all is to accept a mistake. Nikhil is a living example of how ideas debilitate a man. I have not seen another male like him, he is nothing but a whim of nature. It is not possible to even write a reasonable story or play about him, leave alone live with him.

And then there's Bee—it seems the spell she was under has been broken today. She has identified the current she is flowing along. She must now either go forward or go back. But no, from now on she will take one step forward and then one step backward.

That doesn't worry me. When your clothes are on fire, the more you run about in panic the more the flames are fanned. Fear will make her heart beat faster. I have seen this many times. The widow Kusum had submitted to me quaking in fear. And when the English girl near our hostel used to be angry with me, it seemed she would tear me apart in rage. I remember very well the day she threw me out of her room, screaming 'get out', and then as soon as I crossed the threshold she came running up to me, grasping my feet, weeping and banging her head on the floor till she fell unconscious. I know them very well whether it's rage or shame or hatred, all of it acts like kindling to make the fire in their hearts burn everything to ashes. Only ideas can control these flames. Women do not possess it. They perform pious acts, go on pilgrimages, pay homage to men of god the way we go to office but they do not go anywhere near ideas.

I will not tell her much on my own. I will give her some current English books to read. Let her realize that it is modern to acknowledge and respect one's nature as reality. It is not modern to be ashamed of one's inclinations or to consider restraint more important. Sanctuary from the word 'modern' will make her stronger, because they need their pilgrimages, their men of god and their rituals—mere ideas are meaningless to them.

Anyway, let us watch this play till the fifth act. I cannot claim proudly that I am only a spectator, sitting in the royal seats on the balcony and applauding now and then. I feel a tug in my chest, my nerves ache now and then. When I turn out the lamp at night and go to bed, a small touch, a little wanting, a brief conversation circle around me, filling the darkness. When I wake up in the morning a sense of delight sparkles within me. I feel a melody flowing along with my blood.

There was a photograph of Bee's next to Nikhil's on a photo-stand placed on the table. I had taken the photo away. Showing Bee the empty space yesterday, I told her, the miser's parsimoniousness is to blame for theft, therefore the sin of this theft should be shared between the miser and the thief. Do you agree?

Bee smiled. It wasn't such a good photograph, she said.

What's to be done, I asked. A photograph is just that—a photograph. I shall be satisfied with what it is.

Bee opened a book and began to leaf through its pages. If you are angry I will find a way to fill the empty space, I said.

Today I did just that. This photograph of mine is from my youth, my face was undeveloped, as was my mind. I used to believe in life after death and many similar things. Faith does deceieve, but it also has an important quality—it lends a certain grace to the mind.

My photograph shall remain next to Nikhil's. We are friends.

NIKHILESH'S STORY

I had never thought about myself earlier, but now I often try to see myself as others might. I make an attempt to regard myself through Bimal's eyes. It is my nature to consider everything far too serious, far too important.

It is just that it is better to laugh life away than to sweep it away in tears. This is how we survive—only by waving away all the sorrows that pervade the home and the world today, as though they are fleeting shadows, mere illusions. If we had held on to them as the truth for even a moment would we have been able to a eat a morsel or sleep for an instant?

It is only myself whom I cannot include among the swept away and waved away. I feel as though my miseries alone are piling up into an eternal burden for the world. Hence my serious demeanour; that is why my eyes stream with tears when I look at myself.

Why not stand at the court of the universe and compare yourself with everyone else for once, you wretch? What relationship does Bimal have with you in this multitude of billions gathered at the confluence of every era of time? She is your wife! Whom do you refer to as your wife? You have blown up that word with puffs of your own breath and nurtured it carefully day and night, but do you not know that a single pinprick can let all the air out of it, deflating it in an instant?

My wife, therefore she is mine. If she wishes to say, 'No, I am me,' I will respond, how can that be possible, for you are my wife. Wife! Is this even logical? Is this even true? Can an entire human being be fitted inside this word in entirety and locked within?

Wife! I have cherished this word in my heart with everything that is wonderful, everything that is sacred; I have not allowed it to be besmirched for even a single day. So much incense, so many seasonal flowers, so much music, all for that one name. And now if she were to suddenly sink in the murky waters of the drain like the plaything that is a paper boat, my . . .

There we are, so serious again. Whom are you referring to as the drain, and whom as the murky water? These are expressions of rage. Do you expect things to stop because you are angry about them? If Bimal is not yours, she is not yours—the more you insist, the more you are enraged, the more strongly you will prove this truth. But my heart is breaking! Let it. The world will not be bankrupted, and nor will you, for that matter. Man is greater than everything he loses in life; even after he has crossed an ocean of tears there is a shore. That is why he weeps, he wouldn't otherwise.

But from the point of view of society . . . let society worry about it, let it do what it will. I am shedding my own tears, not society's. If Bimal says she is not my wife, let my social wife stay where she is, I shall leave.

There is always unhappiness. But there is one particular unhappiness succumbing to which will be wrong. I shall save myself from it no matter what I have to do. I cannot imagine, like a coward, that neglect has reduced the value of my life. My life is precious; I was not born so that I could use it only to buy the ladies' chambers in my home. My biggest enterprise will never go bankrupt, the time has come to consider this the truth.

Like myself, I must also view Bimal from an external perspective today. All this time I had adorned her with some of the priceless ideals of my own life. And although this female figure was not identical to the worldly Bimal in every way, still I worshipped her through this figure.

This is not a virtue on my part, it is a grave vice. I am greedy; in my mind I had wanted to take pleasure from my female figure, my Tilottama, the creation of the gods; in the external world, Bimal had become the pretext. Bimal is what she is, no more or no less. There was no compulsion for her to be Tilottama for my sake. Vishwakarma didn't perform my bidding, after all.

Therefore I must examine everything with clarity today; with a firm hand I shall wipe clean everything I painted in the colours of illusion. All this time I ignored much of what I observed. Today it is clear to me that I am only an accident in Bimal's life; the person with whom her entire personality truly matches is Sandip. That is all I need to know.

There is no point in being humble about myself to myself. Sandip has many desirable qualities with which he even attracted me all these days but even if I were to be modest, I have to accept that, all told, he is not a better man than I. If I am not the chosen one, if Sandip is the one who gets the garland, my being passed over will symbolize the gods' judgement of the one who chose, not of me. I do not state this out of pride. If I do not recognize my own worth as a truth, if I do not acknowledge it, if I am forced to consider this blow today as the ultimate humiliation of my life, I will end up in the garbage heap of the world as a discard; I shall no longer be able to achieve anything.

So may the joy of freedom rise through all my unbearable sorrows today. There is familiarity—I have understood the world and I have understood what lies within. What remains after all the accounts are settled is me. And this is not a crippled me, not a poverty-stricken me; the sickly man nurtured on a patient's diet is not me. I have been made by the stern hands of the creator. Whatever had to happen to him has happened, nothing can destroy him now.

Master-moshai came up to me a short while ago, putting his hand on my shoulder and saying, it's past one, Nikhil, go to sleep.

I find it very difficult to go to bed until late in the night, when Bimal is in deep sleep. I do meet her during the day, we even converse, but what can I say to her in the silence of the solitary night in bed? Both my body and heart shrink from it.

I asked Master-moshai, why aren't you asleep yet?

With a smile he said, I am too old to sleep now, I am at the age where people stay awake.

I was considering going to bed when the monsoon clouds in the sky outside my window parted suddenly, and a single star became visible, shining brightly. I felt it telling me, relationships grow and break, just like dreams, but I am constant, I am the everlasting flame in the wedding chamber, I am the undying kiss on the night of union.

With all my heart I sensed at that moment my eternal lover

waiting for me in seclusion behind the screen of the material world. I saw her image momentarily in many mirrors from many lifetimes—so many shattered mirrors, distorted mirrors, dust-coated mirrors. Whenever I said, 'Let me make this mirror mine' or 'Let me put it away in a box', the image vanished. But never mind, what's a mirror got to do with it, and what, the figure in the mirror? Your faith will remain intact, beloved, your smile shall not fade, the vermilion line you have etched for me on the horizon will dazzle every day under the rising sun.

A devil stands in the dark corner, telling me, all this is just an attempt to distract the child. So be it, for the child must be distracted—a million children, a billion children, a host of children. So many children and so many tears. Can such a multitude be deceived with lies? My beloved will not betray me; she is faithful, she is faithful, for this reason I have cast my eyes on her repeatedly, for this reason I shall cast my eyes on her repeatedly. Even through mistakes I have seen her, even through a mist of tears she was visible. I have seen her in the markets of life, I have lost her in them, and then seen her again. I shall see her even after I have slipped through to the other side of death. Do not mock me anymore, cruel one. If, this one time, I have mistaken the address of the street your feet have walked on, of the air which is redolent with the fragrance of your flowing hair, do not make me weep for this error all my life. The unveiled star there is telling me, no, don't be afraid, what is meant to last forever does last forever.

Let me gaze at my Bimal now as she sleeps. Let me plant a kiss on her brow without waking her. This kiss is the fruit of my worship. I believe that I shall forget everything after death—all the mistakes, all the tears—but a pulse will remain somewhere from the memory of this kiss. A necklace of these kisses from every lifetime is being threaded together to be slipped around the beloved's neck.

My sister-in-law entered my room. The clock in the watchroom struck two.

What are you doing here, Thakurpo? Go to bed, my dear. Don't torture yourself so. I cannot bear to look at you.

Her eyes began to stream with tears.

Touching her feet in silent reverence, I went to bed.

BIMALA'S STORY

I had suspected nothing at first, feared nothing; all I knew was that I was surrendering to my country. There was such elation in this complete submission. That was when I discovered for the first time that causing one's own ruination is the greatest of all joys.

I don't know, maybe the trance would have broken on its own once this undefined emotion had played itself out. But Sandip-babu could not wait—he made his intentions clear. The music in his words seemed to touch me physically; his eyes appeared to clasp my feet like a beggar. And yet there was such a strong desire at work within him, as though he wanted to drag me away by a handful of my hair like a cruel bandit.

I shall tell the truth—the destructive force of his irresistible longing attracted me continuously. I began to sense how alluring it was to tear oneself apart. There was such shame, such fear in it, but it was so sharp and sweet.

And there was no end to my curiosity. How enormous, how powerful the mystery of the sullen desire of the man I did not even know well, whom I would not have as mine with certainty, whose abilities were compelling, whose life burnt in a thousand flames. I had never even imagined this. The distant ocean, which I had only read about in my textbooks, leapt over all barriers in the form of a ravenously hungry wave, breaking in a welter of foam, infinite at my feet, at the spot where I had been doing the dishes in the water of the pond behind the house.

I had begun to revere Sandip-babu at first, but my reverence was swept away. I did not even respect him—in fact I am actually full of disrespect for him. I know very clearly that there is no comparison between him and my husband. And I had come to know, gradually, if not at the outset, that what appears to be Sandip-babu's manliness is nothing but restlessness.

But still it was his hands that played on this stringed instrument of my flesh and blood, of my feelings and thoughts. I wanted to loathe these hands and as for this instrument . . . but still, the instrument did play. And when my days and nights were filled with this melody, there was no compassion left in me. Every pulse in my veins, every torrent in my blood kept telling me to submerge myself and everything I had in this music.

I was no longer unaware of the fact that I had something in me which . . . how do I put it? Something because of which I think it would be best for me to be dead.

Master-moshai paid me a visit whenever he got an opportunity. He made me realize that the extent of my life was larger than I had imagined, that its boundaries were not where I had assumed they were.

But what was the use? I did not want to see it that way at all. Nor could I wish, in all honesty, that my intoxication should leave me. Let there be unhappiness in the family, let my truth within me be blackened every moment, but I wanted to be drunk forever. My husband's sister Munu's husband would often drink and beat her up, and then sob repentantly afterwards, swearing never to drink again. But when he did it again the next evening, I would burn in rage and hatred. Today I could see that the wine I was consuming was much more dangerous—it did not have to be purchased or poured into a glass; it was being generated automatically in my bloodstream. What was I to do! Would my entire life pass this way?

Sometimes I look at myself, startled, wondering whether I'm in a nightmare, and whether I will wake up suddenly to discover that this me isn't real; this one is terribly inconsistent, in conflict with herself. Like a sorceress she had painted her dishonour with the shades of the rainbow. I could not understand what had happened, or how.

One day my sister-in-law said with a smile, our Chhotorani is accomplished. She takes care of the guest so well that he has no intention of budging. We entertained guests in our time too, but they were not given so much attention. There was a different custom then—husbands had to be taken care of too. Poor Thakurpo was born so close to the modern era that he's missing out. He should have come to this house as guest, he would have survived for a while. But it's very doubtful now. Don't you even see how wretched he looks these days, you demoness?

Once, such statements made no impression on me. I used to think that they did not understand the vow I had undertaken to fulfil. There was a curtain of passion around me then; I had imagined I was giving up my life for my country, I needed no shame or reserve.

For some time there had been no more talk of the country. The discussions nowadays were about the relationship between men and women in the modern age and a thousand other things. English poetry as well as Vaishnav poems were being imported into all this; the tune to which the verses were being set was rather crude. I had never had a taste of such a melody in my home; I began to feel that this was the music of manliness, of the powerful.

But today nothing was hidden anymore. The question of why Sandip-babu was spending day after day here without rhyme or reason, and why, for that matter, I was needlessly discussing things with him all the time, was answered.

That was why I flew into a rage at myself, at my sister-in-law, at all the arrangements in the world, and said, no, I shall never go out of my room again, not even if you kill me.

For two days I did not go. During those two days I realized how far I had drifted away. I felt as though life had become bland. All I wanted was to throw everything away after a single touch. My entire body, from the hair on my head to the nails on my toes, seemed to be waiting for someone; all the blood in my body seemed to be listening for something outside.

I tried to busy myself with excessive housework. The floor of my bedroom was clean enough, but still I supervised a fresh round of cleaning, with mugs of water being sprinkled on the floor. Things in the cupboard were arranged a particular way. For no particular reason I pulled everything out, dusted and cleaned them, and rearranged them inside. It was two in the afternoon before I could take a bath that day. I couldn't do up my hair that evening. Braiding my loose locks carelessly, I got everyone worked up while cleaning the larder. I discovered a lot of pilfering from the kitchen, but I didn't dare take anyone to task for it lest anyone answered, even if only in their heads, where were your eyes all this while?

The first day passed in a frenzy, as though I was possessed. The next day I tried a book. I remembered nothing of what I read, but now and then I discovered myself, book in hand, wandering absent-mindedly to the window looking out on the corridor leading out of the ladies' chambers and peering through a slat. A row of rooms to the north of the yard could be seen. One of them seemed to have crossed over to the other shore of the sea of life. The ferry would no longer ply there. I couldn't stop looking. I felt like the ghost of myself from day before yesterday, occupying the same spaces but not really here.

At one point I saw Sandip emerge from his room into the veranda, holding a newspaper in his hand. I could clearly see the agitation on his face. Now and then it appeared as though he was losing his temper with the yard and the railings. He flung the newspaper away. He was ready to rip the sky apart if he could. As I was about to go to the drawing-room, I discovered my sister-in-law behind me.

You astonish me, she said and left immediately. I couldn't leave the room.

The maid appeared the next morning and said, it's time to get the things out of the larder, Chhotoranima.

Tell Harimati to get them, I told her, tossing the keys at her and sitting down by the window with my English embroidery. A servant came in and handed me a letter, saying, it's from Sandip-babu. How bold he was, what must the servant have thought! My heart began to tremble. Opening the letter, I found no form of address in it—only these words: 'Very important. For the country. Sandip.'

My embroidery was forgotten. Stepping to the mirror quickly, I patted my hair into place. Without changing my sari, I slipped on a different jacket. I knew this jacket had a special significance for him.

My sister-in-law was slicing betel-nuts as usual in the corridor along which I had to go the drawing-room. I did not hesitate in the least. Where do you think you're going, she asked.

To the drawing-room, I answered.

So early? Time for games with Krishna?

I continued on my way without a word. My sister-in-law began to sing

Radha swoons as she passes
As though she lives in deep waters
She cannot tell salt from sweet

In the drawing room I discovered Sandip standing with his back to the door, carefully examining a catalogue of paintings exhibited at the British Academy. He considered himself an expert on art. One day my husband told him, if artists needed a teacher, they would never lack for one as long as you are alive.

My husband was not in the habit of taunting people this way, but his disposition had changed a little these days; he never refused an opportunity to dent Sandip's pride.

Sandip said, do you think artists do not need teachers anymore?

My husband replied, people like us will have to learn afresh about art from artists all the time, for there is no one fixed lesson.

Laughing derisively at my husband's humility, Sandip said, you consider poverty your capital, Nikhil. You think the more you invest it, the more your wealth will grow. I can tell you that he who has no pride is mere moss in the current, floating about aimlessly.

I was in a strange frame of mind. On the one hand I wanted my husband to win the argument so that Sandip's pride was lessened, but on the other, it was Sandip's unabashed arrogance that attracted me. He glittered like a priceless diamond; nothing could disconcert him. He was not even willing to concede defeat to the sun—on the contrary, his audacity actually increased.

I entered the room. I knew Sandip had heard my footsteps, but pretending not to, he continued reading the catalogue. I was worried lest he began to converse about art. For, the paintings and the aspects of those paintings that Sandip liked discussing with me using art as a pretext still embarrassed me. And to hide my embarrassment I had to behave as though there was nothing to be embarrassed about.

For a moment I considered going back, but suddenly Sandip sighed deeply, looked up and seemed startled to see me. Here you are, he said.

His words, his tone, his eyes all held a suppressed reprimand. Such was my sorry state that I accepted this too. The right over me that Sandip had acquired seemed to make even two or three days' absence a crime. I knew that his arrogance was humiliating for me, but I lacked the power to be angry.

I was silent. Although I was looking away, it was obvious that the allegation in Sandip's eyes was on a vigil in front of me, refusing to move. What a situation! If only Sandip would start a conversation for me to hide behind in relief. When such mortification grew unbearable after five or ten minutes, I said, why did you send for me?

Starting in surprise, Sandip said, must there be a reason? Is friendship a crime? How can there be so much neglect for the most important thing on earth? Must my devotion be shooed away like a street dog from the door, Queen Bee?

My heart began to tremble. Calamity was approaching—it could no longer be kept at bay. Elation and fear grew in equal proportion in my heart. How would I ever be able to shoulder this burden of ruination? I would fall flat on my face in the dust.

My arms and legs shook. Standing firm, I told him, you sent for me saying there was something important for the country, which is why I abandoned my household work.

With a smile he said, that's just what I was telling you. Don't you know I am here to worship you? Have I not told you that I clearly see the power of my land personified in you? Geography is not real—no one can lay down their lives for a map. Only when I see you do I realize how beautiful, how cherished it is, how much it brims over with life and spirit. Not till you have put the mark of victory on my forehead with your own hand will I know that I have received my country's orders; only then will I know, if I were to slump to my death with this memory, that my country is not just land demarcated on a map, it is a protective cover. Do you know of what kind? Like the sari you were dressed in the other day, the colour of red earth, its wide borders as crimson as a stream of blood. Will I ever forget it? These are the things that make life pulse, that make death so thrilling.

Sandip's eyes blazed as he spoke. I could not tell whether the fire in them came from hunger or from devoutness. I was reminded of the day I first heard him give a speech. That day I had forgotten whether he was a man or a flame. Ordinary people can be dealt with as they are—codes of behaviour are available. But fire is a different thing altogether. It mesmerizes in an instant, it makes the apocalypse beautiful. Truth, lying neglected and unnoticed amidst the dry kindling, appears to take on a radiant form, chortling in glee as it races to burn everything the misers have hoarded.

I had no strength to say anything after this. I feared Sandip would rush to me this very moment and take my hand. For his hand was trembling just like a restless flame, while his glance fell on me like sparks from a blaze.

Will you women make all these small domestic rules bigger than everything else, said Sandip. Your spirit can make us disdain life and death at the smallest of signals. Is this spirit to be kept wrapped up inside a room? Hold back no more, pay no heed to whispers, dismiss all the restrictions with a snap of your fingers and run towards freedom.

When Sandip-babu combined his praise for the nation with his praise for me, my reserve could no longer restrain me, my blood began to tingle. My heart had grown weary through the analysis of art and Vaishnav poetry, of the relationship between men and women, of what was real and what was not. But today the blackened embers were reignited, their glow mitigating my embarrassment. I began to feel that my femininity was incomparably beautiful—a divine majesty.

But if only my hair would emit this majesty now like a visible luminescence! Why could I not say a single word that could indoctrinate the entire nation in the principle of fire at once?

Suddenly Khema the maid entered my room wailing. Give me my dues, she said, I have never in all my life . . . she kept sobbing.

What is it? What's the matter?

Mejoranima's maid Thako had gone out of her way without provocation to quarrel with Khema, hurling abuse at her.

No matter how much I assured her I will resolve this, Khema wouldn't stop weeping.

Someone seemed to have poured the water used to wash dishes over the music I had been enveloped in all morning. The slime from which women bloom like lotuses rose to the surface, muddying the waters. I had to rush inside the house to hide this from Sandip. I found my sister-in-law still slicing betel-nut with great concentration in the corridor, a faint smile on her lips, humming 'Radha swoons as she passes'. There was no sign of any crisis anywhere.

Why does your Thako abuse Khema unnecessarily, Mejorani, I asked her.

Oh, really, she said, raising her eyebrows in surprise. I'll kick the hussy out. Just see how she's spoilt your drawing-room tete-a-tete so early in the morning. And that Khema too—when she knows her mistress is busy with the gentleman, why does she have to turn up there—no shame, that woman. But Chhotorani, don't bother yourself with all these domestic things; you can go back, I'll take care of everything.

How strange the human mind is. The wind in its sails can reverse its direction in a moment. Abandoning my morning tasks to discuss things with Sandip suddenly seemed so out of place in my usual daily routine that I went to my room without responding.

I was sure that Mejorani had seized the opportunity to instigate Thako's quarrel with Khema. But I was in such a shaky place that I could not protest. Just the other day I had argued insolently with my husband in the first flush of anger over asking Nanku to leave, but my rage didn't last. I was soon ashamed of my own agitation. And in the middle of all this, Mejorani appeared to tell my husband, it's my fault, Thakurpo. We're old-fashioned people, see, we can never approve of the way your Sandip-babu conducts himself. That's why I had sent Nanku, thinking it would be for the best—but I didn't even imagine this would be an insult to Chhotorani; in fact, I had thought just the opposite. My wretched luck, my accursed brains!

When things that appear glorious from the perspective of the nation and its worship turn murky because of the muck rising from the bottom, I am first enraged, and then pained.

Going into the bedroom, I shut the door and sat by the window, pondering over how simple life could actually be if it was in harmony with the surroundings. There Mejorani was, slicing betel-nuts at peace with herself but I could no longer perform such simple tasks naturally. Where will this end, I ask myself every day. Will I die, will Sandip leave, will I forget all this forever like the delirium of a sick person when cured—or will I break my neck, sinking into such damnation that there can be no rescue in my lifetime? I had not accepted my fortune with ease—how had I managed to ruin it so?

All the walls and the ceiling of this bedroom, which I had stepped into as a new bride nine years ago, stared at me in surprise. After passing his MA examinations, my husband had got an extremely expensive parasitic plant from an island in the Indian Ocean. Just a few leaves, but the tall cluster of flowers blooming on it looked like a cup of beauty emptied out, a shimmering rainbow peeping through the scanty foliage. We had hung the blooming plant up near this bedroom window. It had flowered just once, but never since then—we hope that it will flower again. How strange that I was still watering it, as was my custom. How strange that the bonds of these few leaves tightly coiled with hemp rope had not been severed, that they were still green.

I had placed a photograph of my husband in an ivory frame in the niche in the wall over there. When my eyes fell on him, I couldn't tear them away. Even six days ago I had placed flowers in front of the portrait after my bath and bowed to it. My husband and I had often argued about this.

I am very embarrassed because you make me appear greater than I am and pay homage to me, he told me one day.

Why the embarrassment, I asked.

Not just embarrassment, but envy too, my husband replied.

Listen to you, I said. Whom are you envious of now?

Of that false me, he said. You're not satisfied with the everyday me—you want someone extraordinary who will overwhelm your reason. So you have created another me from your imagination to please yourself.

I get angry when you say such things, I told him.

What's the use of being angry with me, he said, keep your anger for your fate. You did not select me, after all, you had to blindly accept whoever was chosen for you—which is why you are improving me as much as you can with godliness. Damayanti was able to choose a man instead of a god because she was allowed to select her own husband, but because you and other women are not, you choose gods instead of men.

I began to cry in rage. Today this memory does not allow me to look at the alcove anymore.

There was another photograph in my jewellery box. On the pretext of dusting the drawing room, I had picked up the photostand which held a picture of Sandip next to my husband. I did not worship the photograph, I could not show my reverence to it; it remained concealed among my diamonds and pearls—the joy it gave me came from it being hidden. I opened the box to look at it only after shutting all the doors in the room. At night I turned the kerosene lamp up slowly and held the picture in its light. Every day I thought of burning it to ashes in the flame and being done with it forever; every day I sighed and slowly buried it under my diamonds and pearls, locking it back in place. But who gave you all these jewels, you wretched woman? The love of so many years was wrapped around them. Where would they hide their faces now? If only I could die.

Sandip had told me once that it is not in women's nature to hesitate. They have no left or right, only ahead. He would say over and over, when the women in the land awake, they will say much more directly than men, 'We want'. No argument about the good and the bad of it, or about the possibility or impossibility will hold before this wanting. They will have just the one thing to say: 'We want.' 'I want.' This is the fundamental statement of creation; it is this statement that brooks no principles, blazing as a fire in the sun and the stars. The partiality of its passion is irresistible; because it desires man, it has burnt billions of creatures over the aeons to sacrifice them at this altar of desire. This tempestuous 'I want' of creativity-devastation is personified in women today. That is why cowardly men try to dam this primitive flood of creation lest it sweep away the fences around their pumpkin fields, laughing raucously as it dances on its way. The male imagines that the dam he has constructed is permanent. It is gathering, the water is gathering—the lake may be placid and solemn today; it neither moves nor speaks, only filling the pitchers in the men's kitchens in silence. But the pressure cannot be resisted, the dam will break; then the mute force of all this time will race along, roaring, 'I want, I want'.

Sandip's words thundered like a drum in my heart. Whenever I was at conflict with myself, whenever shame cast aspersions on me, I recalled what Sandip had said. I realized then that this shame was only social shame, taking the form of my sister-in-law sitting outside my room, slicing her betel-nuts and looking askance at me. What did I care for it? To say 'I want' without reservation, at home and in the world, with all my power was the complete expression of myself—and not to do so would be my failure. Who cared for the plant or the alcove? Who dared mock this new inspired me?

At that moment I wanted to fling the plant out the window, to take the photograph out of the alcove—let the apocalyptic force be exposed in all its shameless nakedness. My arm did rise, but something struck at my heart, bringing tears to my eyes—flinging myself on the floor I began to sob. What was going to become of me? What did fate hold for me?

SANDIP'S STORY

When I read the story I have written about myself, I wonder, is this Sandip? Am I made of words? Am I a book within covers of flesh and blood?

The earth is not dead like the moon. It breathes; vapour rises from all its seas and rivers, enveloping it, while dust swirls all over. It is shrouded in this curtain of dust. Anyone who views the earth from space will see only the light reflected by this dust and vapour. Will he be aware of the existence of countries and continents?

Just like this earth, the sentient man constantly exhales ideas whose vapour makes him indistinct. The land and water within him, all the variety, is not visible; he only looks like a sphere of light and shade.

I feel as though I am creating the sphere of my ideas like a sentient planet. But it isn't as though I don't exist beyond my wants, my thoughts, my decisions. I am also what I do not love, what I do not wish for. I was created before I was born; I could not choose my qualities, I am having to make do with whatever I've got.

I know very well that the privileged are cruel. Justice is for ordinary people, and wrongdoing, for the extraordinary. The ground is flat, but the volcano gores it with a horn of fire to make it rise like a mountain. It does not care for justice for all; its judgements are for its own benefit. Both human beings and countries have become billionaires and rulers by successfully dispensing injustice and unadulterated brutality. No. 2 becomes one by swallowing No. 1 without hesitation, so that No. 1 cannot continue as before.

That is why I propagate the worship of injustice. I tell everyone that injustice is salvation, injustice is the flame which burns itself out when it cannot burn others. Whenever a nation or a human being cannot dole out injustice, it is consigned to the dustbin.

But still, this is only my idea, this is not all of me. No matter how much I boast of being unjust, there are holes in the fabric of the idea, there are gaps, through which one fact emerges—it is raw, tender. The reason is that most of what I am was created before me.

Sometimes I test the cruelty of my cohorts. We went to a garden for a picnic once. A goat was grazing. I asked them, which of you can cut off one of his legs with this axe? When everyone hesitated, I did it myself. The cruellest amongst us fainted at the sight. When they saw my calm, unruffled expression, all of them acknowledged me respectfully as a great man. In other words, they all perceived the circle of vapour around my idea that day. But the real me—by my own fault or misfortune—was weak and wretched; it was best to keep myself concealed when my heart was breaking in secret.

Things are coming to a head in this chapter of my life involving Bimala and Nikhilesh, but this, too, conceals many things. But there's an idea working away inside me, forcing this concealment. This idea is shaping my life to meet its own objective, but much of my life lies beyond this. My objective does not match the rest of my life, which is why I have to keep it concealed, else it spoils everything.

Life is not well-defined—it is a collection of numerous contradictions. We want to pour a man with ideas into a specific mould so that we can recognize him clearly in a particular form; the clarity of such a life is its success. Everyone from the world-conquering Alexander to today's American billionaire Rockefeller considers themselves successful because they have been able to pour themselves into a special mould—of the sword or of money.

This is where I have conflicts with Nikhil. I say, know yourself, and so does he. But according to him, not knowing yourself is self-knowledge. What you refer to as the getting the fruits of your labour, he said, is like finding success without oneself in it. The soul is greater.

This is extremely vague, I replied.

There's no alternative, he answered. Life is not as well-defined as a machine, but that doesn't mean that making life as simple as a machine will make you understand it. In the same way, the soul is not as distinct as success, but I cannot say that equating the soul with success amounts to seeing the soul for what it really is.

Then where do you see the soul, I asked. On the tip of which nose, between which eyebrows?

Where the soul knows it is infinite, where it surpasses success.

Then what do you have to say about your country?

The same thing. Where the country makes itself its objective, it might achieve success but it loses its soul; where it considers the greatest truly greater than everything, it might not achieve success but it finds itself.

Does history offer examples of this?

Man is so great that he can ignore examples just as he can ignore success. There may not be examples, just as there is no evidence of the flower within the seed; but the seed does contain the flower's agony at not having bloomed yet. And yet, it isn't as though there are no examples at all. Do you think that the Buddha's extreme endeavour over centuries, which awakened all of India, was an endeavour for success?

It's not that I do not understand Nikhil at all. But that is just what my problem is. I have been born in India and the poison of austerity in my blood refuses to die. No matter how much I claim that walking the road of self-deprivation is madness, I do not have the power to dismiss it altogether. That is why strange things are happening in our country today. We're playing both the refrain of religion and the refrain of patriotism at full volume. We want both the Bhagavad Gita and Vande mataram. We don't understand that neither of the two can be heard clearly as a result; that the military drums and the shehnai are being played simultaneously. The mission of my life is to stop this cacophonous confusion; I am going to keep the military drums going. The shehnai has been the cause of our ruin. We shall not bring shame upon the flag of victory with which the goddesses of nature, of power, of everything there is, have sent us forth into the battlefield. Natural urges are beautiful, natural urges are untarnished, as untarnished as the flower buried in the earth, which does not run to the bathroom on any pretext to bathe with a bar of Vinolia soap.

A question that has been running around in my head over the past few days is why am I allowing my life to be involved with Bimal's? My life is not a leaf set adrift on the current, stopping here, there and everywhere.

That's what I was saying—life transcends the mould of the single idea by which I want to contain my life. People are deflected from the idea now and then. This time I'm the one who's been deflected too far in the distance.

I have no false shame about the fact that Bimal has become an object of my desire. I can tell clearly that she wants me; she is my partner. Just because the fruit hangs from the stalk, the claim of the stalk is not permanent, is it! All the juice in her, all her sweetness has ripened for her to fall into my hands; her success lies in letting herself go his way—this is her duty, her principle. I shall pluck her, I shall not let her ripen in vain.

But my concern is that I'm getting involved. It seems to me that Bimal will become a big burden in my life. I have come into this world to be authoritarian, I shall direct people through my commands and my actions. The gathered masses are my battle-steed. My place is in the saddle with the reins in my hands. My mount does not know the destination, only I do. Its feet will bleed on thorns, its flanks will be caked in mud, I shan't allow it to decide, I shall make it gallop.

My horse is standing at the door today, stamping its hooves in impatience, the skies trembling from its cries, but what am I doing? What are my days occupied with? My most auspicious hours are passing me by.

I was under the impression I could storm along; that I could tear out flowers and drop them on the ground without letting them impede my progress. But this time I am circling the flower like a honeybee, not like a tornado.

That's why I say today that the colours in which I paint myself with my ideas are not permanent and the ordinary person shows through in several places. Had some omniscient power written my biography, it would certainly have revealed how few differences there are between Panchu and me—or even between Nikhilesh and me. Last night I was reading the notebook where I have been setting down my own story. I had just passed my BA examinations and my brain was practically bursting with philosophy. From that time I had vowed not to allow any illusions—created by myself or someone else—into my life. I would ensure that my existence was solid with reality. But what have I seen in my life-story since then? Where is that compactness? This is like a net. The thread runs continuously, but the gaps are larger. I have fought with these gaps but not been able to vanquish them completely. For some time I had been making assured progress, but now I see a big gap again.

Today I find myself in pain. 'I want, it is within reach, I shall pluck it' was the clear-cut, shortest route. I have always maintained that those who can walk this path with conviction can achieve salvation. But the king of the gods does not allow this devotion to proceed unimpeded, despatching agonizing nymphs to blur the devotee's vision.

I can see Bimala thrashing about like a deer caught in a trap; so much fear and pity in her wide eyes, her body mutilated by her attempts to break out of the trap by force—this is what pleases the hunter. I feel happiness, but I feel pain too. That is why I keep waiting instead of tightening the noose.

I know there have been two or three moments when Bimala would not have protested had I taken her hand and drawn her to my breast. She would have known that the significance of the entire world would change after this. Standing at the mouth of this cave of uncertainty her face was pale, while her eyes held fear and yet an inspired glow. In this brief moment a decision would be taken, for which the entire universe was holding its breath. But I let those moments pass; I did not allow the near-inevitable to become inevitable. Clearly the inhibitions lurking within me are blocking my way now.

The Ravana whom I admire as the hero of the Ramayana also died the same way. Instead of bringing Sita home, he kept her in the forest. Because of this raw uncertainty in such a brave hero, the entire battle for Lanka proved a failure. Had he not hesitated,

Sita would have forsaken her chastity and worshipped Ravana. And for the same reason, instead of killing Vibhishana as he should have, Ravana ignored him mercifully and died himself.

This is where the tragedy of life lies. It curls up unobtrusively in a corner of the heart and then fells the important things in an instant. Man is not what he thinks he is, that's what makes unexpected things happen.

Nikhil is so odd, someone whom I laugh so much at, but deep inside I cannot deny that he is my friend. I didn't take him into account particularly at first; but the more time passes, the more I am embarrassed in front of him, the more I feel pain. On some days our conversations progress into arguments but my eagerness becomes unnatural and I even do what I never do normally, which is to pretend to agree with him. But this deception does not suit me, nor Nikhil. Here, we are in accord.

That is why I prefer to avoid Nikhil these days. I am relieved if I can somehow escape meeting him. All these are signs of weakness. As soon as the spectre of wrongdoing is acknowledged it becomes a truth; and then it weighs us down no matter how much we deny it. I want to inform Nikhil without mincing my words that these things must be viewed as important, as real. The truth should not come between genuine friendship.

But I cannot deny anymore that all this is weakening me. Bimal was not charmed by my weakness. The moth burnt its wings in the flames of my unbridled manliness. When I am overcome by the fumes of passion, Bimala is moved as well, but she feels hatred; while she cannot withdraw the garland she gave me, she would like to shut her eyes on seeing it.

But there's no going back now for either us. Nor do I see the strength in myself to leave Bimala. But I cannot abandon my own road either. My way lies amidst the masses, not through the back door leading into the inner chambers. I cannot desert my land, especially not today. I shall make my country and Bimala converge into one. The storm from the west that has blown away the veil of right and wrong drawn over my goddess, my country, will also blow away the bridal veil covering Bimala's face—there will be no disgrace in this uncovering. The ship will sway on a human wave, flying the victory flag of Vande mataram, the sea roaring and frothing all around it—this craft will be the vessel of our power and of our love at the same time. Bimala will see freedom in such noble form that its sight will make her sever all her bonds even without knowing it. She will not baulk for a moment at turning cruel under the spell of this apocalypse. This ruthlessness is the natural force of nature and I have noticed this breathtakingly beautiful form of mercilessness in Bimala. If women had found release from their artifical bond with men, we would have seen Kali the destroyer for ourselves on earth—the brazen, heartless goddess. I worship Kali. Drawing Bimala into this destruction, I will make her revere Kali too. Let me make the arrangements now.

NIKHILESH'S STORY

The world seems to be trembling in the September floods; the glow of the tender paddy is like the sweetness of a small boy's undeveloped body. The water has stretched to the garden of our house. The morning sunlight falling on the earth is boundless, like the love in the blue sky.

Why can I not sing? The water in the canals is glittering, the leaves on the trees sparkling, the rice fields quivering and glinting every now and then; amidst this morning music of autumn, only I am mute. Melody is blocked within me; every brightness in the world remains trapped inside me, unable to escape. When I see myself, without light and without radiance, I realize why I am deprived. Why should anyone bear my company day and night!

Bimal is brimming over with life force, after all. She has not appeared old to me for a single moment in these past nine years. But if I have anything within me it is only mute depression, not lively vigour. I can only receive, but I cannot move anyone. My company is like fasting—when I look at Bimal now I can see the famine she was living through all this time. Whom can I blame?

> Alas . . .
> *Flowing rain, moist air*
> *But my temple is bare*

My temple has been created to remain empty for its door is closed. My god had been sitting outside the temple, but I had not realized it all this time. I had assumed that he had accepted the offerings and granted his boon too but my temple is bare, my temple is bare.

During the fullness of the earth's youth in September every year we would go for a boat ride just before the full moon to our lake in Shamaldaha, returning only when the evening moonlight had dwindled to darkness a week later. I used to tell Bimal, a song has to keep returning to its refrain; in life the refrain of the song of union is here, amidst open nature. The first communion between man and woman had taken place here on this water lapping at the shores, where the breeze blows from the east, where the green earth draws a shady veil over its head to lay its ear on the edge of the moonlight and eavesdrop constantly. It had not taken place within the confines of four walls. That is why we return once a year to the refrain of very first union from ancient times between Shiva and Parvati amongst the jungle of lotus in Mansarovar in Kailash. The first two years after my marriage were spent on the troublesome task of taking examinations in Calcutta; for the seven years since then, the September moon has played its silent, auspicious notes by our watery honeymoon chamber next to the blooming lotuses. One phase of seven years of my life had passed this way. The second seven-year phase began today.

We are close to the full moon in September, a date I simply cannot forget. The first of the fifteen days leading up to it have passed. I don't know whether Bimal remembers or not, but she has not reminded me. Everything has fallen silent, the music has stopped.

Flowing rain, moist air
But my temple is bare

In the temple emptied by parting, a melody plays even in the void; but the temple emptied by separation is so silent that even the sound of weeping is discordant.

Today my weeping is discordant too. I must stop weeping. Let me not be a coward who uses his tears to keep Bimal imprisoned here. Let tears not try to hold back the lie that love has become. Bimal will not be released entirely as long as my agony finds expression.

But I shall release her completely, or else I shall not be released from falsehood either. To bind her to myself now is to keep myself entangled in a web of illusion. Nobody will benefit from it, leave alone be happy. Set her free, free yourself—you will treasure your sorrow if you can free yourself from what is untrue.

I feel myself on the brink of a realization. All of us have inflated the love between a woman and a man so much beyond its natural claims that we cannot bring it under control today even for the sake of all of humanity. We have turned the lamp into a flame. No more indulgence, it is now time to ignore it. Being worshipped by our inclinations has turned it into a goddess; but we must not accept the kind of worship that makes a man sacrifice his manhood to let this goddess sip on blood. The chimera that it has created with its adornments and coyness and music and laughter and tears must be destroyed.

I have always nurtured a hatred for Kalidasa's *Ritusamhara*. Can a man possibly lay every cluster of flowers, every basket of fruit in the world at his beloved's feet to feed the worship of lust while demeaning the joyous dance of the universe? What is this intoxicant that has made the poet's eyes droop? The wine I had been drinking all this time was not as red, but its effect was just as intense. It is under its haze that I have been humming in despair since this morning ...

Flowing rain, moist air
But my temple is bare

Bare temple! Aren't you ashamed? How could such a large temple of yours be empty? Just because I have learnt of one falsehood, has every other truth in life been eliminated?

I had been to my bedroom this morning to fetch a book from the shelf. It has been a long time since I went into my bedroom during the day. When I looked at the room by daylight, I felt something twisting my heart. Bimal's sari, the folds set lovingly in it, was coiled on the clothes-stand, while the chemise and blouse she had discarded lay in a corner, waiting to be washed. On the dressing table lay her hairpins, hair-oil, comb, vials of essence and even her tin of vermilion. Her tiny pair of embroidered slippers were beneath the table. Once, when Bimal simply refused to put on shoes, I had had this pair of slippers sent for her by a Muslim classmate of mine from Lucknow. She had died of embarrassment even from the short walk from the bedroom to the veranda with these slippers on her feet. Bimal had worn out many pairs of sandals since then, but she had kept this pair lovingly. I had told her jokingly, while I'm asleep you touch the dust gathered on my feet as a mark of your adoration, I have now wiped away all the dust from your feet to worship my living goddess. Bimal said, don't talk that way, I'll never put those slippers on in that case. This was my long-familiar bedroom. It had a smell which I knew with all my heart, but which no one else probably got. Today I sensed, as I had never sensed before, how many delicate roots my thirsty heart had put down in all the tiny objects in this room. It isn't as though life is released as soon as the tap root is severed— even that pair of slippers tries to hold it back. That is why the mind wanders around the torn petals left behind by the feet of the goddess even after she has forsaken the place. Glancing around the room, I suddenly spotted the alcove, where I noticed my photograph placed as it had always been, but with flowers that had dried and turned black over several days. Despite this grotesque worship, the portrait was unmoved. Those withered, darkened flowers were my true gifts from this room today. They were still here because there hadn't even been any need to discard them. Never mind, I accepted the truth in this desiccated, blackened form but when would I grow as indifferent as the photograph in the alcove?

Suddenly Bimal rushed into the room behind me. Turning my eyes away quickly, I said, walking towards the shelf, I came to get *Amiel's Journal*. I don't know why it was necessary to offer an explanation. But here I felt like a thief, a tresspasser, as though I had come to gaze at something concealed, that deserved to be hidden. I could not bear to look at Bimal and I hurried out.

When it grew impossible to read in the drawing room, when everything in life seemed impossible, when I had not the slightest inclination anymore to see or to hear anything, to say or to do anything, when my entire future pressed down on my heart like an inert, massive stone, Panchu appeared with a basket of ripe coconuts and knelt before me reverently.

I said, what's all this, Panchu? What is it for?

Panchu was a subject of my neighbour Harish Kundu. I had met him through Master-moshai. For one thing, I was not his zamindar, and for another, he was very poor—I had no right to accept gifts from him. I assumed the poor fellow was here out of desperation, trying to make some money by claiming a tip.

As I was about to take two rupees out of my bag and give it to him, he joined his palms and said, no, huzoor, I cannot take this.

Why not, Panchu?

Let me tell you everything. Once, when I had absolutely no money, I stole coconuts from your garden. Who knows when I'll die, so I'm here to return them.

Reading *Amiel's Journal* would have given me no pleasure today, but this one statement of Panchu's cleared my mind. This world is much larger than the joys and sorrows of coming together with, and being separated from a woman. Human life is vast; unless I stand at its centre, I must not measure my laughter or tears.

Panchu was a devotee of Master-moshai's. I knew how his household ran. He woke up with the sun, filled a wicker basket with paan, tobacco, coloured ribbons, mirrors, combs and other things that the women in peasants' families desired, and crossed the knee-deep water in the lake to arrive at the locality where the Shudras lived; there he bartered these things for rice from the women. This made for a better income than money. Whenever he could return home early, he ate a quick meal and then went to the batasha-seller to help him slice his batasha. Back home again, he worked late into the night crafting the light shell bangles that women wear. Even after such backbreaking labour he could seldom afford two square meals a day for his children and himself. His meals started with a pot of water to stuff his belly, while a significant portion of his food was the cheap seed-infested banana. At least four months a year he didn't get more than one meal a day.

I had wanted to give him some money. Master-moshai told me, you can destroy a man with your money but you cannot destroy his suffering. Panchu is not the only one of his kind in Bengal. The milk is drying in the breasts of the entire state. You cannot provide for this mother's milk with money.

These were important considerations. I had decided to dedicate my life to them. That day I told Bimala when I returned, Bimal, I want to use our lives, yours and mine, to eradicate the roots of suffering in our country.

Smiling, Bimal said, you seem to be my Prince Siddhartha, make sure you don't cast me adrift and disappear.

I said, Siddhartha's mission did not include his wife, but I want my wife in mine.

Thus we laughed it away. Actually Bimal's nature was what is termed feminine. Although she came from a poor family, she was a queen. She knew that the yardstick of happiness and satisfaction for the lower classes were always cheap. They would always want for things, but this paucity was not a real want for them. They were well-protected by the barriers of their poverty—just like the water of a small pond, which is suitable only for its current edges. Try to enlarge the pond and the water runs out, revealing sludge. The pride of nobility runs strongly in Bimala's blood, the nobility which has led India to fragment itself into little seats of glory to ensure a dignity and uniqueness consistent with their limitations. She is indeed a descendant of the noble Manu, while the plebian bloodlines of Guhak and Eklavya probably run in my veins; I cannot push away those who are socially lower than me just because they are lower. My India is not the India of just the upper classes. I know clearly that the more the people below me sink, the more India sinks; the more they die, the more India dies.

I could not include Bimal in my mission. I had made her so important in my life that not getting her shrank my mission. I moved the goals of my life into a corner in order to make room for Bimal. The outcome was that I spent all my time preparing her, dressing her up, teaching her—she was the centre around which I orbited; I had forgotten how important human beings are, how noble life is.

But Master-moshai saved me; he was the one who ensured, to the best of his abilities, that I grew in the direction of what is important or else I would have sunk into ruination today. An extraordinary man. I call him extraordinary because there is a strong difference between him and this land and the times. He has caught sight of the almighty, which is why nothing can distract him. When I draw up the accounts of my life, a grievous error, a massive loss, can be detected on one side, but I hope I can state with conviction that I do have some gains to transcend my losses.

By the time I completed my education with him, I had already attained freedom, having lost my father. I asked Master-moshai, why don't you stay with me and not work anywhere else?

He said, look, I have been recompensed for all I have taught you. If I accepted payment for anything more I gave you, it would be like selling my god in the marketplace.

Rain or shine, Chandranath-babu had always walked from his home to mine to teach me. I had never succeeded in inducing him to use our carriages. He would say, my father walked from Battala to work at Laldighi all his life to bring us up. He never even took a seat on a carriage. We are walkers by heredity.

I said, why not take a job related to our affairs?

He said, no, my son, don't trap me with the generous ways of the wealthy, I want to remain free.

His son was looking for a job after passing his MA examinations. I said, he might find some work in my affairs. The son was very keen. First he had let his father know of his choice, without much of a response. Then he hinted it to me in private. Encouraged, I told Chandranath-babu of this with great excitement. He said, no, he cannot work with you. The son was furious with the father for depriving him of this opportunity. In a rage he abandoned his widower father and went off to Rangoon.

He had told me repeatedly, look, Nikhil, I am free when it comes to you, you are free when it comes to me—such is our relationship. Making a relationship of well-being subservient to money is to insult the greatest truth of all.

He was now the headmaster of the Entrance School here. All this while he had never spent a single night at our house. For some time now, I had been visiting him at home every evening, staying till eleven at night to discuss various things. Perhaps he decided that his small room was uncomfortable for me in the sultry monsoon weather, which is why he had now started living here in this house with me. Remarkably, he is as compassionate with the rich as with the poor; he does not disregard their hardships either.

The more we consider reality a personal affair, the more it takes hold of us. But the moment we glimpse even a hint of the truth, the winds of freedom seem to blow. Bimal has made this reality so sharp a presence in my life today that the truth is all but obliterated. This is why I cannot see the end of my suffering anywhere in the universe. And so I have scattered this emptiness in my life on the winds to sing through this autumn morning . . .

Flowing rain, moist air
But my temple is bare

When I view the truth from the window of Chandranath-babu's life, the meaning of this song is transformed. For then it is . . .

How will you pass the hours
Without god, asks Vidyapati

All our suffering, all our errors result from not grasping the truth. How will the days and nights pass without pouring this truth into one's life? I cannot cope anymore—fill my empty temple now, truth.

BIMALA'S STORY

I cannot describe how the consciousness of Bengal changed suddenly. The water of the Bhagirathi seemed to touch the ashes of sixty thousand sons of Bengal at the same instant. Ashes that had been lying at the bottom, wasted, no fire could ignite them, no storm could stir them, spoke up: here I am!

I've read of the Greek sculptor who was given a boon by a god that enabled him to breathe life into his own statue but there was a gradual development from form to life there, a certain dedication at work. The scattered heaps of ashes in our country's burning grounds never had such unity of form. If only it had even been as firmly bound as a rock. After all, Ahalya was turned into stone but regained human form. But these ashes lay dispersed, always slipping through the fingers of the creator, flying in the wind, gathering in a heap but never joining together. And yet this very substance suddenly appeared in our front yard, thundering like a cloud: here I am!

That was why we felt all this was miraculous. The present moment fell into our hands like a precious stone from the crown of a god maddened by wine; there was no natural tradition binding this present with our past. It was like the medicine which we have not sought out or purchased, which is not available with any doctor, which we get in a dream.

And so it seemed that all our sorrows, all our resentment would be cured by this incantation. Nothing separated the possible from the impossible. Our constant thought was, any moment now, any moment now.

On that day I was convinced that history needs no one to draw its vehicle, that it propels itself like the chariot of the gods. At the very least, its charioteer needs no payment; no one has to worry about his sustenance, only his wine glass has to be refilled every minute. And then, suddenly, direct ascent to heaven.

It wasn't as though my husband was unmoved. But amidst all the fervour he seemed assailed by a melancholy, apparently seeing something over and above all that was directly visible. I remember him telling Sandip in the course of an argument that fortune appears at our door only to prove that we lack the power to accept it, that we have made no arrangments to entertain it in our homes.

Sandip said, look, Nikhil, you don't believe in the gods, which is why you talk like an atheist. We have seen the goddess for ourselves, bearing boons for us, and still you are sceptical?

My husband replied, I believe in god, that is why I am convinced in my heart that we have not been able to demonstrate our reverence. God has the power to grant boons, but we must have the power to accept them.

I became very angry when my husband spoke this way. You consider this firing up of the nation nothing but a kind of infatuation, I told him. But does infatuation not provide strength?

It does, he replied, but it does not provide weapons.

I said, the gods give us power—that is what is hard to attain. Even ordinary blacksmiths can give us weapons.

With a smile my husband said, but they don't give them free, they have to be paid for.

We shall pay, I promise, asserted Sandip.

When you do, I shall book lights and music for celebrations, answered my husband.

We aren't waiting for you, Sandip told him. Our priceless celebrations cannot be bought with money.

He sang in his hoarse baritone:

My priceless lover roams the arbour
Playing his priceless flute with ardour

Smiling at me, he said, when music invades the soul, not being able to hold a tune is no obstacle, Queen Bee. I sang to prove just this. When you sing full-throated, the weight of the song is eased. Our country is suddenly filled with song. Let Nikhil practise his scales from the beginning; meanwhile our tuneless singing will overwhelm everyone.

Where will you go, asks my home
You'll lose all you call your own
My heart says why not let it all
Be swept and burnt away?

Very well, we shall all be ruined. Nothing worse, right? I'm willing, I'm willing to be ruined.

If it must, then let it go
I'll just smile, and watch it flow
And then I'll drink the wine of death
With all my heart

The truth, Nikhil, is that we have been converted, we can no longer stay within the limits of what can be accomplished with reason; we shall embark on a path to achieve the impossible.

Our dear ones would hold us close
But this love that no one knows
Twisted on the twisted path
It calls me far away
Let this twisted attraction
Shatter all that's straight

I thought my husband had something to say about this, but he did not. He left on slow footsteps.

The powerful passion that had burst in on the nation had entered my own life with a different tune. The chariot of the god of my destiny was approaching, its wheels rumbled in my heart day and night. At every moment I felt as though something extraordinary was about to take place for which I was not in the least bit responsible. Sin? The road to move away from the arena of sin and salvation, of judgement and conscience, of kindness and compassion, had suddenly opened up on its own. I had never desired it, I had never waited expectantly for it; look at my entire life—I had nothing to justify for this. I had worshipped one god all this while but when it came to benediction, a different god stood in front of me. And so, just as the entire country has been roused to look at what lies ahead and cry 'Vande mataram', my heart has made every one of my arteries and veins resonate to the cry of 'Salute!' to an unknown, exquisite, extraordinary being.

There is a strange harmony between the music of the nation and this melody of my life. Late at night I sometimes left my bed quietly to stand on the open terrace. The half-ripened fields of rice beyond our garden walls, the river visible through the gaps in the dense trees in the village to the north, and the line of the forest even further away were all asleep like the indistinct form of the embryo of a future being. When I look ahead, I see my country standing there—a woman just like me. She is in a corner of her own yard, but today she has been called towards the unknown. She has had no time to reflect, she is advancing into the darkness and she does not even have a lamp. I know how her breast heaves on this sleeping night. I know her heart wants to rush to the source of the distant music, so that she can say, I have found it, I have reached, there is nothing to fear now. I can even walk on with my eyes shut. No, this is not the mother. She does not consider feeding her child, lighting the lamp when darkness falls, or sweeping the floor. Tonight she is on a tryst. This is the land of our Vaishnav poetry. She has left her home, put her duties behind her. All that drives her is boundless passion; it propels her along, and she does not care what lies in her path. The means and the end have both turned unclear, all that remains is passion and progress. When the night turns crimson and ends, nightwalker, you will see no trace of the way back. But why should I return? I shall die instead. If the darkness of the music ruins me, if it leaves nothing of me, why should I worry? All will be destroyed, not even a speck of me will remain, not a sign, all my blackness will merge into the blackness; and then, what will good and evil matter, or laughter and tears?

That day Bengal's machine was fully charged with steam. And so what was not meant to have taken place easily materialized in an instant. Even in this corner where we live, it felt as though nothing could be kept at bay. All this while there had been less of a turmoil here. The primary reason was that my husband did not wish to pressure anyone. He used to say that those who make sacrifices for the country are worshippers, but those who resort to oppression are the enemy: they want to slice off the roots of freedom to water its tip.

But when Sandip-babu settled down here, and his followers began to frequent this place, with public speeches being made, the wave intensified here as well. A group of local young men joined hands with Sandip. Many of them were the black sheep of the community, but the glow of inspiration made them brighter both within and without. It became clear that when there is joy in the air of patriotism, aberrations in human nature are cured on their own. It is exceedingly difficult to be healthy, capable and uncomplicated when there is no happiness in the nation.

At this time everyone noticed that imported salt, sugar and garments had not yet been banished from my husband's estate. Even his officers grew troubled and embarrassed. And yet, when my husband had brought local products into the market here some time ago, people of all ages had laughed both openly and privately. When local products were not related to our pride, we were contemptuous of it in heart and soul. My husband still sharpens his pencils on his locally-made knife, writes with a quill, drinks his water in a brass tumbler, and reads and writes by the light of local lamps but this pallid, colourless swadeshi of his gives me no joy. On the contrary, I have always been embarrassed by the shabby furniture in his drawing-room, especially when magistrates or other white men gathered at the house. My husband would laugh, asking me, why are you so perturbed by such inconsequential things?

They will consider us uncivilized barbarians, I said.

If they do, I shall also conclude that their civilization runs only as far as the white polish on their skin, it has not reached as deep as the red blood that flows in the citizen of the world.

He was in the habit of using an ordinary brass pot as a flower-vase on his desk. Whenever I knew that a white man would be visiting, I would hide it, arranging the flowers in an imported crystal vase instead.

My husband would say, my brass pot is as unselfconscious as the flowers themselves, Bimal. But your imported flower vase announces its identity far too loudly. You should put silk flowers instead of natural flowers in it.

His only supporter in all this was Mejorani. She would go to him, flustered, and say, I believe you have local soap now, Thakurpo. My days of using soap are over, of course, but if there's no fat in your soap I can use it. That's one habit which has taken hold of me ever since I came to your house. I gave it up long ago, but even today I don't feel my bath is complete when I haven't used soap.

This was enough to make my husband happy. Cases of local soap began to arrive. Was it soap or lumps of clay? As if I don't understand these things. The imported soap that Mejorani used in her husband's time was being used even now, every single day. The local soap was for washing clothes.

Another time she said, I believe you get local pens now, Thakurpo? I need them. I beg of you, get me a bundle . . .

Thakurpo was extremely enthusiastic. All the tooth-cleaning sticks claiming to be pens that had been produced began to be piled up in Mejorani's room. This caused her no trouble, for she had virtually no link with the written word. The laundry lists could be scrawled even with drumsticks. Yet I did see her ancient ivory pen in her writing box, on the rare occasion that she felt like putting pen to paper, this was what she used.

The fact was that she did all this only in retaliation against my refusal to join my husband in his whims. But the question of informing my husband of this deception on her part did not arise. If I tried, he would lapse into such a sullen silence that it was obvious I had achieved the opposite of what I had intended to.

Any attempt to save such people from being cheated only led to being cheated yourself.

Mejorani was fond of embroidery. When she was sewing one day, I told her clearly, what do you think you're doing? In your Thakurpo's presence you practically salivate at the prospect of using local scissors, but when it comes to embroidery, you cannot manage a moment without the imported ones.

And what's wrong with that, said Mejorani. Haven't you seen how it pleases him? I've grown up with him, known him since childhood, I cannot cause him pain with a smile on my face. He's a man but still he has no other vices—only this game with local products, besides his dangerous addiction to you, which will drown him.

Say what you like, I told her, being two-faced isn't good.

Mejorani burst out laughing. Oh my dear simple girl, you're so straight—as straight as the teacher's cane. Women aren't as straight as you think. They give way a little because they're soft by nature, but there's nothing wrong with that.

I shall never forget what Mejorani had said—his dangerous addiction to you, which will drown him.

Today I feel constantly that a man must have an addiction, but it mustn't be a woman.

Our market at Shuksayar is one of the largest in this district. On this side of a large lake on the estate, the market is open every day, while on the other side it is set up every Saturday. This market becomes more active after the rains, when the lake links up with the river, making passage easier. The import of yarn and of warm clothes for the coming winter increases in this season.

There was great trouble at the time due to the opposition to local garments and local salt and sugar in every market in Bengal. All of us were adamant. Sandip told me, we have such a large market under our control, it must be turned completely swadeshi. The inauspicious commerce of imported goods must be driven out of this area.

Of course it must, I said with determination.

I've had several arguments with Nikhil about this, but I could not convince him, said Sandip. He said that it is all right to make speeches, but no one must be forced.

Very well, I'll see to it, I said with some pride.

I knew how deep my husband's love for me was. Had I been of sound mind that day I would have died of shame before making such claims on his love so brazenly. But I had to demonstrate my abilities to Sandip! I was the embodiment of power to him, after all. He had repeatedly explained to me in his irresistible way that the ultimate force presents itself to certain people in the form of specific human beings; he said that we are so desperate to see this force that whenever we catch a glimpse of it we realize the meaning of the music in our hearts. Sometimes he would break into song:

You didn't show yourself, Radha, when my flute was playing
Now that our eyes have met my melody has gone missing
With every note I looked for you
On land and then on water too
Having seen your beauty, Radha, my tears are now smiling

When he says all this, I forget that I am Bimala. I am power, I am love, I have no ties, everything is possible within me, I re-create whatever I touch. I am re-creating my world—the autumn morning did not have so much gold before my magic wand touched it. And in an instant I have renewed the hero, the disciple—my devotee—the brilliant genius radiant with knowledge, fired up by his spirit, crowned by passion. I can sense clearly that I am pouring new life into him every moment, he is my own creation. The other day, Sandip had entreated me to meet one of the young men especially faithful to him—Amulyacharan. In a few moments I discovered a new fire glowing in his eye. I realized he had had a glimpse of the original force. I knew that my power to create was at work in his bloodstream. The next day Sandip told me, what is this magic of yours, the boy is no longer a boy, his wick is flaming now. Who can keep this fire of yours contained within the home? All of them will come, one by one. One by one, the lamps will be lit to celebrate Diwali across the land.

Drunk on my own greatness, I had decided that I would bestow a gift on my devotee. I also knew that no one could prevent what I wanted.

When I came back from Sandip, I undid my hair and did it up

again. My Englishwoman had taught me to draw my hair up from my neck and make a high bun with it. My husband was very fond of this hair-do; he would say, god has decided to reveal the beauty of the neck to a non-poet like me instead of Kalidasa. The poet may have termed it a lotus in the lake, but to me it is a torch, with the black flames of your hair blazing at the tip. And then he would come close to my exposed neck and . . . but why talk of all that now?

I sent for him. Earlier he used to be summoned on many small pretexts, some true and some made up. But for some time now all occasions for sending for him had ended. Nor did I have the strength to fabricate any.

NIKHILESH'S STORY

Panchu's wife has died after a prolonged bout of tuberculosis. Panchu must make amends. Society has calculated the cost as twenty-three and a half rupees.

Never mind your atonement, I told Panchu angrily. What are you afraid of?

Raising patient eyes like an exhausted cow's, he said, I have a daughter whom I have to get married. And I have to do something about my wife too.

I said, if you have indeed done something wrong, you've made enough amends for it all this time.

Yes, sir, no small amends, he said. I had to sell some of the land and pawn the rest to pay the doctor's fees. But unless I feed Brahmins, her soul won't be released.

What was the point of arguing? To myself I said, how will the Brahmins who feast on your offerings atone for their sins?

Panchu had in any case always lived on the edge of constant hunger. Now his wife's treatment and last rites plunged him into utter destitution. To seek some comfort, he began to frequent the circles of a holy man, deeply oblivious to the fact that his children were starving. He was convinced that the world amounts to nothing; just as there is no happiness, sorrows are also a dream. Eventually he abandoned his four children in his dilapidated home one night and gave up a householder's life.

I did not know any of this. The gods and the demons were waging a battle in my mind at the time. Master-moshai had not even informed me that he had moved Panchu's children into his own home, where he was bringing them up. His own son had left with his wife for Rangoon; he was alone at home with school duties all day.

When a month had passed this way, Panchu arrived. The haze of other-wordliness had lifted. When his two eldest children nestled up to him on the floor and asked, where did you go, baba, while the youngest son claimed his lap and the third child, a girl, clambered on to his back with her arms around his neck, he simply could not contain his tears. He kept saying, Master-babu, I don't even have the ability to give them two square meals a day; nor do I have the freedom to abandon them and run away. Why must I be tied down and tortured this way? What wrong have I done?

Meanwhile, the business that he had been ekeing out a living from had collapsed. For the first few days, he stayed on at Master-moshai's house where he had been given shelter, showing no inclination to go back to his own home. Eventually Master-moshai told him, go home, Panchu, or else your house will fall apart. I am lending you some money, you can start a garment business and pay your debt back in instalments.

Panchu was unhappy at first; he felt there was no such thing as compassion in the world anymore. Then, when Master-moshai made him write a note for the money, he told himself, I have to return this. What use is such a favour? Master-moshai was absolutely unwilling to make anyone a recipient of charity on the surface and a borrower at heart. A man loses his identity when he loses his honour, he said.

After accepting the money in return for a handnote, Panchu could not show a grand gesture of respect. He touched Master-moshai's feet only perfunctorily. Master-moshai smiled to himself, for he was usually relieved by as brief a display of reverence as possible. He said, I will respect and be respected—this is the purest form of my relationship with other people. Veneration is more than I deserve.

Panchu procured some dhotis, saris and winter clothing and

began to sell them to peasants. While he was never paid in cash, he did extract payment in the form of paddy or jute or some other crops. Within two months he paid back one instalment of interest and even some of the principal. His display of reverence dropped proportionately. Panchu must have concluded that he had been wrong in considering Master-moshai his guide—the man obviously had an eye on the silver.

Panchu's days were passing this way. Suddenly the flood of swadeshi strengthened in force. All the young men from our village and nearby villages who used to study in schools and colleges in Calcutta came home for the holidays and several of them decided not to go back. Making Sandip their leader, they became involved in propagating swadeshi. Many of these young men had passed their entrance exams from my free school; I had given them scholarships to study in Calcutta. One day they came to me in a group. You must stop the sale of shawls and other garments made with imported yarn at our market in Shuksayar, they demanded.

I cannot do that, I told them.

They asked, why, do you fear losses?

I realized that this was meant to be an insult. Not my losses but the poor people's, I was about to say.

But Master-moshai was present; he said, yes, of course; it's his loss, not yours.

They said, for the sake of the country . . .

Master-moshai interrupted them, the country isn't the earth beneath our feet, it is the people. Have any of you ever spared them a glance? Today you have suddenly decided to enforce the choice of salt and clothes on them. Why should we tolerate this, and why should we let them tolerate this?

We have also taken to salt and sugar and clothes made in our own country, they argued.

He said, you people are angry and adamant; drunk on these, you're doing as you please. You have money, you can pay a couple of paise extra for local products. These people are not coming in your way. But what you want them to do is strictly by force. Caught in a battle for survival every single day, they are fighting to their last breath. None of you can even imagine what this couple of paise means to them—how can any of you be compared to them? In the building of life you have always occupied a different floor from theirs; and today you want them to shoulder the burden of your responsibility? You want to use them to appease your anger? I consider this cowardice. Travel as far on the road as you can yourselves. I am an old man, but I am willing to acknowledge all of you as leaders and march behind you. But when you trample over the freedom of the poor and brandish your flag of victory, I will oppose you even if I have to die for it.

Since most of them were Master-moshai's students, they could not be openly abusive, but their blood seethed with anger and began to boil. Addressing me, they said, look, why should you be the only one to come in the way of the vow that the entire country has made today?

Do you think I have the power to come in the way, I said. Instead I will help as much as I can.

With a contemptuous smile the MA student said, what sort of help?

I answered, I have stocked locally made yarn and clothes in our market; I will send this yarn to other markets in the area too . . .

The same student said, but we saw at your market that no one is buying your local yarn.

That's neither my fault nor the market's, I responded. The only reason is that the entire country has not made your vow.

Master-moshai said, not just that, those who have, have only taken a vow to harass people. Those who have not made the vow must buy the yarn and those who have not made the vow must weave fabrics from it and those who had not made the vow must buy that fabric. How will you ensure this? With brute force and through the zamindar's army? In other words, the vow is yours, but they will starve, and you will eat the first meal after the fast.

The science student said, very well, tell us which part of the fast you are on yourself.

Master-moshai said, you really want to know? It is Nikhil who has to buy the thread from the local mill. It is Nikhil who has to have the fabric woven. It is Nikhil who has set up a school for them. And then these people are so adept at business that the gamchhas they make will cost as much as brocade, so Nikhil will buy the gamchhas himself and use them as curtains in his drawing room—curtains that will veil nothing at all. If your vow has been fulfilled by then, all of you will laugh loudly at this example of local embroidery and if at all there is anyone who values and places orders for these colourful gamchhas, it will be Englishmen.

In all the years I had spent in Master-moshai's company, I had never seen him so agitated. I realized that his heart was aching in silence, simply because he loved me. It was this agony that had eroded the bulwark of his patience internally.

The student from the medical college said, you are older, we shall not argue with you. Tell us simply whether you will remove foreign goods from your market or not.

I said, no, I shan't, because they are not mine.

The MA student said with a faint smile, because that will mean losses for you.

Master-moshai said, yes, it will mean losses for him, and therefore it is his business.

The students left, shouting 'Vande mataram' at the top of their voices.

Master-moshai brought Panchu to me a few days later. What was it?

Their zamindar Harish Kundu had fined Panchu a hundred rupees.

Why, what is his crime?

He has been selling foreign clothes. He pleaded with the zamindar, saying that he had bought these with borrowed money, and that he would not do it again. The zamindar refused, saying, I shan't let you go unless you burn the clothes here in my presence. Unable to contain himself, Panchu said, I do not have the means, for I am poor; you do, why don't you buy them and burn them? Furious, the zamindar said, so you can talk back, you bastard! Flog him with a shoe. Not only was Panchu humiliated, but he was also fined a hundred rupees. And these are the people who follow Sandip around, screaming Vande mataram. These people will serve the country!

What happened to the clothes?

They were burnt.

Who else was present?

Innumerable people. All of them screamed, Vande mataram. Sandip was present too; picking up a handful of the ashes, he said, my brothers, this is the first pyre in your village for the funeral of foreign enterprise. These ashes are sacred; you must smear them on your bodies like naked holy men and break through the net of Manchester to pursue your mission.

You have to file a criminal case, Panchu, I told him.

No one will agree to be a witness, Panchu said.

No one? Sandip! Sandip!

What is it, said Sandip, coming out of his room.

This man's zamindar burnt the sack of clothes he was selling. Won't you be a witness?

Smiling, Sandip said, of course I will. But I am a witness for the zamindar.

I said, what do you mean, witness for the zamindar? Witnesses are for the truth!

Sandip said, is what happened the only truth?

I asked, what are the other truths?

Sandip answered, the events that should take place, the truth that we will have to create. This truth needs many lies, just as this world is created through illusions. Those who are here to build things do not care for the truth, they create it.

And therefore . . .

Therefore I shall do what you refer to as bearing false witness. Those who have established kingdoms, expanded their empires, developed society and created religious communities are the people who have boldly given false testimonies in your courts of fettered truth. Those who shall rule do not fear lies; the iron chains of truth are only for those who shall be ruled. Have you not read history? Do you not know that the ingredients of the political pishpash being cooked in the biggest kitchens of statecraft in the world are all adulterated? Enough pishpash has been cooked in the world, now it's time for . . .

Oh no, why should you people make pishpash—you will only force it down people's throats. You will split Bengal, and say it is for the benefit of the people; you will bar the doors against education and claim that it is with the noble intention of elevating the people's ideals; you will shed tears pretending to be pious, while we will be unholy and strengthen the fortress of lies. Your tears will not last, but our fortress will.

Master-moshai told me, this isn't worth arguing over, Nikhil. An overwhelming truth lives within all of us, down to our roots. Those who cannot realize this for themselves cannot be expected to believe that the ultimate objective of man is to peel all the layers off this deepest of truths and reveal it and not to make a pile of material possessions.

Laughing, Sandip said, spoken like a true teacher. All this is to be found only in books. With my own eyes I can see that piling up material possessions is indeed the ultimate objective of mankind. And those who have dedicated themselves to fulfilling this objective scream out their lies in capital letters every day in the course of publicizing their business. They fabricate accounts in bold letters in the books of state policy. Their newspapers are ships laden with falsehoods. And their clergymen spread lies the way the fly propagates the typhoid germ. I am their disciple. When I belonged to the Congress, I had absolutely no hesitation in diluting an ounce of truth with fifteen ounces of water. I have left that party today, but I have discovered that the fundamental principle is that truth is not the objective of mankind, results are.

The fruits of truth, said Master-moshai.

Sandip said, yes, but this harvest can ripen on the soil of falsehood. It ripens only after the ground beneath the feet is split open and pounded into dust. And the truth, which ripens on its own, is weeds and thistles. Those who expect fruits from it belong to the ranks of worms and insects.

Sandip marched out. Smiling, Master-moshai said, you know what, Nikhil, Sandip is not against righteousness, he is outside of it. He is the moon on the dark night. A moon, but placed by circumstances on the opposite side of fullness.

I said, that is why I have never agreed with his views, although I am attracted to him for his nature. He had done me immense harm, and he will do more, but I cannot disrespect him.

He said, I am realizing as much. I have often wondered in astonishment how you have tolerated Sandip all this time. Sometimes I have even suspected a weakness within you in this matter. Now I see that your ideas do not match his, but your rhythms do.

In jest I said, stress between friends creates a poetic pentameter. Maybe the poet of our destiny is preparing to write an epic like *Paradise Lost*.

Master-moshai asked, what do we do with Panchu now?

You said that Panchu has acquired hereditary rights to the land on which his house stands, I said. The zamindar has been trying for ages to take away these rights. Why don't I buy that land of his and let him live there as my subject?

And the hundred-rupee fine?

What fine? The land will be mine.

And his sack of clothes?

I will get some for him. As my subject let him sell whatever he wants. I'd like to see anyone stopping him.

Joining his palms respectfully, Panchu said, kings will fight, huzoor, and everyone from police inspectors and lawyers will gather like vultures and be amused, but I will be the one to perish.

But why, what can they do to you?

They will set my house on fire, I will burn to death with my children.

Master-moshai said, very well, let your children stay with me for some more time, don't be afraid. You can run your business the way you want to, no one will be able to lay a finger on you. I will not allow you to be defeated by injustice and flee. Let the load be heavier still, I shall bear it.

I purchased Panchu's land and had it registered the very same day. And then the conflict began.

Panchu's property belonged to his mother's mother. Everyone knew that there was no other descendant of hers besides Panchu. Suddenly someone claiming to be Panchu's aunt—his mother's brother's wife—came from nowhere and installed herself in Panchu's house along with her clothes, trunk, prayer books and an adult, widowed niece, claiming lifetime rights.

But my mother's brother's wife died a long time ago, said Panchu in astonishment.

The response, his first wife had indeed died, but he had no hesitation in marrying again.

But the uncle's wife had died long after him there was no time for a second marriage.

The woman admitted that the second marriage had taken place before the death of the first wife, not after. She used to live with her parents because she was afraid to share a house with her husband's first wife. When he died, she gave everything up and went off to Vrindavan. Some of those who managed Kundu's zamindari knew all this, perhaps some of the subjects too. And if the zamindar so desired, no doubt some people would have averred they had actually been guests at the wedding.

When I was very busy with Panchu's predicament that afternoon, Bimala sent for me from the inner chambers.

Who's calling me, I asked, startled.

Ranima, said the servant.

Bororanima?

No, Chhotoranima.

Chhotorani! She had not sent for me in a hundred years.

Asking everyone to remain in the drawing room, I went off to the inner chambers. I was even more surprised when I saw Bimala in the bedroom, because I saw she had dressed up, not excessively, but subtly. I had seen this room left in a state of neglect for some time. Everything had turned so awry that it seemed as though the room too had stopped caring. But today I saw some of the old neatness there.

I looked at Bimala without a word. She reddened slightly, and, twisting the bangle on her left wrist furiously with her right, she said, look, ours is the only market in all of Bangladesh where foreign clothes are being sold. Do you think that's right?

I asked, what's the best course of action?

Why not tell them to take those things away?

But those things are not mine

The market belongs to you though.

The market belongs much more to those who use it.

Let them buy local products.

I'll be happy if they do, but what if they don't?

What! Would they dare? If it were you . . .

My time is limited, what is the point of arguing about this? I cannot oppress people.

The oppression is not for your own benefit but for the country's . . .

The Home and the World

Oppression for the sake of the country is oppression of the country. But you won't understand.

With these words, I left. The entire world suddenly appeared illuminated in front of my eyes. I felt in my blood that this clay earth had lost its daunting weight, even after its task of nurturing living things, even through every phase of its own continuous development, it was rolling day and night like prayer beads under an extraordinary force, all the while hurtling through the sky. Its responsibilities were unlimited, but so was the momentum of its quest for freedom. No one could stop it, nothing could stop it. An enormous joy seemed to erupt from the depths of my heart like a towering column of water from the ocean reaching up to the clouds.

What has happened to you suddenly, I asked myself repeatedly. I didn't get a clear answer at first; then I realized that the bond that had inflicted such agony on me these past few days had revealed itself as badly frayed today. I was surprised to discover my mind cleared of fog. Everything about Bimala was revealed to me just the way a photograph is revealed on a plate. It was obvious that she had dressed up specially to extract what she wanted. Till now, I had never separated Bimala from the way she was dressed. Today I saw her Western bun as nothing but coils of hair; those coils had seemed priceless once, but today I found her ready to sell it cheaply.

I have conflicts with Sandip over our country at every step, but these are genuine conflicts. However, what Bimala was saying, claiming to speak for the country, only echoed what Sandip says—they were not original ideas. If Sandip said something else, so would she. I saw all this very clearly, without the slightest fog obscuring my view.

When I came out of the broken cage of my bedroom into the open daylight of the autumn afternoon, a flock of mynahs were squawking with great excitement beneath one of the trees in my garden. Rows of butterfly trees on either side of the gravel path leading southwards from the garden had overwhelmed the sky with the volubility of their pink flowers. Not far away, at the end of the trail winding through the field, an empty bullock-cart lay face down, its tail pointing to the sky. One of the two cows set free was grazing, while the other lay in the sun, a crow perched on its back picking worms out with its beak. The cow's eyes were closed with pleasure. Today I felt so close to the beating heart of everything simple—and yet big—in the world that I could feel its warm breath mingled with the scent of those pink flowers on my breast. My existence, combined with everything else's, had created a music spanning the sky—generous, intense, indescribably beautiful.

And then I remembered Panchu, trapped between poverty and cunning; I seemed to see Panchu lying across all of Bengal's wistful fields in the autumn sun just like that cow with his eyes closed, not from pleasure, but from exhaustion, disease, starvation. He was the symbol of every impoverished ryot in the state. I could see too the corpulent Harish Kundu, devoted to rituals and with sacred marks on his forehead. He was not small either, he too was enormous, an unbroken mass of oily green scum stretching across a pond enclosed in a bamboo grove.

Eventually we shall have to combat the gigantic darkness which, emaciated with starvation, blind with ignorance, and worn out with fatigue on the one hand, and bloated with the blood of the dying on the other, torments the earth lying beneath its unperturbed inertness. This task has been postponed for centuries. May my infatuation be dispelled, may the covers be drawn back, may my manliness not be entangled in failure in the dreamlike web of the inner chambers. We are men, freedom is our mission, we shall surge forward at the call of the idea, we must scale the walls of the demon's palace to rescue the goddess. The woman who weaves our flag of victory with deft hands is our true partner. And may we break through the disguise and discover the real identity, free of fascination, of the woman who weaves a web of illusion for us—may we not turn her into a voluptuous nymph with the passions and colours of our own desire and despatch her to disrupt our devotion. Today I feel I shall be victorious. I stand on the road to lucidity, I see everything with clear eyes. I have found freedom; I am giving freedom too. My salvation lies in the work that I must do.

I know my heartstrings will ache in agony now and then. But I have become familiar with this agony too—I cannot respect it. Whatever is mine alone has no value. The pain of the world must adorn my throat. Save me, truth, save me. Do not allow me to go back to the false heaven of deception. If you must make me a solitary traveller on the road, let that road be yours. Your drums of victory are playing in my heart today.

SANDIP'S STORY

The dam of tears was about to break that day. Bimala sent for me, but not a word escaped her lips for some time, after which her eyes began to shine. I realized she had had no success with Nikhil. She had been confident of getting her way with him, but I had no such hope. Women know men inside out when it comes to their weaknesses, but when they are pure, women cannot quite penetrate their mystery. The fact is that men are a mystery to women, and women a mystery to men. If it were not so, the differences between the genders would have been rather a waste for nature.

Ah, pride! What should have happened did not, but the reason does not matter. The regret is that what I had asked for explicitly did not materialize. Women's demands for what the 'I' wants are conveyed through a wealth of sentiment and gestures and tears and tricks and mannerisms; that, in fact, is where their appeal lies. They are far more individualistic than we are. God was a schoolmaster when he created us; his bag was stuffed with books and learning. But in their case he gave up teaching and became an artist, turning to his paint and brushes.

So when Bimala stood in silence like a water-laden, flame-packed cloud in the red glow of tearful pride, she looked very appealing to me. Going close to her I grasped her hand; she did not withdraw it, instead she trembled uncontrollably. I said, we are fellow-travellers, Bee, we have the same objective. Sit down.

I made Bimala sit down. How strange! Had such an irresistible current dwindled to such a trickle? The Padma in the rains, roaring and destroying everything in its way, as though it would leave nothing unscathed, had suddenly abandoned its destructive path for no obvious reason and crossed over to the other side. The force itself did not know what obstacles lay beneath. I held Bimala's hand tightly and every string in my body resonated inside her. But why did they stop at the opening bars, without reaching the middle section? I realized that the deepest trenches along which my life flowed had been formed by ancient currents. When the flood of desire grows very strong, this channel at the bottom gives way in some places, but throws up obstacles at others. Something is still holding me back somewhere, but what is it? It is not any one thing; it's a multitude of things. I cannot identify it clearly, although I do realize that it is an obstacle. Court testimony will never convert what I really am into a codifed document. I am a mystery to myself, that is why I love myself. Complete self-knowledge would have led me to fling everything away and reach a beatific state.

Bimala turned pale in an instant. She understood that she had averted a crisis. The comet may have sped past her, but her heart and soul seemed to have been rendered unconscious by a blow from its tail. To dispel the trance, I said, there are impediments, but we shan't rue them—we shall fight them. Do you agree, Queen?

Clearing her throat, Bimala only said, yes.

We must draw up a clear plan for our work, I told her.

I took paper and pencil out of my pocket, discussing how to divide up the work between the boys in our group who had arrived from Calcutta. Suddenly Bimala said, not now, Sandip-babu, I'll be here at five, we'll talk it over then. She left the room quickly.

I realized that Bimala had not been able to concentrate despite her efforts; she needed to be alone with her heart for some time now.

When Bimala left, the air seemed to grow even more intoxicating. Just like the clouds soon after sunset, my heart also acquired a multitude of colours after her departure. I felt I had been right in letting the moment pass. What cowardice was this! Bimal may have left out of my contempt for my strange hesitation. Well she might.

While the passion of this intoxication was tingling in my blood, the servant appeared to inform me that Amulya wanted to meet me. For a minute I was inclined to send him on his way, but before I could make up my mind he arrived in the room.

Then came the news about the battle over salt and sugar and

clothes. The rapture vanished from the air. I felt as though I had woken from a dream. I straightened my back and then, off to the battlefield. May the gods be praised.

The subjects of the Kundus who sold goods at the market had submitted. Most of Nikhil's officers were secretly on our side, pulling strings on our behalf. The Marwaris were saying, take a penalty from us and allow us to sell imported clothes, or we'll go bankrupt. The Muslims were refusing to fall in line.

A peasant had bought cheap German shawls for his children. One of the young men from our group in this village snatched the shawls away and set them on fire. There was trouble over this. We told him, we'll buy you homemade warm clothes. But where would we get cheap warm clothes made in India? We could hardly buy him cashmere shawls. He appealed tearfully to Nikhil, who ordered that a complaint be filed against the young man who burnt the shawls. The officers took the initiative to ensure that the complaint was not lodged properly—even the legal people were on our side.

Now the thing is, if we have to buy homemade clothes for those whose clothes we burn, and then there is litigation too, where will we get the money for all this? And burning imported clothes will only increase demand. When the nawab, entranced by the sound of cut-glass chandeliers shattering, smashed chandeliers in every room, the chandelier seller's business flourished.

The second question is this—there are no cheap but warm local clothes in the market. Winter is upon us, should we keep our imported shawls and flannels and merino wool or get rid of them?

I said that those who insist on buying imported clothes cannot be recompensed with local garments. It is they who must be punished, not we. Those who try to litigate will have their granaries set on fire; it's no use trying to coax them. Surprise won't do, Amulya. I have no interest in creating bonfires with farmers' grain. But this is a battle. If you are afraid to hurt people, then drown yourself in sugar syrup, spend your days making love, not war.

And imported warm clothing? It will never be allowed, whatever the difficulties. In no circumstances can we compromise on the matter of foreign goods. When there were no imported shawls, the farmer's son would wrap a sheet of plaited cotton around his head to keep the chill out. He can do the same now. I know it won't catch their fancy, but this isn't the time for such fancies.

Many of those who come to the market in their boats have been coaxed and cajoled and coerced into toeing our line. The most influential among them is Mirjan, but he refused to relent. We asked the treasurer Kulada whether he could sink the boat. That's not difficult, he said, I can; but what if I'm blamed afterwards? I said that we should not keep be so careless as to have anyone held responsible, but if at all it came to that I would take the blame.

After the market had closed for the day, Mirjan's empty boat was lying tethered near the bank. The boatman was not there either for the treasurer had craftily arranged to have them invited to the jatra. That night the boat was let loose and allowed to drift out into the currents with a hole punched into its bottom and sacks of rubbish placed in it.

Mirjan understood clearly. He came weeping to me, saying, I made a mistake, huzoor, now . . .

How did this realization dawn on you, I asked.

Instead of answering my question, he said, the boat is worth nothing less than two thousand rupees, huzoor. I have come to my senses now, if you can just forgive me this time . . .

He grasped my legs. I told him to come back ten days later. If I can give him two thousand rupees now, I would be buying him out. Drafting people like him into our group will be useful. I won't get results unless I can get hold of lots of money.

As soon as Bimala arrived in the room in the afternoon, I rose from my seat and said, everything's arranged, Queen, there's not much time, now I need money.

Bimala asked, money? How much?

Not much, I said, but I must have it.

How much do you need, asked Bimala.

For now, only fifty thousand, I told her.

Bimala jumped mentally in consternation, but she hid it well. How could she say, 'I cannot,' yet again?

You can make the impossible possible, Queen, I told her. You have done it already. If only I could have shown you what you've done, you'd have known. But this is not the time, perhaps the time will come later. For now, I need money.

I shall provide it, Bimala responded.

I realized that Bimala had decided to sell her ornaments. You must keep your jewellery for now, I told her. You never know when we might need it.

Bimala stared at me.

You have to get this money from your husband, I told her.

Bimala was even more stupefied. A little later she asked, how can I get his money?

Isn't it your money too, I asked her.

No, she answered with a sense of injury.

Then it isn't his either, I said, it belongs to the country. Nikhil has stolen this money from the country at a time the country needs it.

How will I get my hands on this money, Bimala said.

In whatever way possible. You can do it. You shall bring the money to whom it belongs. Vande mataram! Vande mataram are the magic words that will open the door of the safe and demolish the wall of the treasury while those who do not believe in the great power on the pretext of piety will have their hearts cleaved down the middle. Say it, Bee, Vande mataram!

Vande mataram!

We are men, we are the kings, we shall claim our taxes. We have been looting the earth ever since our arrival here. The more demands we have made of it, the more it has submitted. Right from the beginning we men have plucked fruits, chopped trees, dug the earth, slaughtered beasts, hunted birds, caught fish. Extraction—that is all we have ever done from beneath the ocean, from beneath the soil, from the jaws of death. We are the male race. We have not made an exception for any iron safe in the creator's treasury; we have broken into all of them and plundered them at will.

The earth takes pleasure in meeting men's demands. It has turned fertile in the process of meeting these constant requirements, turned beautiful, been fulfilled, or else, smothered in jungles, it would not have come to know itself. All the doors to its heart would have remained shut. Its diamonds would have remained in the mines, its pearls would not have been purified by the light of day.

We men have unveiled women simply on the strength of our demands. Giving themselves to us continuously, they have discovered their own selves in a greater way. Only after depositing all the diamonds of their joys and pearls of their sorrows in our royal coffers have they found these gems. Taking things in this manner is the true form of giving for men, and giving, the true gain for women.

I have made a high bid to Bimala. Apparently the propensity of the mind is to argue with oneself, hence my doubts. Perhaps I have set her too difficult a task. I considered telling her, no, there's no need for you to go to all this trouble; why should you disrupt your life so much? For a moment I had forgotten that this is what makes the male tribe industrious. It is our job to disrupt and foment trouble among the indolent to make them fulfil their existence. Had we not made women weep all this time, the door to their wealth of sorrows would have remained barred forever. Men are meant to gratify all the three worlds by making them shed tears. Why else should their arms have been so strong, their fists so resolute?

Bimala's inner self wants me, Sandip, to make an impossible demand of her, to call her out to die. She won't be happy with anything less. It was because she had not wept properly all this time that she had been waiting for me. It was because she had been happy all this while that clouds of sorrow gathered in a blue intensity on the horizon as soon as she set eyes on me. If I have to stop her tears out of compassion, what am I needed for?

The primary reason for my pinch of doubt was the amount of money I had demanded. Money belongs to men, after all, asking for it is a little like begging. That is why I had to increase the amount. A thousand or two would have smelt of theft, but fifty thousand is robbery.

Besides, I should have been very rich. Only the lack of money has repeatedly prevented me from fulfilling my wishes. All said and done, this does not befit me. If it had only been unfairness on the part of fate, I would have forgiven it, but it is tasteless, and therefore unpardonable. It is not sad but laughable for someone like me to have to worry about how to pay the rent or to prudently buy intermediate class tickets when travelling by train. I can see clearly that ancestral wealth for people like Nikhil is an extravagance. He would not have looked out of place had he been poor. He could easily have paired with his teacher to pull a ramshackle carriage of scarcity.

At least once in my life I want to hold fifty thousand rupees in my hand and squander it in a couple of days on my own comforts and the needs of the country. I am wealthy—I have a desire to banish this disguise of a poor man even if only for a day or two and look at myself in the mirror.

But I do not believe that Bimala will get her hands on fifty thousand rupees easily. Maybe it will eventually boil down to three or four thousand. So be it. 'The wise man forsakes half of what he gets,' they say; but since the forsaking is not out of choice, the hapless wise man forsakes three-fourths, or even nine-tenths.

I have written about myself thus far—of which more at leisure. But there was none now. The treasurer had sent word I must visit him immediately. I was told there's trouble.

The treasurer said that the man whom we had persuaded to sink the boat was suspected by the police; he was an old convict, and they were interrogating him. He was too canny to divulge information easily, but one never knew, with Nikhil angry, the treasurer could not act openly. The treasurer told me, look, if I get into trouble I shan't spare you.

Where is the proof to implicate me, I asked him.

I have one letter from you and three from Amulya-babu, he answered.

I realized now that the letter which the treasurer had insisted I write in reply to his was necessary for this reason alone. I was learning new tricks. The treasurer respected me enough to know that I could sink an ally as easily as the enemy's boat. His respect would have increased manifold had I replied orally and not in writing.

Now the thing was, the police had to be bribed, and if things went further, compensation for the sunken boat would have to paid, too. This would result in a fat share of the profits for the treasurer—but I had to keep these thoughts to myself for both of us were users of the Vande mataram slogan.

The tools with which one has to accomplish such tasks are mostly damaged, with large parts worn away. Since righteousness is supposed to be embedded in one's bones, I was very angry with the treasurer at first and was on the verge of writing something strong about the deception practised in this country. But if there's a god I must acknowledge my gratitude to him, for he has enabled me to think clearly; there is no possibility of anything within or without me remaining vague. I may fool others, but I never fool myself. This is why my anger did not last. Science says that what is true is neither good nor bad—it is the truth. The lake is made of the water that is left over after the earth has absorbed what it has to. The earth beneath Vande mataram would absorb the water that it had to; so would I, and so would the treasurer. What remained after that was Vande mataram. Maligned or not, this was the truth, and it had to be accepted. Beneath every great deed in the world is a layer of slime; it exists below the oceans too.

When embarking on an important task, therefore, the demands of this slime must be taken into account. The treasurer would take some money and I had some needs too, part of the larger need. For it isn't enough to feed the horse, the wheels must be oiled too.

Anyhow, I needed money. I could not afford to wait for fifty thousand—I had to gather what I could right away. I know that when such compulsions make their claims you have to abandon the future. Today's five thousand would swallow the seeds of tomorrow's fifty thousand. That is why I tell Nikhil, those who walk the path of sacrifice do not even have to conquer greed; but those who walk the path of greed have to sacrifice their greed at every step. I had to sacrifice fifty thousand rupees, but Nikhil's teacher Chandranath-babu did not have to.

Of the six vices, the first two and the last two belong to the male, while the middle two are the coward's. I shall desire, but I shall have no greed, no infatuation. In their presence, desire shall be spoilt. Infatuation exists around the past and the future, both adept at making the present lose its way. Those who are unable to concentrate on what is required right now, who listen to a melody from another time, are like Shakuntala riven apart by the pain of parting; they cannot hear the call of the visitor who is at hand, and because of this curse, they lose the distant visitor whom they desire in their infatuation. Enchantment is a hammer for devotees of desire. Who is your wife, and who your son?

I had held Bimala's hand tightly the other day—the strains were still playing in her mind. The resonance had not stopped in mine either. This melody would have to be kept fresh. If I kept using it, making the strokes broader, what was a melody now would descend into an argument. At present Bimala did not find the opportunity to question anything I said. What is the use of cutting off the supply of infatuation to those who need it? I had many tasks at hand, so let the superficial flavour of the cup of wine remain for now, there would be trouble if it went down to the dregs. I would not ignore it when the time came. Forsake your desire, you greedy man, and master infatuation like an instrument so that you can play on its strings.

Meanwhile, our work was gathering pace. Our people had spread across the land quietly. Having gone hoarse calling the Muslims our brothers, I had realized that they would never join us. They had to be subjugated and pushed to the bottom and made to comprehend that the power lay in our hands. They did not heed our call today, baring their teeth and howling. I would make them dance like monkeys one day.

Nikhil says, if India is real it includes Muslims.

That's possible, I say, but we have to be clear where they belong, and they must be forced to occupy that space, else they will oppose us.

Do you want to wipe out conflict by instigating it, asks Nikhil.

What's your plan, I ask him.

There is only one way to eliminate conflict, he says.

Just like the stories told by holy men, I knew that every one of Nikhil's arguments would end as morals. Surprising, despite having dabbled in these morals all these years, he still believed in them. It's not for nothing that I say Nikhil was born a schoolboy. His special quality was that he was the genuine article. Like Chand Saudagar he was devoted to the unreal Shiva; even while dying of real snakebites, he refused to admit it. The problem is that death is not the ultimate proof for these people; they have shut their eyes with the conviction that something more lies beyond death.

I had long nurtured a plan that, if executed, would set the country on fire. Our countrymen would not awaken until they saw their country with their own eyes. The country needed a goddess. My friends liked the idea. Let us create an idol, they said. It won't do for us to create one, I said, we must turn the established idol into a goddess representing the country. The road to worship was well-laid in our land, we had to force the people's adoration to walk this road.

I had a serious argument over this with Nikhil some time ago. Nikhil said, we cannot draft illusions to our cause in order to accomplish a task that we respect as the truth.

I said, the inferior classes cannot do without illusion. And three-fourths of the people of the world are inferior. Gods have been created in every country to keep this illusion alive—human beings know themselves only too well.

The gods are for smashing illusions, said Nikhil. Only the demons preserve them.

Very well, let them be demons then, but our work cannot progress without them. Sadly, illusion remains a strong factor in our country. We keep feeding it continuously, but we do not extract what we need from it. Take the fact that we revere Brahmins, show our respect to them always, give them money and other things—and yet we are allowing such ready power to go waste without putting it to use. If their rights were to be given to them in entirety, we could achieve the impossible with it. For there is one set of people on earth who live beneath the feet of others and they are the majority; they can achieve nothing without the dust of those others' feet either on their backs or on their heads. Infatuation is a formidable weapon to make them toil. We have only honed these lethal weapons in our armoury all this while, now the day has come to wield them. How can we possibly set them aside today?

But explaining all this to Nikhil is very difficult. Truth has lodged itself in his mind like pure prejudice, as though there is something definite that goes by the name of truth. I have told him many times that where falsehood is true, falsehood is truth. It is because our nation understood this once that it could avow without reservation that to the ignorant, lies are the truth. If he is deflected from this lie, he will be deflected from the truth too. The goddess representing the country will work like truth within the man who can accept this goddess as the truth. Our habits and beliefs do not allow us to accept the entity of the country easily—but we can effortlessly accept a goddess as the country. Since this is well known, the doers must exploit this.

Suddenly Nikhil said in great agitation, you people have lost the ability to pursue the truth. That is why you want to pluck a giant fruit from the sky without putting in any effort. While the things that need to be done for the country have remained undone for centuries, you have turned the country into a deity and are waiting for her boon.

The impossible must be achieved, I said, which is why the country needs to be deified.

In other words, you are no longer satisfied with your commitment to what is within your reach, Nikhil told me. Nothing will change, but the miracles will be achieved.

You are mouthing homilies, Nikhil, I said. They may be useful at a particular age, but they are no good once a man grows teeth. I can see clearly that what we had not sown even in our dreams is ripening at breakneck pace. What made this possible? The fact that we can picture the country as a deity in our minds today. It is the task of today's talents to immortalize this in the form of an idol. Talent does not argue—it creates. I shall give material form to what the country is thinking. I shall tell everyone that the goddess has appeared in my dream, she wishes to be worshipped. We shall tell the Brahmins, you are the priests of the goddess, it is because rituals have been stopped that your downfall is imminent. You might say I am lying. No, this is true. Millions of people are waiting to hear this from me, which is why I say this is true. If I can broadcast my message, you will see extraordinary results.

Nikhil said, I won't live forever. But there may be results beyond the outcome that you will present to the country which may not be visible now.

I want success today, I replied. This success is mine.

I want success tomorrow, answered Nikhil. This success belongs to everyone.

The fact is that Bengalis, including Nikhil, have a valuable asset in the form of their imaginativeness. But the vegetation of righteousness has swamped it, practically killing it. The Bengali has revealed himself in an unexpected way through the improvised worship of Durga and Jagadhatri. I am certain that this goddess is a political goddess. They are two different manifestations of the patriotic force which Bengalis had prayed for to vanquish the enemy during the reign of Muslims. Has any other group of people succeeded in creating such striking embodiments of devotion?

Nikhil's insight of imagination has been completely blinded, which is why he could say, Marathas and Sikhs had sought to end Muslim rule by taking up arms against them. Bengalis, however, only armed the idols of their goddesses and expected results. But the country is not a goddess so all that this led to was the beheading of cattle. Only when we work for everyone's betterment will the true god, who is greater than the country, provide true results.

Trouble is, what Nikhil says sounds good on paper. But my beliefs are not to be written on paper, they are to be etched on the breast of the nation with an iron rod. Not the way the expert writes the laws of farming with ink, but the way the farmer draws his desire on the flesh of the earth with his plough.

When I met Bimala I told her, I could not believe with my heart and soul in the god to worship whom I was born after an endless wait until he showed himself. I have told you many times that had I not seen you, I would not have seen my entire country as one—I do not know whether you understand this. It is very difficult to explain that the gods remain invisible in their own land, revealing themselves only on earth.

Looking at me steadily, Bimala said, I understand you clearly. She used the informal 'tumi' for the first time instead of the formal 'apni'.

I told her, the Krishna whom Arjuna saw constantly as his everyday charioteer had a greater form too, which he witnessed one day—that was when he perceived the entire truth. I have seen your greater form in my entire country. The seven strands of the necklace of the Ganga and the Brahmaputra are draped around your neck; I have seen the black lashes of your dark eyes in the distant line of forests beyond the blue water of the river; your light-and-dark sari sweeps over the fields of tender rice; and I have observed your heartless rage in the summer sun when the sky seems to laugh like a desert lion with its red tongue protruding. Since the goddess has revealed herself to her devotee in this miraculous way, I shall broadcast the need to pay homage to her all over the country, only then will my countrymen live. 'It is your idol I build in every temple.' But not everyone has understood this clearly. So I have resolved to call out to the entire country, build the idol of my goddess with my own hand, and pay homage to her in a way that removes people's scepticism. Grant me this boon, this spirit.

Bimala's eyes closed. She seemed to merge with her seat, becoming as still as a stone statue. Another word from me and she would have fainted. A little later she opened her eyes to say, you have begun your journey, traveller of the apocalypse, no one dares obstruct you. No one can impede the force of your desire today. The king shall cast his sceptre at your feet, the rich shall turn over all their wealth to you, those who have nothing will plead to die for you. All the principles of good and evil shall be swept away. My king, my god, I do not know what you have seen within me, but I have just seen your worldly form in the flower in my heart. What am I in comparison to this force? All shall be ruined, such is its power. I won't live till it kills me completely, I cannot cope anymore, my heart is being torn apart.

As she spoke she toppled over from her seat and grasped my legs. And then, heaving, she sobbed . . . sobbed . . . sobbed.

This is what hypnotism is. This is the power with which to conquer the world. This hypnotism needs no equipment, no ingredients. Who says the truth shall prevail? It is infatuation that shall conquer. The Bengali understood this, which is why he introduced the worship of the ten-armed deity, constructed the figure of the goddess who rides the lion. The Bengali will build the figure again today; he will conquer the world through enchantment. Vande mataram!

Slowly I helped Bimala back into her seat. Before fatigue could follow her exhilaration, I told her, I have been given the responsibility of establishing the worship of the mother in Bengal, but I am poor.

Bimala's face was still red, her eyes still misty. In a throbbing voice she said, you're not poor. Everything here is for you. What have I got trunks full of jewellery for? Take all my gold and precious stones for your worship, I don't need any of it.

Bimala had offered me her ornaments earlier too. I don't baulk at anything, but I had baulked there. I've analysed the reason for my hesitation. Men have always adorned women with ornaments—to accept jewellery from women is a blow to manhood.

But I must forget myself. It is not me who is taking. This is the worship of the mother, everything must be used. It must be conducted with grandeur of a kind that no one has ever seen. This ritual shall be established as the essence of the history of Bengal forever. I shall bequeath it to the country as the finest gift of my life. The fools of the country shall worship the goddess, Sandip shall create her.

The big things were taken care of, but the smaller issues had to be addressed, too. For now I needed at least three thousand rupees—five thousand would make it even better. But how could I bring up money against the background of such inspiration? And yet there was no time.

Smothering my hesitation, I said, meanwhile the treasure-chest is almost emptied out, Queen, our work is grinding to a halt.

A spasm of pain appeared on Bimala's face. I realized that she was under the impression I was demanding the fifty thousand immediately. She was weighed down by this, she must have pondered it all night without a solution. She had no other way to worship of her love. Since she could not openly lay her heart at my feet, she wanted to bring this enormous sum of money to me as a symbol of her thwarted adoration—but could not. I felt her pain in my heart. She was completely mine now; there was no need to uproot her anymore; she had to be nurtured.

I don't need the fifty thousand at present, Queen, I told her. Five thousand, even three thousand, will be enough.

Suddenly the pressure was eased on Bimala, making her joyous. I shall bring you five thousand, she said as though singing.

In the same way that Radhika had sung . . .
Like a bride I'll wear flowers in my hair
They can't be found in the three worlds anywhere

The flute plays so clear
But not everyone can hear
Look, the Yamuna floods its banks over there

This was the same music, the same song, and the same words: 'I shall bring you five thousand.' 'Like a bride I'll wear flowers in my hair.' The flute is narrow and closed on all sides, which is why its melody is lovely. Had I smashed the flute today with excessive greed, I would have been asked, why do you need so much money? And I am a woman, how will I get my hands on so much money? And so on and so forth. Not a word would have rhymed with Radhika's song. That is why I say that infatuation is the truth, that's what the flute is, and without the infatuation it is only the hollow within the broken pipe. Nikhil, of late, had a taste of this pure emptiness, which is clear from his expression. I feel his pain too. But Nikhil boasts of wanting the truth, while I claim that I will never let the infatuation slip out of my grasp. As the thought, so the salvation. Why shed tears over it?

To keep Bimala's heart flying in the upper reaches, I finished the business of the five thousand rupees quickly and went back to planning the worship of Durga. When and where should we do it? Millions of people gathered at the fair of Hossaingazi in Ruimari, which was part of Nikhil's estates, in the middle of December. It would be a grand affair if we did it there. Bimala sounded enthusiastic. She felt that since this was not a case of setting imported clothes on fire or burning people's homes Nikhil would not object to such an excellent suggestion. I smiled to myself—even those who have spent every hour together for nine years know so little of each other. They know each other only in domestic tasks. When things related to the world outside come up, they are out of their depth. Over nine years they had come to believe that the home is identical to the world; today they had to realize that the two were never meant to be similar.

Never mind—those who had not understood this would learn through their mistakes; I didn't have to worry about them. I could not keep Bimala flying high like a balloon very long on this particular inspiration alone so I had to accomplish my immediate tasks as quickly as possible. When Bimala had reached the door, I said very casually, then the money, Queen . . .

Stopping, Bimala turned around to say, at the end of the month . . .
No, I cannot wait, I said.
When do you want it?
Tomorrow.
Very well, I shall bring it tomorrow.

NIKHILESH'S STORY

Reports and letters to the editor about me are beginning to appear in the newspapers; I've been told initiatives are afoot to publish rhymes and a photograph too. The source of jokes has been opened up, and the country is ecstatic over the downpour of innumerable lies. They know that they hold the water gun in this sport of murky Holi; I am the decent man walking along the road, I cannot possibly keep my attire clean.

They've written that every single man on the street is eager to join the swadeshi movement, but they fear me. And that I am taking advatange of my position as the zamindar to terrorize the one or two courageous people who are in favour of using indigenous products. I am secretly connected to the police, I exchange correspondence with the magistrate on the sly, and my efforts to earn a title of my own to add to the one I have inherited will not go waste. They've written, 'All hail the famous, but we have information that people want them to be booted into infamy.' They didn't mention my name explicitly, but it is clearly evident through the obfuscation.

Meanwhile, a series of letters is being published singing praises of Harish Kundu, so enamoured of his mother. Had there been more of such people willing to serve the motherland, wrote the newspaper, every chimney on every factory roof in Manchester would have been trumpeting the tune of the Vande mataram.

In the meantime a letter has arrived, addressed to me in red ink, with details of the zamindars from Liverpool whose offices have been burnt to the ground because of their treachery. God will now use his purifying fire, it says; arrangements are being made to ensure that those who are not true children of the mother are not allowed to remain in her arms.

The letter has been signed by 'The most unworthy claimant to the mother's arms, Ambikacharan Gupta.'

I know that all of this is the creation of my current students. I summoned a few of them to show them the letter. The BA said grimly, we have also heard that a group of people have become desperate. There is nothing that they will not do to remove the impediments to swadeshi.

I said, if even a single person in this land is vanquished by their unjust demands, it will mean a defeat for the entire country.

The MA in history said, I don't understand.

The country is half-dead from fear of everyone from the gods to the guards, I said. If you want to pass off this same fear of the demon under the guise of freedom, if you want to exploit tyranny to plant the victorious flag atop people's cowardice, those who love their country will not bow to this reign of fear.

The MA in history said, is there a single country not under a reign of fear?

I answered, the extent of this reign of fear determines how free the people of a country are. If it is limited to crime and to injustice, it is clear that such a reign seeks only to free people from the threat of attacks from others. But if it seeks to define what garments people will wear, which shops they will patronise, what they will eat and with whom, then people's fundamental wishes are being ignored. This amounts to depriving people of their humanity.

The MA in history asked, are there no attempts in other societies of the world to cut off choice at the very roots?

Who says there isn't, I responded. The stronger the practice of human slavery in a country, the more the people are harming themselves.

So this business of slavery is the nature of human beings, this is what humanity is, remarked the MA.

The BA added, we were quite taken with the example that Sandip-babu gave the other day. Even if you combed the entire area where Harish Kundu is the zamindar, or the Chakrabortys of Sankibhanga, you wouldn't get an ounce of English salt. You know why? Because they have always ruled by force—not having a master is the greatest danger for those who are slaves by nature.

The FA-fail said, let me tell you a story. The Chakrabortys had a Kayasth subject, who got into trouble with them over a market that he had leased. Thanks to constant litigation he no longer knew where his next meal was coming from. When the family had not eaten for two days, he set off to sell his wife's silver jewellery—the last resort. The zamindar's cashier said, I'll buy them for five rupees. The jewellery was worth at least thirty. Having no other choice, the man agreed to five rupees, whereupon the cashier took the bundle and said, I'm adjusting this against the taxes you owe. When we heard this story, we told Sandip-babu, we want to boycott the Chakrabortys. Sandip-babu said, if you eliminate all the living, do you plan to serve the country with corpses? They know how to bend people to their will—they are the lords. Those who cannot make their own wishes come true will live or die according to these people's wishes. Drawing a comparison with you, he said, not a man in the Chakrabortys' realm can raise a finger against swadeshi, but Nikhilesh will never be able to implement swadeshi no matter how much he wants to.

What I want to implement is bigger than swadeshi, I said. That is why it is difficult for me to implement swadeshi. I don't want dead posts, I want living trees. What I want to accomplish will take longer.

The historian smiled. You will get neither dead posts nor living trees. I accept Sandip-babu's precept—you can only get something by snatching it away. It has taken us time to learn this, for it is the opposite of what we are taught in school. I saw for myself the Kundus' rent-collector Gurucharan Bhaduri out to collect dues. One particular Muslim subject had nothing that could be confiscated to pay his taxes. He did have a young wife. Bhaduri said, you must use your wife to pay your dues. A candidate to marry her was brought, and the dues were paid. I confess I could not sleep that night at the sight of the tears in her husband's eyes. But no matter how painful the experience was, I have learnt that the man who can get someone to sell his wife to pay off his debt is a greater man that I; I cannot do it, it makes me weep. If anyone can save my country, it is these rent-collectors, these Kundus, these Chakrabortys.

Astonished, I said, if that is so, it is my duty to save the country from these rent-collectors, these Kundus, these Chakrabortys. Look, when the poison of slavery that lurks in our bones rears its head, it turns into horrifying tyranny—the tortured daughter-in-law turns into the most despotic mother-in-law. When a man who is oppressed by society joins the groom's party at a wedding feast, his demands make it impossible for even the most reputed host to preserve his reputation. Under the rule of terror you have obeyed the authorities out of fear, adopting this as your guiding principle. Which is why you have now made persecution your principle for getting others to submit to your views. My battle is against the severity of this weakness.

What I was saying was quite simple, which ordinary people did not take a moment to understand, but all the MAs in our country were honing their historical skills to defeat the truth.

Meanwhile I was thinking about Panchu's impostor aunt. It would be difficult to prove she was one. The number of witnesses to the truth was limited; it was even possible that there were no witnesses. But there was never a lack of witnesses to what had not happened. This was a trick to annul the hereditary rights that I had purchased for Panchu.

Seeing no other way out, I was considering giving Panchu a plot of land on my own estate and having a house built for him. But Master-moshai said, I cannot accept defeat to unjust forces so easily. I shall make an attempt myself.

You will make an attempt?

Yes, I.

Since it was under litigation, it wasn't clear to me what Master-moshai could do. I didn't meet him at the usual hour that evening. Making enquiries, I learnt that he had left with his suitcase and bedding; all he had told his servants was that he would be back in three or four days. I thought he may have gone to Panchu's maternal uncles' house to gather witnesses. If that was so, I knew his efforts would be in vain. Since his school was closed for a few days on the occasion of Jagadhatri Puja, Muharram and Sunday, he could not even be traced to his school.

When daylight turns murky late on autumn afternoons, the light within the mind changes its colour too. Many people have their minds fixed in their homes, ignoring the object called the 'world' in its entirety. But mine seems to live beneath the trees. I hear everything the winds tell me, every sharp note of light and darkness rings in my heart. In broad daylight the world crowds around me with its numerous tasks—I do not need anything more from life then. But when the sky dims, when a curtain descends on earth from the window of heaven, my heart tells me that evening falls specifically to shroud our surroundings; the only thought in the minds of the land and the water and the sky is to occupy the eternal darkness in the company of the One. The richness of life that blossoms during the day comes to rest within the One in the evening—I cannot remain indifferent to this significance of light and darkness. So, when evening turns into the lover's still black eyes gazing at the universe, my body and soul keep saying, this is not true, work alone cannot be the beginning and the end. Man is not just a labourer, even if his labour is for the cause of truth, the cause of duty. Is the man who is released from his responsibilities under starlight, who is ready to drown in the sweetness of darkness, lost to you forever, Nikhilesh? When the lonely man will not be comforted by the company of the teeming millions on earth, how terribly lonely he must be.

I had no work that afternoon as it flowed into evening nor was my mind on work. Master-moshai was not present either, and my empty heart was trying to reach out to the sky. I went into the garden. I am very fond of chrysanthemums, which I had planted in different colours all over the garden. When all the plants flowered together, the green sea appeared to have waves running through it, frothing with colour. I hadn't been to the garden for some time. Today I smiled and told myself, let me compensate for parting with my grieving chrysanthemums.

When I entered the garden, the moon, fresh from its fullness of the previous night, had just peeped over the wall. The foot of the wall was in dense darkness, over which the slanted moonbeams had fallen on the western side of the garden. It seemed to me that the moon had crept up behind the darkness and covered its eyes, chuckling.

Going up to the side of the wall where rows of chrysanthemum pots were arranged like a gallery, I discovered someone lying quietly on the grass beneath the flights of flowering steps. My heart jumped into my mouth. When I went closer, the person sat up hurriedly.

What should I do now? I was wondering whether to go back, and Bimala must also have been wondering whether to get up and leave. But it was as difficult to go away as it was to stay. Before I could come to a decision, Bimala rose to her feet, drew the end of her sari over head and set off towards the house.

Bimala's unendurable agony materialized in those fleeting moments. The grievances of my own life were swept away. I called out to her, Bimala!

She stopped, startled, but didn't turn towards me. I went up to her. She was in the shadows, while the moonlight fell on my face. She stood with her eyes closed, clenching her fists. I told her, this cage of mine is closed on all sides, Bimala, how can I lock you in here? You will not survive this way.

Still Bimala was silent.

I said, I am telling you the truth—I hereby release you. If I do not mean anything to you, I shall not be your handcuffs for eternity.

I walked away towards the house. No, this was not generosity, and it was certainly not indifference. I would never be released unless I let go. I had wanted her to be the necklace round my heart—I could not make her a burden on my heart forever. All I've been doing is to pray earnestly to the almighty—it is all right if I do not find happiness, I am even willing to accept unhappiness, but do not tie me down. To hold on to a lie as the truth is like throttling yourself. Save me from suicide.

In the drawing room I found Master-moshai waiting for me. I was overcome in both my mind and my heart. Instead of asking him why he was there, I said, release is the greatest thing for man, Master-moshai. Nothing can be compared to it, nothing.

Master-moshai was surprised to see me so agitated. He stared at me without a word.

Books teach us nothing, I said. I read in the scriptures that desire is bondage; it binds itself, binds others too. But mere words are dreadfully empty. Only when I really succeed in setting the bird free from its cage do I realize that it is actually the bird that has freed me. The one I imprison in the cage imprisons me in my desires, and these desires bind more strongly than chains can. No one understands this, I tell you. Everyone thinks reforms must begin elsewhere. But no, they must begin nowhere else except in desire.

Master-moshai said, we believe that getting what we desire is freedom; but actually, freedom is giving up what we desire.

I told him, Master-moshai, putting it in words this way makes it sound like bald advice; but when I catch even a glimpse of it with my own eyes, what I see is the ambrosia that the gods sipped to become immortal. We cannot even see what is beautiful until we let go of it. It was the Buddha who conquered the world, not Alexander but that is a lie when I say it drily. When shall I sing it? When will all the lives in the universe overflow the printed page, like the torrents of the Ganga all the way from its source at Gangotri to the sea?

I suddenly recollected that Master-moshai had not been here for the past few days and I didn't even know where he had been. A little embarrassed, I asked, where did you go?

To Panchu's house, he answered.

Is that where you were the past four days?

Yes, I thought I would talk to the woman who's pretending to be Panchu's aunt. She was a little surprised at first, for she had not even dreamt that someone from a decent family could behave so strangely, for I refused to leave. Then she began to feel embarrassed. I told her, you cannot humiliate me into going away, my daughter. And if I stay here, so will Panchu—I cannot bear to see his young motherless children thrown out of their home. For two days she listened to me in silence, without saying either yes or no. Today, finally, I saw her packing. We will go to Vrindavan, she said, give us money for our travel. I know they're not going to Vrindadvan, but they will need a sizeable amount of money. So I have come to you.

Very well, I shall provide whatever is required.

The old woman isn't a bad sort. Panchu doesn't let her touch the water they drink; he protests when she comes into the room, she was telling me these details. But when she heard that I had no objection to her cooking for me, she took great care of me. She's an excellent cook. Whatever little regard Panchu had for me was wiped out. Earlier he used to consider me at least a simple man; but now he believes that I allowed the old woman to cook for me in order to win her over. Tactics are all very well for survival, but how could I abandon my faith altogether? If I could have borne false witness to outwit the hag, that would have made sense to him. Nevertheless, I'll have to guard Panchu's home for some time even after the old woman leaves, or else Harish Kundu will do something terrible. Apparently he has told his courtier, I found a bogus aunt for him, but he has done one better by discovering a bogus father. I shall see how his father can save him.

He may live or he may die, I said, but if we can wage war against all the different instruments of death that these people have created though religion and society and enterprise, we shall die happy even if we lose.

BIMALA'S STORY

I could not have imagined so much happening in a single lifetime. I seem to have lived seven lifetimes already. A thousand years have passed in these past few months. Time was moving too fast for me to even realize its movement. A sudden jolt the other day woke me up.

When I went to my husband to ask him to get rid of imported products from the market, I knew there would be an argument. But I had not expected to have to combat logic with counter-logic. There was magic in the environment. Even a person of Sandip's stature had washed up at my shore like a wave—not on my invitation, but on the environment's. And then there was Amulya. Oh, how young he was, as innocent and inviting as the tender strains from a flute. When he came to me, his life was flushed with colour, just like the river at dawn. When I looked at Amulya, I realized how a devotee could charm a goddess. This, I discovered, was how my magic wand was working.

And so I had burst in on my husband—but what happened eventually? I had never seen such a dispassionate look in my husband's eyes in all these nine years. It was like a desert sky, without the slightest drop of moisture in it, reflecting something devoid of all colour. I would have been relieved had he been even slightly angry. But I could not touch him. I felt I was a lie. As though I was a dream; as soon as the dream broke, there was nothing but the darkness of the night.

I had envied my pretty sisters-in-law for their beauty all this while. In my mind I knew that the lord had not given me strength—the love of my husband was my only strength. Today, though, I had drunk my fill of the wine of power. But suddenly the cup fell to the ground and was shattered. How was I to live now?

Quickly I had begun to do my hair. Shame! Shame! Shame! As Mejorani passed my room she said, well, Chhotorani, your hair seems to want to leap over you—are you feeling all right in the head?

The other day my husband had told me calmly in the garden, I'm setting you free. But can you set someone—or yourself—free quite so easily? Is freedom a thing? Freedom is emptiness. Like a fish I have swum in a sea of love all my life—when you suddenly held me up to the sky and said, here's your freedom, I could neither move nor live.

When I enter my bedroom today, all I see is furniture, the clothes-rack, the mirror, the bed—but not the heart that was here once. There's freedom, only freedom, a void. The currents have dried, exposing the rocks and boulders. There's no love, only furniture.

Just as I was wondering how much of my truth remained in this world, I met Sandip again. And as heart collided with heart, the same fire was rekindled. What lie? This was the brimming truth, truth overflowing its banks. This emergence of my inner self was a thousand times more true than all these people moving about, talking, laughing—far truer than Barorani counting her beads, or Mejorani giggling with her maid Thako and singing.

I need fifty thousand rupees, said Sandip. My enraptured heart said, fifty thousand is nothing, I shall bring it—it hardly mattered how or from where. I had risen from nothingness to fullness in an instant. A single command was all that was needed. I can, I can, I can. There was no doubt about it.

I came away, but where was the money? Where was the tree of plenty? Why does the world have to inhibit the mind? But still I would bring him the money—there would be no ignominy no matter what means I used. Wherever there is poverty there is injustice—but injustice cannot touch power. Only thieves steal; victorious monarchs plunder. I began to investigate—where was the treasury located? Who was entrusted with the money? Where were the guards posted? In the middle of the night I would go to the public half of the house, gazing at the office from the veranda. How was I to take away fifty thousand rupees from the money protected by those iron bars? I felt no mercy. If the guards were to fall dead miraculously, I might run into the building in a frenzy. Inside the mind of the queen of the house, a gang of robbers danced with naked cleavers in their hands, asking the goddess for a boon. But the sky remained silent, the guards were changed every hour, the clock rang out repeatedly, and the enormous palace lay sleeping in peace.

Eventually I sent for Amulya. We need money for the country, I told him. Can you get the money out of the treasury?

Of course, he said confidently.

Alas, I had said the same thing to Sandip one day. I wasn't the least reassured by Amulya's confidence.

What will you do, I asked him.

Amulya began to outline impractical plans that were not fit to be expressed anywhere except the short story pages of monthly magazines.

No, Amulya, none of this childishness, I told him.

Very well, he answered. I'll buy off the guards.

Where will you get the money to pay them?

By looting people, he replied nonchalantly.

No need, I said. I have some jewellery that you can use.

But the treasurer needn't be bribed, warned Amulya. There's a very simple solution.

Which is?

You'd better not ask. It's very simple.

Still. Tell me.

Taking a pocket-edition of the Gita from the pocket of his kurta and putting it on the table, Amulya pulled out a small pistol and showed it to me without a word.

How dreadful! Not a moment's hesitation in proposing the

murder of our treasurer, an old man! Amulya's face suggested he wouldn't harm a fly, but what he was saying was completely different. The old treasurer didn't even exist for Amulya—he could very well have been a patch of empty sky. A sky devoid of life or pain, and containing only a line: it is not slain when the body is slain.

My goodness, Amulya, I said. Our Roy-moshai is married, he has children, he . . .

How will I find anyone in our land who isn't married and doesn't have children? Look, what we call mercy is nothing but mercy on ourselves. We do not strike out against others lest our own feeble hearts are injured. This is ultimate cowardice.

My heart quaked on hearing Sandip's words being parroted by this young man. He was so tender—this was the time for him to believe in what was good. Poor boy, this was the time for him to live and to grow. The mother in me awoke. Speaking for myself, there was a sense of neither right nor wrong in me—there was only death in its sweetest guise. But I trembled to see this eighteen-year-old boy concluding so easily that killing a blameless old man was his duty. When I saw there was no sin in his heart, it appeared even more horrible. I seemed to see the sins of the parents in their young child.

His innocent eyes made my heart ache. He was about to enter the mouth of the python—who could save him? Why did my country not turn itself into a real mother and clasp this boy to her breast? Why did it not tell him, what use is it your saving me, my son, if I cannot save you?

I know that the greatest powers of the world have signed pacts with the devil for their own benefit, but the mother exists to single-handedly prevent the devil from thriving. The mother does not want accomplishment, no matter how momentous it is—the mother wants to protect. Today my entire being wanted to hold this boy in my arms to protect him.

But I had told him to rob the treasury at the outset—no matter how vehemently I told him otherwise now, he would laugh, thinking of it as a woman's weakness. They accept feminine frailty wholeheartedly only when it enraptures the world.

You don't have to do anything, I told Amulya. It is my responsibility to collect the money.

When he reached the door I called him back. I am your elder sister, Amulya, I told him. In the almanac, it may not be the day when the sister prays for her brother's well-being, but the real date for these prayers comes three hundred and sixty-five times a year. My blessings are for you—may god protect you.

Amulya stopped a moment on hearing me say this. Bending down, he touched my feet in reverence. His eyes were moist when he rose.

I am going to die anyway, my brother, may I die with all your cares transferred to me—may I not cause you to commit a sin.

You must give your pistol to me as a mark of respect, I told Amulya.

What will you do with it, Didi?

I'll practise death.

That's what we need, Didi. Women must kill too, die too. He gave me the pistol.

Amulya left the luminosity on his young face in my life like the first lines of the sun at dawn. Tucking the pistol into my sari, I said, this is my last resort for safety, my compensation for my sisterly duties.

This was the one time that a window had opened on the mother residing in my heart. I had expected it to stay open.

But the road to beatitude was blocked again as the lover put a padlock on the door to the mother's recovery.

I met Sandip again the next day. Madness planted itself on my heart again, naked, and began to dance. But was this my nature? Never!

I had never seen this shameless, selfish side to myself. The snake-charmer had suddenly pulled the snake out of my garments; but it had never really been in there—it had lurked beneath the snake-charmer's shawl. I was possessed by an evil spirit. All this was not my sport but his.

This evil spirit appeared one day with a burning torch and told me, I am your country, I am your Sandip, you have nothing greater than me, Vande mataram. Joining my palms I said, you are my duty, you are my heaven, I shall sweep away all I have in my love for you. Vande mataram!

You need five thousand rupees? Very well, I shall bring five thousand. Tomorrow? Very well, you shall have it tomorrow. Like alcohol, this gift of five thousand rupees will ferment into daring and disgrace. Then will come the drunkard's celebrations. The firm earth will tremble beneath my feet, fireballs will run through my eyes, storms will rage in my ears. Oblivious of what lies ahead, I will totter towards my death. All the flames be put out at once, all the ashes will fly in the wind . . . nothing will remain.

I had made no plans whatsoever to secure the money. But the heightened excitement of the day suddenly threw a pool of light on how I could get it.

My husband gave three thousand rupees to each of his two sisters-in-law as a mark of respect during Durga Puja. The money had accumulated in their bank accounts every year, earning interest. This time he had given them their gifts already, but I knew that it hadn't yet been put in the bank. And I also knew where it was. There was an iron safe in a tiny chamber adjacent to our bedroom, in which the money had been locked away.

My husband went to Calcutta every year with the money to deposit it in the bank; but this year he hadn't been there yet. This is why I believe in fate. The money was still where it had been because it was earmarked for the country. Who could possibly take it to the bank? The goddess of the apocalypse held out her hand, saying, I am hungry, give it to me. I gave her the blood from my veins in the form of those five thousand rupees. Mother mine, the owner of this money will hardly be affected, but you have bankrupted me now.

Mentally I had often dubbed Barorani and Mejorani thieves, accusing them of exploiting my gullible husband for his money. I had often told my husband that they had spirited away many family possessions after their respective husbands' deaths. He would never reply. I would get angry, telling him, if you want to offer charity, go ahead—why must you let them steal? The almighty had chuckled at my accusation that day, for today I was about to steal Barorani's and Mejorani's money from the safe.

My husband kept his clothes in the same room at night, with the keys in the pocket. Taking the keys out, I unlocked the safe. The slight sound made me fear that the whole world had woken up. A chill suddenly froze my limbs, making my heart tremble violently.

There was a drawer in the safe. Pulling it open, I found not currency notes but guineas arranged in paper packets. There was no time for calculations—I bundled all of twenty packets into the end of my sari.

It wasn't a light load! The shameful burden of my theft made me want to sink through the floor. Perhaps currency notes would not have seemed like theft, but this was all gold.

When I entered my own room as a thief that night, it no longer remained mine. I had such an uncontestable right to this room, but I had forfeited it through my crime.

In my head I repeated the incantation, Vande mataram, Vande mataram. This land, my land, my golden land. All the gold belonged to the country, not to anyone else.

But the heart becomes weak at the dead of night. My husband was asleep in the bedroom. Screwing my eyes shut, I left his room. Going out to the uncovered terrace over the inner chambers, I dropped to the floor, my breast shielding the stolen money bundled at the end of my sari, the wrappers striking at my heart. The silent night raised its accusing finger at me. I was not able to separate my home from my land. I had looted my home, and so I had looted my country. My sin had simultaneously taken my home away from me and alienated my country. If, instead, I had begged to gather the money and died in the process, the unfinished service would have been my own offering; the gods would have accepted it. But theft was not worship—how would I offer this to my country? My land would sink under the weight of stolen goods. I was close to dying, but why take my country down with me and tarnish its purity?

Returning the money to the safe was impossible. I was not strong enough to go back to that room this very night and unlock the safe. I would faint at the doorstep to my husband's room if I had to do that. There was no other path now but the one that lay in front of me.

I was too ashamed to count how much money I had taken. Let it all remain as much a secret as it was now—I wasn't going to calculate how much I had stolen.

There wasn't the slightest haze in the dark sky of the winter night—all the stars were glittering. Lying on the terrace, I told myself, if I had to steal these stars for the sake of my country, all these stars gathered in the breast of the darkness, the night would be a widow and the night sky, blind. And my theft would have amounted to stealing from the entire world. I had not stolen money today, I had stolen the light from the sky forever, a theft from the entire world. I had stolen faith, I had stolen righteousness.

I spent the entire night on the terrace. In the morning, when I was sure that my husband had left, I covered myself completely in my shawl and trudged off to my room. Mejorani was watering her potted plants in the veranda. As soon as she saw me she said, have you heard the news, Chhotorani?

I stopped, my heart quaking. The guineas gathered at the end of my sari seemed to be making a lump in my shawl. I felt as though the fabric would tear any moment, sending the guineas ringing across the floor of the veranda. A thief who had stolen her own wealth and lost everything in the process would now be revealed even to the maids and servants.

Your Devi Chowdhurani gang has written an anonymous letter threatening to rob Thakurpo's treasury, said Mejorani.

I stood like a thief, in silence.

I was telling Thakurpo to seek your help. Be merciful, goddess, call your gang off. We shall accept your offer of Vande mataram to the gods. All sorts of strange things are happening—now please don't allow your home to be plundered.

I hurried away to my bedroom without a word. I had stepped into quicksand. I could not extricate myself anymore. The more I struggled, the more I'd sink.

I'd be relieved if I could get rid of this money and hand it over to Sandip at once. I could not bear this burden anymore—my ribs seemed to be breaking.

A little later I was told that Sandip was waiting for me. I didn't bother to dress—I went out to the drawing-room quickly, wrapping myself in my shawl.

I found Amulya sitting with Sandip. Whatever little self-esteem I still had left my body through my soles, sinking into the floor. I would have to suffer the ultimate humiliation that a woman could, in the presence of this boy. They were discussing my theft amongst themselves—they had not allowed the thinnest of curtains to remain over my act.

We women will never understand men. When they pave the road along which the juggernaut of their ambition will roll, they do not hesitate to shatter the heart of the universe and use its pieces. When they are maddened by the passion of creating with their own hands, their joy comes from destroying god's creations. My shame would not even catch their eye; they have no compassion for the heart, all they want is to fulfil their objective. Who am I to them anyway? Merely a wild flower in the path of a flood.

But what did Sandip gain from putting out my light this way? Was it just for these five thousand rupees? Did I have nothing more than those five thousand rupees in me? Of course I did. Sandip had told me as much, which had enabled me to disregard the wide world. I was the giver of light, of life, of strength, of immortality—it was with this faith, this joy, that I had set out, flooding my banks. If someone had made my happiness complete, I would have lived even in death; I would not have lost anything even if my entire world were swept away.

Do they now want to say that all this is a lie? That the goddess in me lacks the power to offer her disciples the gift of strength? Were the paeans of praise they sang to make me descend from heaven to earth not meant to turn this earth to heaven? Or was it to reduce paradise to clay?

Pinning his usual penetrating glance on me, Sandip said, I need money, Queen.

Amulya gazed at me. He wasn't born in my womb but in his mother's—a mother just like me. Oh, such an innocent face with gentle eyes, such youth. I am a woman, I belong to the breed of mothers—am I supposed to hand him poison when he tells me to?

I need money, Queen!

In my rage and shame I wanted to hurl my load of gold at Sandip's head. My fingers trembled so much that I simply couldn't untie the knot at the end of my sari. When the paper-wrapped packets finally fell on the table, Sandip's face fell. He was sure they contained nothing but small change. So much hatred! Such extreme contempt for incompetence! He looked ready to strike me. Sandip thought I was trying to haggle with him, that I wanted to settle his demand for five thousand rupees with two or three hundred. At one moment I thought he would throw the packets out of the window. Was he a beggar, after all? He was a king.

Amulya asked, No more, Ranididi?

Pity dripped from his voice. I thought I might burst out crying. Controlling my heart with all my strength, I shook my head. Sandip was silent—neither touching the packets, nor saying a word.

I wanted to leave, but my feet wouldn't move. If only the earth would part and draw me in, this lump of clay would have been relieved to have found refuge.

My humiliation struck at the boy's heart. Feigning joy, he said, this is no small amount. This will be enough. You have saved us, Ranididi.

He unwrapped one of the packets, and the guineas inside began to glint.

Sandip's face lost its black hue at once. His eyes shone with happiness. Unable to withstand this sudden reversal of the wind, he jumped out of his seat and ran towards me. I did not know what his intention was. I flashed a glance at Amulya—he looked as though he had been whipped; his face seemed to have been robbed of all colour. Summoning all my strength, I gave Sandip a shove. His head hit the marble table with a thump, after which he slumped to the ground, not stirring for a while. I had no strength left after this extreme effort and I sat down. Amulya's face glowed with joy and without sparing Sandip a glance, he sat down at my feet after touching them reverently. My brother, my dear, this show of respect from you is the last drop of sweetness in the empty cup of my life. I could not contain myself any longer, I began to weep. Covering my mouth with the end of my sari, I was wracked with sobs. Every time I felt Amulya's distressed touch on my feet, my tears flowed even more strongly.

When I had recovered, I opened my eyes to discover Sandip sitting at the table, making a bundle of the guineas with his handkerchief as though nothing had happened. Amulya rose from his position near my feet, tears welling in his eyes.

Raising his eyes towards us without hesitation, Sandip said, six thousand rupees.

We don't need so much, Sandip-babu, said Amulya. My

calculations say three and a half thousand is all we need at the moment.

Our work isn't limited to what we're doing now, said Sandip. How can our needs be measured with a specific number?

Amulya said, still, I'll take responsibility for securing our future needs. Return the two and a half thousand to Ranididi.

Sandip looked at me. No, I don't even want to touch that money anymore, I declared. Do whatever you like with it.

Turning to Amulya, Sandip said, can men ever give anything the way women can?

Women are goddesses, said Amulya ecstatically.

We men can give our strength at best, said Sandip, but women give themselves. They give birth to children and bring them up from within their heart, not as an act for the world to see. This giving is a real giving.

Looking at me, Sandip said, if what you have given us today were just money, I wouldn't even have touched it. You have given me what is greater than your own life.

Human beings probably have two different ways of understanding things. In my case, one of them told me that Sandip was deceiving me, but the other one chose to be deceived. Sandip was characterless, but he had power. Which was why the moment he aroused the heart was also the moment he fired the arrow of death. He had the quiver of the gods, which could not be depleted, but it was a demon's arsenal.

Sandip could not fit all the guineas into his handkerchief. Can you give me a handkerchief of yours, Queen, he asked.

When I gave him one, he touched his forehead with it, and then squatted near my feet to touch them reverently, saying, it was to offer you this respect that I had come running up to you, goddess, but you knocked me down to the floor. Your blow is my boon, I accept it humbly. He showed me the spot of impact.

Had I really misunderstood? Was Sandip coming up to me with outstretched arms only to touch my feet? The sudden passion on his face had been visible to Amulya too. But Sandip set his flattery to such magnificent tunes that I could not argue—the eyes with which I should have seen the truth seemed to close under the influence of some unknown opium. Sandip's blow was twice as hard as mine—the wound on his head made my heart bleed. When he offered me his adoration, my theft was graced by nobility. The guineas on the table smiled alluringly, ignoring all public criticism, all righteous reasoning.

Just like me, Amulya was converted, too. Although his respect for Sandip had been diminished for a few moments, it surged again, the obstacles gone. The bowl of flowers to worship Sandip and me with was refilled. Like Venus at dawn, his eyes radiated the pure grace of simple faith. I worshipped, I was worshipped, my sins grew luminous. Looking at me, Amulya joined his palms and said, Vande mataram.

But I could not keep hearing my praises being sung. In my heart I had no means to preserve my self-respect. I could not enter my own bedroom. The iron safe scowled at me, while our bed seemed to raise a forbidding hand. I wanted to run away from this self-humiliation; all I wanted was to hear Sandip singing my praises. This was the only space for self-esteem in my endless, agonizing darkness; all else was a void. I wanted to cling to it all the time. Praise, praise, I wanted praise day and night. I could not survive if the cup of wine ran empty even for a moment. And so my heart longed all day to go to Sandip and listen to him; I needed Sandip so much just to discover the worth of my existence.

I could not bring myself to sit down opposite my husband when he came for his lunch; but not doing this was so embarrassing that I had to be present—I sat behind him, so that our eyes did not meet. That was how I was seated the other day during his meal when Mejorani arrived. You may laugh away all those threats of being robbed, Thakurpo, but I'm afraid, she said. You still haven't deposited the money you gave us this time in the bank?

No, I haven't had the time, my husband replied.

Look, you're very careless, said Mejorani. This money . . .

It's in the iron safe in the room next to my bedroom, my husband told her with a smile.

You never know, they could take it from the safe.

If a thief gets into that room of mine, you might be stolen some day too.

Oh no one will take me, don't worry. What's worth taking is in your own room. No, it's not a joke—don't keep the money at home.

The taxes have to be paid in about a week, I'll send the money to Calcutta at that time.

Don't forget, all right? You're so absent-minded, one never knows.

If any money is stolen from the room it will be mine, Mejorani—why should it be yours?

You make me ill when you say such things, Thakurpo. Do you think I differentiate between you and me? I'll feel the pain just as much if your money is stolen. The accursed lord may have robbed me of everything but he has let me keep my wonderful brother-in-law—don't you think I know his worth? I cannot immerse myself in the gods day and night like Barorani—what the gods have given me is greater than the gods. And you, Chhotorani, why are you as silent as a doll? You know, Thakurpo, Chhotorani thinks I flatter you. I would have if I had to but you're not the kind of brother-in-law who waits to be flattered. If you'd been another Madhab Chakraborty our Barorani would not have been worshipping her gods and goddesses today—she would have been spending her days pleading with you for a little money. It would have been good for her, though, she would not have had the time to make up so many things about you.

Mejorani kept chattering, while drawing her brother-in-law's attention to the different items served for lunch. My head was spinning by now—there was no time, I would have to do something. As I kept asking myself over and over what could happen or what could be done, Mejorani's voice appeared absolutely unbearable to me. Especially because I knew nothing escaped her notice. She kept staring at me—I don't know what she could see, but it seemed to me that everything was written on my face.

My daring knew no bounds. I laughed, seemingly amused in the most natural way, and said, the truth is that it's me whom Mejorani doesn't trust, thieves and robbers are just a pretext.

Chuckling, Maejorani said, you're right, when women steal they can destroy everything. But then I'm bound to find you out, since I'm not a man. What will you fool me with?

I told her, if you're so afraid, I'd better deposit all my possessions with you—if I cause you any losses you can deduct the amount.

Listen to you, said Mejorani, smiling. There are losses that you cannot recover even if you deposit everything in this life and the one that comes after.

My husband didn't say a word during this conversation. He left after completing his meal—he no longer went to the bedroom to rest a while as he used to.

Most of my valuable ornaments were with the treasurer. But still, what I had at home was not worth less than thirty or thirty-five thousand rupees. I held this jewellery box open to Mejorani, telling her, I'm keeping my ornaments with you, Mejorani. You can be reassured now.

Putting her hand to her cheek in astonishment, she said, oh my god, you surprise me. Do you really think I can't sleep nights worrying that you're going to steal my money?

And what's wrong if you do, I said. Do we really know one another well enough, Mejorani?

Is that why you're trying to teach me a lesson by trusting me? I can't keep track of my own jewellery and now you expect me to die worrying because I've taken change of yours? Maids and servants are on the loose everywhere—you'd better take your ornaments away.

As soon as I came away, I asked for Amulya to be fetched to the drawing-room. Sandip appeared along with him. I had no time to waste; I told Sandip, I have something important to discuss with Amulya, if you could...

With a wooden smile Sandip said, do you see him as distinct from me? If you want to win him over from my side I shan't be able to stop him.

I didn't reply. Very well, said Sandip, after you've finished your important discussion with Amulya, you must make time for an important discussion with me as well—or else I will face defeat. I can accept anything, but not defeat. My share is greater than everyone else's. I have fought with the lord all my life over this. I shall defeat him, I shall not be defeated.

Hurling a burning glance at Amulya, Sandip left the room. I told Amulya, my dearest brother, you have to do something for me.

I'll lay down my life to do whatever you ask me to, Didi, he said.

Taking the jewellery box out from under my shawl, I set it down before him, saying, pawn these ornaments or sell them, but get me six thousand rupees as quickly as you can.

Pained, Amulya replied, No, Didi, I shan't pawn these—I shall get you six thousand rupees.

Annoyed, I told him, forget all that, I have no time. Take this box and take the night train to Calcutta—you must get me six thousand rupees the day after tomorrow.

Taking the diamond necklace out of the box, Amulya held it up to the light before putting it back dismally. It won't be easy to sell this diamond jewellery at the correct price, I said, which is why I'm giving you jewellery worth more than thirty thousand rupees. I don't care if everything goes, but I must have six thousand rupees.

Look, Didi, said Amulya, I have quarrelled with Sandip-babu for taking six thousand rupees from you. I cannot tell you how shameful it is. Sandip-babu says shame must be forsaken for the country. Perhaps. But this is different. I am strong enough not to be afraid to die for my country, not to show pity when killing for my country; but I simply cannot rid myself of the agony of taking this money from you. Sandip-babu is far stronger than me here— he does not have an ounce of regret. He says we must rid ourselves of the illusion that money actually belongs to the one in whose safe it is locked away, or else what's Vande mataram worth?

Amulya grew animated as he spoke. His eagerness to speak increased when I was the listener. He continued, Krishna says in the Gita, no one can destroy the soul. Killing is just a word. So is theft. Whom does money belong to? No one creates it, no one takes it along when they die, it is not a part of anyone's soul. It's mine today, my son's tomorrow, the moneylender's the day after. Since this money is not anyone's on principle, will it really turn evil just because it is vilified for being used for the country instead of falling into the hands of your unworthy son?

My heart trembled as I heard Sandip's words from this boy. Let the snake-charmers blow on their pipes and play with snakes; let them die knowingly if they must die. But oh, these boys were so tender, the benediction of the entire world wanted to protect them at all times. When they reached out laughing to play with the snake, not knowing its identity, I could see clearly what a terrible curse this was. Sandip had rightly concluded that I might choose to die at his hands, but I would win this boy over from Sandip's grasp and save him.

With a smile I asked Amulya, is the money needed for the service of those who serve the nation?

Of course it is, answered Amulya proudly. They are our kings—poverty makes their power waste away. Do you know that we never allow Sandip-babu to travel except by first class? He never hesitates to accept luxuries. He has to maintain this status not for himself, but for all of us. Sandip-babu says, the magic of wealth is the strongest weapon for the gods of this world. To take on the mission of living in poverty is not to accept misery, but to commit suicide.

Suddenly Sandip entered, silently. I quickly covered my jewellery box with my shawl. Isn't the important discussion with Amulya over yet, he asked with a sneer.

A little embarrassed, Amulya said, no, we've finished. Nothing important.

No, Amulya, we haven't finished, I said.

Sandip asked, then a second exit for Sandip?

Yes, I said.

Then Sandipkumar's re-entry . . .

Not today, I have no time.

Sandip's eyes blazed. There's time only for important things, but not to waste on anything else.

Envy! When the strong turned weak, how could the powerless woman not blow her trumpet of victory? Therefore I said quite firmly, no, I have no time.

Sandip left with a dark face. A little perturbed, Amulya said, Sandip-babu is annoyed, Ranididi.

I answered spiritedly, he has neither reason nor the right to be annoyed. Let me tell you something, Amulya—you must not tell Sandip-babu about selling my jewellery even if threatened with death.

No, I shan't.

Then don't delay anymore, take the train tonight.

I left the room along with Amulya, and discovered Sandip in

the veranda outside. I realized he was going to pounce on Amulya. To prevent this, I had to talk to him. What is it you wanted to say, Sandip-babu?

I don't have anything important tell you, only small talk, since you have no time . . .

I have time, I said.

Amulya left. As soon as he entered, Sandip said, Amulya had a box of some sort, what's in it?

The box had not escaped his attention. Strengthening my resolve, I said, if I had any intention of telling you I'd have given it to him in your presence.

Do you think Amulya won't tell me?

No, he won't.

Sandip didn't suppress his rage anymore; flying into a temper, he said, you think you can dominate me, but you're wrong. This Amulya would die happy if I trod on him—as long as I'm alive, I shall never let you win him over.

Such weakness! Sandip had finally realized that he was a weak man in front of me—hence this sudden unrestrained rage. He knew that he could not bend my force to his will, that I could demolish the walls of his fortress with one look. Hence all this bluster. I merely smiled without a word. Finally I had reached a level higher than his; I mustn't lose this place, I mustn't descend. Even in my disgrace let me maintain some of my dignity.

I know it's your jewellery box, Sandip said.

You can guess whatever you please, I shan't tell you, I said.

You trust Amulya more than me? Do you know he's nothing but the shadow of my shadow, the echo of my echo—that he's nothing if he deserts me?

Where he is not your echo he is Amulya. That's where I trust him more than your echo.

You must not forget that you are committed to giving up all your ornaments so that the goddess may be worshipped. In fact you have given them up already.

If the goddess spares any of my ornaments I shall give them to her. How can I give her stolen ornaments?

Look, don't try to slip through my fingers. I have work to be done, let me finish it—there will be time for all your feminine guile afterwards. I shall join the game too.

The moment I had stolen my husband's money and handed it to Sandip, the music in our relationship had turned discordant. Not only had I sold myself, turning as worthless as a counterfeit coin, but Sandip also could not exercise his power over me anymore. You can hardly fire an arrow at what's already in your grasp. That was why Sandip was no longer the hero. His words were filled with the harsh, vulgar noises of combat.

He remained sitting, training his bright eyes on me, eyes that soon began to blaze like the parched noonday sky. His legs stirred restlessly; I realized he was about to rise to his feet, that he would take me in his arms now. My heart lurched, my nerves began to jangle, the blood pounded in my ears. I knew that if I continued to sit here I wouldn't be able to move. Using all my strength to tear myself away from my seat, I ran towards the door. Sandip's muffled voice groaned, where are you running away, Queen?

He leapt up to take me in his arms, only to rush back to his seat on hearing the sound of footsteps outside. Turning towards the bookshelf, I began to scan the spines.

As soon as my husband entered, Sandip said, don't you have Browning on your shelves, Nikhil? I was telling Queen Bee about our college-club—remember the competition between the four of us over translating that poem? Really? You don't remember? That one...

> She should never have looked at me
> If she meant I should not love her!
> There are plenty... men, you call such,
> I suppose... she may discover
> All her soul to, if she pleases,
> And yet leave much as she found them: But I'm not so, and
>   she knew it
> When she fixed me, glancing round them...

I did force out a Bangla version, but it didn't turn out to be the kind that 'the people of Bengal will joyfully sip the nectar of eternally'. At one time I was on the verge of becoming a poet, but the lord helped me avert the trap. But had our Dakshinacharan not become a salt inspector, he would surely have been a poet. His translation was excellent—it read as though it was written in

Bangla, not the language of a country outside geography.

No, Queen Bee, you are searching in vain; Nikhil has given up reading poetry completely since his marriage—he probably doesn't need to anymore. I had given it up because of the pressure of work, but it seems that the epidemic of verse is about to claim me.

I came to warn you, Sandip, said my husband.

Sandip said, about verse-fever?

Not amused, my husband said, some Maulvis from Dhaka have started visiting our area. There are plans afoot to instigate the Muslims in this region. They are unhappy with you—they may do something unpleasant suddenly.

Do you advise me to flee?

I came to inform you, I have no wish to advise you.

If I had been the zamindar hereabouts, the Muslims would have been worried, not I. If you made them anxious instead of making me worry, it would be worthy of both of us. Do you know that your weakness is weakening your neighbouring zamindars too?

I did not offer you any advice, Sandip, and you needn't have offered me any either. It will be fruitless. There's something else I have to say. Your gang has started quietly terrorising my subjects. This cannot go on—you have to leave my estate now.

Out of fear of Muslims, or is there something else to be afraid of?

Something else, which makes the absence of fear cowardice. It is from this fear that I am saying that you must go, Sandip. I am going to Calcutta in a week, you must come too. You can stay at our house in Calcutta, I have no objection to that.

Very well, I have a week to think it over. Meanwhile, Queen Bee, let me hum the song of farewell from your beehive. O modern Bangla poet, open your door, let me plunder your words— the theft is yours, for you have made my song your own. The fame may be yours, but the song is mine.

He started singing in Raga Bhairavi in his almost tuneless baritone...

The honeyed season is eternal in your kingdom
With smiles and tears of meeting and of parting
Some have to go, but the flowers keep on blooming

Only those that have to die do fall to ground
I gave you many songs when I was near you
Now that I am going, I have a gift for you
So I leave this hope, hidden in your flowers
That the rains of June soften your fiery spring

His boldness was unbounded and unconcealed—as naked as flames. There was no opportunity to stop him; to ask him to desist was like asking the thunder to cease, the sort of request that lightning dismisses with a laugh.

I left the room. As I was returning to the inner chambers, Amulya suddenly appeared from somewhere. Don't worry, Ranididi, he said. I'm going now, I shall not fail.

Looking at his dutiful young face, I said, I won't worry for myself, Amulya, but I hope I can worry for all of you.

He was about to leave, but I called him back to ask, is your mother living, Amulya?

She is.

Your sister?

I have none—I am the only child of my mother's. My father died when I was a child.

Go back, go back to your mother, Amulya.

But, Didi, when I'm here I see both my mother and my sister.

You must have your meal here tonight before you leave, Amulya, I said.

There's no time, Ranididi, he said. Give me food blessed by your touch to take along.

What do you like eating, Amulya?

I would have had my fill of sweets had I been with my mother now. When I'm back I'll have sweets you'll make for me yourself.

NIKHILESH'S STORY

Waking up at three in the morning, I had the sudden notion that the world which I lived in once had died, and its ghost now possessed this bed of mine, this room, all my possessions. I realized why we are afraid even of the ghosts of people we knew. It's horrifying when the familiar turns into the unknown in an instant. It is perplexing when the familiar currents of life need to be diverted into a new channel. Protecting one's own nature becomes difficult; we appear to be strangers to ourselves.

I had known for some time that Sandip's group was fomenting trouble in our area. If I had remained steadfast to my character, I would have told Sandip with conviction, leave this place. But my recent troubles were making me behave uncharacteristically. The path I was treading was no longer a simple one. I felt a rush of embarrassment at the prospect of asking Sandip to leave. There was an additional factor now; I looked petty to myself.

Conjugality is instrinsic to me, it is not merely a matter of my household or family or daily routine—it is the flowering of my life. That was why I could not put any pressure on Sandip. I would have been insulting my god in the process. I could not explain this to anyone. Maybe I am a strange man, which is why I was deceived. But how could I be untrue to my nature just to protect my external self?

I have been indoctrinated in a truth that creates everything from the heart. That is why I had to snap the web today. My god shall free me from the slavery of my external life. I may have to secure my release by shedding blood from my heart, but when I do get it the kingdom of my heart shall be mine.

I am getting a taste of this freedom already. The bird within me bursts into song through the darkness now and then. No harm will be done even if the illusory dream that is Bimala were to be broken, assures the man inside me.

From Master-moshai I heard that Sandip has joined hands with Harish Kundu to conduct the Mahishmardini puja with great pomp. Harish Kundu has begun to extract the costs of the ceremonies from his subjects. Our learned poet laureate has been commissioned to compose a eulogy that can be interpreted in two ways. Sandip has even had an argument with Master-moshai about this, stating that gods evolve; unless the descendants can mould the gods created by their ancestors to their own requirements, they will turn into atheists. My mission is to modernise the ancient gods; I have been born to free the gods from the bonds of the past. I shall rescue them.

I have observed from childhood that Sandip is a conjuror of ideas. He has no need to discover the truth, his joy lies in weaving magic around it. Had he been born in central Africa he would have loved to prove that human sacrifice followed by cannibalism is the finest form of intimacy. The man whose calling is to delude others cannot help but delude himself too. I believe that everytime Sandip casts ever-new spells of black magic with the enchantment of his words, he concludes, 'I have discovered the truth', even if each of his creations are at conflict with the others.

Be that as it may, I cannot assist in the construction of this distillery of illusions in the country. All these young men want to serve their country—I shall not be involved in luring them into addiction. Those who wish to accomplish their tasks by tricking people with slogans may value the tasks, but they do not value the minds they deceive. If I cannot save the country from intoxication, worshipping the country will only harvest a poisonous fruit. Like a misguided missile, all the effort will only strike the country at its heart.

I have told Sandip in Bimala's presence, you must leave my home. Perhaps both Bimala and Sandip will misunderstand my objective. But I want to be released from this fear of being misunderstood. Let Bimala misunderstand me too.

Maulvis from Dhaka are here, preaching. Muslims in this area used to hate cow-slaughter almost as much as Hindus. But now cows have begun to be slaughtered in some places. It was one of my Muslim subjects who informed me, and protested too. An artificial fanaticism lies behind it now, but trying to stop it will make the fanaticism real. And that is what the opposition wants.

Summoning my most influential Hindu subjects, I tried my utmost to explain to them. I said, we can maintain our faith, but we have no control over other people's faith. The hunter will not stop killing animals because I worship them. What's the way out? The Muslims must be allowed to be guided by their faith, too. Please don't create trouble.

They said, we didn't have this nuisance all these years, maharaj.

I said, no, but that was their choice. Find a way to make them stop it by choice too. And that is not the road of conflict.

They said, no maharaj, those days are gone, they will never stop unless they are forced to.

I said, force will certainly not stop cow-slaughter, but it may lead to violence between people.

One of them had studied English, he had learnt to chant the latest jargon. He said, look, it isn't just a matter of tradition. Our country is an agricultural one, the cow is . . .

I answered, in our country the buffalo also gives milk and is used to plough the land, but we cavort in the temple courtyard smeared in blood and holding severed buffalo heads, don't we? When we join issue with Muslims for the sake of our religion—our dharma—we make Dharma, the god of justice, laugh. And the quarrel intensifies. If it is only the cow that must not be slaughtered and not the buffalo, then it isn't a question of faith, but only of blind tradition.

The English language expert said, don't you see who's behind this? The Muslims have come to know that they will not be punished. You've heard of their exploits in Panchurey, haven't you?

I said, these attacks on ourselves using Muslims as weapons have been made possible because we have forged the weapons with our own hands; such is the ruling of the god of justice. We will pay for everything we have done all this time.

The English language expert said, so be it, let us pay. But we take pleasure in the fact that victory is ours this time; we have demolished the very law that is their greatest strength. They had ruled all this while, but now they will be forced to become plunderers. History will not record this, but we shall remember it forever.

Meanwhile, I became famous for being infamous in every newspaper. I'm told that people in the service of the nation erected my effigy near the crematorium on the Chakrabortys' estates and burnt it with great ceremony; several other forms of humiliation were also arranged. These people had approached me to buy shares in their partnership for starting a cotton mill. I told them, I would have no regrets if all I lost was the paltry sum involved, but if you set up your mill many poor people will lose their livelihood, which is why I shall not buy your shares.

But why? Aren't you in favour of what is good for the country?

Enterprise may lead to the good of the country, but merely saying we want 'what is good for the country' does not make for an enterprise. When we were calm our enterprises did not thrive, are they going to be successful now just because we are enraged?

Why not just tell us you won't buy the shares?

I will buy them, but only when I consider your enterprise nothing but a business venture. I don't see any obvious evidence that just because your revolutionary fires are burning, your table will be laden with the food cooked on it.

These people considered me a penny-pinching miser. I was tempted to show them the account books of my swadeshi enterprise. And they probably did not know of my attempts to improve the quality of the crops in my motherland. For several years I had imported sugarcane from Java and Mauritius and cultivated them here; on the advice of the agricultural department of the government, I left no stone unturned in experimenting with tilling and irrigation. But what was my harvest? Only the muffled laugher of the peasants on my estate. It remains muffled still. After that, whenever I proposed planting Japanese beans or imported cotton on reading government journals on agriculture, the muffled laughter was heard openly. There was neither hide nor hair of those working in the service of the country then, the slogan of Vande mataram was silent. And as for my mechanical ship . . . but then why talk of all these distant things? If the flames of national service were to be satisfied by burning my effigies, we would actually be saved.

What was this I was hearing! Our office in Chakua had been robbed! Seven thousand rupees to be paid as tax was deposited there last night. We were to have left for the district headquarters by boat at dawn. To make the despatch easier, the rent-collector had had bundles of ten and twenty-rupee notes made. At midnight a band of robbers with guns and pistols plundered the treasury. Kasem Sardar was injured by a pistol shot. Strangely, the robbers had taken only six thousand rupees, leaving the rest scattered around the room. They could easily have taken the entire amount. In any event, after the robbers, it was now the turn of the police. The money was gone, now our peace would follow it on the way out.

When I went into the inner chambers, I discovered that they had been told already. Mejorani said, what a thing to happen, Thakurpo!

To make light of her concern, I said, there's a lot more waiting to happen. I'll survive a while longer.

No really, it's not a joke. Why are they so angry with you of all people? Perhaps you'd better keep them happy, Thakurpo. Can so many people in the country be . . .

I cannot destroy the country for the sake of the people.

Just the other day I heard they did something awful with you by the river. How horrible! I was dying of fear. Chhotorani has studied with an Englishwoman, she's not afraid of anything. But I had to get the priest to perform a peace ritual. Go to Calcutta, Thakurpo, I beg of you. Who knows what they'll do to you if you stay here.

Mejoranididi's fears and apprehension put a balm on my soul. We will never stop begging at the door to your heart, goddess.

It isn't wise to keep your money in that room, Thakurpo. They will get to know somehow and eventually . . . it's not the money I worry for, but who knows whether . . .

To calm her down, I said, very well, I will take the money out at once and send it to the treasury. I'll deposit it in the bank in Calcutta the day after tomorrow.

About to enter my bedroom, I found the door to the next room shut. When I knocked on it, Bimala said, I'm dressing.

Mejorani said, Chhotorani dressing up so early in the morning—how strange! Oh, are they having their Vande mataram meeting today? Tell me, Devi Chowdhurani, are the stolen goods being gathered?

Telling her that I would return later for the money, I went to the drawing room to discover the police inspector there. Any news, I asked him?

I have my suspicions.

On whom?

That Kasem Sardar.

What? But he's the one who has been injured.

Hardly an injury; he just bled a little from his leg, it's a self-inflicted wound.

I cannot suspect Kasem in any circumstances, he's trustworthy.

I'm willing to accept that he's trustworthy, but that doesn't mean he's incapable of theft. I know people who don't break the trust reposed in them for twenty-five years, and then suddenly . . .

If that's the case I cannot put him in jail.

Why should you? That's somebone else's job.

Why did Kasem take only six thousand and leave the rest behind?

In order to plant this doubt in your mind. Whatever you may say, he's a hardened criminal. He may be the guard at your office, but I'm sure he's behind all the thefts and robberies nearby.

The inspector provided several examples of how these stick-wielding robbers could commit a crime twenty-five or thirty miles away and return the same night to be present at their employer's office in the morning.

Have you brought Kasem, I asked.

He answered, no, he's at the police station, deputy-babu will be here soon to investigate.

I want to meet him, I said.

A weeping Kasem clutched my feet the moment he saw me. I swear on the lord, maharaj, I didn't do it.

I don't suspect you, Kasem, I told him. Don't worry, I will not allow you to be punished if you're innocent.

Kasem could not describe the robbers very well; he kept exaggerating, four or five hundred people, with enormous guns and swords, and so on. I realized he was making things up, either fear had amplified all he had seen, or he was embellishing the details to suppress the shame of his cowardice. He felt that Harish Kundu was my enemy, and this must have been his doing. He was even convinced that he had clearly heard the voice of Ekram Sardar, who worked for the Kundus.

Look, Kasem, I said, don't implicate anyone on conjecture. It is not your job to speculate whether Harish Kundu is involved or not.

I returned home and sent for Master-moshai. Shaking his head, he said, no one cares anymore to do what's right. We have replaced duty with patriotism—now all the sins committed in this land will be in shameless evidence.

Do you think this robbery . . .

I don't know, but there is an explosion of sin. Get rid of them from your estate at once.

I have given them one more day; they will all leave the day after tomorrow.

Let me give you some advice—take Bimala to Calcutta. Here, she looks at the world through a narrow perspective; she is unable to size up people correctly. Show her the real world for once; let her see human beings and their work from a vantage point that offers a wide view.

That is what I was thinking, too.

But don't delay this. Look Nikhil, the history of mankind includes every country and every race, which is why, even in politics, the country cannot be more important than what is right. I know Europe does not believe this with all its heart, but I shall not accept Europe as our mentor. People attain immortality by dying for the sake of the truth—if a race were to die for the same reason, it too would become immortal in history. Let our Bharat be the one country in the world where truth attains purity, defying the devil's sky-splitting laughter. But what is this epidemic of sin that has entered our country from foreign lands!

The day was spent on these troublesome things. I went to bed at night exhausted, having decided to take the money out of the safe tomorrow morning instead of tonight.

I woke up in the middle of the night. The room was dark. I could hear a sound. Someone sobbing.

Like gusts of monsoon winds, I heard intermittent tear-laden sighs. It felt as though my room was weeping from its heart.

There was no one else here. For some time now, Bimala had taken to sleeping in one of the adjoining rooms. Getting out of bed, I went to the veranda outside to discover her lying face-down on the floor.

I cannot put it in words. Only he who absorbs all the world's agonies from his position at the heart of the universe knows what it is. The sky was mute; the stars, silent; the night, speechless—and in the midst of them all, this sleepless crying.

We label all our joys and sorrows in keeping with the ways of the world and the scriptures before disposing of them. But what name could there be for this suffering that rose through the heart of the darkness? When I looked at her in the silence of the millions of stars on that black night, my fearful heart told me, who am I to judge her! I bow before the unknowable that resides within life, within death, within the infinite universe and its god.

I considered turning back, but I could not. In silence I sat down at Bimala's side and put my hand on her head. At first she stiffened into a block of wood, but then the stiffness seemed to melt into a thousand streams of tears. It is impossible to comprehend how a human being can store so many tears in their heart.

I stroked Bimala's head gently. A little later she groped for my feet, pressing them upon her breast so hard that I thought their pressure would tear her heart apart.

BIMALA'S STORY

Amulya was to return from Calcutta this morning. I had told the servants to inform me as soon as he arrived. But calmness eluded me, and I went to the drawing room to wait.

When I had sent Amulya to Calcutta to sell my jewellery, I was not concerned with anything in the world besides myself. It never even occurred to me that he was a mere boy, whom everyone would be suspicious of for trying to sell such expensive jewellery. We helpless women inevitably impose our own problems on others. When we die, we take several others down with us.

I had averred with great pride that I would save Amulya. But can someone who is herself sinking possibly save others? It is I who killed him. My brother, I am so wretched a sister that the god of death must have laughed, unseen, the day I put the sister's mark of love for her brother on your forehead. I return today with a burden of ill fortune.

People seem afflicted by a plague of misfortune at times, its germ arrives from nowhere to bring death in just one night. Can it not be kept far away from the entire world? I can clearly see how dangerous its contagion is. It is like a torch of destruction, burning just to set the world on fire.

It was past nine. I had a presentiment that Amulya was in trouble, that he had been captured by the police. There was trouble over my jewellery box at the police station—whom did it belong to, how did he get it? I would have to answer all these questions eventually. What would I say in the presence of all the people in the world? I had only been contemptuous of you all this while, Mejorani. But your day had dawned now. You would take on the form of the entire world to avenge yourself. Save me now, o god—I will abandon all my pride and seek a place at Mejorani's feet.

I could not contain myself. I went inside the house and met Mejorani. Seated in a pool of sunlight in the veranda, she was making paan, with Thako by her side. I felt a twinge of inhibition at the sight of Thako; but I overcame it to drop at her feet and touch them in deference. What's the matter, Chhotorani, what's wrong with you, she exclaimed. Why this sudden reverence?

I was born on this day, Didi, I answered. I have often done you wrong—bless me, Didi, so that I may never hurt any of you again. I am small-minded.

Touching her feet once more, I left hurriedly. She called out to my retreating back, why didn't you tell me earlier that it's your day of birth, Chhutu? You must eat with me this afternoon. Don't forget, my dear girl.

Do something to make today my day of birth, god. Can't I turn into a new woman today? Wipe out my past and test me again from the beginning, lord.

As I was about to enter the drawing room once more, Sandip appeared. My heart turned bitter with abhorrence. In the morning light his face did not hold the slightest magic of genius. Please go, I exclaimed.

Amulya isn't here, Sandip smiled. It is my turn for a personal conversation.

My wretched luck! How was I to withdraw the privilege that I had given him myself? I would like to be left alone, I told him.

The presence of another person in the room does not prevent anyone from being left alone, Queen. Don't confuse me with the crowd, I am Sandip, even amongst a million I am alone.

Please come another time, this morning I am . . .

Waiting for Amulya?

I was about to leave the room in annoyance when Sandip drew my jewellery box out of his shawl and set it down on the marble table with a clatter.

I was startled. Didn't Amulya go, then, I asked.

Go where?

To Calcutta.

No, said Sandip with a smile.

I was relieved. The sister's mark on Amulya's forehead had not been proved false. I was the thief, let the lord's punishment be limited to me, let Amulya be spared.

Observing the expression on my face, Sandip said mockingly, so pleased, Queen? Is the jewellery box so valuable? Then how did you have the heart to dedicate it to the service of the goddess? And now that you have given it, do you want it back from her?

Pride will not desert you even at death; I felt an impulse to prove to him that I did not have the slightest attachment to these ornaments. If you have your eyes on this jewellery, why don't you take it, I said.

Sandip said, today I have my eyes on all the wealth in every corner of Bengal. Is there a calling more noble than greed? Covetousness is the steed of the divine kings on earth. All these ornaments are mine, then?

As soon as Sandip picked up the case and tucked it under his shawl, Amulya entered. He had dark circles under his eyes; he looked haggard, and his hair was dishevelled. All the youthfulness of his tender years seemed to have vanished in a single day. My heart ached when I saw him.

Without a look at me, Amulya went up to Sandip, asking, did you take the jewellery box out of my trunk?

Is the jewellery yours?

No, but the trunk is.

Sandip burst into laughter. Your sense of thine and mine over the ownership of the trunk is very subtle, I observe. You will turn into a missionary before you die.

Sitting down heavily, Amulya hid his face in his hands and lowered his head on the table. Going up to him, I put my hand on his head, asking, what's the matter, Amulya?

Jumping to his feet, he said, I had set my heart on bringing this jewellery box back to you myself. Sandip-babu knew this, which is why he . . .

What will I do with those ornaments, I said. Let them go. It will do no harm.

Where will they go, asked Amulya in wonder.

This jewellery is mine, said Sandip, an offering from my queen.

No, never, screamed Amulya like a mad man. I have brought it back, Didi, you cannot give it to anyone else.

I shall remember your gift all my life, Amulya, I told him, but let he who has his eye on the jewellery take it.

Throwing angry glances at Sandip like a wild beast, Amulya fumed, look, Sandip-babu, you know very well I do not fear the gallows. If you appropriate this jewellery . . .

Trying to summon a derisive smile to his face, Sandip said, you too should have known by now that I do not fear authority, Amulya. I did not come here today to take this jewellery, Queen Bee, I came to give it back to you. But to mitigate the injustice of your accepting from Amulya what is rightfully mine, I made you admit my claim to it. Now I shall bequeath on you what is mine. Here it is. You can settle accounts with the boy. I am leaving. The two of you have been having personal conversations for some time, which I am not part of. If something untoward happens now you cannot blame me. Amulya, I have sent all your belongings that were lying with me—your trunk, books, and everything else—to your house near the market. You must not keep any of your things in my room.

Sandip strode out.

I haven't had a moment of peace since I gave you the jewellery to sell, Amulya, I said.

Why, Didi?

I was worried lest you got into trouble over the jewellery. What if someone suspected you of stealing it? I do not need the six thousand rupees. And now you must do as I tell you, you must go home at once, to your mother.

Pulling a bundle out from beneath his shawl, Amulya said, I have brought six thousand rupees, Didi.

Where did you get this, I asked.

Without answering, he said, I tried my best to get hold of guineas, but I could not. So I have brought currency notes.

I beg of you, Amulya, tell me the truth. Where did you get this money?

I shan't tell you.

I was panic-stricken. What have you gone and done, Amulya? Is this money . . .

I know you think I've got this money by wrongful means—very well, I admit it. But the greater the wrongdoing, the bigger the price, and I have paid it. This money is mine now.

I was no longer inclined to know the details of how the money was procured. My nerves felt pinched, making my body shrink. Take it away, Amulya, return this money wherever you got it.

That is very difficult.

No, it isn't, Amulya. What an inauspicious moment it was when you came to me. I have done more harm to you than even Sandip.

Mentioning Sandip seemed to sting him. He said, Sandip! It was because I came to you that I discovered his real self. Do you know, Didi, he hasn't spent a paisa out of the six thousand rupees that he took from you the other day? After he left you, he shut the door of his room and piled all the coins on the floor from his handkerchief, staring at them, mesmerized. This isn't money, he said, these are the petals of the eternal amaranth, these are notes that have hardened after dropping off the flute of Kuvera's kingdom of riches—they cannot be exchanged for currency notes. Don't view this with materialistic eyes, Amulya, this is the smile of the goddess of wealth, the grace of the queen of heaven. No, these have not been created to be handed over to that crass treasurer. Look, Amulya, he is lying, pure and simple. The police have no information that the boat was stolen; he is merely using the opportunity to make some money. We have to get those three letters out of the treasurer, Amulya. How, I asked. Sandip said, by force, by terrorising him. I'm willing, I said, but these guineas must be returned. Very well, said Sandip, it shall be done. How I browbeat the treasurer into parting with those three letters and burnt them is a long story. That same night I went back to Sandip and said, give me the guineas. I shall return them to Didi tomorrow morning. What is this obsession, Sandip asked me. Is the nation to cower beneath the end of your Didi's sari? Say with me, Vande mataram, let the spell be broken. You know Sandip's ability to sway people, Didi. The sovereigns stayed with him. In the darkness of the night I sat next to the lake, paying homage to Vande mataram. When you gave me the jewellery to sell yesterday, I went to him again in the evening. I realized he was furious with me. He did not reveal his anger; he said, check for yourself, if you find the sovereigns in any of my cases, take them. He tossed his bunch of keys at me. Where have you put them, I asked. Sandip said, I shall tell you only after your infatuation has been broken, not before that. When I realized that I would not be able to shake him in any circumstances, I had to adopt a different route. Even after this I tried to offer him these currency notes worth six thousand rupees to recover the sovereigns from him. Then, pretending to bring me the sovereigns, he deceived me by breaking into my trunk which was in his room to bring you your jewellery box. And he claims these ornaments are his gift to you! How do I explain what he has deprived me of? I will never be able to forgive him. His spell has been broken, Didi. You have broken it.

My life has found fulfilment, Amulya, I said. But there's more. It is not enough to overcome the delusion. The stains I have acquired must be cleansed too. Don't delay anymore, Amulya, return the money now. Can't you do it, my dear boy?

With your blessing, I can, Didi.

This is not just a test of your ability, but of mine too. I am a woman, which means the path to the world outside is closed to me, or else I would have gone myself instead of letting you go. My harshest punishment is that you have to shoulder the burden of my wrongdoing.

Don't say that, Didi. The path I was treading is not for you. I was drawn to it because it was difficult to negotiate. Now you have called me to your path, Didi, even if it is a thousand times more inaccessible, with your benediction I shall be victorious. I am not afraid. Then why do you order me to return this money where it came from?

It's not my order, it's from the one above.

I don't know all that. It is enough that the order from the one above has come through you. But, Didi, you owe me a feast. I shan't leave before I claim it today. I need the food blessed by my goddess. And then, I'll be back before evening falls if I can.

Trying to smile, I shed a tear instead. Very well, I said.

My heart sank when Amulya left. Who knew which mother's

son I had cast adrift into danger? God, why do I have to atone for my sins with such a destructive ceremony? Why are so many people invited? Why am I not enough? Why must you make so many others bear the burden of my sin? Why oh why will you cause a boy to be killed?

Amulya, I called him back. My voice rang out so faintly he could not hear me. Going up to the door I called him again, Amulya! He was gone by then.

Bearer, bearer!

Yes, Ranima?

Fetch Amulya-babu.

Maybe the servant did not know who Amulya was—he returned with Sandip a little later. Sandip said on entering, when you threw me out I knew you would call me back. The moon that causes the low tide also causes the high tide. I was so sure you would send for me that I was waiting by the door. When I saw your servant I said before he could speak, very well, I'm coming, I'm coming at once. The Bhojpuri fellow stared in astonishment. He thought I can read minds. The biggest battle in the world is this battle of reading minds, Queen Bee. Hypnosis versus hypnosis. Its arrow seeks its target out by sound. There's also the arrow that seeks its target by silence. Finally Sandip has met his match in this battle. You have many arrows in your quiver, battlefield heroine. In this whole wide world you alone have been able to send Sandip back according to your will, and then bring him back too. The quarry is here. Now tell me what you will do with it. Will you kill it entirely, or lock it in your cage? But I'm warning you beforehand, Queen, it's as difficult to kill this creature as it is to lock it up. Therefore do no tarry in testing the divine weapons you wield.

A sense of defeat had taken root in Sandip, making him so garrulous today. I was sure he knew it was Amulya I had sent for. The servant had in all probability mentioned the correct name; but Sandip had hoodwinked him and arrived himself. He did not give me the opportunity to point out that I had sent for Amulya, not him. But his bluster was a sham, for I had seen his weakness. I was not prepared to relinquish even a sliver of the land I had conquered.

How do you manage to speak incessantly, Sandip-babu? Do you prepare beforehand?

Instantly Sandip's face turned red with anger. I've been told that professional speakers have long descriptions of different kinds in their notebooks, which they apply as needed. Do you also have a notebook like that?

Speaking through clenched teeth, Sandip said, by the grace of god you women do not lack for posturing and tricks, on top of which the tailor and jeweller also come to your service, while the creator has ensured we are unarmed, so . . .

Consult your notebook, Sandip-babu, I told him. What you are saying is not working. I've observed you say most unsuitable things sometimes, that's the drawback of memorising from notebooks.

Unable to contain himself any longer, Sandip roared, you! You think you can insult me! Is there anything about you that I don't know! That you . . .

He could not speak anymore. Sandip was a merchant of spells. Once the spells no longer worked, he had no power. The king turned into a cowherd. Weak! Weak! The more boorish he became, saying harsh things, the more my heart was filled with joy. The coils in which he had bound me had fallen off—I was free. I'd been saved, I'd been saved. Insult me, insult me now, this is your truth. Do not sing my praises, that is a lie.

My husband entered. Today Sandip no longer had the power to control himself in a moment, as he was wont to do. My husband was a little surprised when he looked at Sandip. Earlier, I would have been embarrassed, but today I was pleased, no matter what conclusion he drew. I wanted to measure this man's weakness.

Observing that both of us were silent, my husband took a seat after a little hesitation. I was looking for you, Sandip, he said, and I was told you're here.

Emphasizing his response, Sandip said, yes, Queen Bee had sent for me in the morning. I am the worker drone of the honeycomb, so I had to abandon all other responsibilities and present myself.

I am leaving for Calcutta tomorrow, said my husband. You must come too.

Why, asked Sandip. Am I part of your entourage?

Very well, you go to Calcutta then, I shall be part of your entourage.

I have nothing to do there.

Which is exactly why you need to go to Calcutta. You have too much to do here.

I'm not budging.

Then I shall have to make you budge.

By force?

Yes, by force.

All right, I shall budge then. But the world is not divided into Calcutta and your estate alone. There are other places on the map.

Your behaviour suggested there was no other place in the world besides my estate.

Rising to his feet, Sandip said, there comes a time in the life of a man when the entire world shrinks to a single spot. I have seen my world in this drawing-room of yours, which is why I did not shift from it. None of these people will understand what I am saying, Queen Bee, perhaps you won't either. I worship you. I am going to continue my worship of you. My incantation has changed since I saw you. It isn't Vande mataram anymore—it is Vande priyang, Vande mohining. I worship thee, my beloved, my enchantress. The mother protects us, but the beloved destroys us and how beautiful this destruction is. You have sounded the bells of this dance of death in my heart. In an instant you have changed the form of this komala sujala suphala malayasheetala Bengal, this tender, moist, fertile, pleasant land of ours, in your devotee's eyes. You have no compassion; you are the enchantress with a cup of poison. When I sip this poison, when I am stricken by it, I shall either die or conquer death. My beloved my beloved my beloved! You have rendered god and heaven and duty and truth irrelevant—everything else on earth is a shadow, all the shackles of rules and restraint have been snapped. My beloved my beloved my beloved! I can light a fire everywhere on earth except the land on which you have planted your feet and dance with the joy of annihilation on the ashes. They are good people, they are innocent, they want to do good for everyone, as if all of this is true! Never, there is no such truth in this world, my only truth is that I worship you.

Giving my heart to you has made me heartless, my devotion to you has ignited the flames of the apocalypse within me. I am not good, I am not dutiful, I conform to no rules, I only believe in the one that I have seen more clearly than anyone else.

How extraordinary! I had loathed this man with all my heart just a short while ago. I thought only ashes were left, but there is a fire beneath. There was no doubt about the purity of these flames. Why does god make man such a mixture? Is it only to demonstrate his miraculous magical powers? Just half an hour ago I had been telling myself that I had indeed mistaken this man for a king, but only as a king in a play. But that was not the case—a real king might be found even among costumed actors on stage. His weaknesses included much greed, coarseness and insincerity; he was wrapped in layers of flesh; and yet, we know that we do not know the ultimate truth—it is best to acknowledge this. We do not know ourselves. Man is so unusual; only the destroyer, god knows, can plumb the depths of his mystery. Caught in between, we are burnt to cinders. Apocalypse! Shiva is the god of the apocalypse, and he is the one who brings joy, who will break our fetters.

For quite some time now I had felt that I had two minds. One told me that this apocalyptic form of Sandip's was destructive, while the other averred that this was where sweetness lies. When a ship sinks it draws in those swimming around it; Sandip was like this figure of death, before fear can repel, he attracts—away from all light, all goodness, from the freedom of the sky, the air of one's breath, from all that one has amassed over life, from everyday thoughts. Destruction was intense and instant. He came as the herald of an epidemic, walking the roads with the incantation of the ungodly on his lips, and all the boys and young men in the land were rushing towards him. The mother sobbed; breaking through the doors of her storehouse of nectar, they set up a drinking den with their bottles of alcohol. They wanted to pour all the sweetness into the dust and smash these eternal goblets into smithereens. But although I understood all this, I could keep my own enthralment at bay. The god of truth does this to test how unwavering our allegience to the truth is—drunkenness dresses up in heavenly robes to prance in front of the worshippers. You are foolish, it declares, dedication and devotion cannot achieve anything. This road is long, and progress, slow; that is why the god who wields thunderbolts has sent me, I shall welcome you. I am beautiful, I am madness, my embrace can achieve all you want in a flash.

After a pause Sandip continued, it is time to go away, goddess. Just as well. I have accomplished what I had to in your company. If I stay any longer, it will all be destroyed again one by one. To cheapen the most important thing in the world out of greed can only lead to disaster; what is eternal in a single moment only shrinks from the attempt to extend it over a length of time. We were about to destroy this eternity when your weapon raised itself to strike; you saved both the worship of you and the worshipper. Today my adoration of you transcends everything through my departure. I too am releasing you today, goddess; you could no longer be accommodated in my earthen temple, it was on the point of collapse. Today I am leaving to worship your greater figure in a greater temple. I shall get you as the truth only from a distance. Here I had received your indulgence, there I shall receive your boon.

My jewellery box was lying on the table. Holding it out, I said, place my ornaments at the feet of the one to whom I am giving them through you.

My husband remained silent. Sandip left.

I was cooking for Amulya when Mejorani arrived to ask, well Chhutu, are you preparing to feed yourself on your day of birth?

Do you think there's no one else to feed, I asked.

You're not the one who should we doing all this today, it's our responsibility, said Mejorani. As I was making the arrangments, I was given the shocking news; apparently some five or six hundred bandits had attacked one of our offices and robbed six thousand rupees. People were saying they will rob our home now.

A load was lifted off my mind when I heard this. This was our own money, then. I could send for Amulya at once and tell him to return the six thousand rupees to my husband in my presence. I would then explain to him.

Observing my expression, Mejorani said, how strange! Aren't you even a little afraid?

I cannot believe that they will rob our house, I said.

Cannot believe it! Who could have believed they would have robbed the office, for that matter?

Without answering, I went on stuffing the sweets with mashed coconut, my head bent. Staring at me for a while, she said, I'd better send for Thakurpo, those six thousand rupees of ours must be taken out at once and sent to Calcutta, we cannot afford any delays.

As soon as she left, I dropped the tray and hurried off to the room with the steel safe and locked the door. My husband is so absent-minded that the garment in whose pocket he kept his keys was still hanging from the clothes-rack. Taking the key to the safe out of the ring, I hid it in my jacket.

Someone banged on the door. I am changing my clothes, I said. I heard Mejorani say, just a few minutes ago she was making sweets, and now she's dressing up. So capricious! Do they have a Vande mataram conference today? Listen, Devi Chowdhurani, are you gathering stolen goods?

On an impulse I quietly unlocked the safe. Perhaps I was wondering whether it was all a dream, whether I would open the small drawer to find the bundle wrapped in paper still in place. But all in vain—like the trust destroyed by a traitor, it was empty.

I had to change my clothes after all, though unnecessarily. There was no need, but still I redid my hair. Mejorani asked as soon as we met again, what's all the dressing up for? For my day of birth, I said.

You just need an excuse, Mejorani smiled. You're the vainest person I know.

As I was looking for the servant to send for Amulya, he handed me a note written with a pencil. Amulya had written, you had invited me to a feast, Didi, but I couldn't wait. I shall perform your bidding first, and then accept your offering. It might be evening before I'm back.

Whom was Amulya going to return the money to now? What web was he getting entangled in? I could fire him like an arrow, but I could not call him back if my aim is wrong.

I should have confessed at once that I was at the root of all this trouble. But women live on trust at home, for that is their world.

It is very difficult for us to survive once we have confessed to betraying this trust. We have to plant our feet on the very thing that we break. The splinters will hurt us constantly. Sinning is easy, but no one finds it as difficult as women do to make amends for it.

For some time now, the process of easy conversation with my husband had stopped. So I simply could not decide how or when to break the news to him. He was very late for lunch today—it was two o'clock before he came. His mind elsewhere, he hardly ate. I had lost my right to entreat him to eat well. Turning my face away, I wiped my tears.

I considered overcoming my hesitation to tell him, rest awhile in the bedroom, you look exhausted. Just as I was about to clear my throat and speak, the servant arrived to say that the inspector had brought Kasem Sardar. My husband hurried out, looking anxious.

Soon after he had left, Mejorani arrived and said, why didn't you inform me when Thakurpo came to eat? When I saw he was late I went for my bath, and meanwhile . . .

Why, what is it?

I've been told you and he are going to Calcutta tomorrow. I cannot stay here in that case. Barorani will not forsake her favourite gods, but I cannot guard your empty house while robbers are on the prowl, scaring myself at every sound. You're definitely leaving tomorrow?

Yes, definitely, I answered. To myself I said, who knows what history will be wrought in these hours before we leave. Perhaps it will make no difference whether we go to Calcutta or not. No one knows what the world and life will be like afterwards. It's all wrapped in fog, a dream.

Only a few hours remained before my unseen fate became visible, could no one stretch this period out from one day to the next, making it last much, much longer? Then I could use the time to prepare calmly. At the very least I could brace myself and my household for the blow that was about to fall. The seeds of the apocalypse stay under the earth for a long time, so long that sometimes it appears there's nothing to be afraid of. But once the sapling breaks through the surface, it grows furiously; there is no time anymore to smother it with one's heart or life.

I tried to tell myself not to think, to remain numb, to allow the sword to fall on my head. Everything would be over and done with by the day after tomorrow—public knowledge, laughter, tears, questions and answers, everything.

But I simply cannot forget Amulya's boyish face, so radiant with the glow of self-sacrifice. He did not await fate silently, he plunged into danger. Even as the worst among women, I salute him. He is my boy-god, he is here to playfully take away my burden of disgrace. He will take my punishment on himself to save me but how can I bear such kindness from the almighty? I salute you, my boy. You are pure, you are wondrous, you are brave, you are fearless, I salute you. I pray that you come to me as my son in another lifetime.

Meanwhile rumours are rife everywhere, the police are here all the time, and all the maids and servants at home are worried. Khema the maid told me, here are my gold necklace and bracelet, lock them away in your safe. There was no one I could tell that Chhotorani herself had created this web of anxiety and then trapped herself in it. I had to accept Khema's ornaments and Thako's savings innocently. Our milkman's wife left an expensive sari of hers, along with other valuables in a tin trunk with me; I got this sari as a gift at your wedding, Ranima, she told me.

When the safe in my own room was unlocked, what would Khema and Thako and the milkman's wife . . . never mind, why speculate about all this. Let me imagine instead that a year has passed. Would all the wounds in my household still be as gaping as they were today?

Amulya had written that he would be back before evening. I could not sit quietly in my room until then. I went off again to make more sweets. I had made enough already, but I would have to make more. Who would eat all this? I would give them to all the servants and maids. Tonight. My day lasts till tonight. Tomorrow is no longer in my hands.

I fried one sweet after another without pausing. Now and then it seemed there was trouble brewing on the floor above. Maybe my husband was trying to unlock the safe but could not find the keys, and had summoned Mejorani and the servants and maids to turn the house upside down. No, I wouldn't listen to the sounds, I would bolt the door. As I was about to, I saw Thako rushing in my direction. Panting, she said, Chhotoranima! Go away, don't disturb me, I exclaimed, I have no time. Thako said, Mejoranima's sister's son Nanda-babu has brought a machine from Calcutta, it sings like a human being. Mejoranima has sent for you.

I didn't know whether to laugh or to weep. A gramophone in the middle of all this! Every time it is wound up, it apparently emits the music we hear at the theatre—it has no concerns. When machines imitate life, it turns into such terrible mockery.

Evening fell. I knew there would be no delay in informing me as soon as Amulya came, but still I could not wait. Calling the servant, I said, fetch Amulya-babu. He returned a little later to say, Amulya-babu isn't here.

Simple words, but suddenly there was an upheaval in my heart. Amulya-babu isn't here—it sounded like a wail in the darkness of the evening. Not here, he wasn't here. He had appeared like the golden line of the sunset, and now he wasn't here. Thoughts of mishaps both plausible and improbable began to gather in my head. I was the one who had sent him to his death. It was the greatness of his heart that kept him from being afraid, but how was I to live after this?

I had no mementos of Amulya's, except his gift to me when I had put the sister's mark on his forehead—the pistol. I felt it was a divine signal. My god had vanished somewhere, but not before appearing in the guise of a boy to give me the means to wipe out the dishonour my life was marked by all the way to its roots. There was such love in this gift. How evident its purifying power was.

Taking the pistol out of his box, I raised it to my forehead reverently. At that very moment the bells pealed for evening prayers at our temple. I prostrated myself on the floor.

At night everyone at home was treated to the sweets I had made. Mejorani said, I must say you have organized a grand celebration. Aren't you going to allow us to do anything for you? She proceeded to play the songs of every actor in the world in their falsettos and their baritones on her new gramophone; horses seemed to be neighing musically in the stables of the singers of heaven.

It was late at night by the time everyone had eaten. I had

meant to touch my husband's feet in respect tonight. When I went to the bedroom I found him sound asleep. Absorbed in worry, he had spent the entire day rushing about. Getting under the mosquito net very carefully, I gently laid my head close to his feet. At the touch of my hair he pushed my head away with his foot, still sunk in sleep.

I went to the western veranda and sat down. In the distance a silk-cotton tree stood like a skeleton in the darkness; all its leaves had been shed. Behind it, the crescent moon set gradually.

Suddenly it seemed to me that all the stars in the sky were afraid of me, that this enormous universe of the night was staring at me warily. For I was alone; no one is more of an outsider in this world than a solitary person. Even someone who has lost all his family is not alone—he feels their presence from the other side of death. But someone who is surrounded by people but has no one close by, someone who has been excluded from every aspect of a fulfilled home, makes all the constellations tremble in fear. I was not where I was physically, I was far removed from those around me. I was moving about, going from place to place, balancing precariously, like a dewdrop on a lotus leaf, on a chasm of parting that had split the earth.

When a person changes, why doesn't everything about them change? When I look at my heart I see everything is intact, though shaken. The flawless configuration has been disturbed; what had been threaded in the necklace around my throat is rolling in the dust today. That is why my heart is breaking. I wish I could die; but it all lives on in my heart, it does not seem to be that death will end it. On the contrary, the suffering will worsen. Only through life can I finish what must be finished—there is no alternative.

Excuse me this time, my lord. I have turned all wealth of life you had given me into a burden. Today I can neither bear it, nor forsake it. Play the same music that you did the other day by the crimson sky at dawn—let all problems be simplified. Nothing but the tune of your flute can mend what is broken, or purify what has been tainted. Create my world anew with this melody. I see no other way.

Throwing myself on the floor, I wept. I needed a little kindness from somewhere, a sanctuary, the promise of forgiveness, an assurance that everything might actually be all right. I told myself, I will keep a vigil day and night, lord, I shan't eat, shan't take a sip of water, until I receive your benediction.

I heard footsteps. My heart lurched. Who says the gods don't show themselves. I did not raise my eyes, lest they repel him. Come, come, come, let your feet touch my head, stand upon my fluttering heart, my lord, let me die this instant.

He sat down near my head. Who was it? My husband. In his heart the god who could not bear my tears had been moved. Then the knots in my veins snapped, the agony in my breast emerging in a torrent of weeping. I clutched his feet to my breast; was it not possible to leave a permanent imprint of these feet here?

I could have told him everything. But there was nothing to say after all that had happened. Let all that be.

He caressed my head tenderly. I had received my benediction. Now I would be able to bear the humiliation coming my way tomorrow, and pay simple obeisance at my god's feet.

But my heart broke at the thought that the wedding tunes that had been played nine years ago would never again be played in this lifetime. I had been welcomed to this house. Was there any god in the universe to whom I could plead so that the bride could appear again on the threshold in all her wedding finery, awaiting her reception? How much longer would it take, how many ages, how many eons, to go back but once to that day nine years ago? God can create new things. But did he have the power to rebuild his own shattered creation?

NIKHILESH'S STORY

We shall go to Calcutta today. Accumulating happiness and sorrows continuously only makes the burden heavier. For inactivity is a lie, gathering is a lie. That I am the head of this household is a made-up idea—the truth is that I am a traveller on the road of life. That is why this head will suffer blows repeatedly, with death as the final blow. Your union with me was for the length of the journey; it is best to travel together only as long as we can; going any further will turn the union into chains. Let the chains be left behind now. I am on my way; the meeting of eyes and touching of hands during the journey are of value only as long as the journey lasts. Afterwards? There is the road to the infinite universe, the pace of eternal life. How much can you deprive me of, my love? If I pay attention to the flute playing up the road, I can hear its sweetness pouring out through every crack that led to our separation. Since the goddess's store of nectar will never be depleted, she breaks our pot sometimes, laughing when we weep. I shall not bother to gather the broken pieces, I shall carry on with my unfulfilled heart.

Mejoranididi told me, why have all your books been packed into the bullock-cart, Thakurpo? What does this mean?

This means that I have not been able to give up my fondness for those books.

I'd be delighted if some affection remained. But are you planning not to return?

I shall come and go, but I must not cling to this place.

Really? Then come with me, take a look at the things I cannot give up my fondness for. She dragged me along by the arm.

In her room I discovered boxes and bundles of different shapes and sizes. Opening one of the boxes, she said, here are my ingredients for making paan, Thakurpo. Ground powder in this bottle, and here are the different tins of flavours. Here are my cards—I haven't forgotten how to play. Even if you don't play with me I shall find others. This comb is made in India, and this . . .

But what is it Mejorani? Why have you packed all this?

I'm going to Calcutta with you, you see.

What?

Don't worry, I shall neither consort with you, nor quarrel with your wife. Since death is inevitable, it's best to take shelter on the bank of the Ganga while there's still time. I hate the thought of being cremated under that barren tree of yours after my death, which is why I have been plaguing all this time.

Finally my home had acquired a voice. I was six when Mejorani became part of our family at the age of nine. Every afternoon I used to play with her on the roof in the shade thrown by the walls. Climbing the hog-plum trees in the garden I would throw the fruit down for her to slice, add salt and chillies, and serve up an unhealthy delicacy. The responsibility of raiding the kitchen in secret for the ingredients needed for the wedding of the dolls was mine, for under my grandmother's jurisdiction there was never any punishment for my crimes. Later on, I was the messenger who conveyed her demands for luxuries to my brother; I would goad him into accepting her demands. I remember, too, that getting a fever in those days meant a strict diet of nothing but warm water and cardamom under the watchful eyes of the kaviraj. Unable to bear my misery, she often brought me better food furtively, swallowing the admonitions that came her way when she was found out. As I grew older, the shades of our joys and sorrows deepened. We quarrelled often, with jealousy, mistrust and even conflict creeping in over matters of property and business. Sometimes Bimal was caught up in it, and it felt as though the rift would never heal. But then it was proved that the affinity between souls ran far deeper than the external wounds. In this manner a true, unbreakable relationship had grown since my childhood, its branches and boughs casting their soothing, proprietorial shadows over every room and corridor and veranda and terrace of this enormous house. When I saw Mejorani ready to leave our home, all her effects packed into cases and trunks, each and every root of this eternal relationship in my heart seemed to tremble. I understood perfectly why Mejorani, who had not left this house for a single day since her arrival here at the age of nine, was ready to cut off all her moorings and set herself adrift amongst strangers. And yet she refused to state the real reason explicitly, offering all kinds of trivial excuses instead. Deprived by destiny, this childless widow had nurtured this one single relationship with all the emotion in her heart—standing amidst her possessions scattered around the room, I grasped the depth of her agony more strongly than I ever had before. There I realized that material interest was not the reason for the repeated conflicts between her and me or Bimal over the allocation of money or property, or over petty household details. The reason was that she had not been able to strengthen her claim on this one relationship in her life. Bimal had materialized from nowhere to make the significance of this one pale. Hurt at every step of the way, she was powerless to complain. Bimal had also comprehended that Mejorani's claim on me was not just a social one, but much deeper. That was why she was so envious of this childhood bond between us. Today my heart began to beat faster. I sank down on a trunk, saying, Mejoranididi, I wish we could go back to the day we had met each other for the first time in this house.

Sighing, Mejorani said, no, I don't want to be born a woman again. Let all that I have endured be limited to a single lifetime, I cannot bear it again.

The freedom that comes through sorrow is greater than the sorrow itself, I exclaimed.

She said, that's possible, Thakurpo; you are men, freedom is for you. We women want to tie you down, and we want to be tied down too; you will not get freedom from us easily. If you want to take wing you must take us along, you cannot leave us behind. That is why I have prepared this burden for you to carry. We have no hope once we allow you to travel light.

Smiling, I said, so I see; the burden of your song is that it is a burden. But we don't complain because all of you compensate us for bearing this burden.

Mejorani replied, our burden is a load of small things. If you try to leave any of them out they will say, 'I am a trifle, how heavy can I possibly be?' This is how we use a number of light loads to increase your burden. When do you have to leave, Thakurpo?

Eleven-thirty at night, there's plenty of time.

Listen to me, Thakurpo, my dear boy, you have to heed my request. Have an early lunch today and take a nap in the afternoon; you won't sleep well on the train at night. You look as though you might collapse any moment. Come on, you must bathe at once.

At that moment Khema entered with the end of her sari covering half her face and said softly, the inspector is here with someone, he wants to meet Maharaj.

Flying into a rage, Mejorani said, is Maharaj a thief or a dacoit? Why does the inspector chase him constantly? Go tell him Maharaj is taking a bath.

I said, let me meet him, maybe it's important.

Mejorani said, impossible. Chhotorani made a pile of sweets yesterday, I'll send the inspector some to keep him happy.

She pushed me into the bathroom and shut the door.

I said from within, but my fresh clothes aren't yet . . .

I will take care of everything, she said. Take your bath meanwhile.

I did not dare flout such an imperious command; it came far too rarely. Let the inspector eat his sweets. Never mind if important things were neglected.

The inspector had detained several people over the robbery. Every day he would arrest one innocent person or another and make a scene. He must have arrested another such hapless fellow today. But would the inspector eat the sweets all by himself? That wouldn't be right. I hammered on the door.

Mejorani said, go on, take your bath, don't work yourself up.

I answered, send sweets for two. Whoever the inspector has arrested deserves the sweets more. Tell the servant to give him a larger share.

Finishing my bath as quickly as possible I came out to find Bimal sitting on the floor at the door. Was this my Bimal, the proud, spirited Bimal? With what prayer in her heart could she actually be waiting outside my door? When I stopped abruptly, she rose to her feet, lowered her eyes and said, I have something to talk to you about.

Then come to our room, I said.

Were you going out for something important?

Yes, but never mind that. First let's . . .

No, finish what you have to. We'll talk after you've eaten.

In the drawing-room I found the inspector's plate empty. The person he had arrested was still eating his sweets.

Astonished, I said, Amulya! You here!

Speaking through a mouthful of sweets, he said, yes. I've eaten my fill. If you don't mind, I'll take the rest home.

He proceeded to make a bundle with his handkerchief.

I turned to the inspector. What's all this?

Laughing, the inspector said, the mystery of the thief remains a mystery, Maharaj. Now I'm racking my brains over the mystery of the stolen goods.

Unwrapping a bundle of tattered rags, he held out a bunch of currency notes. Here is Maharaj's six thousand rupees, he said.

Where did this come from?

For now, from Amulya-babu. He went to the treasurer at your office in Chakua and said, the stolen notes have been found. The treasurer was not as worried about the theft as he was about recovering the stolen money. He was afraid that everyone would suspect him of having taken it, and coming up with an impossible story to protect himself. Keeping Amulya-babu waiting on the pretext of giving him something to eat, the treasurer sent word to the police station. I went to meet him on horseback and have been at it since early this morning. He said, I will not tell you how I got the money. I cannot release you if you don't tell me, I answered. I will lie, he said. Very well, lie then, I told him. I found it in a bush, he said. I answered, it isn't so simple to lie. Where is this bush? Why were you there? You will have to explain everything. Don't worry, I will have plenty of time to make up the details, he responded.

Why drag a decent man into all this, Haricharan-babu, I asked.

He not only belongs to a well-known family, retorted the inspector, he's also Nibaran Ghoshal's son. Nibaran Ghoshal was my classmate. I'll tell you what happened, Maharaj. Amulya found out who stole the money—thanks to this Vande mataram business he knows who it is. He wants to shoulder the blame himself to save the culprit. All this is the result of his valour. I was also eighteen once, my son; I studied at Ripon College. One day I almost went to jail in an effort to save the driver of a bullock-cart from the oppression of a policeman, and I escaped imprisonment by the skin of my teeth. It might be difficult to catch the thief now, Maharaj, but I can tell you who's behind this.

Who? I asked.

Your treasurer Tinkari Dutta and the guard Kasem Sardar.

After the inspector left, having presented the arguments to support his assumptions, I told Amulya, no one will come to harm if you tell me who took the money.

I did, he said.

How? They said it was a gang of robbers . . .

I was alone.

Amulya related a strange tale. The treasurer was washing his hands outside the room in the darkness after dinner. Amulya had a pistol in each pocket, one loaded with bullets and the other with blanks. Half his face was covered with a black mask. When he suddenly flashed the light of a bull's-eye lantern on the treasurer and fired a blank from his pistol, the treasurer started shrieking and fainted. A pair of guards came running up, whereupon he fired over their heads, which made them race into the first available room and lock the door. Kasem Sardar ran up with a stick, but fell to the ground when Amulya fired at his legs. Then Amulya made the treasurer unlock the iron safe, took out six thousand rupees, rode one of the horses from the office to a spot five or six miles away, abandoned it there, and came here to my house the next morning.

Why did you do this, Amulya, I asked him.

There was a reason, he said.

Then why did you return the money?

Call the person who ordered me to return it, I will explain in her presence.

Who is it?

Chhotoranididi.

I sent for Bimal. She appeared on faltering footsteps, her head covered in a white shawl. She wasn't even wearing slippers. I felt I had never seen her this way before; like the moon in the morning, she seemed to have covered herself with daylight.

Prostrating himself in front of her, Amulya touched her feet respectfully. Rising, he said, I have obeyed your instructions, Didi. I have returned the money.

Bimal said, I am relieved.

Amulya continued, out of regard for you, I have not uttered a single lie. I am laying my war cry of Vande mataram at your feet. I have eaten the food you have blessed.

Bimala didn't understand. Taking his handkerchief out of his pocket, Amulya untied it to show the sweets packed inside. He said, I didn't eat all of them, I put a few aside for you to put on my plate with your own hands.

I realized I was no longer needed here; I left the room. All I did was talk myself to death, I reflected, while they garlanded my effigy with torn shoes and burn it. I could not force someone to turn back from the road of death but those who could only used the right signals. My words did not hold such authoritative influence. We weren't flames, we were embers—we had been extinguished, we could not light lamps. The story of my life had proved just that. The lamps I had set out could never be lit.

I returned slowly to the inner chambers. Possibly my heart sought out Mejorani's room once more. I had to assure myself that my life had left a real and palpable mark on someone else's, for one cannot validate one's existence within oneself, one has to look for signs elsewhere.

When I reached Mejorani's room she said, here you are Thakurpo, must you be late today as well? There's no time, your food is ready, it's coming.

Let me get the money out meanwhile, I said.

As we walked towards my bedroom, Mejorani asked, has the inspector solved the theft?

I did not feel inclined to tell her about the recovery of the six thousand rupees. That's what they're all busy with, I said.

Going into the room with the iron safe, I reached into my pocket to discover the keys missing. How absent-minded I was. I had used this very key-ring to unlock drawers and cupboards, but not once had I noticed that this particular key was missing.

Where's the key, asked Mejorani.

Without answering I rummaged in my pockets, pulling everything out. I had no difficulty realizing that the key was not lost—someone had taken it out of the ring. Who could it have been? In this room . . .

Don't worry, said Mejorani, why don't you eat first? I suspect Chhotorani has put the key away because she knows how careless you are.

Something was wrong. Bimal was not in the habit of removing the key from the ring without informing me. She was not present while I ate—she had fetched food from the kitchen and was attending to Amulya's meal. Mejorani was about to send for her, but I stopped her.

I had just finished my meal when Bimala came. I had not wanted to discuss the lost key in Mejorani's presence, but I could not avoid it. As soon as Bimal arrived she asked, do you know where the key to Thakurpo's iron safe is?

With me, answered Bimal.

Mejorani said, I told you! With all these thefts everywhere, Chhotorani wanted to be cautious even though she pretends she's not worried.

Bimala's expression planted a doubt in my mind. I said, keep the key for now, I'll take the money out in the evening.

Mejorani said, why leave it till the evening, Thakurpo, get it now and send it off to the treasurer.

Bimala said, I've taken the money.

I was startled.

Where have you put it, asked Mejorani.

I've spent it, answered Bimal.

Oh my god, exclaimed Mejorani. What did you spend so much money on?

Bimal did not answer. I didn't ask her any questions either. I stood in silence, my hand on the door. About to say something to Bimal, Mejorani stopped; looking at me, she said, good for her if she's taken it. I used to steal all the money in my husband's wallet and hide it; I knew the money would be squandered otherwise. You're no different, Thakurpo, you know a hundred ways to waste money. Your money will be saved only if we steal it. Now come, take a nap.

Mejorani took me to my bedroom. I had no awareness of where I was going. Sitting by the bed, she said cheerfully, can you bring a paan, Chhutu? You've become such a Western woman. Don't you have any paan here? Have one fetched from my room then.

You haven't eaten yet, Mejorani, I said.

I ate ages ago, she replied.

This was a barefaced lie. Sitting by my side she prattled away—all sorts of nonsense. The maid appeared outside the door to inform Bimal that her food was getting cold. Bimal did not respond. Mejorani said, what, haven't you eaten yet? It's so late.

She took Bimala away by force.

I realized that there was a connection between the six thousand rupees that had been robbed and the money that had been taken out of the safe. I had no desire to find out what kind of connection. I would never ask.

The creator draws the pictures of our lives hazily; his intention is that we change some of it ourselves and fill in the gaps to create a clear image according to our own choices. I have always ached to create my own life following the lead of the creator, to express a big idea through everything I call my own.

I had spent all this time on that quest. Only god knew the internal history of how I had starved my inclinations and restrained myself. What made it difficult was that life is not anyone's own property alone; he who creates is bound to fail if he cannot include everything around him. That was why I had an ardent desire to draw Bimal into this creation. Since I loved her with all my heart, why would I not succeed? Such was my conviction.

This was when I saw clearly that those who can naturally include their environment as they create themselves belong to a breed that I do not. I had taken up a mission, but I had not given anyone one. Those to whom I submitted myself totally took everything of mine except this one thing that lay deep within. I would now be tested more severely. I was isolated precisely when I most needed help. But I had vowed to pass this test. I would travel alone on this remote road till the last moment of my life.

Today I suspected that a certain tyranny had been at work within me. There was an obstinacy in my desire to cast my relationship with Bimal in the mould of an uncompromising, flawless goodness. But human lives were not for pouring into moulds. And when you tried to build goodness like an inanimate object, it took revenge by dying.

We had not realized that it was this insistence that had made us diverge from each other in our hearts. Because of the pressure I put on Bimal, her potential was not fulfilled. And this constant grinding existence had eroded the dam. She had to steal these six thousand rupees today; she could not be transparent with me, for she knew where our differences lie. Those who are at one with people like us—possessed by single-minded ideas—can understand us, but those who are not only deceive us. We force even straightforward people to keep things from us. In trying to build partners for ourselves, we distort the lives our wives lead.

Could we not go back to the beginning? I would take the route of simplicity this time. Instead of trying to bind my travelling companion with the chains of an idea, I would only play her my love-flute, saying, love me, and let your real self blossom fully in this love. Let my blueprint be buried, let the creator's intent for us win, let my wishes retreat in shame.

But the rift that had been gathering within had emerged in the form of such a virulent wound that it was doubtful whether the soothing touch of habit could heal it. The curtain behind which nature performs its silent repairs had been torn apart. Wounds had to be covered; I would cover this wound with my love; I would wind the layers of my heart around the agony and protect it. A day would come when there would not be a single sign of this wound. But was there time anymore? After such a long time living under a mistake, it took this day to arrive for my mistake to be realized. How much longer would it take to be corrected? And after that? The wound might heal, but would there ever be recompense?

There was a sound. I looked up to find Bimala going back from the door. Maybe she had been standing by it in silence all this while, unable to decide whether to enter or not. Jumping to my feet, I called out to her, Bimal. She halted, her back to me. I took her hand and drew her into the room.

The moment she entered she flung herself to the floor and, burying her face in a pillow, began to weep. I sat near her without a word, holding her hand.

When she sat up after her sobs had died down, I tried to draw her to my breast. Forcing my arm away, she knelt on the floor and touched my feet with her forehead repeatedly. When I tried to withdraw my feet she grasped them, saying in an overwhelmed voice, no, don't take your feet away, allow me to worship them.

I was silent. Who was I to stop her? When the worship is real, so is the god to whom it is addressed—since I was not the god, there was no need for me to shrink back.

BIMALA'S STORY

Come on, come on, set out now for the confluence where all love flows into an ocean of worship. All the mud and grime will be washed away in its pure blue depths. I am not afraid anymore— not of myself, nor of anyone else. I have passed through fire; whatever had to burn has been reduced to ashes, what remains cannot die. I now offer myself at the feet of the one who has accepted all my sins in his immense suffering.

We have to go to Calcutta tonight. All the disturbances within and without had prevented me from paying attention to packing. Pulling the trunks out, I sat down to pack. A little later I discovered my husband next to me. No, that's not allowed, I told him. You promised to take a nap.

I may have promised, my husband replied, but sleep hasn't. No sign of it.

No, you cannot do this, I said. Go to bed.

How will you manage alone, he asked.

Of course I will.

If you want to boast that you can do without me, go ahead, but I cannot do without you. I simply couldn't sleep alone in the room.

He got down to work with me. A little later the bearer arrived to announce, Sandip-babu is here, he asked me to inform you.

I did not have the strength to ask whom he had asked the bearer to inform. In an instant the light in the sky withdrew like a shrinking violet.

My husband said, come, Bimal, let us find out what Sandip has to say. He said goodbye and left, since he has returned he must have something important to tell us.

Because it would be more embarrassing not to go, I accompanied my husband outside. Sandip was standing in the drawing-room, looking at the paintings on the wall. As soon as we entered he said, you must be wondering why the man's back. The ghost cannot leave until the last rites are completed.

Taking out a bandle wrapped in a handkerchief from beneath his shawl, he held it open over the table. The sovereigns. Make no mistake, Nikhil, he said, don't imagine I have suddenly become a saint in your company. Sandip is not one to shed tears of remorse and return these sovereigns worth six thousand rupees. But . . .

He did not finish. After a pause, he looked at me and said, Queen Bee, a but has finally entered Sandip's unsullied life after all these years. Waking up at three a.m. every morning I have engaged in hand-to-hand combat with it and discovered it is not ephemeral. Sandip will not be released till he has paid its dues. So

I offer my respects to this fatal 'but' of mine. I tried my utmost, only to discover that she is the one person on earth whose wealth I cannot take. I can bid you farewell only after I have been bankrupted in front of you, goddess. Here.

Pulling out the jewellery case as well and putting it on the table, Sandip made to leave quickly. Just a minute, Sandip, my husband told him.

Stopping at the door, Sandip said, I don't have time, Nikhil. I've been told that the Muslims are conspiring to snatch me away like invaluable jewels and bury me in their graveyard. But I need to stay alive. The train to the north is leaving in twenty-five minutes, so I shall be on my way for now. If I get the opportunity later I will complete all unfinished discusssions with you. If you take my advice, you shouldn't delay either. Queen Bee, I bow to the queen who breaks hearts.

Sandip left at a run. I was silent. I had never realized as I did today how valueless the sovereigns and the jewellery were. A few minutes ago I had been wondering what to take on the journey and how to fit it all in, now I felt there was no need to take anything. It was only necessary to leave.

Leaving his seat, my husband took my hand and said softly, there's not much time left, let us finish our tasks.

Chandranath-babu entered, pausing for a few moments when he saw me. Excuse me, he told me, I couldn't send word beforehand. The Muslims are enraged, Nikhil. Harish Kundu's treasury has been looted. That itself is no cause for alarm, but what they are doing with the women cannot be tolerated.

Then let me go there, my husband said.

What can you do, I said, taking his hand. Stop him, Master-moshai.

There is not enough time to stop him, my child, Chandranath-babu said.

Don't worry, Bimal, my husband said.

Going up to the window, I saw him disappear on horseback. He was unarmed.

Mejorani ran in a few moments later. What have you done, Chhutu, what have you done? Why did you let him go?

To a servant she said, call the Dewan at once.

Mejorani had never appeared in the Dewan's presence but she had no qualms that day. Sent a rider to bring Maharaj back at once, she said.

All of us told him not to go, said the Dewan. He won't come back.

Tell him Mejorani has cholera, her death is imminent.

When the Dewan had left, Mejorani began to heap abuses on me. Murderer! You wouldn't die yourself, but you sent Thakurpo to his death!

Daylight waned. The sun set on the western horizon behind the blossoming drumstick tree in Goalpara. I can see every line of that sunset even today. With the setting sun in the middle, a thick canopy of clouds spread in two halves to the left and the right like an enormous bird unfurling its wings, its flame-coloured feathers set in layers. The day seemed to be speeding on its way in order to cross the sea by night.

Darkness fell. Like flames that leap to the sky sporadically when a distant village is on fire, occasional waves of noise seemed to swell in the darkness.

The bells signalling the evening rituals rang out in the prayer room. I knew Mejorani was seated there, her palms joined in supplication. I could not move an inch from my position by the window. The road and the village in the foreground, the fields shorn of crops further back, and the line of trees even further, all grew dim. The big lake next to the palace kept looking at the sky with a blind man's eyes. The music room above the gate on the left stood erect, seemingly observing something.

The sounds of the night donned multiple disguises. A branch rustled nearby—someone seemed to be fleeing in the distance. A door banged suddenly in the wind—it sounded like the heart of the sky leaping into its mouth.

At intervals I could see lights beneath the rows of black trees by the side of the road, but not for long. I heard hoofbeats, and then saw the rider emerge from the palace gates and gallop away.

I was convinced that all dangers would pass if I died. As long as I was alive, my sins would keep killing the world. I remembered the pistol in my trunk, but my feet wouldn't let me abandon my place by the window to fetch the gun. I was waiting for fate, after all.

The palace clock struck ten.

A little later I saw several lights on the road and a number of people. An entire crowd seemed to have cleaved together in the darkness to become a huge black serpent winding its way towards the palace gates.

Hearing the noise, Dewanji rushed to the gate and asked one of the riders apprehensively, what news, Jatadhar?

It isn't good, he answered.

I could hear every word clearly from where I was.

Then they began to whisper, and I could no longer hear them.

A little later a palanquin entered, followed by a litter. Mathur the doctor was walking alongside. What do you think, doctor, Dewanji asked.

Impossible to say, the doctor replied. A terrible head injury.

And Amulya-babu?

He was shot in the chest. He's done for.

I KNOW WHO YOU ARE
আমি চিনি গো চিনি

I know who you are
Faraway woman
You live across the ocean
Faraway woman
On autumn dawns I've seen you
On honeyed nights I've seen you
In my heart I've seen you
Faraway woman
In the skies
I've heard your song
I've pledged myself to you
Faraway woman
I've travelled the world
I've reached a new land
I'm the guest at your door
Faraway woman

Poems

Camellia

Kamala was her name
    I saw it on the cover of her book.
She was on the tram, going to college with her brother.
    I was on the seat behind hers.
The perfect line of her profile was visible,
    Tender wisps of hair straying on her shoulder.
In her lap were her books and notes.
I didn't get off where I should have.

Since then I've been timing my departure—
    Though it doesn't match my working hours,
Frequently it coincides with their hour of travel,
    Frequently I get to see her.
I tell myself, what if there's nothing between us
    She's a fellow passenger at least.
A pure intelligence
    Seems to shine through her appearance,
The hair swept back from her young forehead,
    Her bright eyes fearless.
I wished a crisis would erupt right now,
I could fulfil my existence by rescuing her—
    An assault of some sort on the road,
A goon trying to get fresh with her.
It happened all the time these days.
But my luck was like a shallow, murky pool,
Incapable of holding anything historic.
Ordinary days croaked drearily like frogs—
Sharks and alligators weren't invited, nor swans.

One day there was a crowd, some jostling.
A half-Englishman was seated next to Kamala.
Without provocation, I was dying to knock his hat off,
    And throw him out by the scruff of his neck.
I couldn't find a pretext, my fingers itched.
At that moment he lit a fat cigar
    And began to puff on it.
Going up to him, I said, 'Throw it away.'
Pretending not to hear,
    He blew smoke-rings deliberately in the air.
Plucking it from his mouth I tossed it out.
Balling his fists he glared at me—
Then leapt off the tram without another word.
He probably knew who I am.
I was well known as a footballer,
    A bit of a loud reputation.
Her face turned red,
    Opening her book, she pretended to read.
Her hands trembled,
    She didn't even glance at the hero.
The office clerks said, 'Good for you.'
Soon afterwards she got off, before her destination,
    Took a taxi and went on her way.

I didn't see her the next day
    Nor the day after.
On the third day I spotted her
    Going to college in a rickshaw.
I realized my bull-headed error.
She was quite capable of looking after herself
    I needn't have intervened at all.
I told myself again,
    My luck's like a shallow, murky pool—
The memory of my heroism echoed in my mind
Like a mocking bullfrog.
I decided to make amends.

I'd heard they usually vacationed in Darjeeling.
I needed a holiday urgently that year.

They had a tiny home, it was named Motia,
    In a corner down a slope from the road
        Behind a tree,
            Facing the snow peaks.
I was told they weren't coming this time.
Contemplating return, I ran into a fan
        Mohonlal—
A little sickly, tall and bespectacled,
His weak constitution perked up only in Darjeeling.
He said, 'My sister Tanuka
    Won't let you go without meeting you.'
The girl was like a shadow,
    Her physical existence the barest minimum—
        Not as keen on her meals as she was on books.
And hence such unusual admiration for a football captain
She thought it generous of me to meet her.
What games destiny plays!

Two days before my return to the plains, Tanuka said,
'I'll give you something to remember us by—
    A flowering plant.'
Such a nuisance. I was silent.
Tanuka said, 'A rare, expensive plant,
    Needs a lot of care to survive on our soil.'
'What's it called?' I asked.
'Camellia,' she answered.
I was startled,
    Another name flashed in the darkness of my mind.
I smiled. 'Camellia.
    Its heart isn't to be won easily, is it?'
I don't know what Tanuka made of this,
She was embarrassed suddenly, pleased too.
I set off, along with the potted plant.
It turned out she wasn't an easy co-passenger.
In a carriage with two compartments
    I hid the pot in the bathroom.
Never mind the details of the journey,
    Forget, too, the triteness of the months that followed.

The curtain rose on the farce during the autumn vacation
    In an area where tribal people lived.
A tiny village. I'd rather not reveal its name—
Compulsive holiday-makers aren't aware of its existence.
Kamala's uncle was a railway engineer.
He had set up home here
    In the shade of a sal wood, in squirrel country
Where the blue mountains could be seen on the horizon,
    A stream coursed across a bed of sand nearby,
        Silkworm were cocooned amidst the flame of the forest
      Oxen wandered about beneath the trees,
        Unclothed tribal boys perched on their backs.
There were no houses to stay in
    So I pitched my tent by the river.
I had no companion
    Only the camellia in its pot.

Kamala was here with her mother.
Before the sun was overhead
    While the dew-soaked breeze blew
    She strolled in the sal wood with her parasol.
The wild flowers bowed in prayer at her feet
    She didn't even spare them a glance.
Crossing the stream with its thin trickle of water
    She went to the other bank,
    To read beneath a tree.
That she had recognized me was obvious
    From the fact that she didn't notice me.

One day I saw them picnicking on the sandbank.
I had the urge to ask, don't you need me for anything.
    I can fetch water from the stream
      Chop wood and bring it from the forest,
      Besides, isn't it possible to find
        A decent bear in the jungle nearby?

I spotted a young man in the group
    In shorts and an imported silk shirt,
    Sitting beside Kamala with outstretched legs
Smoking a Havana cigar.
While Kamala absently shredded
    The petals of a white hibiscus
    An English monthly magazine
    Lying by her side.

In this desolate corner, I realized,
I was unbearably redundant, I wouldn't fit.
I would have left immediately, but for an unfinished task.
The camellia would bloom in a few days
    Only after sending it to her would I be free.
I roamed the jungle all day with my gun,
Returning at dusk to water the plant
    And check on the progress of the bud.

It was time, finally.
    I had sent for the tribal girl
    Who brought me firewood every day.
I would send it with her
    In a leafy box.
I was reading a detective story in my tent
When a melodious voice wafted in, 'You called for me?'
Emerging from the tent, I saw
    The camellia tucked behind her ear
    Lighting up her dark-skinned face.
'Why did you call for me?' she asked again.
'Just for this,' I replied.

And then I journeyed back to Calcutta.

An Ordinary Girl

I'm the girl from the inner chambers
    You don't know me.
I read your last storybook, Sarat-babu,
    'A Garland of Stale Flowers'.
Your heroine Elokeshi was close to self-destruction
    At thirty-five.
She was at loggerheads with twenty-five
You're generous, I saw—
You gave her victory.

As for myself,
    I'm young.
The enchantment of my green years
    Had touched someone's heart
    Knowing this I danced with joy—
        I forgot that I'm a very ordinary girl.
Thousands more like me everywhere,
    The allure of youth in their age.

I beg of you,
    Write a story about an ordinary girl.
    She's so unhappy.
Even if something extraordinary
    Hides somewhere in her depths
      How will she prove it,
        How many can even see it.

Their eyes are clouded by the magic of tender years,
   Their minds do not seek the truth,
   We're sold off at the price of a mirage.

Let me tell you how all this came up.
Let's say his name is Naresh.
He had said he hadn't seen another like me.
I didn't dare believe something so momentous,
   But where was the strength not to?

One day he went abroad.
I got a letter now and then.
God, I thought to myself! So many girls over there,
   Such jostling crowds of them!
And are they all brilliant—
   So clever, so dazzling?
And had they all discovered one Naresh Sen
   Who was just another name back home?

In the last letter he wrote that he had
   Been to the seaside with Lizzie to bathe.
He quoted a few lines from a Bangla poem—
The ones where Urvashi rises from the ocean—
   Then they sat side by side on the sand
   Blue waves rolling in the sea before them,
   Unsullied sunshine spread across the sky.
Very softly Lizzie told him,
   'You came the other day, you'll go away soon;
   Two seashells
      Let them be filled
         With a perfect teardrop—
         Rare and priceless.'
What a marvellous way to talk.
Naresh also wrote,
   'No harm even if it's all made up . . .
   It's beautiful—
   Are gold flowers with diamonds real? And yet they are.'

As you can see
    A hint of comparison in his letter pierced my heart
    Like an invisible thorn, telling me—
    I'm such an ordinary girl.
I don't possess the riches
    To pay the full price for what's priceless.
So be it, then
    Let me be in debt all my life.

Write a story, Sarat-babu, I plead with you
    A rather ordinary girl's story—
        An unfortunate girl who must compete at a distance
            With at least half a dozen matchless women
                Beaten back by a circle of enemy forces.
I realize my luck is wretched
I have lost.
But the girl you write about—
    Make her win for me,
        So that I feel proud when I read.
        May your pen be blessed.

Name her Malati.
It's my name.
No one will know.
There are many such Malatis in Bengal,
    All of them ordinary girls.
They don't know French or German,
    They know how to weep.

How will you make her win?
High is your thinking. Your writing, generous.
Maybe you will steer her along the path of sacrifice,
    To the edge of sorrow, like Shakuntala.
Have mercy on me
    Come down to my level.
In my bed under the darkness of night
    The impossible boons I seek from the gods
    Shall never be mine,
    But may your heroine get them.

Why not keep Naresh in London for seven years,
    Let him fail his examinations repeatedly
    And live amidst the adulation of his devotees.
Let Malati get her MA degree meanwhile,
    And come first in Calcutta University
    In mathematics, with one stroke of your pen.
But if you stop there
Your fame as the emperor of literature will suffer.
Let my state be what it might
    Do not curb your imagination.
You're not a miser like god.
Send the girl to Europe
    Let the erudite, the scholarly, the valorous,
    Those who are poets, artists, kings,
    Gather around her in groups.
Like astronomers let them discover her
    Not just for her learning, but as a woman.
The magic power she has to conquer the world . . .
    Let its mystery be realized, not in the country of fools,
    But where there are connoisseurs and the cognoscenti,
The English and the German and the French.
Why not give Malati a reception for honours won,
    A gathering of famous people.
Assume that praises are being rained on her incessantly,
    While she negotiates a path between them carelessly—
    Like a sailboat on the waves.
Her eyes are the subject of their whispers
    Everyone's saying India's moist clouds and bright sun
    Have combined in her mesmerizing gaze.
(Here I should tell whom it may concern
    That the creator has indeed been kind to my eyes.
I had to say it myself
    Not having had the fortune to have met
    An aesthete from Europe.)
Let Naresh appear in one corner,
    Along with his entourage of extraordinary women.

And then?
Then my story draws to a close,
    My dreams end.
Oh, you ordinary girl!
Oh what a waste of the almighty's powers.

An Unexpected Meeting

We met suddenly on a train,
   I hadn't thought it possible.
I'd seen her many a time
   In a red sari—
      Crimson like a dahlia;
      Today she was in black silk,
         It covered her head in a cowl
            Cupped her face, lustrous and fair like a lily.
She seemed to have enveloped herself
   In a deep dark distance,
   The distance to the edge of the mustard fields
   To the blue-grey of the sal wood.
   My senses came to a sudden stop,
      I knew her once, now she wore a stranger's solemnity.

Throwing aside her newspaper
   She greeted me suddenly.
Social mores could now be followed;
   We began to converse—
      'How are you?' 'How is everyone?'
Etcetera.
She continued to gaze out of the window
      As though she had overcome the contagion of intimacy
     She answered in monosyllables,
   Some, she didn't even respond to.
Conveyed with an impatient wave—
   Why talk of all this,
   Silence is so much better.

I was on another bench with her companions.
After a while she beckoned with her finger.
Such boldness, I thought
    I sat down on the same bench.
Under the sound of the train
    She said softly,
        'Please don't mind,
        Where's the time to waste time!
I have to get off at the next station;
    You're going further,
    We'll never meet again.
So, I want your answer to the question
    That hasn't been answered all this time,
    You'll tell the truth, won't you?'
'I will,' I said.
Still gazing at the sky outside she asked,
    'Are those days of ours that are gone
  Gone forever—
    Is nothing left?'

I was silent for a while;
    Then I said,
    'All the stars of the night
    Remain under the glare of the day.'

I felt doubtful, had I made it all up?

'Never mind, go sit over there now.'
Everyone got off at the next station.

                        I journeyed on alone.

Deprived

The moment I returned from Phooli's
    I found the postcard in front of the mirror,
    I didn't know when it had arrived.
It felt as though I had no time,
    I'd probably miss the train.
    Trying to get money from the drawer
    I spilled several coins,
    Some I retrieved, the rest remained on the floor,
    I didn't manage to count them.
When was I to change?
    The blue silk handkerchief
    I pinned to my head
    Braided my hair somehow
    Picked up, from the pot,
    A flaming chrysanthemum.
At the station the train was nowhere in sight,
    I don't know how many minutes passed—
    Maybe five, or perhaps twenty-five.
About to enter the train I found
    A bride in wedding finery, surrounded by people;
    I didn't seem to see any of it,
    A mass of red mist, a faded picture.
The train trundled on, the whistle blew,
    Coal-dust flying in the air,
    I kept wiping my face.

Milkmen crowded around with their wares
    At some unknown station
    Delaying the train needlessly.
The whistle blew at last,
    The wheels made a grating noise, the train moved.
    Trees, houses, ponds
    Raced backwards on both sides of the window—
    The world seemed to have left something behind,
    Which it couldn't retrieve anymore.
The train trundled on.
It stopped for a long time during the journey, without reason
    Like food sticking in the throat while eating. The whistle blew
        again,
    The train began to move again.
Eventually we reached Howrah Station.
I didn't look out through the window
    I had decided that
    Someone would come searching and discover me,
    And then we would laugh together.
The bride and the relatives with the groom's headgear
    All went away.
The porter arrived, looked at me,
    Peered inside the compartment
Nothing.
Those who had come to receive the bride left.
The humans streaming towards the train
    Turned round towards the exit.
Marching past on the platform
    The guard threw a glance at my window,
    Wondering why the woman wasn't getting off.
So the woman had to.
Amidst the crowd of strangers
    I was the odd one out.
Both ends of the platform
    Seemed to ask me a question
    Which I answered in silence,
    'I shouldn't have come.'

I read the postcard once more . . .
    I hadn't made a mistake, had I?
Not a single return train now.
And even if there had been, so what . . .
    In my heart, twisting and turning
    A thousand 'perhaps'es—
    All of them dreadful.
Going out of the station I gazed at the bridge.
I don't know what the pedestrians surmised.
A bus came up, I got in,
    Throwing the chrysanthemum away.

The Other Side

There was simply no time.
Where had the red velvet shoes gone;
    They were found beneath the bed.
I was at the door, doing the buttons up to my neck
    When my father appeared suddenly,
Starting a leisurely conversation.
He had heard of two suitable boys for Mini
    And was oscillating between the two of them.
I kept glancing at my watch and perspiring
    I went out;
    Twelve minutes for the train to arrive at Howrah
    The blood in my heart tried to spur on slothful time.
The taxi broke the legal speed limit.
Harrison Road, Chitpore,
    Howrah Bridge, nine minutes to go.
When bad luck and bullock carts strike
    They strike in a group.
Carts piled with jute—pandemonium.
The constable shouted and shoved;
    The solid obstacle offered no opening.
I got out of the taxi,
Striding along quickly,
    I reached Howrah Station.
    Who knew, maybe my watch was fifteen minutes fast?
Who knew, maybe the arrival
    Had been delayed starting today?
I entered.

An empty train stood there—
Like the skeleton of an enormous prehistoric reptile,
A long word sequence in the Sanskrit dictionary
Strung together with tedious meaning.
Like a fool I peeped into the women's compartments
Called out her name,
No reason except 'I wonder if'
For this madness.
Broken hope lay in the dust of the empty platform.
I came out—
Not knowing where to go.
Only fate saved me from going under a bus.
I had no wish to thank
The gods for this kindness.

Writing a Letter

You gave me a gold fountain pen,
    Suitable furniture for writing.
A small desk
    Of walnut wood
    Stamped notepaper
    Of different sizes.
Enamelled silver paper-cutting
Scissors and knives. Sealing wax, red ribbons.
A glass paperweight,
    Red, blue and green pencils.
You must write me letters, you told me,
    On alternate days.

I've sat down to write a letter,
    I've bathed already
    But I cannot think of anything to write about.
    There's only one piece of news—
    You've left.
Which you know too.
But still it feels as though
    You don't know it well enough.
    So I think I will let you know that
    You've left.

Every time I start writing
    It becomes obvious that this news isn't so simple.
I'm no poet;
    I cannot lend voice to words,
    Nor can I picture them
    The more I write, the more paper I rip.

It's past ten.
Your nephew Boku must go to school,
    Let me give him his meal.
For the last time let me write—
    You've left.
Everything else
    Is just scribbles and doodles on the blotter.

WITH YOUR WIND IN MY SAIL
তোমার পালে হাওয়া

With your wind in my sail
I'll snap the rope
I'm ready to sink
I'm willing to sink
My morning is wasted
My evening too
Don't hold me back
Close to the shore
I stay up all night
For the boatman
The waves just
Play with me
I'll befriend the storm
I shan't fear its fury
Set me free
The storm will save me
For I'm willing to die
With your wind in my sail

The Monk-king

রাজর্ষি

A NOVELLA

1

The stone ghat of the temple to Bhuvaneswari led down to the Gomti. Govindamanikya, the king of Tripura, had arrived one summer morning to bathe in the river, accompanied by his younger brother Nakshatraray. A young girl appeared on the steps with her little brother. 'Who are you?' she enquired, tugging at the king's garments.

'I am your son, ma,' answered the king with a smile.

'Please pick me some flowers for my prayers,' the girl entreated him.

'Very well,' said the king.

His entourage grew restive. 'Why should you go, maharaj,' they said, 'we will do it for you.'

'No,' answered the king. 'It was me whom she asked, and it is I who shall do it.'

The king looked at the girl. Her face resembled the unblemished sun. When she strolled about the flower garden adjacent to the temple, holding the king's hand, her face glowed like the white jasmines blooming around them, an immaculate radiance that spread across the garden. Her little brother trailed her, clutching her sari. His sister was the only one he knew—the king could not win him over.

'What is your name, ma?' the king asked the girl.

'Hashi,' she answered.

'And yours?' the king asked the boy.

He looked at his sister with wide eyes, silent.

Smiling, Hashi put her hand on his shoulder and said, 'Why don't you say, my name is Taataa.'

Parting his tiny lips a little, the boy echoed his sister solemnly, 'My name is Taataa.'

He clutched her sari even more tightly.

'He's a child, you see,' Hashi explained to the king, 'so everyone calls him Taataa.'

Turning to her brother, she said, 'Say temple.'

'Ladamp,' declared Taata, looking at her.

Laughing, Hashi said, 'Taataa cannot say temple, he says ladamp . . . how about story, Taataa?'

'Moly,' responded Taataa gravely.

Hashi laughed again, announcing, 'Our Taataa can't say story, he calls it a moly.'

She began to rain kisses on him.

Unable to discern the reason for his sister's laughter and affection, Taataa only gazed at her with wide eyes. Indeed it could not be denied that his pronunciation of temple and story was flawed; at Taataa's age, Hashi most certainly did not refer to a temple as a ladamp—she called it a paalu; and while one cannot be sure whether she called a story a moly, she did refer to a cart as a ghaa. Therefore it was hardly surprising that she should be vastly amused at Taataa's strange diction. She began to relate various exploits of her brother's to the king. Once, an elderly man wrapped in a blanket had approached them, whereupon Taata had mistaken him for a bear, such was his poor intelligence. On another occasion, he had mistaken the castor apples on a tree for birds and attempted to make them fly away by clapping his small, plump hands. With myriad examples, Hashi made it abundantly clear that Taataa was far more of a child than she was. An unruffled Taataa listened to this account of his mental prowess, unable to discover anything to protest at in the bits that he did understand. And thus the flowers were picked for the day. When the king filled the end of the little girl's sari with the blooms, he felt as though he had completed his prayers; the sight of the love between these simple souls, and being able to offer the flowers to fulfil the wish in the girl's pure heart, made him feel as though he had just paid homage to the gods.

2

The next day onwards, mornings did not mean waking up and the rising sun for the king, but meeting the little brother and sister.

He did not bathe till he had picked flowers for them. They sat on the steps leading down to the river, watching him perform his ablutions. His rituals seemed incomplete on the mornings they did not appear.

Hashi and Taataa were orphans, their only relative being their father's younger brother, whose name was Kedareshwar. The two children were the sole happiness and support in his life.

One year passed. Taataa could now say the word temple, though not the word story yet. He was not particularly voluble—merely listening with bulging eyes to whatever story his sister told him as she sat beneath the chestnut tree by the Gomti with her legs splayed out. The stories made no sense at all, and only the boy could tell what he made of them, but then what do we know of the thoughts and images that surfaced in the tiny heart of the child as the sunlight and the breeze played on him? Taataa did not run about with other boys, following his sister everywhere like a shadow instead.

It was the month of Ashadh. The skies had been overcast since morning. It was not raining yet, but a shower was imminent. A cold wind blew in from a distant land on the raindrops. The darkened sky cast its shadow on the Gomti as well as on the forest on either side of the river. There had been a new moon on the previous night, when a ritual had been conducted for the goddess Bhuvaneswari.

The king appeared at the appointed hour for his ablutions, holding Hashi and Taataa's hands. A streak of blood ran down the white stone steps, flowing into the river—the blood of one hundred bulls that had been sacrificed the night before.

Retreating in confusion at the sight of this blood, Hashi asked the king, 'What is this, baba!'

'Blood, ma!' answered the king.

'Why so much blood?' she asked. The girl uttered her question so plaintively—'Why so much blood?'—that it kept echoing in the king's heart. 'Why so much blood?' He trembled. Ever since he could remember, he had seen this stream of blood every single year, but now a little girl's question rose in his mind, 'Why so much blood?' He forgot to answer. Bathing absently, he pondered this very question.

Soaking the end of her sari in the water, Hashi began to wipe the bloodstains slowly. Her little brother Taataa copied her. The end of Hashi's sari turned red with blood. By the time the king had completed his ablutions, the siblings had wiped off the line of blood.

Hashi ran up a fever when she went home. Taataa sat near her, trying to prise her eyes open with his tiny fingers, calling out to her now and then, 'Didi!' Jolted into wakefulness briefly, his sister drew Taataa close; then her eyes closed again. Taataa looked at his sister without a word for a long time. Eventually he put his arms around her and said, bringing his face close to hers, 'Won't you get out of bed, Didi?' Waking up with a start, Hashi clasped Taataa to her breast, saying, 'Why shouldn't I, my love!' But his sister no longer had the strength. The light went out in Taataa's tiny heart. The eager joy of playing with his sister all day was dulled. The sky was completely dark, the rain could be heard falling incessantly on the thatched roof, the tamarind tree in the yard was drenched, the roads were deserted. Kedareshwar fetched a doctor. Checking her pulse, he found the reading ominous.

When the king went to the river to bathe the next day, he found the brother and sister missing. He assumed that the torrential rain had kept them home. Completing his ablutions and rituals, the king got into his palanquin and instructed the bearers to take him to Kedareshwar's cottage. His entourage was astonished, but they dared not contradict the royal order.

A commotion broke out in the hut when the king's palanquin entered the yard. Everyone forgot about the patient in the uproar. Only Taataa did not budge, sitting silently near his sister with the end of her sari stuffed into his mouth.

When the king entered, Taataa asked, 'What's the matter?'

Anxious at heart, the king did not answer. Tilting his head upwards again and again, Taataa repeated his question, 'Is Didi hurt?'

'Yes, she is,' his uncle Kedareshwar answered in irritation.

At once Taataa went closer to his sister, attempting to lift her head and putting his arms around her, asking, 'Where does it hurt, Didi?'

His intention was to soothe his sister with his love, using his warm breath on the injured spot to rid her of all agony. But when she did not answer, he could not endure it anymore—his small lips began to pout, and he wept in indignation. He had been sitting here since yesterday, and still not a word! What had Taataa done to deserve such neglect? Kedareshwar grew frantic at Taataa's behaviour and dragged him into the other room in annoyance. Still Taataa's sister did not speak.

The royal physician arrived and expressed his apprehension. The king visited Hashi again in the evening. The little girl was delirious. 'Why so much blood?' she said.

'I shall stop this torrent of blood, ma,' declared the king.

'Come, Taataa, let's wipe this blood off, you and I,' said the girl.

'I'll join you,' said the king.

Soon after evening fell, Hashi opened her eyes just the one time. She seemed to be searching for someone. Taataa had cried himself to sleep in the next room. Unable to find whoever she was looking for, Hashi closed her eyes. She did not open them again. At midnight, Hashi died with her head in the king's lap.

Taataa was asleep, dead to the world, when Hashi was taken away from the hut forever. If he had come to know, he might have accompanied his sister like a little shadow.

3

The royal court was in session. The priest of the temple to the goddess Bhuvaneshwari had sought an audience with the king.

The priest's name was Raghupati. The priest was referred to as the chontai locally. Fourteen days after the ceremony for Bhuvaneshwari, fourteen other gods were worshipped in a special midnight ritual. No one, not even the king, was allowed outdoors for one day and two nights during this particular ceremony. If the king ventured out, he had to pay a fine to the chontai. Legend had it that a human sacrifice was conducted in the temple on the night of the ceremony. The beasts, which were sacrificed first, were accepted as gifts from the royal palace. The chontai had arrived in the king's presence to receive the animals earmarked for the sacrifice. The ceremony was twelve days away.

'Animals shall not be sacrificed at the temple from now on,' declared the king.

Everyone at the court was astonished. The king's brother, Nakshatraray, was transfixed.

'Am I dreaming?' asked Raghupati.

'No, thakur,' answered the king. 'It is we who had been dreaming all these days, but we have woken up now. The goddess came to me in the guise of a little girl. She told me that as a compassionate mother she cannot bear to see the blood of her creatures on earth being shed.'

'Then how has the goddess been drinking the blood of the beasts all this while?' challenged Raghupati.

'No, she did not drink it,' responded the king. 'She averted her face when all of you drew blood from the creatures.'

'There is no doubt of your prowess in matters of state, maharaj,' said Raghupati, 'but you know nothing about worship. Had the goddess been unhappy about something, I would have been the first to know.'

Nodding knowledgeably, Nakshatraray said, 'That is correct. Had the goddess been unhappy about something, the priest would have been the first to know.' The king replied, 'One cannot hear the goddess if one's heart has turned to stone.'

Nakshatraray looked at the priest, as though a response was essential. Blazing with anger, Raghupati averred, 'You speak like a godless heretic, maharaj.'

'Yes, you speak like a heretic,' echoed Nakshatraray softly.

Gazing at the impassioned figure of the priest, Govindamanikya said, 'You are wasting your time at court, thakur. Go to the temple, there is work to be done there. Spread the word on the way—anyone in my kingdom who sacrifices an animal to the gods will be banished.'

Shaking with anger, Raghupati rose to his feet, touched his sacred thread and announced, 'In that case, may you rot in hell.'

The courtiers pounced on Raghupati in protest. The king signalled to them to desist, whereupon they stepped aside. Raghupati continued, 'You are the king, and you can usurp everything that your subjects own if you so wish, but that does not mean you can usurp the sacrifice meant for the goddess. The temerity! Let us see how you can hinder the ceremony for the goddess so long as I, Raghupati, remain at her service.'

The minister was very well aware of the king's nature. He knew that the king could not be shaken from what he had determined to do. 'Your departed ancestors have always offered sacrifices to the goddess, maharaj,' said the minister slowly and apprehensively. 'There was never any deviation from this practice.'

The minister paused.

The king was silent. The minister said, 'If the ceremonies established by your forefathers are stopped after all these years, they will be unhappy in heaven.'

The king began to ponder. 'Yes, they will be unhappy in heaven,' Nakshatraray said with the air of one who knew.

'Why not have the number of sacrifices reduced from one thousand to one hundred?' continued the minister.

The courtiers were still thunderstruck. Govindamanikya was still thinking. The enraged priest was about to leave the court.

Suddenly a little boy, bare-bodied and barefoot, appeared in the court, having evaded the attention of the sentries. Stopping in the middle of room, he raised his large eyes towards the king and asked, 'Where's Didi?'

At once the king got off his throne to take the little boy in his arms. He told the minister firmly, 'There will be no more animal sacrifice in my kingdom today onwards. Do not contradict me any further.'

'As you wish,' responded the minister.

'Where's Didi?' Taataa asked the king.

'With ma,' the king answered.

Taataa sat in silence for a long time, sucking his thumb. He seemed to have finally understood where his sister had gone. The king had Taataa move into the palace thereafter. His uncle Kedareshwar was also installed in the royal palace.

'What kind of lawless land are we turning into?' the courtiers began to murmur amongst themselves. 'Only the Buddhist Mogs don't shed blood, are we now going to follow the same law in our Hindu land as well?'

Concurring, Nakshatraray said, 'Yes, are we now going to follow the same law in our Hindu land too?'

Everyone considered the decision a palpable sign of degeneration. No difference between Mogs and Hindus anymore!

4

Jaysingh, the attendant at the temple of Bhuvaneshwari, was a Kshatriya. His father Suchetsingh was an old retainer at the royal palace of Tripura. Jaysingh was a mere child when his father died. The king had engaged the orphaned boy to work at the temple. Jaysingh had been educated and brought up by Raghupati. Having grown up in the temple, he loved it like his own home, and was closely familiar with every stone, every step, of this edifice. His mother being dead, he considered the goddess Bhuvaneshwari his own mother, often sitting down in front of the idol to talk to her. He never felt alone, for he had other companions too. He had nurtured several plants in the temple garden with his own hands. His plants flourished around him by the day, the vines twined themselves around the stems, the flowers blossomed, the trees threw longer shadows, the clusters of leaves on the green creepers suffused the bower with their splendour. But not many people knew of these matters in Jaysingh's heart; it was his indomitable strength and valour that he was renowned for.

His work at the temple completed, Jaysingh sat down at the door of his hut. The garden stretched out before him. It was late in the afternoon. Dense clouds had gathered in the sky, and it was raining. Jaysingh's plants bathed in the fresh water, the leaves celebrating the dance of the raindrops, hundreds of little currents coming together and gurgling into the Gomti. Jaysingh sat in happy silence, gazing at his garden. The soothing darkness of the clouds, the shadows of the forest, the green beauty of the dense foliage, the croaking of frogs, the incessant clatter of raindrops—his heart overflowed at the grandeur of the monsoon.

Raghupati arrived, drenched. Jaysingh quickly fetched dry clothes and water to wash his feet with.

'Who asked you for clothes?' said an annoyed Raghupati.

He tossed the garments away.

Jaysingh advanced to pour water on his feet. Irritated, Raghupati said, 'Never mind your water.'

He kicked the pitcher of water away.

Puzzled by such unexpected behaviour, an astonished Jaysingh was about to pick the clothes off the floor and put them back when an irked Raghupati said again, 'Leave them alone, do not bother.'

He went away to change his clothes without help, drawing the water to wash his feet without Jaysingh's assistance.

Softly, Jaysingh asked, 'Have I done something wrong, my lord?'

'Who said you did anything wrong?' countered Raghupati belligerently.

Jaysingh lapsed into an injured silence.

Raghupati paced up and down restlessly. The night deepened, the rain continued unceasingly. Finally Raghupati put his hand on Jaysingh's shoulder, saying tenderly, 'Go to bed, son, it is late.'

Responding to the affection in Raghupati's tone, Jaysingh said, 'I will go only after my lord goes to bed.'

'It will be a while before I retire for the night,' Raghupati told him. 'Do not be upset at my harsh behaviour, my son. I was disturbed. I shall tell you all the details in the morning. Go to bed tonight.'

'As you desire,' responded Jaysingh.

He departed. Raghupati paced up and down all night.

In the morning Jaysingh touched his guru's feet in respect and stood in front of him. Raghupati said, 'Sacrifices to the goddess have been stopped, Jaysingh.'

'What, my lord!' exclaimed Jaysingh in surprise.

'Such is the king's order,' said Raghupati.

'Which king?' asked Jaysingh.

'Do we have dozens of kings here?' replied Raghupati testily. 'Maharaj Govindamanikya has decreed that there shall be no animal sacrifice at the temple.'

'Human sacrifice?'

'Aren't you listening! I'm talking of animal sacrifice, but what you're hearing is human sacrifice.'

'No animal sacrifice will be permitted?'

'No.'

'This is Maharaj Govindamanikya's order?'

'Yes, how many times must I tell you?'

Jaysingh did not speak for a long while, only muttering to himself, 'Maharaj Govindamanikya!' Ever since his childhood, he had considered Govindamanikya a god, attracted to the king in the way that children are attracted to the full moon. Whenever Jaysingh set eyes on the monarch's pleasant and serene visage, he felt he could lay down his life for Govindamanikya.

'This must be remedied,' declared Raghupati.

'Of course,' said Jaysingh. 'Let me go to the king and plead with him to . . .'

'Fruitless endeavour,' declared Raghupati.

'What must be done, then?' asked Jaysingh.

After some thought Raghupati said, 'I shall inform you tomorrow. You must go to Prince Nakshatraray in the morning and request him in confidence to meet me.'

5

Nakshtraray arrived the next morning and touched Raghupati's feet in respect, asking, 'What is your command, thakur?'

'Ma has given orders for you,' answered Raghupati. 'Come and pray to her first.'

They went to the temple, accompanied by Jaysingh. Nakshatraray prostrated himself in front of the idol of Bhuvaneshwari.

'You shall be the king, prince,' declared Raghupati.

'I shall be the king?' responded Nakshatraray. 'What on earth are you talking about, thakur-moshai?'

He began to laugh uproariously.

'I aver that you shall be king,' announced Raghupati.

'You aver that I shall be king?' asked Nakshtraray.

He glanced at the priest.

'Do you think I am lying?' questioned Raghupati.

'Do I think you are lying?' said Nakshatraray. 'How can this be possible? Look, thakur-moshai, I dreamt of a frog last night. What does it signify to dream of a frog?'

Suppressing his laughter, Raghupati said, 'What sort of frog? It had a mark on its head, did it not?'

'Of course it had a mark on its head,' avowed Nakshtraray proudly. 'How could it not have a mark?'

'Indeed!' said Raghupati. 'This means you shall be coronated.'

'Then I shall be coronated,' responded Nakshatraray. 'You say I shall be coronated? And if I am not?'

'Are you suggesting my prediction shall not be fulfilled?' queried Raghupati.

'Oh no, that is not what I'm suggesting,' replied Naskshatraroy. 'You are saying I shall be coronated, but suppose I am not. Is it not possible that by chance . . .'

'No, it shall not be otherwise,' said Raghupati.

'It shall not be otherwise,' echoed Nakshatraray. You are assuring me it shall not be otherwise. If I become king, thakur-moshai, I shall make you my minister.'

'I care nothing for the post of a minister,' Raghupati told him.

'Very well, I shall make Jaysingh my minister,' offered Nakshtraray generously.

'We can discuss all that later,' said Raghupati. 'Let me tell you what you have to do in order to become king. Ma desires royal blood—such is the command that has been issued to me through a dream.'

'Ma desires royal blood—such is the command that has been issued to you through a dream,' echoed Nakshatraray. 'Excellent.'

'You must offer her Govindamanikya's blood,' announced Raghupati.

Nakshtraray's mouth fell open. He did not consider this statement 'excellent'.

'Do I sense a sudden burst of brotherly love?' asked Raghupati sharply.

'Ha ha, brotherly love!' Nakshtraray laughed mechanically. 'Well said, thakur-moshai, brotherly love indeed!'

Vastly amusing—nothing could be funnier. Brotherly love! Shameful! But the omniscient divinity knew how strongly brotherly love was welling up in Nakshtraray's heart—it simply could not be laughed away.

'Then tell me what you will do,' Raghupati asked Nakshtraray.

'Tell me what I should do,' Nakshtraray said.

Raghupati said, 'Listen carefully. You will have to bring Govindamanikya's blood and present it to ma.'

Nakshtraray repeated like an incantation, 'I will have to bring Govindamanikya's blood and present it to ma.'

'No, this is beyond you,' declared Raghupati with utter contempt.

'Why should it be beyond me?' countered Nakshatraray. 'I shall do as you say. It is your order, isn't it?'

'Yes, it is my order.'

'What is your order?'

Annoyed, Raghupati said, 'Ma wishes an offering of royal blood. My order is that you must present her Govindamanikya's blood to fulfil her wish.'

'I shall engage Fateh Khan at once,' promised Nakshatraray.

'No, you must not breathe a word of this to anyone else.' Raghupati warned him. 'I shall appoint Jaysingh to assist you. Visit me tomorrow morning, when I shall inform you how to accomplish this task.'

Nakshatraray breathed a sigh of relief at escaping from Raghupati's presence, leaving as quickly as he could.

6

When Nakshatraray had left, Jaysingh said, 'I have never heard anything so terrible, gurudev. You just proposed fratricide in the presence of the goddess, invoking her name—and I was compelled to be a witness.'

'What alternative do we have?' said Raghupati.

'Alternative? To what?' asked Jaysingh.

'You are behaving just like Nakshatraray,' complained Raghupati. 'Weren't you listening?'

'What I heard is not fit to be heard. Even hearing it is sinful.'

'What do you know of sin and salvation?'

'After all these years of learning from you, how could I have remained completely ignorant about sin and salvation?'

'Then let me give you another lesson, my son. There is no such thing as sin or salvation. Who indeed is your father, and who your brother? Who is anyone? If killing were a sin, all killing would be considered equal. But who can claim that killing is a sin? People are killed every day. Some are slain by a rock falling on their heads, others are killed in floods, yet others by epidemics or at the hands of men who stab them. We tread on hundreds of ants every day, killing them—are we really greater living beings than they are? The life and death of all these tiny creatures are nothing but sport, nothing but an illusion created by the supreme force. The lives of millions of creatures are being sacrificed to the death-faced goddess every day—streams of blood from every corner of the world are flowing into her divine bowl. What if I added another drop to the stream? Once upon a time she used to accept the sacrifices offered to her personally, what if I am an intermediary now?'

Turning to the idol of the goddess, Jaysingh said, 'Is this what everyone addresses you as ma for, ma? Are you so heartless! Does your greedy tongue protrude only to lap up the blood you wring out of the entire world, you demoness?

'Are love and compassion and beauty and righteousness all untrue, then? Is your infinite lust for blood the only truth? Must men plunge daggers into one another's throats, must brothers murder each other, must fathers and sons cross swords, only to gorge your appetite? If this really is your wish, why do the clouds not rain blood upon us, why does the compassionate river not bear a current of blood into the sea? No, ma, tell me clearly—this lesson is false, this dictum is false—I cannot bear it if ma is not to be called ma but a demoness thirsty for her children's blood.'

Tears streamed from Jaysingh's eyes—he was lost in his own thoughts on what he had just said. These things had not sprung to his mind before—and had Raghupati not attempted to impart a new lesson to him, they would never have occurred to him.

With a faint smile Raghupati said, 'Then the practice of animal sacrifice should be abolished altogether.'

Jaysingh had been witness to the sacrifices every day since his childhood. Therefore, he could not acknowledge the possibility that sacrifices at the temple could ever be stopped, or that they should be stopped. Even the thought of it cut him to the quick. So he responded to Raghupati, 'That is another matter. There is a different significance to this practice. There is no sin in it. But from there to fratricide? From there to killing Maharaj Govindamanikya ... my lord, I beseech you to tell me, do not mislead me, has ma really said in your dream that she will not be satisfied without royal blood?'

After a brief silence, Raghupati said, 'Do you think I am lying? Do you doubt me?'

Touching his feet in reverence, Jaysingh said, 'May my trust in my guru never weaken. But Nakshatraray is of royal blood too.'

'The gods only leave signals in our dreams,' answered Raghupati. 'Not everything is clarified—a great deal must be interpreted. It is obvious that the goddess is unhappy with Govindamanikya, for which there is adequate reason. Therefore, when the goddess seeks royal blood, it must be understood to be Govindamanikya's.'

'If this is true,' declared Jaysingh, 'I shall bring royal blood this very day—I shall not let Nakshatraray commit a sin.'

'There is no sin in obeying the orders of the goddess,' said Raghupati.

'But there is salvation, my lord,' responded Jaysingh. 'I shall earn salvation.'

Raghupati replied, 'Then let me tell you the truth, my son. I have nurtured you from childhood with greater care than I would have my own son, loving you more than I love myself. I cannot lose you. No one would protest if Nakshatraray were to assassinate the king and occupy the throne, but if you attacked the king I would never get you back.'

Jaysingh said, 'Your love for me—I am not worthy, my father—will not allow you to harm a fly. If you were to commit a sin, I shall not be able to enjoy your love very long, for such love shall never auger well.'

'All right, all right, we shall talk about this later,' Raghupati replied hastily. 'We shall see once Nakshatraray arrives tomorrow.'

'I shall bring the king's blood on my own,' Jaysingh vowed to himself. 'I shall not allow fratricide for the sake of the goddess.'

7

Jaysingh did not sleep all night, his discussion with his guru branching quickly into innumerable new thoughts. Most of the time, the beginning is in our control, but not the end. This holds true for our thoughts as well. Jaysingh's mind was assailed irresistibly by notions challenging the very roots of the beliefs he had held since childhood. He was stricken and weary.

But like nightmares, the thoughts refused to die down. Why has my mentor robbed the goddess—whom I have always considered my mother—of her motherhood? Why has he interpreted her as a heartless force? What gives satisfaction to such a force, and what, for that matter, dissatisfaction? Where are her eyes, where her ears? Like a gigantic rumbling chariot, this force is merely grinding the world to dust under a thousand wheels—what does it know of those who use it for sustenance and those who are pulverized by it, of those who have clambered on it to celebrate and those who have fallen under it to cry in agony? Does it have no charioteer? Is it my calling in life to extract the blood of all the helpless innocent frightened creatures of the world in order to quench the thirst of this cruel force with a face of death? Why? It is performing its task on its own in any case—it has famines, floods, earthquakes, pestilences and epidemics, conflagrations, even the violence within merciless human hearts. Why does it need an insignificant individual like me!

The morning which dawned the next day was a beautiful one. The rain had ended. The eastern sky was cloudless. The sunrays seemed washed and softened by the rain. The sunlight and raindrops combined to make the air sparkle. Joyous beams of light appeared in the sky over the fields and the forest and the river, like fully-bloomed white lotuses. Kites floated across the blue firmament—a flight of cranes flew below the archway of the rainbow. Squirrels scampered about on trees. A frightened rabbit or two shot out from the cover of bushes, only to dart back into hiding. Lambs grazed on the remote slopes of hills. The cows were wandering happily all over the meadows. The goatherds sang. Children were outdoors, clutching the ends of their mothers' saris as the mothers went off to fetch water in their pitchers. The elderly were plucking flowers for their rituals. Several people had gathered at the river to bathe, chattering like the river, which murmured incessantly. Gazing at the vibrant, joyful earth on this Ashadh morning, Jaysingh sighed before entering the temple.

Joining his palms in reverence to the goddess, he said, 'Why so displeased today, ma? Must you frown because you have not been presented with the blood of your creatures for just one day? Look into our hearts, do you see a dearth of faith? Can you not be satisfied with the hearts of the devout? Must you have the blood of innocents too? Tell me truly, ma, is it your intention to eliminate Govindamanikya, the embodiment of virtue, to establish a kingdom of demons here? Must you absolutely have royal blood? I will never allow the king to be assassinated unless I hear the answer from your own lips, I will prevent it. Yes or no, tell me.'

Suddenly a sound rose in the desolate temple. 'Yes!'

Startled, Jaysingh looked over his shoulder, but he could not see anyone, although he sensed something like a shadow flit away. His first thought on hearing the voice was that it was his mentor's, but later he reasoned that it was more likely that the goddess had answered him assuming the priest's voice. He felt a thrill run through his body. Bending in supplication before the idol of the goddess, he departed, fully armed.

8

At a particular point on the southern side of the Gomti, the bank was exceedingly high. The flow of rainwater and several tiny rivulets had riddled this area with hollows and cavities. A semicircle of giant sal and beachwood trees surrounded the pitted expanse of land, but not a single large tree was to be found in the middle. Only a few sal trees, unable to grow on the mounds on which they had sprung up, stood bent over and black. Small currents of water, a foot or two wide and strewn with rocks, meandered hundreds of times, splitting and joining, before flowing into the river. The spot was completely desolate—and the sky here was not obscured by trees. Standing here, one could see not only the Gomti but also beyond it, far across the multicoloured patchwork of crop-laden fields across the river. King Govindamanikya visited this spot every morning, without any companions or members of his entourage. The fishermen would sometimes see their serene king from a distance, sitting as still as a yogi with his eyes closed. It was not obvious whether the glow on his face was bestowed by the dawn or by his soul. Now that the monsoon was here, he could not visit every day, but whenever he did, once the rain had relented, he brought little Taataa along.

One is not inclined to refer to him as Taataa anymore. The only person whom it befitted to address him by that name was gone, after all. The word Taataa means nothing to readers. But when Hashi would hide impishly behind the sal trees in the morning, calling out Taataa's name in her sharp sweet voice, the thrushes on every tree would answer, and her call would echo across the distant gardens. Charged with meaning, the sound of 'Taataaa' would spread across the garden. Abandoning the loving nest of the little girl's tiny heart, it would fly heavenward, silencing all the songbirds and pointing to the unity between the joyous loveliness of nature in the morning and the girl's ecstatic love. She was no longer there. The boy was, but not Taataa. He belonged to thousands of people and thousands of things—but Taataa had belonged only to his sister. King Govindamanikya now addressed the boy as Dhruva, and so shall we.

Earlier, the king used to visit the bank of the Gomti alone, but now he brought Dhruva along. His simple, pure visage spoke of the abode of the gods to the king. When Govindamanikya entered the vortex of the material world at noon, he was surrounded by his learned ministers, who advised him on various matters. And when morning dawned, a child took him out of this world—every complexity was simplified by his large, silent eyes. Holding the child's hand, the king stood on the straight, wide path leading to the infinity that lay at the centre of the universe. Here the greatest gathering of the cosmos was visible under the boundless blue sky and the glow of the moon; here the strains of music from the earth and the sky and the heavens—all the seven worlds—could be heard; here everything appeared simple, straightforward, perfect; the urge to move forward was strong; monstrous thoughts and worries, illnesses and disquiet, all disappeared. On that morning, on the banks of the river by the secluded forest, beneath an open sky, absorbed in his love for a child, the king discovered the way to the infinite ocean of adoration.

Holding Dhruva in his arms, Govindamanikya was telling him the story of the legendary Dhruva. It wasn't as though the boy understood a great deal, but the king wanted to hear Dhruva lisp the tale back to him.

As he listened to the story, Dhruva said, 'I want to go into the forest.'

'To do what?' asked the king.

'To see gaw,' answered Dhruva.

'We are in the forest, we're here to see god,' responded the king.

'Where's gaw?' enquired Dhruva.

'Here,' responded the king.

Dhruva asked, 'Where's Didi?'

Jumping to his feet, he looked behind him—under the impression that his sister was creeping up on him as before to cover his eyes with her hand. Finding no one there, he lowered his head and raised his eyes to ask, 'Where's Didi?'

'God has called her to himself,' answered the king.

'Where's gaw?' asked Dhruva.

'Pray to him, my son. Let me hear you say the words I taught you.'

Dhruva recited, swaying back and forth . . .

I seek you god—a lonely boy,
The forest's dark by day
It's so black, with tears in my eyes
I cannot find my way.

I do not know what I should do
Or when death's night I'll see
That is why I call your name
There's no one else by me.

My tears shall not go in vain
You are kind to those who love you
That is why I am still alive
This is the hope that I hold true.

Loving you, we're never lost
Your eyes shine brightly in the night
Dhruva needs you, guiding star
Who else will show me the light.

Confusing the Rs, Ls and Ds with one another, swallowing half the words and pronouncing the rest, Dhruva said the lines out aloud with a charming lilt. The king sank into happiness, the morning grew twice as pleasant, and the river and the garden and the trees and leaves all began to smile. In the blue sky tinged with honey gold, he seemed to see a rare, smiling face. Just like Dhruva on his lap, someone else was drawing the king into his own lap, encircling him with his arms. He saw himself and everyone around him, even the entire expanse of the earth, held in someone's arms in this way. Happiness and love radiated in all directions like the rays of the sun, filling the sky.

Suddenly an armed Jaysingh emerged from a tunnel and appeared in front of the king.

'Come, Jaysingh,' said the king, holding out his arms.

The king was one with the child, his royal reserve forgotten.

Jaysingh prostrated himself in reverence in front of the king. 'I have a submission, maharaj,' he said.

'What is it?' said the king.

'The goddess is unhappy with you,' Jaysingh told him.

'What have I done to earn her displeasure?'

'The king is hindering the rituals by putting a stop to animal sacrifices.'

'Why this penchant for violence, Jaysingh?' exclaimed the king. 'Do you want to shed the blood of the baby in its mother's arms to please the goddess?'

Jaysingh sat down slowly near the king's feet. Dhruva began to play with his sword.

'But, maharaj, the scriptures do accommodate animal sacrifice,' said Jaysingh.

'Does anyone follow the scripture scrupulously?' questioned the king. 'We interpret the texts according to our own proclivities. When people smear themselves with mud and blood from sacrifices to dance in the temple yard before the goddess with grotesque cries and violent jubilation, do they worship her or do they worship the lusting demoness within their own hearts? Sacrificing beasts to bloodlust is not a tenet from the scriptures—sacrificing this lust is what the scriptures dictate.'

Jaysingh was silent for a long time. This very thought had turned his mind upside down the previous night.

Finally he said, 'I heard it directly from the goddess's own lips—there can be no more doubts about it. She told me herself that she wants the king's blood.'

Jaysingh recounted the morning's events at the temple to the king.

Smiling, the king said, 'This is not the goddess's command, this is Raghupati's. It was he who answered your question without your seeing him.'

Jaysingh was startled to hear the king say this. A similar suspicion had flashed through his mind too, appearing and vanishing like a streak of lightning. But the king reignited his doubts.

'No, maharaj, do not lead me continuously from confusion into deeper confusion,' pleaded Jaysingh in utter despair. 'Do not push me from the shore into the sea—you are only deepening the darkness around me. Let the faith and trust I had remain. I do not desire this mist that has replaced them. Whether it is the mother goddess's command or my mentor's makes no difference—I shall fulfil it.' Swiftly he unsheathed his sword, which gleamed like lightning in the sunlight. Dhruva burst into tears at the sight, wrapping his tiny arms around the king with all his might—without paying any heed to Jaysingh, the king clasped Dhruva to his breast.

Jaysingh flung his sword into the distance. Comforting Dhruva with his hand on the child's back, he said, 'Don't be afraid, my son, don't be afraid. You are safe in the generosity of your sanctuary, make this big heart your home, no one will separate you from him. I am leaving.'

Bidding goodbye to the king, he prepared to depart.

On a sudden thought, however, he turned back to say, 'Allow me to warn you, maharaj, that your brother Nakshatraray is conspiring to kill you. Be on your guard on the twenty-ninth of Ashadh, on the night of the ceremony for the fourteen gods.'

Smiling, the king said, 'Nakshatra could never kill me, he loves me.'

Jaysingh departed.

Turning to Dhruva, the king said in admiration, 'It was you who saved the earth from bloodshed today, this was why your sister left you behind.'

He wiped Dhruva's cheeks, which were wet with tears.

'Where is Didi?' Dhruva asked solemnly.

A cloud obscured the sun, casting a black shadow on the river. In the distance, the edge of the forest grew as dark as the cloud. Noting the signs of incipient rain, the king returned to the palace.

9

The temple was not very far. But Jaysingh took a long detour along the secluded river, approaching the temple slowly. Myriad thoughts crowded his mind. He sat down beneath a tree by the side of the river. Covering his face with his hands, he mused, 'I have taken a step, but my doubts will not leave me. Is there anyone to dispel my doubts from now on? Who will teach me to distinguish between right and wrong? Poised here at the confluence of a million paths in this world, whom do I ask which is the correct one? I am alone, blinded, in the wilderness, my guiding stick is shattered.'

It had started raining by the time Jaysingh resumed his journey. He proceeded towards the temple, drenched in the rain, and discovered a multitude of people speaking loudly on their way back from the temple.

An old man was saying, 'It's been going on from the time of my ancestors, but the king knows better than all of them today.'

A young man added, 'I no longer care to go to the temple, the rituals have lost all their pomp and glory.'

'Have we turned into the nawab's kingdom?' someone added.

He seemed to think that only a Muslim could have doubts about animal sacrifice, but for a Hindu to experience such doubts was extraordinary.

'This kingdom will not thrive,' said the women.

One of them said, 'The priest himself said that the goddess has said in his dream that we will be wiped out by an epidemic within three months.'

Haru said, 'Take Modho—he survived a year-and-a-half despite his illness, but died the moment the animal sacrifices were stopped.'

'Not just that,' said Khanto, 'who'd have known my nephew was going to die? He had fever for only three days, but the moment the doctor gave him a pill he dropped dead.'

Khanto was overcome with grief for his nephew and anxiety about the ill fate awaiting the land.

'The fire at Madhurhat town didn't leave a single hut untouched,' said Tinkori.

Chintamani the farmer told a companion, 'No need to go so far, just see how paddy prices have fallen this year—they've never been so low. Who knows what lies in store for us farmers this year.'

All the mishaps that had taken place after—and even before—the sacrifices had been stopped were unanimously attributed to the king's decision. There was general agreement that it was best to abandon this kingdom. While this opinion simply would not change, everyone continued living here.

Jaysingh was distracted. Without paying the slightest attention to any of them, he arrived at the temple to discover Raghupati sitting outside, having completed the rituals.

Going up to him quickly, Jaysingh asked in a stricken but determined tone, 'When I asked ma a question before accepting her command this morning, why did you answer, gurudev?'

Hesitating, Raghupati answered, 'The goddess replies through me, after all, she doesn't speak for herself.'

'Why did you not tell me openly, then?' queried Jaysingh. 'Why did you deceive me by concealing yourself?'

An enraged Raghupati retorted, 'Be quiet! How do you expect to understand my actions? Do not say the first thing that comes to mind like a garrulous fool. You shall obey my orders alone and no one else's—do not ask any questions.'

Jaysingh lapsed into silence. But his doubts mounted instead of subsiding. A little later he said, 'This morning I told the goddess that unless she issued her orders personally, I would never allow the king to be killed—I would prevent it. When I was certain that the command was not hers, I was compelled to reveal Nakshatraray's intention to the king. I have warned him.'

Raghupati did not speak for some time. Restraining his growing anger, he said firmly, 'Enter the temple.'

Both of them entered.

Raghupati said, 'Touch ma's feet and swear—I shall lay down royal blood at your feet before the twenty-ninth of Ashadh.'

Jaysingh was silent, his head bowed. Then he looked in turn at his mentor and at the idol. Touching the image of the goddess, he said slowly, 'I shall make an offering of royal blood at your feet before the twenty-ninth of Ashadh.'

10

Returning to his residence, the king completed his duties of state. The morning sun had been obliterated, the day growing dark again under the clouds. The king seemed rather inattentive. Nakshatraray was usually present at court, but not today. The king sent for him, but he gave an excuse of ill health. The king went to Nakshatraray's chamber. Nakshatraray could not look him in the eye, pretending to be busy with a sheet of paper with something written in it. 'Are you not well, Nakshatraray?" asked the king.

Turning the sheet of paper over and over and examining the ring on his finger, Nakshatraray said, 'Not well? No, not exactly . . . I had something urgent to attend to—oh yes, I was ill, something like an illness.'

Nakshatraray grew exceedingly restless, while Govindamanikya looked at him unhappily. 'Alas,' he told himself, 'envy has penetrated even the abode of love, trying to conceal itself like a serpent, unwilling to reveal itself. Do we not have enough wild animals in our forests? Must human beings fear one another too? Cannot brothers sit next to each other without trepidation? Have jealousy and greed outstripped everything else in this world—is there no room for love and affection anymore? This is my brother, we live in the same house, share the same seat, exchange smiles— but he too is whetting his knife as he sits by my side.' To Govindamanikya, the world appeared to be a jungle full of ferocious beasts. All he could see in the impenetrable darkness were glowing claws and teeth. Sighing, the king told himself, 'My existence in this loveless, hostile kingdom is only stoking the flames of violence and greed and hatred amongst my brothers—the members of my family, dearer to me than my own heart, are grimacing at me around my throne, grinding their teeth. Like a dangerous pack of trained dogs, they're waiting for an opportunity to pounce on me. It would be better to be torn apart by their teeth and claws, satisfy their thirst for blood, and thus make my exit.'

The countenance of love that Govindamanikya had seen in the morning sky had vanished.

Rising to his feet, the king declared grimly, 'You and I shall visit the desolate forest on the bank of the Gomti this afternoon, Nakshatra.'

Nakshatraray did not dare contradict the king's stern order, but his heart was flooded with doubt and apprehension. He felt as though the king had silently been probing his mind all this time—squirming at the sudden light, the thoughts wriggling like worms in the dark cavities of his brain had emerged. Nakshatraray glanced fearfully at the king and saw on his face only a deep, melancholy tranquillity, without a trace of fury. The harsh cruelty of the human heart had only led to intense sadness in his own heart.

The sun declined. The skies were still overcast. The king proceeded on foot towards the forest with Nakshatraray. Evening was still a few hours away, but the darkness induced by the clouds made it appear that evening had descended. The crows had returned, cawing incessantly, though a falcon or two still swam about in the sky. When the brothers entered the remote forest, Nakshatraray felt his skin prickling with fear. Large, ancient trees stood in clusters—they did not utter a word, but seemed to hear even the footsteps of insects in their stillness. They only stared unblinkingly at their own shadows, and at the darkness beneath. Nakshatraray's feet refused to carry him further into the unknown mysteries of the forest, his heart quaked at the sullen silence that enveloped everything. A deep suspicion and fear rose within Nakshatraray; he could not fathom where the king was leading him in silence this evening, away from the eyes of the world, like a remorseless destiny. He must have felt that he had been found out by the king, and had been brought into the forest to be punished severely. Nakshatraray would have been relieved if he could have run away as fast as his legs could carry him, but he felt as though he was being dragged along, his hands and feet in chains. Nothing could save him now.

There was a clearing in the centre of the forest, with a natural lake, now brimming with rainwater. Turning towards him suddenly on the bank of this lake, the king said, 'Stop!'

Nakshatraray stopped, startled. Time itself seemed to have stopped flowing at the king's order—every tree in the forest seemed to lean forward—the earth beneath and the sky above were holding their breaths, looking on in silence. The cacophony of the crows had died down, not a sound was to be heard in the forest. Only the single word: 'Stop!' seemed to reverberate for a long time—like lightning the word 'stop' flashed from tree to tree, from branch to twig. Every leaf in the forest vibrated with the sound. Nakshatraray was rooted to the spot in silence, just like the trees.

Casting a long, mournful glance at Nakshatraray that penetrated his brother's soul, the king said slowly in a calm, deep voice, 'You wish to kill me, Nakshatra?'

Nakshatraray stood transfixed, as though struck by lightning. He did not even attempt to answer.

'Why do you want to kill me, my brother?' asked the king. 'Is it out of greed for my kingdom? Do you think a king is nothing but golden throne, diamond crown and royal sceptre? Do you know the weight of this crown, this sceptre, these robes? This diamond crown hides my concern for thousands of people. If you want the kingdom, make the unhappiness of these thousands your own, accept their dangers as your own, bear their poverty on your shoulders as your own—he who does this is the king, no matter whether he lives in a hut or a palace. He who can be close to every person on earth will have all of them close to him. He who takes away the misery of the world is the true king. He who sucks the blood and riches out of the earth is the enemy—the tears of thousands of luckless people rain on him all day and night; no royal canopy can shield him from this stream of curses. The hunger of hundreds of starving subjects is hidden in his royal repast, the gold jewellery he dons is crafted from the poverty of orphans, his flowing robes are stitched from the soiled, tattered covers used by those who succumb to winter. You cannot win the kingdom by killing the king, my brother, you have to win the world over.'

Govindamanikya stopped. A deep silence reigned. Nakshatraray bowed his head without a word.

The king unsheathed his sword. Offering it to Nakshatraray,

he said, 'There is no one here, no witness, no human being—if a man wants to plunge a knife into his brother, then this is the time and place to do it. No one will ask you to desist, no one will speak ill of you. The same blood flows in your veins and mine, the blood of the same father, the same ancestors—shed this blood if you must, but not where human beings reside. For wherever the drops of blood fall, the sacred bond of brotherhood will quietly be loosened. There's no telling where the chain of sin leads. Wherever a seed of wrongdoing is planted, a thousand trees spring up swiftly and secretly—no one even realizes how an honourable human society is gradually converted into a jungle. Therefore, do not spill the blood of your brother in a place where brothers live together in perfect harmony. That is why I summoned you into the forest today.'

The king handed Nakshatraray his sword, which slipped from Nakshatraray's hand and fell on the ground. Covering his face with his hands and weeping, Nakshatraray said, his voice choking, 'I'm not guilty of this, my brother—it never occurred to me that . . .'

Embracing him, the king said, 'I know. You could never hurt me—you have been badly advised by others.'

'Raghupati alone advised me thus,' answered Nakshatraray.

'Keep your distance from Raghupati,' the king told him.

'Tell me where I should go,' said Nakshatraray. 'I do not wish to stay here. I want to escape from this place, from Raghupati.'

'Stay with me, you needn't go anywhere else,' said the king. 'What can Raghupati do?'

Nakshatraray clutched at the king's arm firmly, as though he were worried that Raghupati might draw him away.

11

There was still some light in the sky as Nakshatraray returned through the forest, holding the king's arm—but inside the jungle it was extremely dark. It was like a deluge of darkness, with only the tips of the trees rising above the floods. Gradually they would be submerged too, the sky and the earth merging into one vast darkness.

The king took the road to the temple instead of the palace.

Raghupati and Jaysingh were seated in the hut, the evening rituals at the temple completed. Each was sunk in his own thoughts. Only the shadows on their faces were visible in the faint lamplight. Nakshatraray could not raise his eyes when he spotted Raghupati; he stood behind the king, staring at the ground. The king drew him to his side, taking his hand firmly and giving Raghupati a determined look. Raghupati's eyes bored into Nakshatraray. At last the king greeted Raghupati respectfully, with Nakshatraray following suit. Accepting the greetings, Raghupati said grimly, 'Long live the king—is all well with the state?'

Pausing, the king said, 'Give us your blessings, thakur, so that no ill may come upon the state. May all the children of the goddess in this kingdom live in love and friendship with one another, may no one snatch a man away from his brother, may no one establish violence where there is affection. I am here apprehending trouble in the kingdom. Friction between sinful intentions might set off a conflagration—douse the flames, sprinkle the water of peace, cool the earth.'

'Who can put the fire out when the goddess burns with rage!' exclaimed Raghupati. 'A thousand innocent people are set ablaze because of one sinner.'

'That is indeed my fear,' retorted the king, 'that is why I tremble. Why do people pretend not to understand this? Do you not know that the gods are being invoked in this kingdom in order to violate their own tenets? That is why I am here this evening, apprehending evil—please do not plant the roots of sin here and invite the wrath of the goddess on my well-endowed, happy kingdom. I am telling you this clearly and this is what I came to tell you.'

The king cast a probing look at Raghupati. His solemn, resolute voice had resounded in the hut like a powerful thunderstorm. Without answering, Raghupati toyed with his sacred thread. Offering his respects once more, the king left, holding Nakshatraray by the hand. Jaysingh went out too. Only a lamp, Raghupati, and Raghupati's gigantic shadow remained in the room.

The light in the sky had been extinguished. The stars were submerged in the clouds. Darkness brimmed over. The fragrance of kadam flowers wafted in on the eastern breeze in the impenetrable darkness, and the murmurs of the forest could be heard. Immersed in thought, the king was walking along a familiar path when he suddenly heard someone call him from behind, 'Maharaj.'

'Who is it?' the king asked, turning around.

A familiar voice said, 'I am your unworthy servant—Jaysingh. You are my lord and master, maharaj. I have no one in the world but you. Just as you are leading your younger brother through the darkness, take my hand too, take me with you; I am caught in an intense darkness. I cannot distinguish between the beneficial and the harmful. I am lurching from one side to the other; I have no one to guide me.'

Tears fell in the darkness, which no one saw, but the king heard Jaysingh's voice, moist with those tears, quivering with emotion. No longer still and silent, the darkness trembled too like a sea disturbed by the wind. Taking Jaysingh's hand, the king said, 'Come with me to the palace.'

12

When Jaysingh returned to the temple the next day, it was past the time for the daily rituals. A sullen Raghupati was sitting alone. Such a deviation from practice had never occurred before.

When Jaysingh arrived, he went into his garden instead of approaching his guru, sitting down amidst his plants. They swayed and weaved around him, making their shadows dance. All around him were flower-laden boughs, one green layer after another, offering a dappled canopy of comforting and tender affection, a sweet invitation, the loving embrace of nature. Everything here awaited its turn, not posing questions, not disturbing one's thoughts. It looked only when looked at, it spoke only when spoken to. Sitting at the centre of this silent healing, in this curtained heart of nature, Jaysingh let his thoughts flow, weighing the advice that the king had given him.

Raghupati appeared on slow footsteps, putting his hand on Jaysingh's shoulder. Jaysingh became alert. Raghupati sat down beside him. Looking at Jaysingh, he said, his voice trembling, 'Why such a demeanour, my son? What have I done to make you distance yourself from me?'

Jaysingh tried to speak, but Raghupati interrupted him. 'Have you seen even a moment's lack of affection on my part? Have I been unfair to you, Jaysingh? If I have, I apologize—I am your guru, your father—I seek your forgiveness.'

Jaysingh was thunderstruck. Clutching his mentor's feet, he began to weep. 'I know nothing, my father, I understand nothing, I cannot see where I am going.'

Taking Jaysingh's hand, Raghupati said, 'I have reared you from childhood with the love of a mother, my son; I have taught you the scriptures with the care of a father. Reposing complete trust in you, I have made you my companion in all that I do, just like a friend. Who is taking you away from me today? Who is severing our bond of love and affection? Who is attempting to interfere in my sacred, god-given right over you? Tell me the name of this sinner, my son.'

'No one has separated us, my lord,' answered Jaysingh, 'you have pushed me away. I was at home, you threw me out on the road. No one is my father or mother or brother, you said. There are no bonds in this world, you said, no sanctified claim that love or affection can make. You defined the entity whom I considered my mother as nothing but a force—a hungry power who waits with her bowl in bloodlust wherever there is violence, wherever there is bloodshed, wherever brothers are at war, wherever people are in conflict. What is this kingdom of demons to which you have exiled me from my sanctuary in my mother's arms?'

An astonished Raghupati remained sitting for a long time. Finally he said with a sigh, 'In that case you are independent now, free of your bonds. I withdraw all my claims over you. If that is what makes you happy, so be it.'

He made to rise to his feet.

Clutching his feet, Jaysingh said, 'No my lord, even if you were to abandon me, I cannot abandon you. I shall remain—at your feet, do with me as you please. I have no road to walk except yours.'

Raghupati embraced Jaysingh, his tears dropping on Jaysingh's shoulders.

13

There was a large gathering at the temple, and a hubbub of conversation. 'What are you here for?' asked Raghupati brusquely.

'We want to see the goddess,' rose their voices.

'The goddess?' said Raghupati. 'Where is the goddess? She has left this kingdom. You could not hold her back. She has left.'

There was an uproar now, with different voices being heard.

'What do you mean, thakur!'

'What crime have we committed?'

'Will the goddess not change her mind?'

'I couldn't visit the past few days because of my nephew's illness.' (The speaker was convinced that the goddess had departed because she was unable to accept his neglect.)

'I had meant to sacrifice two goats to the goddess, but I live so far away.' (He was overcome with grief at the delay in offering his goats causing such harm to the kingdom.)

'It's true that Gobordhan did not offer the goddess what he had promised, but ma has punished him too. His liver is the size of a mountain now, he has been bedridden for six months.' (Let Gobardhan and his inflamed organ go to hell, but let the goddess remain—such was this man's prayer. Everyone hoped for the hapless Gobordhan's liver to improve in leaps and bounds.)

A tall man in the crowd berated the others, asking them to be quiet. Joining his palms reverently, he asked Raghupati, 'Why did ma go away, thakur, what did we do wrong?'

'You could not offer her even a single drop of blood,' mocked Raghupati. 'Such is your devotion.'

Everyone was silent. Eventually there were snatches of conversation. A few said haltingly, 'The king has forbidden it, what can we do?'

Jaysingh was as still as a stone statue. The words 'Ma has forbidden it' rose swiftly to his lips, but he restrained himself, not uttering a word.

'Who is the king? Must the goddess's throne be subservient to the king's throne? Then live with your king in this motherless world. Let me see who protects you.'

A buzz rose amongst the crowd. People spoke cautiously.

Rising to his feet, Raghupati said, 'All of you have exalted the king and humiliated the goddess, forcing her out of the kingdom. Don't imagine you will live happily. In three years not a sign of your homes will remain in this huge land—none of your descendants shall be alive.'

The murmurs of the crowd grew louder. The number of people increased. The tall man joined his palms again and told Raghupati, 'If ma's children have made a mistake let her punish them, but how can she abandon them. Tell us what we have to do to bring her back, my lord.'

'Ma will return to this kingdom only when your king leaves it,' answered Raghupati.

The hum ceased suddenly. A deep silence fell on the crowd. People exchanged glances, but none of them dared to speak.

'Do you want to see for yourselves, then?' thundered Raghupati. 'Very well, follow me. You have travelled a long way in the hope of a glimpse of the goddess—come to the temple.'

They gathered fearfully in the temple courtyard. The doors were closed. Raghupati opened them slowly.

No one could speak for a while. The face of the goddess was not visible—her back was turned to the audience. Ma had turned away from them. Wails rose from the crowd suddenly. 'Turn around, ma! Have we done something wrong?' There were cries of 'Where has ma gone?' everywhere. The idol could not turn only because it was made of stone. Many fainted. Confused children started crying. The elderly sobbed like orphaned babies, 'Ma! Oh, ma!' Forgetting to keep their heads covered, the women began to beat their breasts. Young men declared in quavering, high-pitched tones, 'We shall bring you back, ma. We shan't let you stay away.'

A mad man sang:
'Is my mother made of stone
Forsaking her very own'

The entire kingdom seemed to wail 'Ma! Ma!' at the door of the temple—but the idol did not turn. The sun grew merciless at noon, but the starving crowds did not stop their cries of despair.

Walking uncertainly up to Raghupati, Jaysingh said, 'Am I not allowed to say anything at all, my lord?'

'Not a word,' answered Raghupati.

'Is there no room for doubt?' asked Jaysingh.

'None,' said the priest firmly.

'Should I believe everything?" asked Jaysingh, clenching his fist.

'Yes,' Raghupati told him with a piercing glance.

'My heart is breaking,' said Jaysingh, putting his hand on his breast.

He raced away through the crowd.

14

The next day was the twenty-ninth of Ashadh. The rituals for the fourteen gods and goddesses were scheduled for the night. The eastern sky was cloudless when the sun rose behind the palm grove. When Jaysingh took a seat in the garden of joy flooded by the golden rays of the sun, his old memories welled up. Like a pleasant dream, he recollected his childhood amidst the temple and steps of stone here in this forest, here in the shade of the giant banyan tree on the bank of the Gomti, and by the side of the small lake always wrapped in shadows. The charming scenes that infused his childhood days with love were smiling today, beckoning to him again, but his mind told him, 'I have embarked on my journey, I have said my goodbyes, I shall not return.' The beams of the sun fell on the white stone steps, while the shadow of the bokul tree rippled on the floor to their left. When Jaysingh was young this temple of stone seemed to be alive, when he played on this flight of stone steps he used to find companionship in them—by the light of the morning sun, the temple seemed just as alive today; he began to see the steps through the eyes of his childhood. The goddess within the temple appeared to be a mother figure again. But pique overran his heart, his eyes brimmed with tears.

When Jaysingh saw Raghupati approaching, he wiped his tears. Greeting his guru respectfully, he rose to his feet. 'It's the day of the ritual,' said Raghupati. 'You haven't forgotten what you swore with your hands on the goddess's feet, have you?'

'I have not,' replied Jaysingh.

'You *will* fulfil your vow?' asked Raghupati.

'I will,' answered Jaysingh.

'Be careful, my son,' Raghupati warned him. 'There is danger. It was to protect you that I instigated the people to rise against the king.'

Jaysingh looked at Raghupati in silence without answering. Placing his hand on Jaysingh's head, Raghupati said, 'With my blessings you shall accomplish your task without hindrance and obey the goddess's orders.'

Raghupati left.

The king was playing with Dhruva in a room in the afternoon, taking off and putting on his crown on Dhruva's instructions, his plight making the boy laugh uproariously. With a faint smile the king said, 'I am practising, so that I can take off the crown on the instruction of the almighty as effortlessly as I put it on when he commanded me to. Donning the crown is difficult enough, but giving it up is even more so.'

A thought suddenly occurred to Dhruva. Staring at the king for a while, he put his thumb in his mouth and said, 'You are the uler.' Getting rid of the R in its entirety gave him no cause for repentance. Describing the ruler as the uler to his face provided him complete satisfaction.

Unable to tolerate this audacity on Dhruva's part, the king said, '*You* are the uler.'

'You are the uler,' Dhruva retorted.

The argument could not be settled. Neither could provide any proof, the argument proceeding only on the basis of stubbornness. Eventually the king mounted his crown on Dhruva's head, a move which Dhruva could not counter—he was soundly defeated. Nodding his enormous crowned head, he ordered the uncrowned king, 'Tell me a story.'

'What story?' asked the king.

'A story that Didi told,' answered Dhruva. To him, every story was his sister's—as far as he was concerned, there was no story in the world other than those his sister had told him.

The king spun a long mythological tale. 'There was a uler named Hiranyakashipu.'

Hearing a familiar word, Dhruva declared, 'I am the uler,' using the large and wobbly crown on his head to completely disregard Hiranyakashipu's claim to the throne.

Like a smooth-tongued courtier Govindamanikya tried to please the crowned child by saying, 'You are a uler, and so was he.'

Expressing his disagreement clearly, Dhruva announced, 'No, I am the uler.'

When the king finally said, 'Hiranyakashipu was not a uler, he was a ogue,' Dhruva had nothing to protest against.

Nakshatraray entered the chamber, saying, 'I was told the king has summoned me on matters of state. I await his commands.'

'A few minutes more,' said the king, 'let me finish the story,' and proceeded to do so.

'Naughty ogue.' Dhruva expressed his viewpoint briefly on hearing the story.

Nakshatraray was not pleased at the sight of the crown on Dhruva's head. Observing Nakshatraray staring at him, Dhruva told him solemnly, 'I am the uler.'

'No, you mustn't say that,' replied Nakshatraray, trying to lift the crown off Dhurva's head and return it to king. Observing the possibility of losing his crown, Dhruva shrieked like a real king. Govindamanikya rescued him from this imminent danger, stopping Nakshatraray.

Finally the king told Nakshatraray, 'I believe Raghupati is trying to stoke dissatisfaction amongst my subjects through underhand means. Go into the city personally to investigate and report to me whether this is true or not.'

'As you wish,' said Nakshatraray and left, but he simply could not approve of the crown being placed on Dhruva's head.

The sentry appeared to announce, 'The priest's attendant Jaysingh awaits an audience with you.'

The king gave permission for him to enter.

Greeting the king, Jaysingh joined his palms in reverence and said, 'I am leaving for a distant land, maharaj. You are my king, my guru, I have come to seek your blessings.'

'Where are you going, Jaysingh?' asked the king.

'I do not know, maharaj,' answered Jaysingh. 'No one can tell.'

As the king about to speak, Jaysingh said, 'Do not stop me, maharaj, if you do the journey shall not be propitious. Pray that all the doubts I have here are dispelled in this new land, that the clouds are dispersed, that my destination is a kingdom ruled by a king like you, which can bring me peace.'

'When will you go?' asked the king.

'This evening,' said Jaysingh. 'I do not have much time, maharaj, I shall leave now.'

When he bent to touch the king's feet respectfully, two teardrops fell on the feet.

As Jaysingh was about to leave, Dhruva went up to him slowly, tugging at his garments and saying, 'Don't go.'

Jaysingh turned back with a smile, picking Dhruva up in his arms and kissing him. 'Whom shall I stay with, my son? Whom can I call my own?'

'I am the uler,' said Dhruva.

'You children are the emperors of the king, you have imprisoned all of us,' said Jaysingh.

Setting Dhruva down, Jaysingh went out. A grave Govindamanikya pondered for a long time.

15

The night before the full moon . . . There were both clouds and a moon in the sky, which was a mixture of light and dark. The moon emerged occasionally, and remained hidden at other times. The forests on the banks of the Gomti looked up at the moon, their occasional sighs penetrating the intense darkness.

People were forbidden from going out tonight. Who would go out at night anyway? But because it was forbidden, the roads seemed even more desolate than usual. All the citizens had barred their doors and turned out their lamps. Not a single guard patrolled the road—not even thieves came out on this night. Those who had to take the dead to the crematorium were waiting for morning. People with sick children at home did not venture out to fetch doctors. The beggar who normally slept beneath a tree by the road had taken shelter in a cowshed tonight.

Jackals and dogs roamed the streets, a couple of leopards sniffing at the front doors of people's homes. Only one human being was outdoors—no one else. He honed a knife on a rock by the river, distracted by his own thoughts. The knife had a sharp enough edge already, but possibly he was honing his own thoughts too, which was why he simply would not stop. The sharpened, hissing knife grew warm with bloodlust from friction with the rock. A black river flowed in the darkness. The dark hours of night passed over the world. A dark current of dense clouds flowed across the sky.

Only when it began to rain torrentially did Jaysingh return to his senses. It was almost time for the ceremonies. He had remembered his vow. He could not afford to delay another moment.

The temple was illuminated with a thousand lamps. Standing amidst thirteen other goddesses, Kali had extended her tongue for human blood. Having sent the temple attendants on their way, Raghupati sat by himself in front of the fourteen goddesses. A giant blade lay before him. Naked and glittering in the lamplight, the blade was poised like an immobile thunderbolt for the goddess's orders.

The rituals were to be conducted at midnight. The hour was almost at hand. Raghupati was waiting impatiently for Jaysingh. Suddenly a storm blew up, accompanied by a torrent of rain. All the lamps began to flicker in the wind, lightning flashing on the naked blade. The shadows cast by the fourteen goddesses and by Raghupati seemed to acquire a life of their own, dancing to the rhythms of the lamps all over the floor of the temple. A pair of small bats got in, flitting about continuously like dry leaves, their shadows on the walls following them.

An hour passed. Jackals howled, nearby at first, and then from a distance. The storm joined them to sob piteously. It was time for the ceremony. Fearing the worst, Raghupati had turned restless.

Suddenly Jaysingh cut through the darkness of the night like a living embodiment of the storm and the thunder and the lightning to enter the lit-up temple. His body was covered with a sheet, water dripping off every part of his body. He was panting, and a fire blazed in his eyes.

Clutching him, Raghupati took his mouth close to his ears. 'Have you brought royal blood?'

Shaking him off, Jaysingh said loudly, 'I have. I have brought royal blood. Step aside. Let me offer it to the goddess.'

The temple shook at the sound of his voice.

Standing in front of the idol of Kali, Jaysingh said, 'Do you really want your child's blood, ma? Will your thirst not be quenched with anything but royal blood? I have addressed you as my mother ever since I was born, served you, never looked at anyone else, never had any other objective in my life. I am a Rajput, I am a Kshatriya, my father's father's father was a king, my mother's family still rules the kingdom. Here then is the blood of your child, here then is your royal blood.' The sheet slipped off his body. He pulled his dagger out of his belt—a flash of lightning—and plunged it up to the hilt in his own heart, the jagged tongue of death piercing his breast. Jaysingh slumped to the ground at the feet of the goddess. The idol of stone remained unmoved.

Raghupati screamed, trying to raise Jaysingh—but could not. He fell instead on the corpse. The blood flowed over the white floor of the temple. The lamps went out one by one. In the darkness only the breathing of a single living being was heard all night; a long time after midnight, the storm abated, and silence fell. Two hours later, moonlight filtered into the temple through a break in the clouds. The moonbeams fell on Jaysingh's bloodless face, and the fourteen goddesses stood near his head, looking down at it. When the birds sang out from the forest at dawn, Raghupati rose to his feet, leaving the corpse behind.

16

Following the king's instructions, Nakshatraray was out to personally investigate the reason for unrest among the people. How can I go to the temple, he fretted. In Raghupati's presence he lost his equanimity, unable to control himself. He was absolutely unwilling to run into the priest. Therefore he had decided to avoid Raghupati and steal into Jaysingh's chamber to get a detailed account.

Nakshatraray entered Jaysingh's room furtively. And as soon as he did, he wanted to run for his life. He discovered Jaysingh's manuscripts, garments and personal effects scattered all around, with Raghupati sitting amidst them, but no Jaysingh. Raghupati's reddened eyes glowed like embers, his hair was dishevelled. When he saw Nakshatraray, he gripped his hand firmly, forcing him to sit on the floor. Nakshatraray was paralyzed with fear. Boring into

Nakshatraray's heart with his blazing eyes, Raghupati said like a lunatic, 'Where's the blood?'

The blood began to pound in Nakshatraray's chest, he could not utter a word.

'What about your vow?' said Raghupati loudly. 'Where's the blood?'

Nakshatraray moved his arm, moved his leg, shifted to the left, plucked at his own garments, perspiration flowed. With an ashen face he said, 'Thakur . . .'

'Ma has taken the blade in her own hand,' said Raghupati. 'The blood that will flow now will ensure that not a single member of your family survives. Then I will see how deep Nakshatraray's brotherly love runs.'

'Brotherly love! Ha ha ha! Thakur . . .'

Nakshatraray's laughter dried up, his throat felt parched.

'I do not want Govindamanikya's blood,' said Raghupati. 'I want the one person on earth who is dearer to Govindamanikya than his own heart. I want to smear his blood on Govindamanikya—his breast will turn red—he will never be able to wipe the blood away. See.' He took off his shawl, revealing a body streaked with blood, with clots across his chest.

Nakshatraray shivered. His limbs trembled. Holding his arm in an iron grip, Raghupati said, 'Who is it? Who is dearer to Govindamanikya than his own heart? Whose death will turn the world into a graveyard for Govindamanikya and rob him of his reason for living? Whose is the face he is reminded of as soon as he wakes up in the morning, whose is the memory he takes to bed, who occupies his heart in its entirety? Who is it? Is it you?'

Raghupati glared at Nakshatraray the way a tiger glares at a trembling fawn before pouncing on it. 'No, not I,' Nakshatraray said quickly, but he could not free himself from Raghupati's grip.

'Then tell me who it is,' said Raghupati.

'It's Dhruva,' Nakshatraray blurted out.

'Who is Dhruva?' asked Raghupati.

'A child,' replied Nakshatraray.

'I know, I know him,' said Raghupati. 'The king has no child of his own, he is bringing up this boy as his own. I don't know how much people love their own children, but I do know they love their adopted children more than themselves. The king considers the child's happiness more important than all his riches. He is more delighted to see his crown on the child's head than his own.'

'You're right,' exclaimed Nakshatraray in astonishment.

'Of course I'm right,' retorted Raghupati. 'Do you think I do not know how deeply the king loves him? Do you think I do not understand? I want him too, no one but him.'

Nakshatraray stared open-mouthed at Raghupati. 'No one but him,' he mumbled.

'He must be brought to me,' declared Raghupati. 'He must be brought now, tonight.' Nakshatraray echoed, 'He must be brought tonight.'

Fixing his eyes on Nakshatraray for a while, Raghupati lowered his voice and said, 'This child is your enemy, do you know that? You have been born into the royal family—but are you aware that a child whose bloodline no one knows is here to snatch your crown away from you? Can you not see with your own eyes that that the throne which was waiting for you has now been earmarked for him?'

None of this was news to Nakshatraray. He had harboured similar thoughts earlier. Confidently he declared, 'You do not have to spell it out, thakur. Do you suppose I cannot see this?'

'There you are,' said Raghupati. 'Bring him to me, then. Let me get rid of the impediment to your ascending the throne. We just need to pass the intervening hours, and then—when will you bring him?'

'This evening, when it is dark,' answered Nakshatraray.

Touching his sacred thread, Raghupati said, 'The Brahmin's curse will be upon you if you do not bring him. The very lips with which you have made the vow that you do not keep will have their flesh eaten by vultures before three nights have passed.'

A startled Nakshatraray ran his hands over his lips—he found it unbearable to imagine the beaks of vultures feasting on the tender flesh. Bidding Raghupati farewell, he left in a hurry. Returning to the fresh air and light and the sounds of people, Nakshatraray earned a new lease of life.

17

That evening Dhruva came running to Nakshatraray when he saw him, exclaiming, 'Kaka!' Putting his arms around Nakshatraray's neck, he rubbed cheeks with him, whispering, 'Kaka.'

'Don't say that, I'm not your kaka,' Nakshatraray told him.

Since Dhruva had addressed Nakshtraray as uncle ever since he could remember, he was surprised by this sudden disapproval. He sat solemnly for a few moments, and then, raising his large eyes towards Nakshatra, asked, 'Who are you?'

'I am not your uncle,' answered Nakshatraray.

Dhruva suddenly found this very funny—he had never heard anything so impossible. Laughing, he said, 'You are my kaka.' The more Nakshatraray forbade him, the more he insisted, 'You are my kaka,' and the more he laughed. He went on teasing Nakshatraray by addressing him as kaka. 'Would you like to meet your sister, Dhruva?' Nakshatraray asked.

Letting go of Nakshatraray's shoulders, Dhruva jumped to his feet. 'Where's Didi?' Nakshatraray said, 'With ma.'

'Where's ma?' asked Dhruva.

'I know where she is,' answered Nakshatra. 'I can take you to her.'

Clapping his hands, Dhruva said, 'When will you take me, Kaka?'

'Right now,' said Nakshatra.

Shrieking with joy, Dhruva wrapped his arms tightly around Nakshatraray's neck; picking him up in his arms, Nakshatraray covered him with his shawl and left through the secret exit.

People were forbidden from going out tonight, too. So there were no guards on the road, no pedestrians. A full moon hung in the sky.

Arriving at the temple, Nakshatraray was about to hand Dhruva over to Raghupati. But when Dhruva saw Raghupati he clung to Nakshatraray with all this strength, refusing to let go. When the priest snatched him away by force, Dhruva burst into tears, crying, 'Kaka!' Tears sprang to Nakshatraray's eyes—but he was too embarrassed to reveal this weakness in his heart to Raghupati. He pretended to be made of stone. Weeping, Dhruva kept calling out, 'Didi, didi,' but his sister did not appear. Raghupati thundered an admonishment. A frightened Dhruva stopped weeping. But his body was wracked by sobs. The idols of the fourteen goddesses looked on.

Govindamanikya was awakened from his slumber at the sound of sobbing in his dreams. Suddenly he heard someone calling out to him piteously below his window, 'Maharaj! Maharaj!'

Hurrying to the window, the king discovered Dhruva's uncle Kedareshwar in the moonlight. 'What's the matter?' he asked.

'Where is my Dhruva, maharaj?' asked Kedareshwar.

'Is he not in his bed?' asked the king.

'No.'

Kedareshwar continued, 'When I didn't see Dhruva from the afternoon onwards, I asked people. Prince Nakshatraray's servant told me Dhruva was with the prince inside the palace. I was relieved. But when it grew late I became anxious. Making enquiries, I learnt that Prince Nakshatraray was not in the palace. I tried my best to seek an audience with you, but the guards refused to entertain my request. That is why I have been forced to call out to you this way. Pardon me for disturbing your sleep.'

A suspicion flashed through the king's mind. Summoning four of his sentries, he said, 'Arm yourselves and follow me.'

'Going out is forbidden tonight, maharaj,' said one of them.

'I am ordering you to,' answered the king.

Kedareshwar made to accompany them, but, asking him to turn back, the king set off for the temple in the moonlight along the deserted road.

When the doors of the temple opened suddenly, Nakshatraray and Raghupati were found drinking with the blade lying before them. There was not a great deal of light, with only a single lamp having been lit. Where was Dhruva? He had fallen asleep near the feet of the idol of Kali—the tears had dried on his cheeks, his lips were slightly parted, there was not a trace of fear or anxiety on his face. He didn't seem to be lying on a bed of stone, but in his sister's lap. She seemed to have kissed his tears away.

Alcohol had made Nakshatraray's inhibitions vanish, but a still Raghupati was awaiting the appointed hour of the rituals, without paying the slightest heed to Nakshatraray's babbling.

Nakshatra was saying, 'Secretly you are afraid, thakur. And you think I am afraid too. But there is nothing to be afraid of. Fear what? Fear whom? I shall protect you. Do you think I am afraid of the king? I am not afraid of Shah Suja, I am not afraid of Shah Jahan. Why didn't you tell me, thakur—I would have got hold of the king and brought him to you. We could have satisfied the goddess. How much blood can you draw from a little boy, after all?'

Suddenly a shadow fell on the floor of the temple. Turning round, Nakshatraray discovered the king. Sober in an instant, he turned darker than his own shadow. Scooping up Dhruva's sleeping form in his arms quickly, Govindamanikya told the guards, 'Take them prisoner.'

The four guards gripped Raghupati and Nakshatraray by their arms. Clasping Dhruva to his breast, the kind returned to the palace by moonlight along the deserted road. Raghupati and Nakshatraray spent the night in prison.

18

The trial was to be held the next day. The court brimmed over with people. The king was in the judge's seat, with his courtiers around him. The two prisoners stood before him. Neither was in chains, though surrounded by guards. Raghupati stood like a block of stone, while Nakshatraray's head was bowed.

Pronouncing Raghupati guilty, the king said to him, 'What do you have to say?'

'You do not have the power to judge me,' said Raghupati.

'Then who will judge you?' asked the king.

'I am a Brahmin, a servant of the gods, only the gods may judge me,' said Raghupati.

'The gods have numerous attendants on earth to punish wrongdoing and reward goodness,' the king told him. 'We are among them. I do not wish to debate this with you—I am asking whether or not you abducted a child last evening with the intention of sacrificing him.'

'I did,' answered Raghupati.

'You admit your wrongdoing?' said the king.

'Wrongdoing? What wrongdoing? I was fulfilling the order of the goddess, I was performing her bidding and you prevented me. You have transgressed—I hold you guilty in the presence of the goddess, she will judge you.'

Without responding, the king said, 'The law in my kingdom is that anyone who sacrifices or tries to sacrifice a living being to the gods will be exiled. I am sentencing you accordingly. You are exiled for eight years. The guards shall escort you out of my kingdom.'

The guards prepared to lead Raghupati out of the court. 'Stop,' Raghupati told them. Turning to the king, he said, 'My trial has ended, now I shall conduct yours, listen carefully. It is the law of our temple that anyone who goes out during the two nights of the ceremony of the fourteen goddesses shall be sentenced by the priest. According to this ancient law, you are due to be sentenced by me.'

'I am ready for your sentence,' responded the king.

'The sentence cannot involve anything but a financial penalty,' said the courtiers.

'I place a penalty of two hundred thousand coins on you,' said the priest. 'It must be paid at once.'

After some thought, the king said, 'So be it.' Summoning the treasurer, he ordered that two hundred thousand coins be fetched. The guards escorted Raghupati out.

When the priest had left, the king turned to Nakshatraray and asked firmly, 'Do you admit your misdemeanour, Nakshatraray?'

'I am guilty, maharaj,' said Nakshatraray. 'Pardon me.'

Running up, he clutched the king's feet.

Perturbed, the king could not speak for some time. Restraining himself, he finally said, 'Rise, Nakshatraray, listen to what I have to say. Who am I to pardon you? I am bound by my own laws. The judge is a prisoner, too. How can I punish one person but pardon another when both have committed the same crime? You be the judge.'

'Nakshatraray is your brother, maharaj,' exclaimed the courtiers, 'you must pardon him.'

'Be quiet, all of you,' said the king in a determined voice. 'As long as I am on this seat, I am no one's brother, no one's friend.'

The courtiers quietened down. The court fell silent. The king said with authority, 'All of you have heard that the law in my kingdom prescribes exile for anyone who sacrifices—or tries to sacrifice—living beings to the gods. Last evening Nakshatraray conspired with the priest to abduct a child with the intention of performing human sacrifice. This crime having been proven, I sentence him to eight years in exile.'

As the guards prepared to take Nakshatraray away, the king got rose from his seat and embraced Nakshatraray. In a choking voice, he said, 'It is not you alone, my brother, this sentence is mine too. I do not know what sins I committed in my past life. May the gods be with you all the time you are away from your friends, may they ensure your well-being.'

The news spread in an instant. Wails were heard in the ladies' chambers. The king locked himself in a private room. Joining his palms in reverence, he said, 'If I ever sin, do not pardon me, lord, do not show me the slightest mercy. Punish me for my sin. It is possible to endure punishment for wrongdoing, but it is not possible to endure the weight of clemency, lord.'

The king's love for Nakshatraray swelled. He recalled his brother's face as a child. All of Nakshatraray's games, his speech, his exploits rose one after the other in the king's mind. Every day and every night from the past brought an image of the child Nakshatraray amidst the sunlight and the star-studded sky of the days gone by. Tears streamed from the king's eyes.

19

When the guards asked Raghupati, who was about to be banished from the kingdom, 'Which way would you like to go, thakur?' he answered, 'To the west.'

After travelling westwards for nine days, the prisoner and his guards arrived near the city of Dhaka. Here the guards released their prisoner and returned to the capital.

'The Brahmin's curse has lost its power in the Kali Yug,' Raghupati told himself, 'but let us examine what the Brahmin's guile can achieve. We shall see how powerful Govindamanikya is as a king, and I as a priest.'

News of the Mughal Empire did not usually reach the corner of a temple at one extremity of Tripura. Now that he was in the city of Dhaka, Raghupati became curious about the politics and the state of the Mughals.

It was the reign of the Mughal emperor Shah Jahan. His third son Aurangzeb was engaged in attacking Bijapur in the south. His second son Suja was the ruler of Bengal, with Rajmahal as his capital. The youngest son, Prince Murad, was the governor of Gujarat. The eldest, Prince Dara, lived in Delhi. The emperor was sixty-seven. Since he was not well, the responsibility for running the state had fallen on Dara.

Raghupati lived in Dhaka for some time, learning Urdu, and then set off for Rajmahal.

When he reached, India was in turmoil. The word was that Shah Jahan was on his deathbed. As soon as he heard, Suja had set off for Delhi with his troops. All four of the emperor's sons were preparing to snatch the crown off the ailing Shah Jahan's head.

Leaving the anarchy of Rajmahal, the Brahmin dismissed his entourage and bearers and set off behind Suja. Before leaving, he buried in a remote corner of Rajmahal the two hundred thousand coins he had been carrying, leaving a sign to mark the spot. He took only a little money along. Raghupati made ceaseless progress past burnt-down huts, abandoned villages and trampled-upon fields of crops. He donned the robes of an ascetic, but even in this dress, it was hard to get hospitality from anyone. Famine raged on either side of the road along which the soldiers had passed like locusts. They had taken the unripe harvest for their horses and elephants. Not a grain was left in the farmers' bins. The chaotic aftermath of the looting was all that could be seen. Almost everyone had abandoned their villages. The one or two people he chanced upon didn't look happy. Like startled fawns, they were wary, trusting no one, sparing no one. They sat in groups of three or four with their sticks beneath the trees by the road, waiting all day to hunt passers-by. Like the meteors that trail a comet, bandits followed the soldiers to rob whatever they left untouched. Sometimes, like canines, the troops and bandits even fought over corpses. Cruelty was a game for the soldiers—they considered it a mere joke to casually plunge the tips of their swords into the stomach of an innocent passer-by or to slice off a portion of their skull along with their headgear. They were vastly amused when they found the villagers frightened of them. After looting, they took pleasure in terrorizing the people. Making two eminent Brahmins stand back to back, they tied the traditional tufts of hair on their scalps together and stuffed snuff up their noses. Putting one man astride two horses, they whipped the horses, who promptly raced off in different directions, making their rider fall and break his limbs. They invented new games like these every day. Without provocation they burnt down entire villages, claiming to be setting off fireworks in honour of the emperor.

Hundreds of signs of such cruelty were visible in their wake. How could Raghupati expect hospitality here? His days passed either in starvation or on mere morsels. One night he had rested his exhausted body in a rundown, derelict hut. When he awoke in the morning he discovered that he had used a headless corpse as his pillow all night. One afternoon Raghupati arrived at a hut, famished, and found a man sprawled on his shattered iron safe—perhaps mourning his plundered riches. When Raghupati tried to shake him awake, the man slumped to the floor. Merely a dead body, whose life had left it a long while ago.

He was lying in a hut one night. The darkness had not been dispelled, for morning was still some time away. Suddenly the door opened slowly. Along with the autumn moon, several shadows entered. Startled by their whispers, Raghupati sat up.

At once a number of female voices said in fear, 'O maa! Goodness!' Advancing, one of the men said, 'Kaun hai re? Who is it?'

'I am a Brahmin, a traveller,' answered Raghupati. 'Who are you?'

'This is our home. We had abandoned it. We came back when we heard that the Mughal soldiers have left.'

'Which way did the Mughal soldiers go?' asked Raghupati.

'Towards Bijoygarh,' they answered. 'They must have entered the forests of Bijoygarh by now.'

Raghupati set off at once, without prolonging the conversation.

20

The extended forests of Bijoygarh was a den of thuggees. Innumerable human skeletons were buried on either side of the path that ran through the jungle. Wild flowers bloomed on them, and there was no sign of the existence of the skeletons. There were banyans and acacia and margosa, tendrils and vines in hundreds of varieties. Small ponds or lakes were visible here and there, the water turned green by constantly rotting leaves. Narrow trails snaked through the dark jungle. The branches were occupied by hordes of monkeys. Scores of roots hung from the branches of the banyan trees, along with the tails of monkeys. The shiuli tree in the courtyard of the derelict temple was smothered in white flowers, while the bared teeth of the monkeys shone everywhere. The squawking of flocks of parrots on the shaggy tops of the large trees ripped apart the dense blackness of the night. Nearly twenty thousand soldiers had entered this enormous forest tonight. The huge, circular jungle, entangled in branches and leaves and vines and tendrils, had begun to resemble a collective nest for twenty thousand sharp-beaked military hawks. A multitude of crows had risen cawing into the air at the sight of this gathering of soldiers—they didn't dare perch on the branches. The general had forbidden any sort of noise. Having marched all day, the soldiers had gathered dry wood to cook their meals and were whispering amongst themselves—the hum of their conversations reverberating across the entire jungle, so that not even the crickets could be heard. The horses tethered to the tree trunks stamped their feet from time to time, neighing and startling everyone. Shah Suja had set up camp in the clearing near the dilapidated temple. Everyone else would sleep beneath the trees tonight.

It was night by the time Raghupati entered the forest after travelling all day. Most of the soldiers were fast asleep, with only a few keeping watch in silence. Fires burnt here and there—as though the darkness had opened its sleepy reddened eyes with great effort. As soon as he stepped into the forest, Raghupati seemed to hear twenty thousand soldiers breathing. The innumerable trees and branches in the forest had spread themselves out to protect everyone. Like the screech owl that unfurls its wings over its young one, the enormous night beyond the forest was also sitting in silence with its wings wrapped around the deeper night within—while one night slept inside the jungle with its head tucked in, another one outside was wide awake, its head erect. Raghupati spent the night at the edge of the forest.

Prodded into wakefulness in the morning, he sat up with a start to discover several Turkish soldiers with flowing beards and turbans telling him something in a foreign language. Invectives, he assumed, and proceeded to explain their miserable standing in the world to them in the Bengali language. They began to tug at him.

'Is this a joke?' said Raghupati, but their behaviour betrayed no sign of levity. They began to drag him mercilessly through the forest.

Expressing considerable dissatisfaction, he said, 'Why are you dragging me along? I shall go on my own. What did I travel all this way for?'

The soldiers began to laugh and copy his accent. Gradually a crowd gathered around him, and an uproar ensued. He was heckled and harassed continuously. One of the soldiers grabbed a squirrel by its tail and let it loose on Raghupati's shaven scalp, desirous of learning whether it mistook the head for a fruit and tried to consume it. Another one pulled back one end of a thick strip of bamboo, holding it in front of Raghupati's nose as he walked alongside. If he let go, the lofty glory of Raghupati's nose was likely to be exterminated along with its foundations. The laughter of the soldiers rang in his ears. Since they would have to join the battle at noon, Raghupati became the subject of their sport. Only after their appetite for amusement had been sated did they take him to Suja's tent.

Raghupati did not offer a salaam to Suja. He never bowed his head before anyone but the gods and his own caste. He stood with his head held high, raising his arm and saying, 'Long live the shahenshah.'

Suja sat with a goblet of wine, surrounded by his courtiers. In a lazy, negligent tone he said, 'What is it?'

'An enemy spy was here to gauge the strength of our numbers, janab,' said the soldiers. 'We have captured him and brought him to the lord.'

'Oh all right,' said Suja. 'The poor fellow's here for a survey, show him everything properly and release him. Let him go home and tell stories about us.'

'I seek employment under the governor,' said Raghupati in broken Hindustani.

Suja waved him away indolently. 'Hot,' he said, whereupon the man fanning him doubled his speed.

Dara had sent his son Suleiman, under King Jaysingh, to repel Suja's attack. There was information that their huge forces had arrived nearby. Hence Suja was anxious to take possession of Bijoygarh Fort and consolidate his army there. A messenger had been despatched to Vikramsingh, the ruler of Bijoygarh, to surrender his fort, along with taxes due, to Suja. Vikramsingh had sent a message back through the herald: 'I acknowledge nobody but Shah Jahan, emperor of Delhi, and Bhabanipati, the lord of the universe. I do not know who Suja is.'

'How insolent,' slurred Suja. 'Now we have to go to war again. So much trouble!'

Raghupati overheard all this. The moment he escaped the hands of the soldiers, he set off for Bijoygarh.

21

Bijoygarh was situated on a hill. The forest had ended near the fort. Emerging from the jungle, Raghupati saw the tall stone fort leaning against the blue sky. Just as the forest was defined by its network of thousands of trees, the fort was identified by its own stone walls. The forest was cautious, the fort was alert. The forest crouched like a tiger, its tail curled, while the fort stood like a lion with a flowing mane, its neck arched. The forest listened closely with its ear to the ground, the fort watched with its eyes raised skyward.

The soldiers on the ramparts of the fort were startled when Raghupati emerged from the forest. The horn was played to signal a warning. The fort seemed to roar like a lion, suddenly baring its claws and teeth and frowning. Raghupati raised his sacred thread to draw attention to it. The soldiers waited warily. When Raghupati was near the walls of the fort, they asked, 'Who are you?'

'A Brahmin, your guest,' answered Raghupati.

The castellan, Vikramsingh, was a devout man, well disposed towards serving the gods, Brahmins, and guests. A sacred thread was all the identity required to enter the fort. But the soldiers were not sure how to respond on a day they were at war.

'If you do not give me shelter I shall have to die at the hands of Muslims,' said Raghupati.

When Vikramsingh heard this, he gave permission to grant Raghupati refuge within the fort. A ladder was lowered from the ramparts for Raghupati to enter.

Everyone inside the fort was busy preparing for the battle. The aged Khurra sahib took it upon himself to welcome the Brahmin. His name was actually Kharagsingh, but he was variously referred to as Khurra sahib and subedar sahib, without any particular reason. He didn't have a single nephew in the whole world, not even a brother—he had neither the right nor the distant possibility of becoming a khurra—uncle—to anyone. And he had no more subahs—provinces—than he had nephews, but till date no one had objected to, or been suspicious of, the title bestowed on him. Those who were uncles without having nephews or subedars without possessing subahs were not tied down by the inconstancy of the world and the fickleness of wealth. They had no fear of demotion.

When Khurra sahib appeared, he said, 'Wonderful, this is a Brahmin indeed,' touching Raghupati's feet reverently. Raghupati had the appearance of a spirited flame, the sudden sight of which captivated moths.

Saddened by the woeful state of the world, Khurra sahib said, 'How many genuine Brahmins do you see nowadays, thakur?'

'Very few,' agreed Raghupati.

'Brahmins spouted fire earlier,' remarked Khurra sahib, 'but the only fire that rages in them now is the fire of hunger.'

'Even that isn't as strong now,' said Raghupati.

'Correct,' nodded Khurra sahib. 'If Agastya had eaten to the same extent that he drank, can you imagine what would have happened?'

'There are other instances too,' Raghupati told him.

Khurra sahib agreed, 'Of course there are. We have heard of

Jahnu's thirst. His appetite has not been written about, but one can hazard a guess. That he ate nothing but tiny fruits does not automatically make him a frugal eater—an account of just how many of them he consumed every day would have made things clearer.'

Recalling the greatness of Brahmins, Raghupati said gravely, 'No, sahib, they were not particularly interested in food.'

'Oh but what are you saying, thakur?' said Khurra sahib, clicking his tongue in disagreement. 'There is plenty of evidence to prove that the fires in their bellies raged strongly. See for yourself, all other fires have died out over time—even the sacrificial fire is not to be seen burning anymore, but . . .'

Slightly disappointed, Raghupati said, 'How do you expect the sacrificial fires to burn? Where's the ghee? The heathens are exporting all the cows, where is one to get ghee now? And how long will the power of the Brahmin survive if the sacrificial fires are not lit?'

Raghupati felt his own concealed flammability keenly.

'Right you are, thakur,' said Khurra sahib. 'The cows have begun to die and be reborn as people, who cannot be expected to provide ghee, since they have no milk of human kindness. Where are you coming from, thakur?'

'From the royal palace of Tripura,' answered Raghupati.

Khurra sahib knew little about the history or geography beyond Bijoygarh. He did not even believe that anything in India besides Bijoygarh was worth knowing about. On the basis of complete guesswork, he said, 'Oh, the king of Tripura is great.'

Raghupati endorsed this completely.

'What do you do, thakur?' asked Khurra sahib.

'I am the royal priest of Tripura,' answered Raghupati.

'Ah!' declared Khurra sahib, closing his eyes and nodding intensely. His respect for Raghupati grew inordinately.

'And the purpose of your visit?'

'A pilgrimage,' said Raghupati.

An explosion was heard. The enemy had attacked the fort. Smiling and winking, Khurra sahib said, 'It's nothing, they're throwing pebbles.' The stone walls of Bijoygarh were not as firm as Khurra sahib's faith in them. Whenever a foreign traveller visited the fort, Khurra sahib claimed his time entirely, instilling the greatness of Bijoygarh in his mind. Raghupati was here from the royal palace of Tripura—the sort of guest who did not visit frequently. Khurra sahib was in high spirits as he discussed the origins of Bijoygarh with the stranger. There could be no doubt, he claimed, that Brahma's egg, the Brahmanda, and the Bijoygarh fort had come into existence at almost the same time, and that King Vikramsingh's ancestors had occupied the fort directly from the era of Manu, the first man. Raghupati wasn't kept in the dark about the boon granted to this fort by Shiva, and how the mythical Kartavirjarjuna was imprisoned here.

In the evening, news came that the enemy had not been able to inflict damages on the fort. They had fired their cannons, but the cannonballs had not even travelled as far as the ramparts. Khurra sahib glanced at Raghupati with a smile. Its implication—what more obvious proof could there be of Shiva's infallible boon to the fort? Nandi himself must have arrived to intercept the cannonballs in mid-air for Ganapati and Kartikeya to play marbles with in Kailash.

22

Raghupati's intention was to enlist Shah Suja's attention somehow. When he heard that Suja was intent on attacking the fort, he decided that entering the fort as an ally would enable him to help Suja's assault. But, completely unused as he was to warfare, the Brahmin simply could not fathom how he could come to Suja's aid.

The battle was resumed the next day. The opponents used their gunpowder to destroy a portion of the ramparts, but because of continuous firing from the defenders they could not storm the fort. The broken portion was rebuilt quickly. Today cannonballs were falling within the fort now and then, killing and injuring a soldier or two.

'Don't be frightened, thakur, this is just a game,' said Khurra sahib, conducting Raghupati around the fort and showing him the location of the armoury, the stores, the medical centre for treating the injured, the jail, the court, and everything else, all the while glancing at his face to gauge his reaction. Raghupati said, 'Marvellous arrangements. Tripura's fort cannot match this one. But, sahib, there is a miraculous tunnel to escape in secret from the Tripura fort, which I don't see here.'

About to say something in response, Khurra sahib restrained himself suddenly and said, 'No, we have nothing like that here.'

Expressing utter surprise, Raghupati said, 'How is it possible that a fort as large as this one has no tunnel?'

Stricken, Khurra sahib said, 'How can there not be one? I'm sure there is—just that we don't know.'

With a laugh, Raghupati said, 'Then it's as good as not having one. If you don't know, no one else possibly can.'

Khurra sahib maintained a grave silence for some time before yawning suddenly, snapping his fingers in front of his open mouth and invoking the names of the gods. Running his hands over his moustache and beard, he said, 'You are a man of god, thakur, there's no harm telling you—there are indeed two secret paths to enter and exit the fort, but it is forbidden to show them to outsiders.'

'Indeed?' said Raghupati sceptically. 'If you say so.'

Khurra sahib realized that it was his own fault. Denying the existence of a secret tunnel and then confirming it was bound to make people sceptical. It was intolerable for Khurra sahib that Bijoygarh should in some way be demeaned by the fort at Tripura.

'I imagine your Tripura is quite far away, thakur,' he said, 'and you are a Brahmin, whose only occupation is serving the gods. You aren't likely to disclose anything.'

'Never mind, sahib, don't tell me anything if you're unsure,' said Raghupati. 'I'm a mere Brahmin—what need do I have of information about the fort?'

Clucking remorsefully, Khurra sahib said, 'Oh no, how could I possibly doubt you? Come with me, let me show you.'

Meanwhile, there was sudden pandemonium amongst Suja's soldiers. Suleiman and Jaysingh's troops had arrived in the forest unexpectedly and taken Suja prisoner from his camp. Unseen by anyone, they were now in the midst of the soldiers invading the fort. Instead of joining battle with them, Suja's soldiers abandoned their twenty cannons and scattered.

Celebrations began in the fort. As soon as Suleiman's messenger arrived in Vikramsingh's presence, the latter opened the doors to the fort—walking out to welcome Suleiman and King Jaysingh personally. The fort was filled with the soldiers, horses and elephants belonging to the emperor of Delhi. Their flag began to flutter, horns and martial instruments began to be played, and Khurra sahib's smile beneath his white moustache widened.

23

It was such a joyous day for Khurra sahib! The Rajput soldiers of the emperor of Delhi were guests at Bijoygarh today. The redoubtable Shah Suja was a prisoner of Bijoygarh. There hadn't been a prisoner so illustrious since Kartavirjarjuna. Sighing at his recollection of the imprisonment of Kartavirjarjuna, Khurra sahib told Suchetasingh the Rajput, 'Cast your mind back to the effort involved in putting chains on those one thousand arms. Pomp and ceremony is dead in the Kali Yug. Whether it's a king's son or a badshah's, you won't find more than two arms even if you comb the world. It's no fun putting them in chains anymore.'

Looking at his own arms, Suchetasingh said with a smile, 'These two are enough.'

After a little thought, Khurra sahib said, 'That's true, there were so many more responsibilities in those days. But responsibilities have dwindled so much now that even two hands cannot be accounted for. Any more hands and they would have to be used to stroke one's moustache.'

Khurra sahib was dressed flawlessly today. Parting his white beard below his chin, he had wound the ends of each half around his ears. His moustaches had been twirled to the proximity of his earlobes. His turban was set at a rakish angle on his head, and a curved sword adorned his waist. The tips of his embroidered shoes were curled backwards like animal horns. Khurra sahib was strutting about today as though the greatness of Bijoygarh was coursing though him. The sheer joy at the importance of Bijoygarh being demonstrated to all these veterans of war had robbed him of sleep and hunger.

Khurra sahib spent almost the entire day inspecting the fort along with Suchetasingh. Whenever Khurra sahib's companion did not express wonder, he personally tried to stir the valiant Rajput's heart with exclamations of praise. He had to toil greatly to explain the construction of the ramparts in particular. Suchetasingh was as unmoved as the walls themselves—his expression betraying no emotion whatsoever. Khurra sahib took him all over, to the left and to the right, upstairs and downstairs, repeating, 'Superb!' But still he couldn't occupy the fort of Suchetasingh's heart. Eventually an exhausted Suchetasingh said in the evening, 'I've seen the fort of Bharatpur, other forts do not appeal to me.'

Khurra sahib never argued with anyone. Downcast, he said, 'Of course, of course. You could indeed say that.'

Sighing, he abandoned the discussion about forts and brought up the subject of Vikramsingh's forefather Durgasingh. 'Durgasingh had three sons,' he said. 'The youngest, Chitrasingh, had an unusual habit. Every morning he would eat about half a seer of chickpeas boiled in milk. He had a powerful physique too. Tell me, this Bharatpur fort that you're talking about, it must be a very big fort, of course—but the Brahma Vaivarta Purana makes no mention of it.'

With a smile, Suchetasingh said, 'Is that a problem?'

Khurra sahib laughed woodenly. 'Ha ha ha. That's true, that's true. But then, while the fort at Tripura isn't small either, Bijoygarh . . .'

'Where on earth is Tripura?' asked Suchetasingh.

Khurra sahib answered, 'It's a famous kingdom. But why ask me, the royal priest of the kingdom is a guest at our fort, you can hear all the details from him.'

But the Brahmin could not be located anywhere. Khurra sahib's heart began to weep for him. 'He's much better than these rustic Rajputs.' He praised Raghupati to the heavens for Suchetasingh's benefit, even expressing Raghupati's views on Bijoygarh.

24

Suchetasingh did not have to try much harder to escape Khurra sahib. The emperor's army was scheduled to leave the next morning along with the prisoners. The soldiers began to prepare for the journey.

In the dungeon, a thoroughly displeased Shah Suja was telling himself, 'How impertinent these people are. They did not even remember to bring me my hookah from my tent.'

There was a deep canal at the base of the hill on which Bijoygarh was situated. On one of its banks was the trunk of a banyan tree felled by lightning. Raghupati sank into the earth near this tree trunk late at night, disappearing from view.

The tunnel leading to the secret entrance to the fort ran beneath the canal. Pushing hard on a particular rock at the end of the tunnel made it swing open upwards—but it could not be moved from within the fort. Therefore those within the fort could not escape through this route.

Suja was asleep on a bed in the dungeon. There was no other furniture in the chamber besides the bed. A lamp was lit. Suddenly an opening appeared in the floor. Raghupati emerged slowly from it. He was drenched, water dripping from his wet garments. He touched Suja softly.

Startled awake, Suja sat rubbing his eyes for a while, and then said lethargically, 'What kind of torment is this! Aren't these people going to let me sleep even at night? I am astonished at your behaviour.'

'Please get out of bed, shahzada,' said Raghupati softly. 'I'm the Brahmin who met you. Try to remember. You must remember me in future too.'

The next morning the emperor's soldiers prepared to set off. King Jaysingh personally entered the dungeon to awaken Suja, who, he discovered, was still in bed. Going up to him to shake him awake, he discovered that it was not Suja, but only his clothes. The opening to the tunnel lay uncovered on the floor, the stone slab which normally hid it lying to one side.

News of the prisoner's escape spread across the fort. People ran off in different directions to look for him. King Vikramsingh's head was bowed. The court assembled to analyze the method of escape.

Where had Khurra sahib's imperiously ecstatic expression vanished? He rushed about madly, screaming, 'Where's the priest?

Where's the priest?' The priest was nowhere to be found. Taking his turban off, Khurra sahib clutched his head in despair. Suchetasingh sat down by him, saying, 'What a strange place this is, Khurra sahib. Spirits at work!'

Shaking his head glumly, Khurra sahib said, 'No, this isn't the work of spirits, Suchetasingh, this is the combined handiwork of a rather foolish old man and a treacherous rogue.'

Suchetasingh asked in surprise, 'If you know who they are, why don't you have them arrested?'

'One of them has escaped,' answered Khurra sahib. 'I shall arrest the other one and take him to the court.'

He dressed for an appearance at the royal court, donning his turban.

The testimony of the guards was being recorded. Khurra sahib entered, his head bowed. Placing his sword at Vikramsingh's feet, he said, 'Order my arrest, I am guilty.'

'What's the matter, Khurra sahib?' asked an astonished Vikramsingh.

'The Brahmin! This is the work of the Bengali Brahmin.'

'Who are you?' asked King Jaysingh.

'I am the aged Khurra sahib of Bijoygarh,' answered Khurra sahib.

'What have you done?'

'I have betrayed Bijoygarh by giving away its secret. Like a fool I trusted the Bengali Brahmin and told him about the tunnel . . .'

Flaring up in rage, Vikramsingh shouted, 'Kharagsingh!'

Khurra sahib was startled—he had all but forgotten his name.

'Have you turned into a child again after all these years, Kharagsingh?'

Khurra sahib bowed his head in silence.

'You of all people, Khurra sahib!' exclaimed Vikramsingh. Bijoygarh has been humiliated today because of you.'

Khurra sahib stood in silence, his hands shaking uncontrollably. 'Destiny,' he told himself, touching his forehead with trembling fingers.

'The emperor's enemy has escaped from my fort,' said Vikramsingh. 'Do you know that you have made me guilty in the eyes of the emperor?'

'I am the only guilty one,' said Khurra sahib. 'The emperor will not believe that the king is guilty.'

'You're a nobody,' answered an irked Vikramsingh. 'What does the emperor know of you? You represent me. It's as though I have released the prisoner from his chains with my own hands.'

Khurra sahib had no response. He could not control his tears anymore.

'How shall I punish you?' asked Vikramsingh.

'As the king pleases,' answered Khurra sahib.

'You are an old man,' said, Vikramsingh, 'I cannot punish you harshly. Exile is sufficient.'

Clasping Vikramsingh's legs, Khurra sahib exclaimed, 'Exile from Bijoygarh! No, maharaj, I am an old man, I lost my head. Allow me to die in Bijoygarh. Sentence me to death. Do not drive me away from Bijoygarh like a dog at this age.'

King Jaysingh said, 'Maharaj, pardon him on my special request. I shall inform the emperor of all that has taken place.'

Khurra sahib was pardoned. As he was leaving the court, he collapsed, trembling. Khurra sahib was not to be seen very often after this. He seldom left his chamber. His spine seemed to have been crushed.

25

Gujurpara was a tiny village on the bank of the Brahmaputra. Its lowly zamindar's name was Pitambar Roy; the village was sparsely populated. Ensconced in the ancient village shrine, Pitambar referred to himself as the king. So did his subjects. His majesty extended only as far as the almond and mango trees on the periphery of the little village. Reverberating within the gardens of the village, his glory faded before crossing its borders. The might of the most powerful kings and emperors of the world could not percolate into this sheltered nook. The royal family of Tripura did have a large palace on the bank of the river, constructed for the purpose of holy dips, but it had been a long time since any of the kings had bathed here. So the only impression that the villagers had of the king of Tripura were indistinct and second-hand.

One Bhadra day there was news that a prince of Tripura was

coming to live in the old palace by the river. A few days later, a crowd of men in turbans arrived at the palace and turned the place upside down. Almost a week afterwards, Prince Nakshatraray himself arrived in Gujurpara with an entourage of attendants and guards and elephants and horses. The villagers were dumbfounded at the grandeur of it all. Till now they had considered Pitambar an important king—but not anymore. When they saw Nakshatraray, everyone agreed, 'Yes, this is a prince indeed.'

It was true that Pitambar was obliterated, along with his paved terrace and his shrine, but his joy knew no bounds. He acknowledged Nakshatraray as a king of such repute that he was delirious with joy at sacrificing his own royal glory at the feet of the prince. On the rare occasions that Nakshatraray ventured out on the back of an elephant, Pitambar would summon his subjects to tell them, 'Have you ever seen a king? There he goes.' Pitambar visited Nakshatraray every day with an offering of fish and vegetables—his affections overflowing at the sight of Nakshatraray's comely young appearance. Nakshatraray began to be considered the king of the village, while Pitambar enlisted himself among the subjects.

The band played thrice a day, the horses and elephants marched up and down the village roads, naked swords flashed like lightning at the entrance to the palace, and a veritable carnival began. Pitambar and his subjects were delighted. Crowned king in his exile, Nakshatraray forgot all his woes. He was completely independent here—not even at home had he enjoyed such undisputed power. Besides, Raghupati did not cast a shadow over him here. An elated Nakshatraray immersed himself in pleasures. Actors and musicians arrived from Dhaka—he had not the slightest distaste for music and entertainment.

Nakshatraray adopted all the ceremonial practices of the royal court of Tripura. He dubbed some of his servants ministers, appointed one of them general, and bestowed the title of Dewanji on Pitambar. Formal court sessions were held regularly, with Nakshatraray adjudicating proceedings ceremoniously. 'Mathur called me a dog,' Nakur complained. A trial was held, following all the rules. After sufficient evidence had been collected to prove that Mathur was guilty, Nakshatraray announced the sentence with utter gravity from his throne—Nakur should box Mathur's ears twice. The days passed happily this way. When there was simply no work at hand, the ministers were summoned to invent some outlandish new entertainment. Gathering his advisors and courtiers around himself, Nakshatraray anxiously tried to discover a new game, which involved endless pondering and consultation. One day Pitambar's shrine was attacked by a company of soldiers, his tank plundered of its fish and his gardens of their raw coconuts and spinach, and the loot brought back to the palace with great pomp, to the accompaniment of music. All these games further deepened Pitambar's affection for Nakshatraray.

Today was the day of the kittens' wedding at the palace. Nakshatraray had a kitten, who was to be married to the Mandals' cat. Churomoni the matchmaker had earned a fee of three hundred rupees and a shawl for making the match. The pre-wedding rituals had all been completed. The wedding was to be formalized at an auspicious hour this evening. No one in the palace had had a moment's respite over the past few days.

In the evening the roads were lit up and the orchestra took its position. The groom travelled from the Mandal residence in a palanquin, dressed in silk and mewing hopelessly. The Mandals' youngest son accompanied him as the traditional junior groom, holding the rope fastened around the groom's neck—who finally arrived amidst the blowing of conch shells and ululation.

The priest's name was Kenaram, but Nakshatraray had renamed him Raghupati. Because he was afraid of the real Raghupati, Nakshatraray felt happy when he could toy with the make-believe Raghupati. He tormented him continuously, which the impoverished Kenaram had to endure in silence. By ill-luck Kenaram was absent at court today—his son was dying of a fever.

'Where's Raghupati?' asked Nakshatraray impatiently.

'Illness in his family,' answered the servant.

'Summon him at once,' Nakshatraray commanded twice as loudly.

Someone ran to get him. Meanwhile the singing and dancing continued in the presence of the weeping cat.

'Sahana,' ordered Nakshatraray. The music changed accordingly.

A little later the servant returned to say, 'Raghupati is here.'
'Call him,' roared Nakshatraray.
The priest entered at once. Nakshatraray's frown vanished when he saw him, his expression being transformed completely. His face paled, beads of perspiration appeared on his forehead. The music and drums died down, and only the mewing of the cats sounded doubly loud in the silent room.
It was indeed Raghupati. There could be no doubt. Tall, lean and spirited, his eyes blazed like a starving dog's. Placing his dusty feet on the silk rug, he raised his head. 'Nakshatraray!'
Nakshatraray was silent.
'You sent for Raghupati. I am here,' said Raghupati.
'Thakur . . . thakur,' said Nakshatraray faintly.
'Get up,' ordered Raghupati.
Nakshatraray left the court slowly. The wedding of the cats, the music and the instruments ended permanently.

26

'What was all that?' asked Raghupati.
'Music and dance,' answered Nakshatraray in embarrassment.
Shrinking with loathing, Raghupati exclaimed, 'Shame on you!'
Nakshatraray looked guilty.
'We have to set off tomorrow,' said Raghupati. 'Prepare for the journey.'
'Where do we have to go?' asked Nakshatraray.
'We can discuss that later,' answered Raghupati. 'For now, just accompany me.'
'I am happy here,' Nakshatraray told him.
'Happy here! You have been born into the royal family—your ancestors were all kings. You have chosen to be a make-believe king here in the countryside and you claim to be happy here!'
Raghupati employed prickly sarcasm and sharp rebuke to establish that Nakshatraray was not happy. Nakshatraray came to the same conclusion from the vehemence of Raghupati's statement. 'It's not that I'm particularly happy. But what can I do? What alternative do I have?'

Raghupati said, 'There are plenty of alternatives—no dearth of them. I will show you the way, come with me.'
'Let me consult Dewanji,' pleaded Nakshatraray.
'No.'
'All my things . . .'
'No need.'
'I do not have sufficient money.'
'I do. No more excuses. Go to bed now, we leave at dawn.'
Raghupati left without waiting for a reply.

Nakshatraray awoke early the next morning. The worshippers were singing the Lalit ragini. Going into the outer chamber, Nakshatraray gazed through the window. The sun was rising in the east, and a faint streak of light was visible. The vast expanse of the Brahmaputra flowed unimpeded between the dense green currents of trees on either bank, past the doorways of the sleeping village. A small hut was visible by the river. A woman was sweeping the yard—after a short conversation with her, a man draped himself in a shawl, slung a stick with a bundle hanging at one end over his shoulder, and went out somewhere contentedly. Thrushes and robins whistled, while a singing oriole perched amidst the thick foliage of a large jackfruit tree. As Nakshatraray stood at the window looking out, a deep sigh rose from his heart. Suddenly Raghupati appeared behind him, touching his shoulder. Nakshatraray was startled. 'We are ready for the journey,' said Raghupati softly.

Joining his palms together, Nakshatraray pleaded ardently, 'Excuse me, thakur—I don't want to go anywhere. I am happy here.'

Without a word, Raghupati set his blazing eyes on Nakshatraray. Lowering his eyes, Nakshatraray said, 'Where are we going?'

'I cannot disclose that now,' Raghupati told him.

'I shall not be part of a conspiracy against my brother,' declared Nakshatraray.

Flaring up in anger, Raghupati asked, 'What favour has your brother done for you?'

Looking away and scratching the windowpane, Nakshatra said, 'I know that he loves me.'

With a sharp, acerbic laugh, Raghupati said, 'Such love indeed, by the gods. That must be why your brother banished you from the kingdom on a trumped-up excuse, so that Dhruva could become the crown prince without any impediment. After all, his buttery doll of a brother cannot be allowed to suffer under the severe weight of the realm. Do you expect to re-enter this kingdom easily, you foolish creature?'

'Do you think I don't understand?' said Nakshatraray hastily. 'I understand everything—but what can I do, thakur, what is the alternative?'

'It is the alternative that we are discussing,' said Raghupati. 'That is what I am here for. Come with me if you wish, or else stay here in the bamboo grove and meditate about your well-wisher of a brother. I am leaving.'

Raghupati prepared to depart. Running behind him, Nakshatraray said, 'I shall come along too, thakur, but do you have any objection if Dewanji wishes to accompany us?'

'No one but I shall accompany you,' answered Raghupati.

When they left, Nakshatraray's feet refused to move. Where was he going all alone with Raghupati, away from his pleasurable games and Dewanji? Now Raghupati was dragging him along by his mane. But he felt the beginnings of a mixture of fear and curiosity. It held a powerful attraction for him.

The boat was ready. Arriving at the bank of the river, Nakshatraray found Pitambar approaching for his bath, a towel slung over his shoulder. Pitambar smiled widely when he saw Nakshatra, saying, 'Long live the king. I believe some sinister rogue of a Brahmin appeared to disrupt the wedding last evening.'

Nakshatraray became restive. 'I am the selfsame Brahmin rogue,' thundered Raghupati.

Pitambar laughed, saying, 'Then it was not wise of me to describe you in your presence. Which son of his father would have done such a thing had he known? Please do not take offence, thakur, we say so many things behind people's backs. Those who address me as the king to my face refer to me as Pitu behind my back. As long as they do not say it in my presence, I am happy. The truth is that you look extremely unhappy—whenever people see such expressions they spread canards. And why is the king at the riverside at this hour of the morning?'

Nakshatraray answered pathetically, 'I am leaving, you see, Dewanji.'

'Leaving for which destination?' asked Pitambar. 'Are you going to the Mandals', or to some other place?'

'No, Dewanji, not to the Mandals'. Much further.'

'Much further! To Pikeghata for hunting, then?'

Nakshatraray only threw a glance at Raghupati and shook his head morosely.

'It is getting late, you may board now,' said Raghupati.

Looking at the priest with great suspicion and rage, Pitambar asked, 'Who are you, thakur, to order our king around?'

Quickly drawing Pitambar aside, Nakshatraray said, 'He is our royal priest.'

'So what?' said Pitambar. 'Let him live in our shrine, we will take care of his meals, he will get a warm welcome—what does he need maharaj for?'

'We are wasting time needlessly,' announced Raghupati. 'Let me depart alone in that case.'

Pitambar told him, 'Yes, why delay, you had better leave quickly. I will escort maharaj back to the palace.'

Glancing in turn at Pitambar and Raghupati, Nakshatraray said softly, 'No, Dewanji, I'd better go.'

Pitambar told him, 'Then I shall go too—ask your entourage to join us. Travel like a king. How can a king travel without his prime minister?'

Nakshatraray could only stare at Raghupati. 'No one else will go,' declared Raghupati.

'Look, thakur, you . . .' Pitambar turned aggressive.

Nakshatraray stopped him, saying, 'I'd better go, Dewanji, we're getting late.'

Disappointed, Pitambar took Nakshatraray's hand. 'Look, my son, I address you as the king, but I love you like my own child—I have none of my own. I cannot dictate to you. You are going away, I cannot hold you back by force. But promise me this, whereever you go, you must come back before I die. I will hand over my realm to you personally. This is my only wish.'

Nakshatraray and Raghupati boarded their boat, which sailed southward. His bath forgotten, Pitambar returned home in distraction, his towel still slung over his shoulder. Gujurpara was left bereft—all the ceremonies and entertainment ended. Only the constant celebration of nature, the birdsong in the morning, the murmurs of the leaves and the constant applause of the river currents continued ceaselessly.

27

It was a long journey. Sometimes on the river, sometimes through a dense forest, sometimes over an arid expanse with no shade—in turn by boat, on foot, on a pony—under sun and rain, through noisy days and dark, silent nights—Nakshatraray kept travelling. A variety of lands, of scenes, of people—but, as thin as a shadow and yet as dazzling as the sun, the solitary figure of Raghupati was at Nakshatraray's side constantly. Raghupati was present by day, by night, even in his dreams. Pedestrians passed by on the road, little boys played in the dirt, hundreds of people bought and sold things in the marketplace, the old men played dice, the women fetched water from the river, the boatmen sang as they floated along the currents—but the emaciated frame of Raghupati was constantly awake next to Nakshatraray. Strange games were played everywhere, strange events took place—but Nakshatraray's destiny led him on inexorably through all the acts on this stage. For him the familiar was an unknown land, and habitation, a desert.

Exhausted, Nakshatraray asked the shadow by his side, 'How much further?'

'A long way,' answered the shadow.

'Where are we going?'

No answer. Sighing, Nakshatraray kept moving. Whenever he spotted a neat little cottage thatched with leaves, standing in the shade amidst the trees, he thought, 'If only I were the one living there.' When the cowherd with his stick shepherded his flock at twilight, their hooves kicking up dust from the fields, Nakshatraray thought, 'If only I could go along with him and rest in his home in the evening.' Spotting the farmer tilling the land under the merciless noonday sun, Nakshatraray thought, 'Oh how happy he is.'

Worn out and withered by the travails of the journey, Nakshatraray told Raghupati, 'I'm dying, thakur.'

'Who's letting you die now?' said Raghupati.

Nakshatraray felt that he could not even die unless Raghupati permitted him to. A woman had said on catching sight of him, 'Oh poor thing, where's his family? Who has forced him to travel?' Nakshatraray's heart melted, tears sprang to his eyes, he wished he could address her as 'Ma' and go home with her.

But the more Nakshatraray was tormented by Raghupati the more subservient he became to him. His entire existence began to be controlled by Raghupati's desires.

The river narrowed as they journeyed onward. Gradually the soil looked harder, turning red and strewn with rocks. Human habitations appeared few and far between, vegetation was rare. Leaving behind the land of coconut trees, the two travellers arrived in the territory of palm trees. Large embankments, dried river channels, and mountains resembling clouds appeared in the distance. They were approaching Rajmahal, Shah Suja's capital.

28

Finally they arrived in the capital. Suja was engaged in rebuilding his army after his defeat and escape. But the treasury was not full. The subjects were groaning under the burden of taxes. Meanwhile, Aurangzeb had ascended the throne of Delhi after defeating and killing Dara. Suja was exceedingly perturbed at this news. But since his army was not ready, he sent a messenger to Aurangzeb in the hope of buying some time. His message: the fact that the light of his eyes, the joy of his heart, the object of his affection, his favourite brother Aurangzeb, had been successful in gaining the throne had breathed new life into Suja's corpse—now his cup of joy would overflow if only the new emperor gave Suja the responsibility for ruling Bengal. Aurangzeb accorded the messenger a warm welcome. Expressing his special eagerness to learn of the state of Suja's health—both in body and in soul—and of the well-being of Suja's family, Aurangzeb said, 'Since Emperor Shah Jahan himself had engaged Suja to govern Bengal, no second letter of approval is necessary.' Meanwhile, Raghupati arrived at Suja's court.

Suja welcomed his benefactor who had enabled him to escape, with gratitude and warmth. 'What news?' he asked.

'I have a prayer to make of the badshah,' said Raghupati.

Prayer? Suja wondered. What prayer? I hope he's not going to ask for money.

'My prayer is that . . .' Raghupati said.

'I shall definitely fulfil your prayer,' said Suja. 'But wait a while. There is not enough money in the treasury.'

'I do not seek gold or silver or precious metals, shahenshah,' answered Raghupati, 'I need sharpened steel. Listen to my grievance, I seek justice.'

'That's a problem,' said Suja. 'This is not the time for me to dispense justice. You are here at the wrong moment, Brahmin.'

Raghupati replied, 'Right and wrong moments exist for everyone, shahzada. For you, the badshah, as well as for me, the impoverished Brahmin. If you intend to wait for the right moment to dispense justice, how will I get justice in good time?'

Giving up, Suja said, 'Most upsetting. It is easier to entertain your grievance than to have to listen to all this. Tell me.'

Raghupati began, 'Govindamanikya, the king of Tripura, has sent his younger brother Nakshatraray into exile without his being guilty of any crime . . .'

Annoyed, Suja said, 'Why are you wasting my time with someone else's grievance, Brahmin? This is not the time to consider all this.'

'The plaintiff is present in the capital,' said Raghupati.

'We shall consider the case when he presents himself and states his grievance personally,' said Suja.

'When should I present him at court?' asked Raghupati.

'This man is relentless,' observed Suja. 'Very well, present him one week from now.'

'If the badshah so desires I shall present him tomorrow,' responded Raghupati.

'All right, bring him tomorrow,' said an irritated Suja.

Suja earned himself a day's respite. Raghupati left.

'What do I take as an offering for the nawab?' asked Nakshatraray.

'Don't concern yourself about that,' answered Raghupati. He presented one-and-a-half lakh rupees for the royal offering.

Raghupati arrived with a tremulous-hearted Nakshatraray at Suja's court the next morning. When the one-and-a-half lakh rupees were placed at the nawab's feet, his expression no longer seemed as unpleasant. He comprehended Nakshatraray's grievance quite effortlessly. 'Tell me what your intentions are,' he said.

'Let a command be issued exiling Govindamanikya from the kingdom and installing Nakshatraray as the king in his place,' said Raghupati.

Although Suja did not shrink in the least from setting his sights on his brother's throne, he felt qualms in this case. But fulfilling Raghupati's request appeared to be the easiest course of action for now—else the priest would bully him, he feared. Moreover, he considered it unbefitting to object after the gift of one-and-a-half lakh rupees. 'Very well,' he said, 'I shall issue a warrant declaring exile for Govindamanikya and coronation for Nakshatraray. You may take it with yourselves.'

'We will need some of the badshah's soldiers too,' declared Raghupati.

'No, no, no, that's impossible,' announced Suja firmly. 'I cannot go to war.'

'I am depositing an additional thirty-six thousand rupees to pay for the expenses of warfare,' said Raghupati. 'And as soon as Nakshatraray is coronated in Tripura, I shall send a year's taxes through the general.'

This proposal appeared entirely fair to Suja, and his courtiers agreed. Raghupati and Nakshatraray set off for Tripura with a company of Mughal soldiers.

29

Two years had passed since this story began. Dhruva was two years old then, he was four now. He had learnt many new words. He considered himself a very important person now; although he could not articulate everything clearly, he spoke with extreme conviction. He frequently enticed and comforted the king with promises of 'I shall give you a doll', and whenever the king displayed signs of naughtiness, he terrified him with threats of 'I shall lock you in your room'. Thus the king was under a strongly disciplinary regime—he did not dare take a single step without seeking Dhruva's opinion.

Meanwhile Dhruva suddenly gained a companion. The daughter of a neighbour—six months younger than he was. Within ten minutes they became lifelong friends. The possibility of falling out had cropped up too. Dhruva had a large sugar drop in his hand. In the first flush of love, he carefully broke off a small piece with two fingers and put in his companion's mouth, nodding with great kindness and saying, 'Eat.' Pleased with the sweet taste, she said, 'Want more.'

At this Dhruva felt somewhat beleaguered. Such excessive demands on friendship did not seem justified. With his usual superiority and gravity, he shook his head, widened his eyes and said, 'No more. Will fall thick. Ma beath you.' Without further delay he transferred the rest of the confectionery into his own mouth and consumed it completely. The little girl's facial muscles changed shape suddenly—her lips began to pout, her eyebrows began to dance, and every sign of imminent weeping became apparent.

Dhruva could not bear to see anyone cry. So he offered deep consolation at once. 'More tomorrow.'

As soon as the king arrived, Dhruva indicated his new companion knowledgeably, saying, 'Don't scold, will cry. No, mustn't beath, no.'

While it was true that the king had no evil motive, Dhruva still considered it necessary to take the initiative and warn him. The king did not beat the girl up, and Dhruva clearly saw that his advice had not gone to waste.

After which he put on a patronizing air and proceeded to assure the little girl with utter solemnity that there was nothing to fear.

Not that the assurances were remotely necessary. For the girl went up to the king fearlessly without being prompted, turning the bracelet on his arm round and round and inspecting it curiously and covetously.

Having established peace and love on earth in this manner with purely his own efforts, Dhruva raised his face, as plump and pure and tender as a flower, to the king—a reward for his good behaviour. The king kissed him.

Holding his companion's face up to the king, Dhruva told her in a tone halfway between permission and request, 'Kiss her too.'

The king did not dare disobey Dhruva. Without waiting for an invitation, the girl climbed into the king's lap with practised ease and no change in expression.

There had been no unrest or disorderliness in the world all this while, but as soon as Dhruva's throne came under attack, his universal love became shaky. He concentrated on proving his exclusive claim over the king's lap. His face fell, he tugged at the little girl once or twice, and no longer considered it particularly wrong to beat her in order to secure his position.

With a view to engineering a truce, the king drew Dhruva to the other half of his lap. But this did not dispel Dhruva's objections, and he now mounted a fresh assault against the unlawful occupation. At this point Bilwan, the new royal priest, entered.

Letting both the children down from his lap, the king greeted the priest with reverence. 'Pay your respects to thakur,' he told Dhruva, who did not consider it necessary, adopting a rebellious stance with his thumb in his mouth. The little girl followed the king in showing her reverence.

Drawing Dhruva close, Bilwan asked, 'Where did you find this new friend?'

After some thought, Dhruva said, 'Want to go clipclop.' He was desirous of riding a pony.

'Wonderfully relevant answer to my question,' remarked the priest.

Suddenly Dhruva's attention was drawn to the little girl, whereupon he expressed his opinion and intent succinctly. 'Naughty. Will beath her.'

He punched the sky.

'Very bad, Dhruva,' said the king solemnly.

Dhruva's face fell at once, like a lamp blown out with a puff of breath. At first he began to rub his eyes with his fist to prevent himself from crying; but his tiny, swollen heart could not stand it anymore, and he burst into tears.

Bilwan played with him, scooping him up in his arms, tossing him in the air, setting him down, not letting him be; loudly and quickly he said, 'Listen, Dhruva, let me tell you an incantation . . .

Quarrel quarelong quasi questing
Cotton keaton quitting qumating

That is to say, little boys who weep must be put inside a quarelong and given a taste of quasi questing, followed by cotton keaton with three continuous days of quitting qumating.'

The priest spouted nonsense continuously. Dhruva's tears vanished even before they could be shed completely. Interrupted and surprised by the commotion, he raised his tearful eyes towards Bilwan first. Then, the sight of the priest gesticulating and bobbing his head up and down amused him greatly.

Very pleased, he said, 'Say it again.'

The priest continued with his made-up rhymes. Laughing uproariously, Dhruva said, 'Again.'

The king planted kisses repeatedly on Dhruva's tear-soaked cheeks and smiling lips. The priest, the two children and the king began to play.

Bilwan told the king, 'Maharaj is lucky to be able to spend all his time with children. The company of intelligent people dulls the brain. Honing the knife constantly makes the edge so sharp that the blade vanishes eventually, leaving behind only the butt.'

Smiling, the king said, 'I assume you have observed no signs of my sharp intelligence yet.'

'None,' agreed Bilwan. 'One of the symptoms of a sharp intelligence is that it makes simple things complex. The world would have progressed much more smoothly without the abundance of brainy people in it. In trying to make things easier, they end up making them much more difficult. They cannot determine what to do with their excessive intelligence.'

'Five fingers are enough,' said the king, 'but if by misfortune you are endowed with seven, you have to add to your tasks.'

The king called Dhruva, who had resumed peaceful relations with his companion and was playing with her. Hearing the king, he abandoned the game at once and ran up.

Making the boy sit down in front of him, the king said, 'Sing that new song for thakur, Dhruva.' But Dhruva stared unwillingly at the priest.

The king enticed him, 'You can go clipclop.'

Dhruva lisped . . .

I am lost at every step
For each one wants to guide me
So many seers, so many paths
Only doubt can find me

I wish I could go to you
Your words would clear my qualms
A hundred people with a hundred voices
All of them confuse me

I look for you with sinking heart
They shield me from your sight
My feet just walk the dusty plains
But your feet elude me

My broken bits go different ways
They quarrel and they bicker
Which of them shall I quieten
There are so many of me

Make me whole in bonds of love
Show me one path now
In this maze I weep and die
Your feet are the place for me

Bilwan melted when he heard Dhruva recite the verses in his childlike diction. 'May you live forever,' he said.

'Once more,' he pleaded, picking Dhruva up in his arms.

Dhruva refused firmly and silently. Covering his own eyes, the priest said, 'Then I'll cry.'

A trifle disturbed, Dhruva said, 'Tomorrow. Don't cry. Go home. Baba will beath you.'

'Such a sweet kick,' laughed Bilwan.

Taking his leave, the priest left.

A pair of pedestrians went past, one telling the other, 'I've been knocking my head against his door for three days now, haven't got a rupee out of him. The next time he comes out I'll break his head, let's see if that helps.'

'That won't help either,' said Bilwan from the back. 'You can see very well that the head is nothing but a den of mischief. Break your own head instead, at least you won't have to offer justification to anyone.'

Taken aback, the pedestrians greeted the priest with reverence. 'What you were saying was not nice, my friends,' Bilwan said.

'Yes, thakur,' they agreed. 'We won't say it again.'

Young boys crowded around the priest on the road. 'Come over this evening,' he told them, 'I will tell you stories.' The boys began to jump for joy. On some evenings Bilwan gathered all the children around himself and told them stories from the Ramayana, the Mahabharata and the Puranas in simple language. Occasionally he even tried to insert a few dull morals, injecting them with humour, but when he saw the yawns turning contagious he let them loose in the garden of the temple. There were hundreds of trees in there. With sky-rending shouts the boys would plunder the trees of their fruits like monkeys—Bilwan watched in amusement.

No one knew where Bilwan came from. He was a Brahmin, but he had forsaken the sacred thread. Having stopped the animal sacrifice, he used a new set of rituals for the worship of the goddess. Although people had expressed their opposition and suspicion at first, they had become used to it now. And the way he spoke charmed everyone. Bilwan went around people's houses, talking to them and asking after them. The medicines he administered to the sick had remarkable results. Everyone sought his counsel in moments of crisis—when he mediated and struck a truce between antagonists or solved someone's problem, no one could overrule him.

30

An unprecedented event took place in Tripura this year. The farms were besieged unexpectedly by hordes of rats from the north. They not only destroyed the crops, but they also ate their way through most of the grain that the farmers had stored at home. There was lamentation all over the kingdom. Soon there was a famine. People survived on fruits gathered from the forests. There was no dearth of forests—and there were plenty of edible plants to be foraged. The meat of animals began to be sold at exorbitant prices. People started hunting and eating wild ox, deer, rabbit, hedgehog, squirrel, boar—even elephant when they could. They ate serpents, and there was no lack of birds. Honey was available in the beehives inside crevices on tree trunks. Damming the river and casting intoxicant leaves into the water made the fish float to the surface, their senses deadened. People caught them and either ate them or dried them for storage. They were still managing to get some food, but there was turmoil in the state. Looting began in some places, and the king's subjects began to display signs of revolt.

'All this is the ill effect of the goddess's curse after the animal sacrifices were stopped.' Bilwan laughed their fears away. 'Brothers Kartik and Ganesha have fallen out in Kailash,' he joked, 'and Ganesha's rats have come to the goddess Tripureshwari of Tripura to complain.' The subjects did not quite consider this a joke. They saw, just as Bilwan had said, the flood of rats arriving in a torrent, destroying the harvest, and disappearing just as swiftly—there was no sign of them three days later. No one was left in any doubt about Bilwan's deep insight. Songs were written about brothers falling out in Kailash, children and beggars began to sing them, and they spread everywhere.

But the antagonism towards the king did not entirely dissipate. On Bilwan's advice, Govindamanikya excused the famine-struck subjects a year of taxes. This had some effect. But still many people escaped to the hilly tracts of Chattagram to avoid the goddess's curse. Even the king himself began to have doubts.

Summoning Bilwan, he said, 'Subjects suffer for the king's sins, thakur. Have I committed a transgression by stopping sacrifices to the goddess? Is this the punishment?'

Bilwan dismissed the possibility. 'Didn't human sacrifice claim more victims than the famine has?'

The king did not answer, but his doubts were not dispelled entirely. His subjects were unhappy with him and suspicious—this had not only hurt him but also forced him to question himself. 'I don't understand,' he said with a sigh.

'Is there any need to understand too much?' asked Bilwan. 'Does it matter whether it is clear or not why these rodents appeared and destroyed the harvest? I shall do no wrong, I shall do what's best for my people—it is enough to be clear about these. After that, the almighty will do his job; he will certainly not justify himself to us.'

'You go from house to house, thakur, toiling all day,' said the king. 'Your reward lies in the good that you achieve, and the joy of this achievement dispels all your doubts. All I do all day and night is perch on the throne with a crown on my head, shouldering the burden of responsibilities—I am envious of you.'

'I am but a part of you, maharaj,' said Bilwan. 'Would I have been able to do my work had you not been on the throne? You and I complete each other.'

Bilwan left, while the king pondered, his crown on his head. 'I have plenty of work,' he told himself, 'but I do none of it. I live in contentment with my worries. That is why I cannot earn my subjects' trust. I am not fit to rule.'

31

Appointed the leader of the Mughal army, Nakshatraray was resting in a tiny village on the way named Tentul. Appearing in front of him in the morning, Raghupati said, 'It it time to go, maharaj, get ready.'

Being addressed as king by Raghupati unexpectedly was most gratifying. Nakshatraray was elated. In his head he ascended the highest throne of Tripura, bringing glory to the court. Happily he said, 'You will never be redundant, thakur. You will have to be present at court. Just tell me what you want.' Mentally Nakshatraray granted Raghupati a generous fiefdom at once.

'I do not want anything,' answered Raghupati.

'What do you mean?' said Nakshatraray. 'Out of the question, thakur. You must accept something. I grant you Koylasar pargana—draw up the documents.'

Raghupati said, 'All that . . . we will see later.'

'Why later?' asked Nakshatraray. 'I shall give it to you right now. All of Koylasar pargana is yours—I shan't take a rupee in taxes.' Nakshatraray sat up erect.

'I'll be happy with six feet of land to die in, I don't need anything else,' said Raghupati and left. He had remembered

Jaysingh. He would have accepted a reward had Jaysingh been alive—but with Jaysingh dead, the entire kingdom of Tripura was nothing but a lump of clay.

Raghupati was now trying to get Nakshatraray maddened with the desire of being the king. He was worried lest all his elaborate arrangements go waste, lest the weak-minded Nakshatraray surrender to the king without a fight after arriving in Tripura. But once a vacillating heart was intoxicated by the possibility of power, this would be unlikely. Raghupati was no longer contemptuous about Nakshatraray, on the contrary, he displayed his respect at every opportunity, asking for verbal orders at every step. The Mughal soldiers addressed him as maharaj, jumping to attention when they saw him. Just like an entire field of crops bending when the wind ran through them, rows of Mughal soldiers bowed their heads and saluted Nakshatraray when he appeared. The general greeted him respectfully. He travelled on the back of an elephant—the gold-embroidered seat adorned with the king's crest—by the light of a hundred flashing swords, accompanied by rousing music and the flagbearer holding the royal standard. Wherever he passed, people fled their homes in terror of the soldiers. Their fear made Nakshatraray proud, giving him the impression that he was out to conquer the world. Small zamindars offered him all sorts of gifts when paying their respects. He thought of them as vanquished rulers, and was reminded of the all-conquering Pandavas of the Mahabharata.

One day the soldiers came up to him, saluting and saying, 'Maharaj sahib!' Nakshatraray sat up.

'We have come to lay down our lives for maharaj. We don't care for our lives. It is our tradition to plunder the villages on the way to the battlefield—none of the scriptures considers this wrong.'

'Of course, of course,' Nakshatraray nodded.

'But Brahmin-thakur has forbidden us to loot the houses,' said the soldiers. 'It is grossly unfair that we are on our way to laying down our lives but are not allowed a little looting.'

'Of course, of course,' Nakshatraray nodded again.

'If maharaja orders, we shall loot the villages without paying heed to the Brahmin-thakur.'

'Who is the Brahmin-thakur?' declared Nakshatraray arrogantly. 'What does he know? I am ordering you to plunder the houses.'

He quickly looked around for Raghupati, then felt relieved when he could not see the priest.

But disobeying Raghupati without any qualms gave him a great deal of pleasure. The intoxication of power ran in his veins like wine. He began to see the world in a new light. Riding an imaginary balloon, the earth seemed to disappear, taking many of his problems away with it. Sometimes even Raghupati appeared irrelevant. Suddenly Nakshatraray grew extremely enraged with Govindamanikya, telling himself repeatedly, 'How dare you exile me! How dare you summon me to your court like a common peasant? We'll see who sends whom into exile now. All of Tripura shall know of Nakshatraray's might.'

Nakshatraray was excited and elated.

Raghupati was particularly averse to setting upon and looting innocent villagers. He tried his best to stop the soldiers, but having received Nakshatraray's orders, they ignored him. 'Why this exploitation of helpless villagers?' he asked Nakshatraray.

'You don't understand all this, thakur,' Nakshatraray informed him. 'It isn't right to discourage soldiers in wartime by stopping them from looting.'

Raghupati was a trifle surprised, smiling to himself at this sudden display of self-confidence on Nakshatraray's part. 'If you allow them to loot now, controlling them afterwards will be impossible. They will ransack Tripura.'

'What's wrong with that?' asked Nakshatraray. 'That is just what I want. Let Tripura understand the price it has to pay for exiling Nakshatraray. You don't understand all this, thakur—you've never gone to war.'

Raghupati was vastly amused. He left without a response. He had indeed wanted Nakshatraray to stop being a puppet and turn into something resembling a strong man.

32

The attack of rats in Tripura took place in the month of Sravana. Only corn was growing in the fields at the time, while the paddy was ripening on the slopes. Three months passed somehow—and when it was time for harvesting the rice in the plains, a wave of joy swept over the state. All the peasants, all the women and the boys, all the men young and old, took their sickles to the crops, calling one another loudly with cries of 'heya, heya'. The songs of the harvesting women echoed across the fields. All dissatisfaction with the king vanished and there was peace in the land. And then news came that Nakshatraray had arrived at the border with an army to attack the kingdom, that he had begun plundering and oppressing people. The subjects grew frightened at this information.

The king felt as though a dagger had been plunged into his heart. He sensed its presence all day. Every now and then there was a fresh realization that Nakshatraray was on his way to attack him. He pictured Nakshatraray's guileless, comely face a hundred times, and was reminded at the same time that his brother had gathered an army and was on his way, sword in hand, to attack him. Once in a while he was tempted to face Nakshatraray on the battlefield alone, without a single soldier by his side, and bare his breast to allow Nakshatraray's one thousand soldiers to thrust their swords into his heart at the same time.

Drawing Dhruva to himself, he said, 'Are you also ready to fight with me for this crown, Dhruva?' and flung his crown to the floor. A large pearl was dislodged.

'I want,' said Dhruva, reaching out eagerly.

Putting the throne on the boy's head, the king gathered him in his lap. 'Here you are, he said, 'I do not wish to be in a conflict with anyone.' He embraced Dhruva with great emotion.

All through the next day the king argued with himself, saying, 'I am being punished for my sins.' Why else should a man attack his brother? The thought gave him some comfort. He put it down as god's will. The master of the universe had issued an order which the insignificant Nakshatraray could not disobey on the mere instigation of his mortal heart. He felt less hurt at this realization. He was ready to bear his own sin on his shoulders— that might reduce Nakshatraray's burden.

Bilwan arrived to ask, 'Is this the time to stare at the sky and muse, maharaj?'

'All this is the outcome of my sin, thakur,' said the king.

A little annoyed, Bilwan said, 'I can no longer be patient you when say these things, maharaj. Whoever said sorrows are the result of sins alone? They could be the outcome of virtue too. Many great souls have spent their entire lives in misery.'

The king was silent.

'What sin on the king's part is the cause of these events?'

'I sent my own brother into exile,' said the king.

'You did not send your brother into exile,' answered Bilwan. 'You sent the guilty into exile.'

The king said, 'Even if he was guilty, to exile your brother is a sin. You cannot escape its outcome. Even though the Kauravas were evil, the Pandavas were not able to enjoy their reign in happiness after killing them. They had to perform a ritual penance. The Pandavas took the kingdom from the Kauravas, and in their death the Kauravas took the kingdom away from the Pandavas. I exiled Nakshatraray, now Nakshatraray is coming to exile me.'

'The Pandavas did not go war with the Kauravas to punish them for their wrongdoing,' said Bilwan. 'They did it to wrest the kingdom for themselves. But in sentencing the guilty the king ignored his own happiness to perform his righteous duty. I see no sin in this. But I have no objection to suggesting a method for atonement. I am a Brahmin—pleasing me will be sufficient.'

The king smiled but did not speak.

'Be that as it may, prepare for war now,' said Bilwan. 'Do not delay further.'

'I shall not go to war,' said the king.

'That is absolutely impossible,' said Bilwan. 'You can ponder as much as you like. I will gather an army. Everyone is at harvest, it will be difficult to amass sufficient soldiers.'

He left without waiting for an answer.

Struck by a thought, Dhruva suddenly went up to the king and asked, 'Where's Kaka?'

Dhruva used to address Nakshatraray as kaka.

'Kaka is on his way, Dhruva,' the king told him.

His eyes moistened.

33

Bilwan became very busy. He despatched a swift-footed messenger with gifts to the hilly tract of Chattagram, with a request to the Kuki leaders there for help in the form of Kuki soldiers. The leaders were delighted at the prospect of war. To spread the word, they sent knives wrapped in red fabric through messengers to every village. A wave of Kuki soldiers arrived in no time at Tripura's peaks from Chattagram's. It was impossible to contain them with rules. Bilwan personally travelled around the villages of Tripura, handpicking courageous young men from the harvesting and adding them to the army. He did not consider it wise to advance towards the Mughal soldiers and confront them. He decided to wait till they had crossed the plains and arrived at the relatively inaccessible hills, after which he would catch them unawares by attacking them from hidden vantage points in forests and mountains. He dammed the waters of the Gomti with large rocks—if defeat seemed imminent, as a last step the dam could be destroyed and the Mughal soldiers swept away in the resultant flood.

Looting and plundering, Nakshatraray arrived in the mountainous regions of Tripura. The harvest was over. The peasants were armed for war with knives and bows and arrows. The gushing torrents of Kuki warriors could no longer be restrained.

'I shall not go to war,' declared Govindamanikya.

'That will hardly help,' observed Bilwan.

'I am not worthy to rule,' said the king. 'Every indication points to this. That is why this lack of faith in my subjects, that is why this famine, that is why this war. All these are god's instructions to forsake the kingdom.'

'These are by no means god's instructions. He has entrusted you with the responsibility for ruling the kingdom. So long as there was no crisis in matters of state, you performed your simple duties effortlessly but the moment the burden has become heavy, you want to cast it away and be free. You are deluding yourself by passing it off as god's will so that you can be happy.'

The argument appealed to Govindamanikya. He sat for some

time in silence without answering, before saying, stricken, 'Why don't you assume I have been defeated, thakur, and that Nakshatra has slain me and become the king?'

'If that were indeed to happen, I would not grieve for you. But if the king were to escape his duty and flee, we would have reason for grief.'

'But kill my own brother?' the king asked, a trifle impatiently.

'There are no brothers, no friends, when it comes to duty,' responded Bilwan. 'Try to recollect the advice that Krishna gave Arjuna during the war at Kurukshetra.'

'Are you proposing I strike Nakshatraray with this sword?' asked the king.

'Yes,' said Bilwan.

'Very bad, mustn't say all this,' Dhruva said, appearing suddenly.

The boy had been playing. Hearing the commotion between the king and the priest, he was convinced that they were being naughty, and that it was necessary to scold them before it was too late. Having come to this conclusion, he made an appearance and said, shaking his head, 'Very bad, mustn't say all this.'

The priest was vastly amused. Laughing, he picked Dhruva up in his arms and began to shower kisses on him. But the king did not smile. He seemed to have received a message from god through the little boy.

Without a trace of doubt in his voice he said, 'Thakur, I have decided I will not allow blood to be shed. I will not go to war.'

Bilwan was silent. Eventually he said, 'If maharaj objects to war, you can do something else. Meet Nakshatraray and request him to refrain from waging war.'

'I am ready to do this,' announced Govindamanikya.

'Then let a proposal be sent to Nakshatraray to that effect,' suggested Bilwan.

The king agreed.

34

Nakshatraray advanced with his soldiers without meeting the slightest resistance anywhere. Every village he entered welcomed him as the king. With every step he tasted the feeling of being the king—his hunger was sharpened, he thought of all the fields, villages, mountain ranges and rivers spread out around him as 'mine'. And as his sense of ownership grew, so did his self, making him most generous. He gave an unconditional approval to the Mughal soldiers to take whatever they wanted. All this is mine, he felt—they are in my own kingdom. They must not be deprived of any pleasure at all. When the Mughals return home, they will praise my hospitality and regal munificence. 'The king of Tripura is no ordinary king,' they will say. He was constantly eager to earn accolades from the Mughal army. He melted whenever they addressed him in a way that was music to his ears, and worried all the time lest he give cause for complaint.

'I see no preparation for warfare, maharaj,' Raghupati told him.

'No, thakur,' Nakshatraray replied. 'They are frightened.'

He burst into laughter.

Raghupati saw no reason for laughter, but joined in nevertheless.

'Nakshatraray is here with the nawab's army,' said Nakshatraray. 'No laughing matter.'

'Now we shall see who is at the receiving end of a sentence of exile, shan't we?' said Raghupati.

Nakshatraray said, 'I may exile him if I like—or imprison him, or even have him executed. I have not decided as yet.'

He proceeded to ponder knowledgably.

'Do not think about it so deeply, maharaj,' Raghupati told him. 'There is plenty of time. But I fear that Govindamanikya shall vanquish you without fighting.'

'How can that be possible?' said Nakshatraray.

Raghupati said, 'Keeping his soldiers hidden, Govindamanikya will display excessive brotherly love. Embracing you, he will say: my little brother, come home now, here's your glass of milk. Weeping, maharaj will say: yes, sir, at once, won't take long. Putting on his best shoes, he will follow his brother like a pony, his head bowed. The badshah's Mughal army will laugh heartily at this farce and go home.'

Nakshatraray was stricken by Raghupati's sharp, mocking tone. Making an unsuccessful attempt to smile, he said, 'Does he think

I'm a child who can be distracted? Not a chance. It will not happen, thakur, mark my words.'

Govindamanikya's letter arrived that day. Raghupati opened it. Showering affection on Nakshatraray, the king had requested a meeting. Raghupati did not show Nakshatraray the letter. He told the messenger, 'There is no need for Govindamanikya to take the trouble of travelling all this way. King Nakshatramanikya will himself meet him shortly along with his sword and army. Govindamanikya should not suffer too much for this separation from his brother during this short period. The separation would have lasted longer had the exile lasted eight years.'

'Govindamanikya has written a most loving letter to his exiled younger brother,' Raghupati informed Nakshatraray.

Pretending to laugh contemptuously, Nakshatraray said, 'Indeed? What letter? Let me see.' He held his hand out.

'I did not consider it necessary to show maharaj the letter,' Raghupati told him. 'I tore it up at once. I have said that we have no reply besides war.'

Laughing, Nakshatraray said, 'Well done, thakur. So you said we have no reply besides war? Excellent response.'

Raghupati said, 'When he gets the reply, Govindamanikya will wonder how the brother who had gone off to exile without protesting is now creating so much trouble on his way back.'

'He will conclude that his brother is not an easy man to deal with,' said Nakshatraray. 'He cannot exile or recall me at will.'

He began to laugh again with great enjoyment.

35

Govindamanikya was heartbroken at Nakshatraray's response. Bilwan assumed that the king would no longer baulk at war. But Govindamanikya told himself, 'This cannot be Nakshatra speaking. This is the priest's doing. Nakshatra could never have said such a thing.'

'What have you decided to do now, maharaj?' asked Bilwan.

'If I could just meet Nakshatra, peace would be ensured,' said the king.

'And if you cannot?' asked Bilwan.

'In that case I shall leave the kingdom and go away.'
'Very well, let me try,' Bilwan told him.

Nakshatraray's camp was set up on the hillside. A dense forest—clusters of bamboo, cane and reeds. The soldiers had followed the trail used by wild elephants to climb to the top. It was late in the afternoon. The sun had declined behind the mountain in the west. The western sky had darkened. The fading light of dusk and the shade from the trees had combined to usher in the evening prematurely to the forest. Mist rose from the earth as the winter day drew to a close. The silent forest was loud with the sound of the crickets now. By the time Bilwan reached Nakshatraray's camp, the sun had set completely, although the line of red in the western sky had not yet disappeared. The dense forest tinged by gold in the flat valley on the west looked like a silent green sea. The army was to set off tomorrow. Raghupati was out with the general and a group of soldiers to survey the route—he was not back yet. Although no one was allowed to visit Nakshatraray without Raghupati's knowledge, nobody stopped Bilwan, who was dressed like a monk.

Bilwan told Nakshatraray, 'Maharaj Govindamanikya has written you this letter,' handing it to him. Nakshatraray received it with trembling hands, feeling both frightened and embarrassed to open it. He felt secure as long as Raghupati stood like a bulwark between him and Govindamanikya. He did not want a direct encounter with the king in any circumstances. With Govindamanikya's messenger appearing in front of him, Nakshatraray shrank back, and was annoyed too. He wished Raghupati were present and had prevented the messenger from meeting him. He opened the letter with great hesitation.

It held not the slightest of rebukes. Govindamanikya had not written a single thing to embarrass him. He had not expressed the least unhappiness with his brother, making no mention of the fact that Nakshatraray was on his way with an army to attack the king. It was as though the affection between them was intact. The letter was soaked in deep love and regret, and because this had not been stated specifically, it hurt Nakshatraray even more.

His expression changed gradually as he read the letter. The layer of stone around his heart cracked at once. The letter shook in his trembling hands. He placed the sheet on his forehead for a few minutes—his brother's blessings rained on his agitated heart, soothing it. For a long time he sat still, gazing steadily at the green forest in the distant west, touched by the colours of dusk. The silent evening stayed awake around him like a bottomless, soundless, tranquil ocean. Eventually tears welled up in his eyes, and soon they began to fall furiously. Nakshatraray hid his face in sudden shame and repentance.

Weeping, he said, 'I do not want this kingdom. Forgive me all my sins, my brother, and let me live at your feet, let me stay near you, do not banish me.'

Without a word, Bilwan watched, his own heart moist with emotion. Finally, when Nakshatraray had calmed down, Bilwan said, 'Govindamanikya is waiting eagerly for you, do not delay any further.'

'Will he forgive me?' asked Nakshatraray.

'He is not in the least angry with the prince,' Bilwan told him. 'The journey will be arduous if it gets late. Secure a horse for yourself quickly. The king's people are waiting at the base of the hill.'

'I shall escape in secret,' said Nakshatraray, 'there is no need to inform the soldiers. Let us not tarry another moment, the sooner we get out of here the better.'

'You are right,' said Bilwan.

Stating that he was accompanying the monk to the three-peaked hill to perform a ritual at the shrine over there, Nakshatraray set off on horseback with Bilwan. His followers wanted to go with him, but he stopped them.

They had barely left when hoofbeats and soldiers' conversations were heard. Nakshatraray shrank back. Raghupati was returning with the soldiers. He asked in the surprise, 'Where is maharaj off to?'

Nakshatraray could not answer. At this Bilwan said, 'He is on his way to meet maharaj Govindamanikya.'

Running his eyes over Bilwan from tip to toe, Raghupati frowned and then controlled himself. 'We cannot bid farewell to the king at such an hour. There is no need for haste. He can journey tomorrow morning. Don't you agree, maharaj?'

'I shall go tomorrow, it is late today,' Nakshatraray murmured.

A disappointed Bilwan spent the night at the camp. Trying to approach Nakshatraray the next morning, he was stopped by the soldiers. He discovered that a cordon had been thrown around Nakshatraray, without the slightest opening anywhere. Eventually he went up to Raghupati, saying, 'It is time to depart, please inform the prince.'

'The king has decided not to go,' Raghupati told him.

'I would like to meet him,' said Bilwan.

'He has said he will not meet you.'

'I need a reply to maharaj Govindamanikya's letter,' said Bilwan.

Raghupati said, 'A reply has been sent already.'

'I would like to hear the response directly from him,' Bilwan said.

'That is impossible,' declared Raghupati.

Bilwan realized that his efforts would be futile—merely a waste of words and of time. As he was leaving, he told Raghupati, 'Brahmin, why are you engaged in this act of destruction? This is not a fit task for a Brahmin.'

36

When Bilwan returned, he discovered that the king had sent the Kuki warriors back. They had begun creating mayhem in the capital. He had all but disbanded the army. There was no readiness for war. Bilwan gave the king an account of all that had happened.

'Then it is time I left, thakur,' the king told him. 'I shall leave the riches of the kingdom to Nakshatra.'

'When I consider that you intend to run away, leaving your helpless victims in someone else's hands, I cannot possibly bid you farewell cheerfully,' said Bilwan. 'How can one imagine the mother handing over her son to the stepmother and feeling relieved?'

'What you are saying cuts me to the quick, thakur,' said the king. 'But excuse me this one time, do not say anything more. Do not try to shake my resolve. I had promised not to shed blood, thakur, I cannot break my promise.'

'Then what does the king intend to do now?' asked Bilwan.

'Let me tell you everything,' said the king. 'I shall take Dhruva with me into the forest. My life is incomplete, thakur. I have not been able to do any of the things I had set out to do. I cannot bring back the days that have passed and start afresh. It seems to me that destiny has shot us out like arrows—but if we deviate even a little from our trajectory, not even our best efforts can bring us back on course. The turn I took at the start of my life has prevented me from finding my destination now. None of the things I expect actually materialize. I did not wake up in time to protect myself—by the time I did, I had already begun to sink. I am clinging to Dhruva the way people cling to flotsam when they fall into the sea. I will resolve everything through Dhruva and be reincarnated in him. I shall make him the kind of man I should have been, right from the beginning. I shall grow along with him. I shall fulfil my birth as a human. When I am not even a man, thakur, what can I accomplish as a ruler?'

The king spoke the final words with a great deal of emotion—at which Dhruva rubbed his head on the king's knees, saying, 'I am the uler.'

Smiling, Bilwan picked Dhruva up in his arms. After a long look at the boy he finally told the king, 'How can you nurture a human being in the forest? You can only grow plants in the forest. A human being has to grow up in human society.'

'I am not going to be a forest-dweller,' said the king. 'I shall only live at a distance from human society, without cutting off ties with it. And this is only for a short while.'

Meanwhile, Nakshatraray neared the capital with his army. The people's crops and property began to be looted. They cursed Govindamanikya, no one else. 'All this is because of the king's sins,' they said.

The king sent word, asking to meet Raghupati. When Raghupati arrived, the king told him, 'Why are you oppressing the people? I shall abdicate in Nakshatraray's favour. Send the Mughal soldiers back.'

'Very well,' said Raghupati, 'I will send them back as soon as you leave—I do not want Tripura to be plundered.'

The king prepared to leave the kingdom the same day. Taking

off his regal robes, he dressed in saffron, and wrote a long letter to Nakshatraray with his blessings, reminding him of all his responsibilities as a king.

Finally he picked Dhruva up in his arms, saying, 'Will you come to the forest with me, Dhruva?'

'I will,' said Dhruva at once, putting his arms around the king.

The king suddenly realized that it was necessary to take Dhruva's uncle Kedareshwar's permission before taking the boy away. Summoning Kedareshwar, he said, 'With your approval, I shall take Dhruva with me.'

Dhruva used to spend all his time with the king, and did not have much to do with his uncle. Which was probably why it had never occurred to the king that Kedareshwar might object.

When Kedareshwar heard the king's request, he said, 'I cannot do this, maharaj.'

The king's illusion was shattered. He was thunderstruck. After some moments of silence, he said, 'You come with us too, Kedareshwar.'

'No, maharaj, I cannot live in the forest,' Kedareshwar told him.

Stricken, the king said, 'I shall not live in the forest, I will live with other people.'

'I cannot leave my land,' answered Kedareshwar.

Without saying anything more, the king sighed. All his hopes dwindled. The face of the earth seemed transformed in an instant. Dhruva was playing by himself—the king gazed at him for a long time without seeing him. Tugging at his clothes, Dhruva said, 'Play with me.'

The king's heart melted, gathering in his eyes in the form of tears. Suppressing them with great effort, he turned his face away and said, heartbroken, 'Then let Dhruva stay. I shall go alone.'

The arid path stretching ahead of him for the rest of his life seemed to be revealed to his eyes in a momentary flash of lightning.

Interrupting Dhruva's play, Kedareshwar said, 'Come with me.'

He drew Dhruva towards him. 'No,' Dhruva wept.

Startled, the king turned to the boy. Running up to him, Dhruva put his arms around the king and buried his face between the king's knees. Taking Dhruva in his arms, the king held him close. His generous heart was being torn apart—pressing Dhruva to his breast, he tried to control his heart. Holding the child, he paced up and down in his chamber. Putting his head on the king's shoulders, Dhruva became still.

Finally it was time to leave. Dhruva had fallen asleep in the king's arms. Handing him over carefully to Kedareshwar, the king began his journey.

37

Nakshatraray entered the capital with his army through the eastern gate, while Govindamanikya left through the western one with a little money and a handful of followers. The people of the city welcomed Nakshatraray with music and drums and conchshells and ululation. No one thought it necessary to bid farewell to Govindamanikya on the path he took out of the city on horseback. The women in the huts on either side of the road heaped loud abuse on him, their tongues honed by hunger and the sobs of their starving children. Even the aged woman who had been given a meal at the king's palace during the famine cursed him now, raising her frail arm. Learning from their mothers, the little boys followed the king, jeering at him loudly.

Without a glance to the right or left, the king proceeded slowly. A peasant on his way back from the fields greeted the king reverently. The king's heart melted. He bade the man goodbye in a voice choked with emotion. Only this one peasant out of all his children, of all his subjects, said farewell to him with respect and regret at the end of his reign. Enraged by the screaming mob of young boys trailing the king, he tried to chase them away. The king stopped him.

Eventually the king arrived in that part of the kingdom where Kedareshwar lived. He glanced southward. It was a winter morning. The rays of the sun had barely penetrated the fog. Gazing at the hut, the king was reminded of an Ashadh morning the year before. The sky was overcast, with torrential rain. Like the faintest crescent moon, a frail Hashi lay unconscious on her bed. Unable to understand, little Taataa looked at his sister, chewing on the end of her sari and stroking her face with his small, plump, hands. Today's dew-soaked, clear Agrahayan morning was concealed in that overcast Ashadh morning too. Was the king wondering whether the same destiny that had humiliated him, forcing him to abdicate and leave his home, had also been lying in wait for him that darkened Ashadh morning? This was where the first meeting had taken place. The king stopped in front of the hut, lost in thought. There was no one on the road besides his followers. The boys had been shooed away by the peasant, but the moment he left, they were back. Brought back to his senses by their shouts, the king resumed his course slowly.

Suddenly a sweet and familiar voice amongst the shouting boys caught his attention. He saw little Dhruva running towards him on his small legs, his arms raised, laughing. Kedareshwar had gone off to demonstrate his loyalty to the new king, leaving just Dhruva and an aged maid behind. Laughing happily, Dhruva leapt upon him. Tugging at his clothes, burying his face between the king's knees, he told the king solemnly, after his first flush of joy had subsided, 'Want ride horse.'

The king put him on the stallion. Perching on horseback, he put his arms around the king, touching his cheek with his own. Even with his limited perceptions, Dhruva had sensed a change in the king. Just like someone trying to awaken a person from deep sleep, Dhruva tried to restore the king to his old self with embraces, kisses and physical effort. Unsuccessful, he finally sat back, putting two of his fingers in his mouth. Realizing Dhruva's intentions, the king planted kisses on him repeatedly.

'Let me go now, Dhruva,' the king told him finally.

'I will go too,' Dhruva told the king.

'How can you go,' said the king. 'You must stay with your uncle.'

'No, I shall go,' said Dhruva.

Now the aged maid emerged from the hut, muttering. Grabbing Dhruva's arm forcibly, she said, 'Come along.'

A frightened Dhruva immediately put his arms around the king tightly, hiding his face in the king's chest. Stricken, the king mused that he could tear out a vein from his heart but not the bond of these arms. But still he had to. Removing Dhruva's arms from around himself slowly, he forcibly handed him over to the maid. Dhruva wept loudly, saying as he held out his arms, 'I want to go, baba.' Without looking backward, the king galloped off. The further he went, the more he could hear Dhruva's ardent cries, the child holding out his arms and saying, 'I want to go, baba.' Finally, tears began to stream from the king's calm eyes. He could no longer see the road. The entire world seemed suffused in a vapour. The horse galloped forward on its own.

A group of Mughal soldiers spotted the king on the road and began to laugh at him, even misbehaving with his followers. One of the king's courtiers was going by on horseback. He raced up when he saw this, saying, 'These insults are intolerable, maharaj. The king's humble apparel has given them courage. Here is a sword, here is a head-dress. Now give me a little time to gather some people and teach these barbarians a lesson.'

'No, Nayanray, I do not need a sword or a head-dress,' the king told him. 'What can these people do to me? I can endure far more humiliation than this. I do not want to earn the respect of people on the strength of a naked sword. Just as ordinary people accept all joys and sorrows, all rewards and punishments, in good times and bad times, so too shall I, with my eyes on the almighty. Once upon a time it might have seemed unbearable that friends were turning against me, that those who had sought refuge from me were becoming ungrateful, that the meek were turning arrogant, but now I feel a joy in my heart at enduring all of this. I have come to know the one who is my friend. Go back, Nayanray, welcome Nakshatra warmly, grant him the same respect that you did me. All of you must keep him on the right path for the welfare of the people. This is my request to you as I leave. Ensure you do not refer to me or demean Nakshatra by comparing him to me—not even by mistake. I shall leave now.'

Embracing his courtier, the king continued on his way. Bidding him farewell, the courtier wiped his tears and left.

When the king reached the raised bank of the Gomti, Bilwan appeared from the forest, raising his hand and saying, 'Long live the king.'

Dismounting, the king greeted him reverently.

'I have come to bid you farewell,' said Bilwan.

'Stay near Nakshatra and advise him well, thakur,' said the king. 'Do good for the kingdom.'

'No,' said Bilwan. 'I am useless where you are not the king. I cannot achieve anything here.'

'Where will you go then, thakur?' said the king. 'Be generous to me, my frail heart will be strengthened if you give me company.'

'I am going in search of a place where there are things for me to do,' said Bilwan. 'Whether I am near you or apart, my love will never leave you. But what will I do in the forest with you?'

'Then let me leave now,' said the king softly. He paid his respects to the priest once more. Bilwan disappeared in one direction, and the king, in another.

38

Nakshatraray ascended the throne with great fanfare, naming himself Chhatramanikya. The treasury was not very well-endowed. The Mughal army had to be sent off with the promised payment by seizing the wealth of the people. Chhatramanikya reigned over a land of deep poverty and famine. Curses and tears rained from all directions.

The seat that Govindamanikya used to occupy, the bed that he slept in, the people who were his closest followers all seemed to rebuke Chhatramanikya silently through the day and the night. Chhatramanikya found it intolerable after some time. He began to obliterate every sign of Govindamanikya—destroying the things that his predecessor used and banishing all his favourite courtiers. He could not tolerate the slightest mention of Govindamanikya. He considered every reference to Govindamanikya personally directed at him, constantly feeling as though people were not giving him his due respect as the king; he would lose his temper suddenly without provocation, making the courtiers anxious.

He understood nothing of statecraft; but whenever anyone offered advice, he flared up. 'Do you think I don't know? Do you consider me a fool?'

He felt as though everyone considered him an unworthy usurper of the throne and was contemptuous of him. As a result he forced himself to become too much of a king—establishing his sole authority through all sorts of excesses. Specifically to establish that he could save or take lives at will, he saved the ones who did not deserve to be saved, and slayed the ones who did not deserve to be slain. His subjects were dying of starvation, but there was no end to festivities—music and dances and feasts every day. No king had ever fanned out the tail of his kingdom in this way for such an exquisite dance.

The people began to express their unhappiness, which made Chhatramanikya even angrier. He considered all this nothing but a demonstration of disrespect towards the king. He used oppression and force to threaten people into silence, doubling their dissatisfaction. The entire state became as quiet as the sleeping night. There was nothing surprising about the meek Nakshatraray behaving this way as Chhatramanikya. Weak-minded people often become harsh and tyrannical when granted power.

Raghupati's work was over. Towards the end, it was not as though the hunger for revenge had burnt as powerfully as ever within him. The need to avenge himself had gradually been replaced by the need to complete the task he had set out to do. He had been experiencing an addictive joy from using all his skills to overcome every obstacle to fulfil this mission. Finally the objective had been achieved. There was no happiness to be found anywhere anymore.

Going to his temple, Raghupati found it deserted. Although he was only too keenly aware that Jaysingh was dead, he seemed to realize the fact afresh when he entered the temple. Now and then he felt as though Jaysingh was alive, but then he remembered that he was not. A sudden gust of wind blew the doors open, but when he turned around, startled, there was no Jaysingh. He might be in the room he had occupied, but Raghupati could not enter the room for a long time—lest he discover that Jaysingh was not in it.

Finally, when the shadow of the forest in the slight darkness of twilight disappeared in the deeper shadows, Raghupati entered Jaysingh's room slowly—the empty, desolate room was as silent as a tomb. In one corner a wooden chest and, next to it, a pair of Jaysingh's footwear lay shrouded in dust. On the floor was an image of the goddess Kali, which Jaysingh had drawn with his own hands. A metal lamp stood on a metal stool in the eastern corner—for a year now no one had lit the lamp, which was covered in cobwebs. A black smear from the flame was visible on the wall nearby. The room held nothing but these objects. Raghupati sighed deeply, the sigh reverberating in the empty room. Eventually nothing more could be seen in the darkness. Only a lizard made a sound from time to time. A cold wind blew in through the open door. Raghupati sat down on the chest, trembling.

He spent a month in the deserted temple, but the days just would not pass. He had to give up his priest's duties. He went to the court, and involved himself in matters of state. He discovered that misrule, oppression and chaos were reigning in the name of Chhatramanikya. He attempted to establish order, and tried to advise the king.

Enraged, Chhatramanikya said, 'What do you know of ruling a kingdom, thakur? You don't understand any of this.'

Raghupati was astonished by the king's confidence. This was not the Nakshatraray he had known. Raghupati and the king had frequent conflicts. Chhatramanikya thought that Raghupati considered himself the kingmaker. So he couldn't bear the sight of Raghupati now.

Finally Chhatramanikya told Raghupati clearly one day, 'Go and take care of the temple, thakur. You have nothing to do here.'

Raghupati cast a blazing glance at Chhatramanikya. Taken aback slightly, Chhatramanikya averted his face and left.

39

Kedareshwar had been to meet Nakshatraray the very day that he had entered the capital, but despite his best efforts he had not been able to catch the new king's eye. The soldiers and guards pushed, shoved and harassed him—so much so that he barely managed to escape with his life. During Govindamanikya's reign he had lived in the palace in royal luxury, even sharing a particularly cordial relationship with Nakshatraray. Being evicted from the palace had made his life miserable; as long as he had lived under the patronage of the king, everyone displayed fear and respect—but no one paid attention to him any longer. Whenever people needed something done at the royal court, they would seek his help—but now they passed him by on the street without pausing for a moment's conversation. On top of all this, he was starving, too. In these circumstances, gaining re-entry into the palace would be of great value. One convenient day he prepared a few gifts and went to the royal court for an audience with Chhatramanikya. He stood in front of the king with a gratified expression, smiling obsequiously.

The king flared up when he saw him. 'What are you laughing for?' he asked. 'Are you joking with me? What is this strange behaviour?"

From the crier to the cleaner, from the ministers to the courtiers, everyone showed their displeasure loudly. The curtain fell at once on Kedareshwar's bared teeth.

'Say what you have to quickly and leave,' Chhatramanikya told him.

Kedareshwar could not remember what it was he had to come to tell the king. The speech that he had prepared with great effort was over even before it could be made.

When the king finally said, 'If you have nothing to say, leave at once,' Kedareshwar considered it necessary to respond quickly. Summoning as much pathos as he could to his expression and his voice, he said, 'Have you forgotten Dhruva, maharaj?'

Chhatramanikya blazed in anger. Not comprehending this, the foolish Kedareshwar said, 'He is pining away for maharaj. "Kaka, kaka," he cries all day.'

Chhatramanikya said, 'How dare you? Your nephew refers to me as "kaka"! Is this what you have taught him?'

Stricken, Kedareshwar said humbly, 'Maharaj . . .'

Chhatramanikya said, 'Banish this man and that boy from the kingdom at once.'

So many hands descended on his shoulders suddenly that Kedareshwar shot out like an arrow. The guards snatched the gifts he was carrying, dividing them amongst themselves. Kedareshwar left Tripura along with Dhruva.

40

Raghupati returned to the temple again. He found no loving soul waiting for him with his garments. The temple of stone stood there, without the trace of a heart. He went to the bank of the Gomti and sat down on the white steps. To the left, the night jasmines planted by Jaysingh with his own hands were blooming. The sight of the flowers reminded Raghupati of Jaysingh's comely appearance, pure heart, spartan life and his natural, honest, sublime self. As powerful and spirited as a lion and as tender as a fawn, Jaysingh appeared in his entirety in Raghupati's heart, claiming all of it. All this while he used to consider himself superior to Jaysingh, but now Jaysingh appeared superior to him. Recalling Jaysingh's simple devotion to him, he now felt devoted to Jaysingh, and a distaste for himself. His heart was torn apart when he recalled all the unfair rebuke he had heaped upon Jaysingh. 'I do not have the right to admonish Jaysingh,' he told himself. 'If I could meet him but once, for even a moment, I would accept my unworthiness and seek his forgiveness.' He recollected every little thing that Jaysingh had ever said or done. Jaysingh's entire life occupied his mind—losing himself in the life of that noble soul, Raghupati forgot all his conflicts and hatred. The world that had weighed him down no longer seemed as heavy and stopped tormenting him. That the very Nakshatraray whom he had been instrumental in installing as king had insulted him today did not elicit the slightest anger in him. Considering all such honours and humiliation mere trifles, he was faintly amused. He felt a desire to do something that would please Jaysingh. But he could find nothing suitable—there was only a wailing emptiness everywhere. The secluded temple seemed to close in on him, choking him. He wanted to undertake a momentous task to calm the agony in his heart, but the vision of the temple in this silent, inert, desolation made his heart as restless as a caged bird. Rising to his feet, he began to pace impatiently amidst the trees. He felt an intense loathing for the idle, insensate, ineffective, inanimate idols inside the temple. Now that his heart was in turmoil, spending the rest of his days as the indolent companion to a set of indolent and crude statues of stone seemed hateful. When the second hour after midnight had arrived, Raghupati used a flint to light a lamp, entering the temple of the fourteen goddesses with the lamp in his hand. Inside, he found the fourteen goddesses standing the same way as always; just as they had stood amidst the blood streaming from their devotee's corpse on that terrible Ashadh night of the previous year.

'Lies!' shouted Raghupati, 'All lies! Oh my son Jaysingh, whom have you sacrificed your priceless heart to? There is no god here, no god. It was the fiend Raghupati who drank your blood.'

Raghupati lifted the idol of Kali from its position, carrying it to the door of the temple and flinging it away with all his strength. Clattering down the stone steps in the darkness, the stone idol rolled into the waters of the Gomti. The inanimate demoness who had taken on the form of stone to drink blood all these years disappeared tonight amongst the thousands of boulders at the bottom of the river, but she refused to vacate the stony human heart. Putting out the lamp, Raghupati set off along the road, leaving the capital that very night.

41

Bilwan had been living for some time in Nizamatpur in Noakhali. It was in the grip of a terrible epidemic.

It was an overcast day at the end of the month of Phalgun, with intermittent rain. Finally a real storm began raging in the evening. At first there were strong winds from the east. Then, during the second hour after midnight, a violent cyclone began to blow from the north and north-east. Finally, the torrential rain made the storm weaker. Suddenly there were cries of alarm— there was going to be a flood. Some people climbed to their roofs, some stood on the bank of the lake, some took shelter on trees or on the spire of the temple. A dark night, continuous rain. The roaring of the floodwaters approached, and the villagers were helpless with terror. The flood reached the village with two successive waves washing over it. After the second one, the village was under twelve feet of water. When the sun rose the next morning and the water receded, very few of the houses and none of the people had survived. The corpses and carcasses of humans and cattle, bulls and goats, jackals and dogs, had floated in from nearby villages. The almond trees had been broken and had floated away, with only bits of their trunks remaining. Large mango and jackfruit trees had been uprooted, and were lying on their sides. The thatched roofs of the houses in other villages had floated in on the water and now lay upside down on the ground. Several pots and pans were scattered about. With most of the dwellings being enclosed by bamboo groves as well as mango, jackfruit, coral and other giant trees, many of the people found themselves snagged in the branches instead of being washed away. Some of them had been battered all night by the force of the flood, buffeted as ferociously as the swaying bamboo groves; some were bruised by the thorns on the coral trees, and some had flowed away on the currents along with the uprooted trees. When the water had receded, the survivors descended from the trees to look for their family amongst the dead. Most of the corpses were unknown, having floated in from other villages. No one cremated them. Flocks of vultures arrived to feed on them. They had no conflict with the dogs and jackals, for all the dogs and jackals had died too. Twelve families of Pathans used to live in the village—because they occupied a high patch of land, almost none of them had come to any harm. Those among the survivors who found houses nearby took sanctuary in them—the rest went off elsewhere in search of shelter. Those who had gone travelling returned home to build new houses. Gradually, human habitation began afresh. But because the water of the lake was infected by the corpses, and for several other reasons, there was an epidemic in the village. It began in the area where the Pathans lived. No one had the time to bury the dead or even look after one another. The Hindus claimed that the Muslims were suffering because of their sin of cow slaughter. None of the Hindus offered them even a glass of water, or provided any other help, because of the difference in caste, and the fear of being banished from their own caste. This was the condition of the village when Bilwan arrived. He had gathered a few followers, who promptly attempted to flee out of fear of the epidemic. Bilwan threatened them with dire consequences to hold them back. He took care of the afflicted Pathans, providing them medicines, sustenance and water, and buried their dead. The Hindus were astonished at this uncharacteristic behaviour from a Hindu priest. 'I am a monk,' Bilwan would say, 'I have no caste. Humanity is my caste. When humans are dying, what does caste matter? When one of god's creations was seeking the love of another, what did caste have to do with it?'

When the Hindus observed Bilwan's impartial attempts to help people, they did not dare hate him or criticize him. They could not decide whether what he was doing was right or wrong. 'Wrong,' declared their incomplete knowledge of the scriptures sceptically. But the human being residing in their hearts said, 'Right.' Be that as it may, Bilwan went about his work without considering the praise or censure of other people. The dying Pathans likened him to a god. To keep the children of the Pathans away from the epidemic, he took them to the Hindus. The Hindus grew extremely agitated—none of them offered shelter. Then Bilwan took sanctuary in a large, dilapidated temple and housed the children there. Every morning he went out begging to get them food. But who was going to give him alms? Where was the grain? Thousands of people were starving to death. The Muslim zamindar of the area lived a long way away. Bilwan visited him, persuading him with great effort to import rice from Dhaka. Sometimes Bilwan went off to play with the children. There would be an uproar when he arrived—passing by the temple in the evening, it seemed that a thousand parrots had nested there. Bilwan possessed an instrument similar to the esraj. When he was exhausted, he would play on it and sing. The children would surround him, listening. Some would pluck at the strings, while others would try to sing like him and end up making a terrible noise.

Eventually the epidemic migrated from the neighbourhood of the Muslims to the one where Hindus lived. Anarchy descended on the village—there was rampant theft and robbery, with people looting whatever they set eyes on. The Muslims began to loot people en masse. Dragging the sick out of their beds, they would even steal their cots and mats and mattresses. Bilwan tried his best to stop them. They heeded his instructions, not daring to flout them. In this way Bilwan tried to maintain as much peace as possible.

One day, one of Bilwan's followers informed him that a man from another land, travelling with a young boy, had taken shelter under a tree. He was afflicted by the epidemic and unlikely to survive. Bilwan discovered Kedareshwar unconscious, and Dhruva lying asleep in the dust. Kedareshwar was dying—the travails of the journey and starvation had weakened him already, and the illness had forced itself on him. No medicine worked on him, and he died beneath the same tree. Dhruva looked as though he had cried himself to sleep from hunger. Picking him up in his arms tenderly, Bilwan took Dhruva to his home for children.

42

Chattagram was part of the Arakan kingdom now. When the king of Arakan heard that Govindamanikya was in Chattagram as an exile, he sent a messenger with great fanfare. If you care to reclaim your throne, he wrote, the lord of Arakan can be of assistance.

'No, I do not want the throne,' said Govindamanikya.

'Then live as an honoured guest at the Arakan court for some time,' said the messenger.

'I shall not live in the royal court,' the king said. 'I shall be indebted to the king of Arakan if I am given some land in a corner of Chattagram.'

'The king may stay wherever he pleases,' declared the messenger. 'Consider this your own kingdom.'

Some members of the ruler of Arakan's entourage remained with the king. Govindamanikya did not dissuade them. He thought it possible that the king was suspicious and wanted to keep him under observation.

Govindamanikya set up home by the river Moyani. As clear as crystal, the tiny river flowed swiftly over the rocks. Black mountains rose sharply on either side, multicoloured moss dangling from the rocks. There were small cavities here and there, occupied by birds' nests. The mountains were so high in places that barely one or two delayed sunbeams fell on the water. Large bushes sporting leaves in different colours were suspended from the hillside. Arms of dense forest stretched a long distance away from the river now and then. A tall white gum tree leant on the crest of the hill, its reflection dancing in the turbulent water of the river beneath, while long vines covered the tree, hanging from it. Pleasant, verdant banana groves dotted the dense green forest. Splitting the river bank at intervals, small waterfalls tumbled into the river like children with eager arms, uncontrollable emotions and pure gurgling laughter. The river ran along stretches of level land before cascading down rocky slopes in a shower of foam. This constant rippling reverberated from the walls of stone on either side.

Govindamanikya began to live in this shade, near the cool currents and the pleasing murmur of the water. Expanding his heart, he absorbed the peace all around him—the deeply comforting love of unpopulated nature slipped in like a thousand mountain streams. He wiped out all petty disaffections in the hollows of his heart, opening its door wide, he imbibed the flow of pure light and air. He forgot who had hurt him or who had caused him pain; who had not reciprocated his love, or who had accepted gifts with one hand and served up ingratitude with the other, or who had been welcomed by him and humiliated him in return. Witnessing the unwavering efficiency and yet the calm, confident youthfulness of ancient nature here amidst the boulders, he too grew just as mature, just as generous, just as serene. He extended his body, now bereft of desire, to the furthest reaches of the universe. Dismissing all wants, joining his palms reverently, he said, 'You have saved me from falling off this pinnacle of earthly riches by drawing me into your lap. I was about to die, but I have survived. I did not know of my own greatness when I became king, but now I can sense my greatness everywhere in this world.' Finally, tears began to stream from his eyes. 'You have taken away my dearest Dhruva, my king. The agony has not yet left my heart. But today I realize that you were right. I was about to sacrifice all my responsibilities, my entire life, out of a selfish love for the little boy. You have saved me from danger. I had accepted Dhruva as a reward for all my virtues—by taking him away, you have taught me that the reward for virtue is nothing but more virtue. That is why I am now experiencing the sacred sorrow of parting from Dhruva as a joy, as your kindness. I shall not work like a servant for a salary, my lord, I shall serve you as one mesmerized by love.'

Govindamanikya observed that the currents of love nurtured by a secluded, meditative nature had turned into the river coursing through human habitation. Those who accepted its offering quenched their thirst, but nature had no quarrel with those who did not. Declaring, 'I too shall venture out to share with people this love that I have nurtured away from everyone,' Govindamanikya left his mountain sanctuary.

Giving up one's kingdom suddenly in favour of detachment is easier said than done. Forsaking the royal robes for the saffron of the monk is no easy task. And while it might be possible to give up a kingdom, we cannot easily give up all the habits we have developed since birth—their sharp hunger and thirst are mingled with our flesh. Unless fed regularly, they keep sucking our blood. Let no one imagine that Govindamanikya spent the days in his desolate hut by the river like a statue, undisturbed. At every step he battled with his habits. He reprimanded himself whenever he suffered from the lack of a daily necessity. He starved each of the hungers in his mind to death, experiencing pleasure at these victories. Just as the turbulent stallion has to be calmed down by being made to gallop at top speed, so too did Govindamanikya quell his heart's complaints of deprivation by forcing it to race unceasingly through the desert of self-denial. For a long time, he had not a moment's rest.

Leaving the hills behind, Govindamanikya travelled southward to the sea. Forsaking all the objects of his desire, he felt an extraordinary freedom in his heart. No one could hold him back, no one could prevent him from going forward. He perceived nature as expansive, and himself as being at one with it. The trees had a new green hue to them, the sun gave off new golden beams—he discovered nature in a new form. In the villages, he saw beauty in every human act, observing in their conversations and movement and daily routine the sweetness of exquisite dances. He derived pleasure in talking with everyone he saw—his heart did not recoil from those who ignored him. Wherever he went, he felt the urge to help the weak and console the unhappy. 'I dedicate all my strength and all my happiness to others, for I have no objectives of my own, no desires,' he told himself. All the scenes that did not usually catch people's eyes appeared to him in a new light. Whenever he saw a pair of children playing on the roadside, whenever he saw two brothers, or a father with his son or a mother with her daughter—be they filthy, poor, or ugly—he sensed in them the deep and infinite love in the heart's ocean. In a mother with her child in her arms he saw every mother of the past and of the future. Whenever he saw friends together, he sensed all of humanity living in fraternal love. The same world that had seemed orphaned earlier now appeared to be in the arms of a demure but eternally alert mother. Not even misery or sadness or poverty, or conflicts and hatred, could make him despondent anymore. The smallest auspicious sign made his hope break through a thousand bad omens to rise heavenward. Which of us has not seen the dawn of a new love and freedom—a day on which we have seen this laughing, weeping world blossom in the arms of an ineffable beauty, of a fine love as tender as a young boy; a day when no one can disappoint us, when no one can deprive us of any happiness in the world, when no one can confine us within walls; a day when a marvellous flute plays, when a glorious spring comes alive, when all the earth overflows with the joy of eternal youth; when sorrows and poverty and dangers seem insignificant. That day had arrived in the life of Govindamanikya, his soul exalted by the happiness of his newfound freedom.

The town of Ramu in south Chattagram was still twenty miles away. When Govindamanikya arrived at a tiny village named Alamkhal a little before evening, he heard the faint sound of a little boy weeping in a hut at one end of the village. His heart suddenly grew uneasy. He went to the hut at once, and discovered the young man who lived in it pacing up and down with a frail young boy in his arms. The boy was trembling violently and crying in a faint voice every now and then. Clasping him to his breast, the owner of the hut was trying to put him to sleep. Turning frantic when he caught sight of Govindamanikya, he said, 'Bless the boy, thakur.'

Taking out his own blanket, Govindamanikya wrapped it around the boy, who raised his worn face to give him a glance. He had dark circles under his eyes—his shrunken face seemed to hold nothing but those two eyes. When he saw Govindamanikya he moved his thin, ashen lips to make a faint, unintelligible sound. The next moment he rested his head on his father's shoulder in silence. Putting him down on the floor, still wrapped in the blanket, his father greeted the king reverently, miming the gathering of dust from the king's feet and putting it on his son's head. Taking the little boy up in his arms, the king said, 'What is the boy's father's name?'

'I am his father,' said the master of the hut, 'my name is Yadav. God has taken away each of my children one by one, this is the only one left.' He sighed deeply. The king told him, 'I am your guest for the night. I shall not eat—do not make arrangements to feed me, therefore. I will only spend the night here.' He stayed the night, while his entourage accepted the hospitality of a wealthy kayasth in the village.

It grew dark gradually. Vapour began to rise from a tank nearby choked with hyacinths. Unable to rise into the sky, the heavy smoke from the bonfire of straw collected from the cowshed and dry leaves rolled forward to cover the extensive swamp that stretched in front. A cacophony of crickets could be heard near the verge of wild trees. The breeze was stilled, and not a leaf moved. A bird called occasionally from the thick bamboo grove on the other side of the swamp. In the faint light, Govindamanikya observed the afflicted boy's pale, shrunken face. Wrapping him up snugly in the blanket, he sat by the boy's side and told him one story after another. Evening made way for night, and a jackal howled in the distance. Listening to the stories, the little boy forgot his suffering and fell asleep.

The king went into the next room and lay down. He could not sleep all night, being reminded of Dhruva continuously. 'After I lost Dhruva, every little boy appears to me as him,' the king told himself. Late at night, he heard the boy in the next room wake up and ask his father, 'What's that music, Baba?'

'A flute,' answered his father.

'Why are they playing a flute?'

'It's Durga Puja tomorrow, my son.'

'Tomorrow? Aren't you giving me a present?'

'What should I give you, my son?'

'Won't you give me a red shawl?'

'Where will I get a shawl? I have nothing, my jewel.'

'Nothing? You have nothing, Baba?'

'Nothing, my son, besides you.'

The heartbroken father's deep sigh was heard from the other room.

The boy said nothing more. Perhaps he put his arms around his father and went back to sleep.

Govindamanikya left before dawn without bidding farewell to his host, riding off towards the town of Ramu. He neither ate nor paused to rest, crossing a narrow river on horseback. He reached Ramu under a scorching sun, not tarrying there for long and returning to Yadav's hut before evening had fallen. Drawing him aside, he took a red shawl out of his bag and handed it to him, saying, 'Give this to your son on this Durga Puja day.'

Weeping, Yadav clasped Govindamanikya's legs. 'You have got it for him, my lord, you give it to him.'

'No, not I,' said the king, 'you must give it to him. Don't mention me. I will leave after I've seen his happy smile.'

The king left after the sick child's wasted, cheerless face had been transformed into a joyous one. Sadly he told himself, 'I can achieve nothing. I have only reigned for some time, I have not educated myself. I do not know how to bring a little relief from his agony to an ailing child. All I know is how to grieve helplessly and ineffectually. If Bilwan had been here he could have done something to help these people. If only I were like him.'

'I will not wander about anymore,' declared Govindamanikya. 'I will live amongst people and learn how to be useful to them.'

With the permission of the Arakan king, he settled down near the fort built by the Mogs near Rajakul, to the east of Ramu.

All the children of the village gathered around Govindamanikya in the fort. He started a school, where he taught them and played with them. Sometimes he even went to their houses to live with them, and always visited them when they were ill. It was not as though all of these young boys had descended directly from heaven and were the children of the gods. There was no dearth of human as well as demonic qualities in them. Selfishness, anger, greed, hatred and envy were strong forces within them, and not all of them had been well brought-up by their parents. For these reasons, the fort built by the Mogs was converted into a kingdom just like them—unruly and untamed. All the wild forces of nature seemed to be living in the fort at the same time. Working with such ingredients, Govindamanikya patiently tried to mould them into worthy human beings. His mind was perpetually alive to the greatness inherent in every human's life, and to the extreme care with which it had to be nurtured and protected. Govindamanikya wanted to immerse his own incomplete life in his attempts to ensure the fulfilment of the immense potential of human life. He could endure all kinds of suffering and aggravation for this. Only now and then did he tell himself with a regretful sigh, 'I am not able to perform my tasks properly. I wish Bilwan were here.'

Thus did Govindamanikya spend his days with a hundred Dhruvas.

43

Meanwhile Shah Suja had fled after being driven back by his brother Aurangzeb's soldiers. He was defeated on the battlefield near Allahabad. Vanquished by the enemy, Suja was unable to trust even his allies in this hour of danger. Frightened and humiliated, he fled all alone, disguised like a common man. Wherever he went, he was followed by the enemy soldiers' flags and the hoofbeats of their horses. Finally he returned to Patna and announced his arrival to his family and his subjects, once again dressed in the robes of a nawab. Aurangzeb's son Prince Mohammad was at the door of Patna soon afterwards with his soldiers. Suja fled to Munger.

Some members of his scattered entourage regrouped in Munger, and he gathered some new soldiers too. Refurbishing the forts at Teriagarhi and Shikligali and building a rampart on the hillside by the river, he dug himself in firmly.

Meanwhile Aurangzeb despatched his wise general Mir Jumla to aid Prince Mohammad. The prince camped not far from the Munger fort, in full view, while Mir Jumla set off for Munger along a secret path. While Suja was engaged in a minor skirmish with Prince Mohammad, Mir Jumla arrived in Vasantpur with a large army. A perturbed Suja left Munger at once for Rajmahal with his soldiers. His entire family lived there. The emperor's soldiers followed him there immediately. Suja battled desperately for six days, not allowing the enemy forces to advance. But when he finally realized he would not be able to withstand them any longer, he fled to Tonda under cover of darkness on a stormy night, accompanied by his family and as much of his wealth as possible, and began repairing the fort there.

Then the monsoon arrived, the river swelled, and the road couldn't be negotiated anymore. The emperor's soldiers could not march on.

Before this war, a marriage had been arranged between Prince Mohammad and Suja's daughter. But the war forced both sides of the family to forget the proposal.

While fighting was in abeyance because of the rains, and Mir Jumla had retreated some way from Rajmahal with his camp, one of Suja's soldiers arrived from Tonda to secretly hand Mohammad a letter. Opening it, the prince saw that Suja's daughter had written, 'Is this what fate held for me, my prince? Is the man whom I have accepted as my husband and surrendered my heart to, who exchanged rings and vowed to marry me, now coming here with a cruel sword in his hand to take my father's life? Is this what I was fated to see? Is this our wedding, my prince? Is that what the ceremonies are for? Is that why our Rajmahal is bathed in blood today? Is that what my prince has brought iron chains from Delhi for? Are these the chains of love?'

Prince Mohammad's heart seemed riven apart by a sudden earthquake when he read this letter. He could not be quiet a moment longer. All his hopes of a kingdom and the badshah's kindness seemed irrelevant. He cast all consideration of gains and losses into the sacrificial fire of the first flush of youth. Each of his father's acts appeared unjust and cruel. He had already opposed his father's conspiratorial and brutal policies categorically, earning the emperor's ire as a result. Summoning some of the key people amongst his generals, he expressed his disenchantment with the emperor's vile baseness and tyranny. 'I shall join my father's brother at Tonda,' he said. 'Those of you who love me may follow me.'

Offering long salutes, they said at once, 'Shahzada is absolutely right. You will see half the army joining you at Tonda tomorrow.'

Mohammad went across the river to Suja's camp that very day. Celebrations broke out in Tonda. Everyone forgot that a war was on. Only the men had been busy all this while, but now even the women in Suja's family found themselves occupied all day and night. Suja received Mohammad with great love and joy. After the continuous shedding of blood, the ties of blood seemed to grow tighter. The wedding was conducted amidst music and dancing. No sooner had the festivities ended, however, than there was news that the emperor's soldiers were nearby.

The generals had sent word to Mir Jumla as soon as Mohammad had left for Suja's camp. Not one of the soldiers joined Mohammad, having realized that he had plunged into a sea of danger out of choice. Any attempt to join him would be madness.

Suja and Mohammad had expected most of the emperor's soldiers to be on the prince's side on the battlefield. With this hope Mohammad entered the battlefield flying his standard. A large group of soldiers advanced towards him. Mohammad was elated. But when they came near him, they began to fire at Mohammad's soldiers, whereupon realization dawned on the prince. But it was too late. His soldiers prepared to flee. Suja's eldest son died on the battlefield.

That same night, the unfortunate Suja and his son-in-law escaped to Dhaka with their families on fast-moving boats. Mir Jumla did not consider it necessary to follow Suja to Dhaka. He busied himself with restoring order in the conquered lands.

Since Suja's friends had turned away one by one in his hour of danger, his heart melted when Mohammad risked his own life to be on Suja's side. He came to love Mohammad with all his heart. At this time a spy of Aurangzeb's, carrying a letter, was captured in Dhaka. The letter came into Suja's hands. Aurangzeb had written to Mohammad, 'My dearest son Mohammad, you have neglected your duties to revolt against your father, smearing your blemishless image. Enticed by the deceiving smile of a woman, you have sacrificed your faith. The man who will shoulder the responsibility for ruling over the entire Mughal Empire tomorrow has become a slave to a woman today. Nevertheless, since Mohammad has sworn by the almighty to repent, I forgive him. But only when he has accomplished the task he had set out for will he regain our favour.'

Suja was thunderstruck when he read this letter. Mohammad repeated over and over that he had certainly not expressed repentance to his father—all this was a ploy on his father's part. But Suja's suspicions were not allayed. He considered the matter for three days. Finally, on the fourth day he said, 'The bond of trust between us has loosened, my son. Therefore I entreat you to leave with your wife—or else we shall have no peace in our hearts. My treasury doors are open for you, take as much wealth as you desire. Consider it your father-in-law's gift to you.'

Shedding tears, Mohammad departed, accompanied by his wife.

'I shall not fight anymore,' declared Suja. 'I shall sail for Mecca from the Chattagram port.'

He left Dhaka in disguise.

44

On a monsoon afternoon, a fakir, accompanied by three young boys and an adult porter, were trudging along the road on their way to the fort in which Govindamanikya lived. The boys looked exhausted. There was a raging wind, and it rained incessantly. The youngest of the boys was no older than fourteen—shivering in the cold, he said in a stricken voice, 'I can't anymore, my father,' and began to weep uncontrollably.

Without a word, the fakir sighed and drew the boy to his breast.

The eldest of the boys reprimanded the youngest one, saying, 'What's the use of crying on the road? Be quiet. Don't make it worse for father.'

The youngest boy controlled his weeping and calmed down.

The third one asked the fakir, 'Where are we going, father?'

'Do you see that tower of the fort over there? That's where we are going.'

'Who lives there, father?'

'I believe a king lives like a monk over there.'

'Why did the king become a monk, father?'

'I don't know, my son,' answered the fakir. 'Maybe his own brother gathered an army and chased him out like a dog, depriving him of his kingdom and his riches. Perhaps the dark crevice of poverty and the saffron robes of the monk are the only place he can hide. There is no sanctuary from his brother's hatred, from his poisoned fang.'

The fakir pursed his lips with great force to control his emotions. The eldest boy asked, 'Which kingdom was this monk the king of, father?'

'I do not know, my son,' answered the fakir.

'What if he does not give us shelter?'

'Then we shall sleep beneath the trees. There is no place for us anywhere else.'

The fakir and the monk met at the fort shortly before evening. Each was astonished to see the other. Govindamanikya realized that the fakir did not seem to be a fakir. He did not see on the fakir's face the unsullied, uncommented radiance that comes from withdrawing the heart from small, selfish desires and sublimating it in a larger mission. This fakir was constantly wary, alert. The unquenched desires of his heart seemed to be sipping fire from his blazing eyes. An uncontrollable ferocity, unable to escape through his clamped lips and clenched teeth, had reentered the black cave of his heart to gnaw away at itself. He was accompanied by three young boys whose pleasant and comely—but exhausted and suffering—appearance, along with their proud reserve, made it appear that they had spent all their lives on a pinnacle of high regard, from which they had set foot on earth for the first time. They did not seem to have known that walking meant getting one's feet dirty. The filthy, miserable poverty of the world seemed to be earning their loathing at every step—observing the difference between carpet and the earth, they seemed to be cursing the world constantly. The earth appeared to have quarrelled with them in particular, rolling up and putting away its largest carpet. To them, everyone was guilty. That the poor man in rags could come up to them was nothing but his audacity; just like people who flung scraps of food into the distance so that hateful dogs could not come near them, they too seemed capable of turning their faces away from a distance at the sight of a wretched, famished beggar and throwing a handful of coins on the ground. In their eyes the deprived and poorly-clothed state of most of the world was a mere case of gross disobedience. If they were not happy and respected in the world, it was nobody's fault but the world's.

It wasn't as though Govindamanikya's thoughts had run quite so far. He had interpreted all the signs to conclude that this fakir was not someone who had sacrificed all his desires to emerge free and strong and ready to work for the world; he was on the road only out of his aversion for the whole world because his desires had not been fulfilled. This fakir believed that everything he wanted was due to him. As for what the world wanted, he would provide it at his convenience—and not care if he did not. Because things had not turned out the way he had wanted them to, he had rejected the world and taken to the street.

To the fakir, Govindamanikya appeared to be both a king and a monk. This was not exactly what he had expected. He had assumed he would encounter either a pot-bellied lump of flesh in a turban, or a filthy monk in humble garments—in other words, an embodiment of aggressive arrogance smeared in ash and lying in the dust. But he observed neither of the two. Govindamanikya looked as though he had forsaken everything, and yet everything belonged to him. He had everything because he wanted nothing— he had them because he had given himself. Just as he had surrendered himself, the entire world had willingly given itself up to him. He was the king because there was no pomp about him, and he was a monk because he had gained proximity to the world. He had not had to play the role of either king or monk.

The king looked after his guests with great attention. They accepted his hospitality carelessly, as though they were completely entitled to it, even informing the king of their requirements. The king asked the eldest of the boys affectionately, 'Are you very tired from your travels?'

Without answering properly, the boy moved closer to the fakir. Smiling at them, the king said, 'Your tender bodies are not for travelling on foot. Stay here at my fort, I will take care of you.'

The boys could not determine whether this needed a response, and precisely how they should behave. So they edged closer to the fakir, perhaps under the impression that this shabby man from an unknown place was about to abduct them.

The fakir said gravely, 'Very well, we are willing to stay at your fort for some time.'

He seemed to be doing the king a favour. To himself he said, 'If you knew who I am, my condescension would have made you infinitely happy.'

The king simply could not win the three boys over. And the fakir remained detached through it all.

'I believe you were a king once,' the fakir told Govindamanikya. 'Of which kingdom?'

'Tripura,' answered Govindamanikya.

At this the boys dismissed him as insignificant. They had never heard of Tripura in their lives. But the fakir was a little perturbed. 'How did you lose your kingdom?' he continued.

Govindamanikya was silent for some time. Finally he said, 'Shah Suja, the nawab of Bengal, banished me from my kingdom.'

He made no mention of Nakshatraray.

Startled, the boys looked at the fakir, who blanched. Suddenly he blurted out, 'So all this is your brother's doing? Is it your brother who has hounded you out of the kingdom and forced you to become a monk?'

The king was surprised. 'How do you know all this?' he asked.

Afterwards he concluded that it was hardly surprising—the fakir must have heard it from someone.

'I don't know anything,' the fakir said hurriedly. 'This is merely my surmise.'

When night fell everyone went to bed. But the fakir could not sleep. He had waking nightmares, starting at every sound.

The next day he told Govindamanikya, 'For certain reasons we cannot stay here. We shall leave today.'

'The boys are exhausted by the journey,' answered Govindamanikya. 'A little rest would do them good.'

The boys were irked—the eldest of them looked at the fakir and said, 'We are not exactly children, we can endure hardship when we have to.'

They were not prepared to accept Govindamanikya's affection. He did not say anything more.

Just as the fakir was preparing to resume his journey, another guest appeared at the fort. Both the king and the fakir were astonished to see him. The fakir could not determine what to do. The king greeted his guest reverently. It was none other than Raghupati. Accepting the king's respects, Raghupati said, 'May you live long.'

A little disturbed, the king asked, 'Did Nakshatra send you, thakur? Is all well?'

'Nakshatraray is well,' answered Raghupati, 'do not worry.'

Pointing to the sky, he said, 'Jaysingh has sent me to you. He is no longer alive. Unless I fulfil his wishes, I shall have no peace. I shall be by your side, as your companion in everything you do.'

At first the king did not know what to make of Raghupati's statement. Wondering whether Raghupati had lost his mind, he was quiet.

Raghupati said, 'I have seen many things, but there is no joy in any of them. No joy in force, no joy in power—only the path you have adopted offers happiness. I have been your greatest enemy, I have resented you, I wanted to ensure you were sacrificed at my feet. Today, I have come to surrender myself to you completely.'

Govindamanikya said, 'You have done me a good turn, thakur. My enemy was chasing me like a shadow, you freed me from it.'

Without paying any attention to this, Raghupati said, 'The demoness whom I served through bloodshed has finally sucked away all the blood in my own heart. I have got rid of the unfeeling bloodthirsty foolishness; it no longer occupies the temple of the gods—it has entered the court and ascended the throne.'

'If it is far away from the temple, it can also recede from people's hearts,' said the king.

A familiar voice said from the back, 'No, maharaj, the human heart is the real temple—that is where the blade is honed and hundreds and thousands of other humans sacrificed. What happens in the temple is a mere enactment.'

Startled, the king turned around to discover the ever-smiling and dignified figure of Bilwan. Offering his respects, the king said, his voice choking, 'This is such a happy day for me.'

Bilwan said, 'Because you have conquered yourself, maharaj, you have conquered everyone else too. Friends and foes alike are gathered at your door today.'

Coming forward, the fakir said, 'I am your enemy too, maharaj, but I surrender to you today.'

Indicating Raghupati, he said, 'The Brahmin there knows me. I am Suja, nawab of Bengal, who banished you unjustly. I have been punished for this—my brother's malevolence follows me everywhere, I have no place of my own in my kingdom. I cannot bear to be in disguise anymore. I am relieved giving myself up to you.'

The king and the nawab embraced. The king only said, 'How fortunate I am.'

'Even being your enemy is beneficial, maharaj,' said Raghupati. 'I have surrendered to you only because I was your foe, or else I would never have come to know you.'

'Just like the noose that tightens around you when you try to free yourself of it,' smiled Bilwan.

Suddenly an uproar rent the sky. The fort was overrun by boys of all ages and sizes. 'There's my Dhruva, thakur,' the king told Bilwan.

He pointed to the boys.

'The one whose benediction has brought you all these boys has not forgotten you either,' said Bilwan. 'Let me bring him to you.'

He went out, returning a little later with Dhruva and depositing him in the king's arms. Clasping him to his breast, the king said, 'Dhruva!'

Dhruva did not speak, simply putting his head on the king's shoulder. This first meeting after a long interval seemed to bring forth an inarticulate embarrassment and hurt in the boy's tiny heart. Putting his arms around the king, he buried his face in his neck.

'I have got so much, only Nakshatra has not addressed me as his brother,' said the king.

'Everyone behaves like a brother, maharaj,' said Suja, 'except one's brother.'

The arrow had not yet been dislodged from Suja's heart.

CONCLUSION

It is necessary to mention here that the three boys were Suja's daughters in disguise. Suja had gone to the Chattagram port with the intention of sailing to Mecca. But unfortunately he could not secure a ship for himself on account of the severe monsoon. While he was returning, disappointed, he met Govindamanikya at the fort. Living in the fort for a while, Suja was told that the emperor's soldiers were still looking for him. Govindamanikya sent him to his friend, the king of Arakan, accompanied by transportation and a huge retinue of people. Before he left, Suja gave Govindamanikya his priceless sword as a gift.

Meanwhile, the king, Raghupati and Bilwan made the village come alive. The fort became its heart.

After six years had passed this way, Chhatramanikya died. A messenger arrived from Tripura to invite Govindamanikya to reclaim the throne.

'I shall not return to the kingdom,' Govindamanikya declared at first.

'This cannot be, maharaj,' said Bilwan. 'When righteousness is at the door with its invitation, do not neglect it.'

Looking at his students, the king said, 'Shall my hopes and my work of all these years remain incomplete?'

'I shall complete your work,' said Bilwan.

'If you remain here my work there will be incomplete,' said the king.

'No, maharaj, you no longer need me,' said Bilwan. 'You can now rely on yourself completely. I shall meet you now and then if I can make the time.'

The king entered his kingdom with Dhruva, who was a little boy no longer. Having learnt Sanskrit thanks to Bilwan, he had now turned his attention to studying the scriptures. Raghupati accepted the priest's position once again. This time he seemed to discover the dead Jaysingh alive one more.

Meanwhile the treacherous king of Arakan assassinated Suja and married his youngest daughter . . .

Govindamanikya mourned when he recalled the cruelty of the king of Arakan towards the hapless Suja. To ensure that Suja's name remained immortal, he exchanged the sword for a purse of money and had a gorgeous mosque constructed in the city of Comilla. It stands to this day with the name of Suja Masjid.

Govindamanikya's care ensured that Meherkul became a settlement of cultivators. He handed over deeds for much of the land to the Brahmins. King Govindamanikya had had a tank made in the village of Batisa, to the south of Comilla. He had planned several tasks for the public good, but he could not complete them. Repenting this, he passed away from his worldly life in the year 1669 Anno Domini.

WE ARE MESSENGERS OF A NEW GENERATION

আমরা নূতন যৌবনেরই দূত

We are messengers of a new generation
Restless and wondrous
We break through barriers
Our passion is red like crimson flowers
We streak through blizzards, we are lightning
When we blunder
We dive in deep and fight our way to the shore
Call us, we are ready—for storms, for life, for death

Stories

Just One Night

I went to school with Surabala, played husband-and-wife with her many a time. Whenever I visited her at home her mother took special care of me, and, pairing us together, said to herself, how well they're matched.

Young though I was, I understood. I developed an ingrained belief that I had some special rights over Surabala compared to everyone else. Intoxicated with that power, I never held back from exercising my authority and inflicting myself on her. For her part, she obeyed me uncomplainingly, endured all my punishment. She was reputed for her beauty—but to the callow philistine that I was, there was no glory in that beauty—all I knew was that Surabala had been born for the precise purpose of acknowledging me as her master, and hence was the object of uncommon callousness on my part.

My father was the secretary to the zamindar, Mr Chowdhury. His ambition for me was to get trained in managing landowners' businesses and to build a career in that direction But I was opposed to the idea. Just like Nilratan from our neighbourhood, who had run away to Kolkata to get an education and become an aide to the Collector, I too harboured a similarly high aspiration—even if I could not become an aide to the Collector, I was determined to at least be head clerk to a judge.

I had always observed my father's obsequiousness towards the above-mentioned judicial professionals, and since childhood I had learnt that one had to worship them with supplies of fish or vegetables or money, which was why even the low officials of the court—even the guard—held a special place in my heart. These were our gods in Bengal—new, miniature versions of the three million gods and goddesses. When it came to material gains, people reposed far deeper faith in them than in Ganesha. Consequently, they were now the beneficiaries of all that used to go to the elephant-headed god in the past.

Inspired by Nilratan's example, I too seized an opportunity to run away to Kolkata. Initially I lived with an acquaintance from the village; subsequently, my father also contributed to my education, which progressed suitably.

I used to attend public meetings, too. I had no doubt that it was absolutely essential to sacrifice your life for the nation. But I did not know how this intricate task could be accomplished, nor were there any examples.

But that did not dampen my enthusiasm. Being village lads, we had not learnt to poke fun at everything the way the precocious Kolkata boys did, so our commitment was stronger. Important people would make speeches at our meetings, while we abandoned our meals to scour the roads with our subscription books, going door to door begging for money, distributing pamphlets on the street, arranging benches at the meetings, ready for a fight if anyone were to utter the slightest word against our leaders. Observing these symptoms, the city boys referred to us as country bumpkins.

I had come to the city to become a clerk, but I prepared to become a Mazzini or a Garibaldi.

At this juncture my father and Surabala's father took the initiative to arrange her marriage with me.

I had run away to Kolkata when I was fifteen and Surabala was eight; I was now eighteen. In my father's opinion, I would soon be past marriageable age. However, I had pledged to myself not to enter into matrimony ever, but to die for my motherland. I informed my father that I would not get married without completing my education.

In a couple of months I was told that Surabala had got married to Ramlochan the advocate. Since I was busy raising funds for my fallen country, the news seemed trite.

My father passed away soon after I cleared my Entrance examinations and was about to take the first Arts examination. I wasn't the only one in the family, there was my mother and two sisters. Hence I had to abandon the thought of college and return home in search of employment. After considerable effort, I secured a job as second master at an Entrance school in Noakhali district.

I decided that I had discovered a suitable vocation. I would use my advice and encouragement to convert my students into troop-leaders for the India that was to come.

I started work—only to discover that the compulsions of the coming examinations were far stronger than those of the India of the future. The headmaster would be enraged if I spoke to the students about anything beyond grammar and algebra. Within a month or two, my passion waned too.

Untalented people like us weave many plans in our dreams, but when we eventually begin our professional lives we find ourselves satisfied playing the beast of burden, toiling patiently every day with our heads down, having our tails twisted when necessary, happy to chew on our single meal of fodder every evening; we have no energy left for any other activity.

In case a fire broke out at the school, it was required for one of the teachers to reside on the premises. Since I lived alone, this responsibility had fallen upon me. I occupied a small hut adjacent to the larger structure in which the school was housed.

The school building was at a little distance from the village, situated beside a large lake. It was surrounded by a variety of trees, with a pair of enormous neem trees virtually next to the building providing ample shade.

What I have not mentioned, for it seemed irrelevant, was that the government advocate Ramlochan Roy lived close to our school. And I was aware that his wife—childhood companion Surabala—lived with him too.

I met Ramlochan-babu. I had no inkling of whether he knew of my childhood connection to Surabala. On my part I did not think it appropriate to mention it when we were introduced. Nor, in fact, did I consider Surabala to have been part of my life in any manner once upon a time.

It was a holiday, and I was visiting Ramlochan-babu at home. I do not recollect what we were discussing, possibly the plight of India at present. It was not as though he was particularly worried or despondent about it, but it was the kind of subject you could spend an hour or two on, expressing casual concern continuously over a hookah.

Suddenly I heard the soft sounds of tinkling bangles, rustling clothes and footsteps in the next room. I realized that a pair of curious eyes were observing me through a window.

At once I recollected her eyes—large, brimming over with trust, simplicity and childlike love, with their black pupils, dark eyelashes and radiant glances. Suddenly someone seemed to wring my heart with an iron fist. My heart ached.

I returned home, but the ache persisted. No amount of reading or writing could lighten the load; my heart suddenly assumed the proportions of an intolerable burden, placing a severe strain on my blood vessels.

Calming myself down by the evening, I began to ponder over the reason for this sensation. The answer came from within: where did your Surabala disappear?

But I relinquished my rights over her voluntarily, I replied to myself. Why should she have waited for me forever?

Someone within me appeared to respond, once she could have been yours whenever you wanted, but now not even the most ardent entreaty will allow you to steal a glance of her. No matter how nearby your Surabala lives, no matter how often you can hear the tinkling of her bangles or sense the fragrance of her washing her hair, there will always be a permanent wall between you.

I said, let there be a wall, Surabala is not mine.

The answer I heard was, Surabala is not yours today, but she could have meant everything to you.

That was true. She could have meant everything to me. She could have been the one I would call my own, the one to share all my joys and sorrows—but today she was so distant, so out of reach, that I was not allowed to see her, that talking to her was wrong, that even thinking of her was a sin. And suddenly this Ramlochan had arrived from nowhere; with just a few ritualistic incantations he had seized her from the grasp of the world in a single moment.

I was not here to propound new philosophies, to tear society apart, to break all relationships. I was merely expressing the state that my heart was in. Did every thought of one's necessarily have to be reasonable? I simply could not disabuse myself of the notion that, rightfully, the Surabala who occupied Ramlochan's home was more mine than his. I admitted that such a notion was inconsistent and incorrect, but by no means unnatural.

I could no longer concentrate on my daily activities. In the afternoon, while the students hummed, the heat baked everything outside, and the warm breeze bore the fragrance of flowers from the trees, I would long for—I don't know what I would long for—all I knew was that I did not feel the slightest desire to spend my life correcting the grammatical errors of all these young hopefuls of India.

When the holidays began, I could not bear to be alone in my enormous room, but when someone paid a visit that seemed unendurable too. As I listened to the meaningless murmur of the trees beside the lake in the evening, human society appeared to me as a web of complex errors. No one did the right thing at the right time, and died of longing afterwards when struck by wrongful desires at the wrong time.

You could have been happy all your life as Surabala's husband, but no, you had to become Garibaldi, though your career culminated in the post of second master at a rural school. And Ramlochan Roy was a lawyer, he had no particular need to be Surabala's husband; up to the moment of his marriage, Surabala was no different from Bhabashankari for him, and here he was, having got married without a thought, now happily earning a salary as a government lawyer. When the milk got burnt he took her to task, when he felt cheerful he bought her jewellery. Plump, well-dressed and incapable of dissatisfaction, he never spent his evenings by the lake, gazing at the stars and bemoaning his fate.

Ramlochan was travelling somewhere for some important litigation. Just like I was alone in my hut, so too must Surabala have been alone in hers.

It was Monday, I remember. The sky was overcast since morning. At ten it began to drizzle. The inclement weather forced the headmaster to close the school early. Fragments of black clouds seemed to be marching up and down the sky in preparation for some gigantic event. The torrential rain began the next afternoon, accompanied by thunderstorms. As night progressed, so did the intensity of the rain and the storm. The wind had started blowing from the east, now it gradually shifted to the north and north-east.

Attempting sleep on such a night was futile. I remembered that Surabala was alone at home on this cataclysmic night. Our school building was far stronger than her hut. A hundred times I thought of fetching her here and passing the night myself by the lake. But I vacillated, unable to decide on a course of action.

When it was one or one-thirty at night, the flood could be heard. The sea was thundering in. I left my home and went towards Surabala's. The lake was on the way, but even before I could arrive on its bank, I was submerged up to my knees. By the time I traversed the distance to the lake, a second giant wave had arrived.

The embankment was some twenty feet high. As I mounted it, so did another individual, albeit from the opposite side. My innermost soul and my entire body, from one extremity to another, knew at once who it was. And I had no doubt that she, too, was aware of my identity.

All else was submerged, only two living creatures, she and I, remained standing on the embankment, which jutted like an island some five or six feet out of the water.

It was an apocalyptic night, there were no stars in the sky, all lights on earth had been extinguished—no convention would have been breached in saying a word, but not a word could be spoken. Neither of us even enquired after the other's well-being.

Both of us fastened our gaze on nothing but the darkness. Beneath our feet, impenetrably black, the frenzied stream of death roared on.

Tonight, Surabala had abandoned the entire world to be by my side. She had no one but me now. In the dim, distant past, when we were infants, Surabala had emerged from another lifetime, from the darkness of some ancient mystery, to be with no one else but me on this planet under the sun and the moon where mankind lived. And now, after all these years, she had left the illuminated world teeming with people to be my side again, all by herself, in this dreadful, desolate, apocalyptic blackness. The current of life had borne the virgin bud to me, now the current of death had once more borne the fully-bloomed flower to me—one more wave and we would be torn asunder from this extremity of the earth, plucked from our separated stalks and united together.

What if that wave never came? What if Surabala lived happily in her home with her husband, her family and her near and dear ones? I had tasted eternal bliss on this single night spent on the edge of the apocalypse.

The night drew to an end—the storm stopped, the flood ebbed—Surabala went home without saying a word, as did I.

I reflected that I had become neither an aide, nor a clerk, nor Garibaldi—I was the second master of a broken-down school. Only for one fleeting moment in my life had an eternal night appeared—of all the days and nights in my lifespan, this one night was the only source of complete fulfilment in my insignificant existence.

The Gift of Vision

I've been told that many Bengali girls these days have to secure husbands through their own efforts. I have done the same, but with the assistance of the gods. Since childhood, I had performed many a penance, offered many a prayer.

I was married by the time I had turned eight. But owing to my sins in a previous life, even after getting a husband as wonderful as mine, I was unable to have him fully. The goddess Durga, with the Third Eye, took away my eyesight. She did not afford me the bliss of seeing my husband till my last day on earth.

My trials by fire began in infancy. Barely had I turned fourteen when I give birth to a stillborn child. I was at death's door too, but it would not do if someone destined to suffer were to die. The lamp that has been made to burn is never endowed with insufficient oil; it shall be extinguished only after it has glowed all night.

I did survive, but because of physical weakness, or the grief in my heart, or some other reason, my vision was affected.

My husband was a medical student at the time. Because of his enthusiasm for his new learning, he was delighted at the opportunity to practice medicine. He proceeded to treat me himself.

My elder brother was in college that year, reading for a Bachelor of Law degree. 'What do you think you're doing?' he asked my husband one day. 'Kumu's about to lose her eyes. Let a good doctor have a look at her.'

'What new treatment can a good doctor offer?' my husband responded. 'I know the medicine perfectly well.'

'Obviously there's no difference between you and the principal of your college,' my brother proclaimed in some anger.

'You're a student of law, what do you know of medicine?'

countered my husband. 'If you are in litigation against your wife over property after you get married, will you come to me for advice?'

When elephants fight, I mused, the grass is trampled. The argument was between my husband and my brother, but I was at the receiving end of both their barbs. Since my brother had already given me away in marriage, I wondered, too, why there should be a battle now over responsibility. My joys and sorrows, illness and recovery were all my husband's concern now.

My husband appeared to develop some bad blood with my brother that day over the trivial matter of treatment for my eyes, which were already streaming with tears frequently; now the flow became stronger and neither my husband nor my brother could fathom the real cause.

Out of the blue, my brother brought a doctor home one afternoon while my husband was away at college. After examining my eyes, the doctor warned that unless I was careful, the affliction could worsen. He prescribed some medicine I was not familiar with, which my brother sent for immediately.

After the doctor had left, I told my brother, 'I beg of you, Dada, do not disrupt my current course of treatment.'

I used to be in great awe of my brother since childhood; it was unthinkable for me to make such an explicit request to him. But I could clearly see that the arrangement for my treatment, which my brother was making behind my husband's back, boded ill rather than well for me.

My brother, too, was probably taken aback by my candour. 'Very well, I shall not bring the doctor to your home anymore,' he said after a pause, 'but let us see what effect the medicine has if you apply it as prescribed.' When the medicine arrived, he explained how to use it and left. Before my husband could return, I flung the bottles, vials, brushes and rules into the draw-well in the front yard.

Seemingly inspired by his altercation with my brother, my husband devoted himself to treating my eye with twice as much zeal. He proceeded to change medicines constantly. I put on eye-patches, tried glasses, applied medicated drops, put medicated powder on my eyelids, even suppressed the urge to expel my intestines after consuming malodorous fish-oil. My husband would ask how I was feeling. Much better, I would respond. I tried to convince myself that I was indeed improving. When my eyes watered too much, I concluded that this was a good sign; when my eyes stropped streaming, I assumed I was on my way to recovery.

But the agony became unbearable after some time. My vision became blurred and the pain in my head would not allow me to stay still. My husband appeared to be somewhat on the defensive now. He was unable to think of a pretext on which to fetch a doctor after all this time.

'Where's the harm in calling a doctor just to keep Dada happy,' I told him. 'He is needlessly upset about this and it makes me unhappy. You're the one who will treat me, after all, but having a doctor as a figurehead is useful.'

'You're right,' said my husband. He proceeded to fetch a British doctor that very same day. I was not privy to their conversation, but the Englishman appeared to be berating my husband, who stood in silence with his head bowed.

When the doctor had left, I took my husband's hand and told him, 'Where did you get this ass of a British doctor, an Indian doctor would have been better. Is he going to diagnose what's wrong with my eye better than you do?'

'Your eye needs surgery,' he said hesitantly.

'You knew all along that it does,' I pretended anger, 'but you hid it from me all this time. Do you think I'm afraid?'

His embarrassment was mitigated. 'How many men are brave enough not to feel afraid on hearing of eye surgery?' he asked.

'The valour of the man is only for his wife,' I joked.

'That is true,' he turned sombre. 'Men can only flaunt their vanity.'

'Do you think you can compete with women on that score?' I said, dismissing his solemnity. 'We'll beat you there too.'

Meanwhile, when my brother came visiting, I drew him aside and told him, 'My eyes were improving once I started following your doctor's prescription, but after I mistakenly applied a medicine to my eyes instead of taking it, things have taken a turn for the worse. My husband says I need surgery.'

'I was under the impression your husband was treating you,'

answered my brother, 'which made me so angry I did not come all this time.'

'No, I was following your doctor's prescription in secret,' I said, 'though I did not tell my husband in case he became angry.'

How many lies one has to tell when one is born a woman! I could not hurt my brother, nor undermine my husband's importance. As a mother she has to keep the child in her arms happy; as a wife she has to keep the father of the child happy—such are the deceptions that women have to resort to.

The outcome of the ruse was that I was able to see my husband and brother reunited before I went blind. My brother surmised that the secret treatment had caused this mishap; my husband concluded that it would have been better to have followed my brother's counsel from the beginning. With these thoughts the two repentant souls sought to make amends and came closer to each other. My husband began to seek my brother's advice; my brother also began to defer to my husband's opinion on every subject.

Eventually, on the basis of their consultations with each other, a British doctor operated on my left eye. Already weak, the eye could not survive this assault, the light in it died suddenly. Then the remaining eye was also gradually shrouded in darkness with every passing day. The curtain was drawn forever on the young figure adorned in sandalwood paste whom I had seen for the first time on my wedding day in childhood.

One day my husband came to my bedside, saying, 'I shall not brag to you anymore, I am the one responsible for you losing your eyes.'

I realized his voice was choking with tears. Seeking his right hand with both of mine, I said, 'I don't care, you have claimed what is yours. Think about it, how would I have consoled myself had I lost my vision because of a doctor's treatment. Since no one can ward off destiny, no one could have saved my eyes. The only joy of my blindness is that I lost my eyes to you. Ramachandra had plucked out his own eyes as an offering to the gods when he had run out of flowers. I offer my vision to my own god—I give you everything, my moonlit nights, my morning light, the blue of my sky, the green of my earth; tell me of whatever appears beautiful to your eyes, I shall accept it as the holy image of what you have seen.'

But I had been unable to say all this, for they cannot be said; I had been thinking of all this for a long time. When I felt weary at times, when my commitment and spirit dimmed, when I thought of myself as deprived, wretched and a victim of misfortune, I used to force such thoughts into my head; I tried to use my devotion to rise above my misery. Through a mixture of words and silence, I may have been able to convey the state of mind to him that way. 'I cannot restore what I have made you lose out of my foolishness, Kumu,' he said, 'but I shall stay by your side to compensate for your lack of vision as much as I possibly can.'

'That is not practical,' I replied. 'I shall simply not allow you to turn your home into a hospital for the blind. You must marry again.'

My voice was close to choking before I could explain in detail why it was absolutely necessary for him to marry. Controlling myself a little after a coughing fit, I was about to continue, when my husband said in an outburst of emotion, 'I may be obtuse, I may be vain, but that does not mean I am heartless. I have blinded you with my own hands. If I forsake you for that handicap and take another wife, I swear by our family deity Gopinath that I shall be branded a sinner who killed a Brahmin, who killed his father.'

I would not have permitted such a dire vow, I would have prevented it, but my tears were threatening to overflow my heart, my throat and my eyes and roll down my face; in trying to restrain them, I was unable to speak. Listening to my husband, I buried my face in my pillow in a tumult of happiness and wept. I was blind, and yet he would not forsake me! He would hold me to his heart like the suffering man embraces his plight! I did not want such fortune, but the heart is selfish, after all.

Finally, when the first torrent of tears had spent itself, I pressed his head to my breast, saying, 'Why did you make such a terrible vow! Do you suppose I was entreating you to marry for your own pleasure? I would have fulfilled my objective through my rival. I would have got her to do the things I cannot do for you because I cannot see!'

'Even maids can do all this. Can I possibly marry a maid for my convenience and put her on the same pedestal as my goddess.' Raising my face with his fingers, he planted a pure kiss on my forehead; this kiss seemed to open a third eye, I was anointed a goddess on the spot. This is better, I told myself. Now that I have gone blind, I can no longer be the housewife, I shall ascend to the position of goddess to ensure my husband's well-being. No more lies, no more deception, I banished all the meanness and pretence of the housewife from my life.

All day long I was in conflict with myself. My husband's momentous oath would keep him from remarrying—my joy at this seemed to gnaw at me; I simply could not shake it off. A day might dawn when it would be more beneficial for your husband to remarry instead of adhering to his vow, suggested the goddess who had arrived that day within my being. So what, the woman of old within me responded, since he has taken this oath, he cannot marry again. Perhaps, said the goddess, but that is no reason to rejoice. That is all very well, the human being countered, but since he has vowed etcetera. The same argument over and over again. The goddess only frowned without answering and my heart and soul were shrouded in the darkness of a terrible fear.

My repentant husband dismissed the servants and maids from my presence and prepared to personally look after all my needs. Initially I revelled in my helpless dependence on him even for the slightest thing. For, in this way I would have him to myself constantly. Because I could not see him, my desire to have him by my side all the time grew inordinately. My eyes' share of the pleasure of my husband's company now became disputed property between the remaining sense organs, each of them trying to increase their own allocation. If my husband happened to be engaged elsewhere for a long time, I felt suspended in mid-air, unable to hold on to anything, as though I had lost my moorings. Earlier, if my husband was late on his way back from college, I used to go up to the window facing the road he took back home and open it a crack to wait for him. With my eyes I had connected myself to the world that he moved around in. Today every part of my sightless body was in search of him. The primary bridge between his world and mine had been destroyed. Now there was an unbridgeable blindness between us; all I could do now was to wait in helpless eagerness for him to cross over of his own volition from his side to mine. That was why, when he left my side for even a moment, I attempted with all of my sightless body to hold on to him, distraught, praying for his return.

But such yearning, so much dependence, was not good. The burden of the wife on the husband was heavy enough, I could not possibly add on the enormous weight of my blindness. I would bear this universal darkness in my life on my own. I took a single-minded oath not to tie down my husband with this eternal blindness of mine.

I learnt to perform all my duties in the darkness, aided by sounds and scents and touch. In fact, I succeeded in accomplishing many of my household chores with greater felicity than before. Now I began to feel that sight distracts us more than it helps. The eyes see a great deal more than is necessary to go about one's activities efficiently. And when the eyes act as sentries, the ears become indolent, hearing far less than they should. In the absence of my restless eyes, all my other sense organs began to perform their tasks with efficiency.

I no longer allowed my husband to look after me, and I began to take care of all his needs as I once had.

'You are depriving me of my atonement,' my husband told me one day.

'I do not know what you are atoning for, but why should I increase the burden of my sins.'

Say what he might, he breathed a sigh of relief when I set him free. No man is fit for the mission of tending to his blind wife all his life.

After passing his medical examinations, my husband took me to live in a village.

Moving to the countryside made me feel as though I had come back home to my mother. I had left my village for the city at the age of eight. Over the past ten years the memories of my land of birth had become as indistinct as a shadow. As long as I had my eyesight, the city of Calcutta had obscured all my other memories. As soon as I lost my vision, I realized that Calcutta could only keep the eyes busy, it could not fulfil the heart. Once my vision was gone, the village of my childhood days became brighter in my mind, just like the stars in the sky at close of day.

We went to Hashimpur in the middle of December. The place was new to me, I could not surmise what it looked like, but the scents and sensations of my childhood wrapped themselves around me. The same morning breeze from the freshly-ploughed earth moistened by the dew, the same sweet fragrance rising from the fields of cascading gold arhar and of mustard to encompass the sky, the same cowherds' songs, even the sound of the bullock-cart trundling along the unrepaired road delighted me. With its indescribable smells and sounds, the bygone memories of my earliest years enveloped me as palpably as the present did; my blind eyes could not protest. I returned to the same childhood, only, my mother was missing. In my mind's eye I could see my grandmother, her sparse hair let loose as she sat in the yard with her back to the sun, putting homemade delicacies out to dry, but I was unable to hear the bawdy songs of Bhajandas, the village hermit, in her slightly quavering, ancient, weak murmur; the same harvest festival came alive in the dew-soaked sky of winter, but there was no longer a gathering of those little girls, my childhood friends, amongst the crowds husking the newly reaped rice! In the evening I could hear a cow mooing close by, I was reminded of my mother taking the evening lamp into the cowshed; the smell of moistened fodder and the smoke from burning straw seemed to seep into my heart and I could hear the sound of brass bells from the temple of the Vidyalankar family who lived by the village tank. Everything corporeal from the eight years of my childhood seemed to have been filtered out, with only the essence and the fragrances having been gathered and heaped around me.

I remembered too, the vows of my childhood and the prayers at dawn to the gods after picking flowers for them. It had to be admitted that the confusion of incursions and intrusions in Calcutta definitely distorted the reasoning of the mind. The innocent purity of prayers and devotion could no longer be maintained. I remembered the day a friend of mine from the neighbourhood told me after I went blind, 'Doesn't it make you angry, Kumu? I wouldn't have set eyes on my husband again if I were you.' 'I certainly do not set eyes on him,' I told her, 'for which I blame these accursed eyes, but why should I be angry with my husband.' Labanya was furious with him for not having consulted a doctor well in time, she was trying to instigate me to anger too. I explained to her that living together meant all kinds of joys and sorrows, sins of omission and commission, deliberate and inadvertent; but if the respect remained intact there was a kind of peace even in unhappiness, else life went by in a spate of temper, competition and conflict. It was bad enough being blind, why increase my load of unhappiness by loathing my husband. Enraged at such an old-fashioned viewpoint from a child like me, Labanya left, jerking her head in contempt. But whatever I might have told her, words are poisonous, they never entirely fail in meeting their objectives. Labanya's angry statements had cast a few embers into my heart, and although I ground them out under my heel, they left a mark or two behind. That was why I was saying that there was so much advice, so many suggestions when in Calcutta that one's reasoning matured and hardened prematurely.

In the village, the fragrance of the cool night-flowering jasmine used for worshipping the gods turned all my hope and trust as fresh and bright as in my childhood. Both my heart and my household were fulfilled by the gods. I prostrated myself, saying, 'No matter that my eyes are gone, o Lord, for you are with me.'

Alas, I was wrong. To claim your proximity was arrogance too. All I was entitled to aver was that I belonged to you. Oh yes, one day my god will force these words out of my throat. I may have nothing of my own that day, but I must be his. I had no claim on anyone, only on myself.

A few months passed happily. My husband acquired a reputation as a doctor. We saved some money too.

But money isn't good. It sucks the mind into itself. When the mind is in control it can create its own happiness, but when wealth takes the responsibility for building happiness, the mind is left with nothing to do. Material objects and furniture and so on occupy the space that was once filled by a happy heart. Joy is exchanged for possessions.

I cannot cite any particular instance or incident, but because the blind sense more, or for some reason I do not know, I could clearly discern the changes that came over my husband with our growing affluence. The sensitivity that he had once had to right and wrong, to morality and immorality, seemed to be dwindling by the day. I remember him saying once, 'I am not studying medicine just to make a living, I shall serve poor people this way.' His voice used to be stifled with loathing whenever he referred to those doctors who would not even check the pulse of an impoverished dying man without taking their fees in advance. I realized that those days were gone. Once, a destitute woman clung to his feet, entreating him to save her son, but he ignored her. Eventually I forced him to go and treat him, but he did not give the patient his full attention. I know what view he had held about illicit income when we were not well off. But now the bank account had swollen, an official representing a wealthy man arrived for two days of secret confabulation. I had no idea what they discussed, but when he came to me the next day, it was to talk about a great many other things with a good deal of cheerfulness. My intuition told me he had disgraced himself that day.

Where was the husband whom I had seen for the last time before going blind! What had I done for the person who had kissed between my sightless eyes and anointed me his goddess. Those who succumb unexpectedly to a tempestuous passion can still rise again under the force of a new fervour, but I could find no antidote to this constant hardening—every moment, every day—in every fibre of his being, this continuous suppression of the conscience under the trappings of external achievements.

The separation that blindness had wrought between my husband and me was immaterial, but I felt things closing in on me when I realized that he was no longer where I was; I was blind, I lived in an internal world, devoid of light, clutching the first love of my green years, my untrammelled devotion, my undimmed faith—the dew had not yet dried on the sapling in the temple to which I had made sacred offerings with my little girl's hands at the beginning of my life; but my husband had now vanished somewhere in the desert of life in his pursuit of money, abandoning this cool, shaded, evergreen land! All that I believed in, all that I thought of as moral, all that I considered greater than every joy and possession in the world were the very things that he looked askance at, laughing at them from a remote distance. But once upon a time there had been no rift between us, in our younger days we had begun our journey on the same road, neither he nor I had realized that our paths had diverged; and now, finally, he no longer responded when I called out to him.

Sometimes I wondered whether I made too much of things because I was blind. If my eyesight were intact, perhaps I would have been able to see the world as it really was.

My husband conveyed as much to me. An old Muslim man had come one morning to request him to treat his granddaughter for cholera. 'I am poor, my son, but Allah will bless you,' I heard him say. 'Allah's blessings will not be enough,' my husband replied, 'first tell me what you will do for me.' My first thought was, why had God only blinded me, why had he not made me deaf as well? The old man sighed deeply, exclaiming 'Allah!' and left. I got the maid to fetch him to the back door at once, telling him, 'Here's some money for your granddaughter's treatment, Baba, please bless my husband and ask Doctor Hari next door to go with you.'

But I could not bring myself to eat the entire day. 'Why do you look so mournful?' my husband asked on awaking from his afternoon nap. I was about to give my customary answer of the past—nothing's the matter. But the time of deception was over, I spoke my mind. 'I keep thinking of telling you, but I simply cannot determine what exactly there is to say. I don't know if I can explain what's in my heart, but I am sure you can sense in yours that although we had started our lives in unison, we walk on different paths today.' 'Change is the principle on which the world runs,' my husband laughed. 'Everyone goes through change when it comes to wealth or beauty or youth, but is nothing meant to be constant?' I asked. Turning grave, he replied, 'Look, other women complain about real things lacking in their lives—some of husbands who don't earn enough, some of husbands who don't love them; you pluck problems out of the sky.' I realized at once that blindness had placed a layer over my eyes and planted me outside this ever-changing world; I was not like other women; my husband wouldn't understand me.

Meanwhile an aunt of my husband's arrived from her village to enquire after my husband. The first thing she said after both of us greeted her was, 'Ill luck has robbed you of your eyesight, Bouma, now how will our Avinash manage his home and household with a blind wife? Get him married again.' Had my husband joked, 'Very well, Pishima, why don't you arrange something,' everything would have been clarified. But he said irresolutely, 'What on earth are you saying, Pishima?' 'Have I said anything wrong?' she said. 'Isn't that right, Bouma, what do you think?' 'You're asking the right person for advice, Pishima,' I laughed. 'Does anyone seek the victim's consent before picking his pocket?' 'Yes, that's true,' she responded. 'You and I will plan this in secret, Avinash. But I must tell you, Bouma, the more wives a high-caste man has, the more his wives can revel in his glory. If our boy had got married instead of becoming a doctor, would he have lacked for an income? Patients inevitably die when they consult doctors, and when they die they cannot pay their fees, but by the curse of God the wives of high-caste men never die, and the longer they live the more their husbands stand to gain.'

Two days later my husband asked his aunt in my presence, 'Can you find a girl from a decent home who can help my wife as a member of the family will, Pishima? She cannot see, if she had a companion by her side constantly I would be relieved.' This might have been applicable when I had become newly blind, but I did not know how either the household or I suffered now because of my blindness; however, I remained silent without protesting. 'That's easy,' my husband's aunt responded. 'My husband's elder brother has a daughter who's as well-behaved as she's pretty. She has come of age, now all she's waiting for is a suitable husband; with a high-caste groom like you, her family will give her in marriage immediately.' 'Who's talking of marriage,' said my husband, startled. 'Do you suppose a girl from a decent family will just come and live in your home unless you marry her?' This was a valid argument, which my husband could not refute suitably.

Standing alone amidst the eternal darkness of my shuttered eyes, I sent my prayers into the sky, protect my husband, o Lord.

A few days later, when I emerged after my morning prayers, my husband's aunt said, 'Hemangini, the niece I was telling you about has arrived from my village. Himu, this is your elder sister.'

My husband appeared suddenly, but prepared to retreat at the sight of an unknown lady. 'Don't go, Avinash,' said my aunt.

'Who is this?' my husband enquired. 'This is my niece Hemangini,' answered my husband's aunt. My husband proceeded to express repeated and superfluous consternation over who had fetched her and when, and other such details.

'I can clearly understand what's going on,' I said to myself, 'but now the deception begins on top of it. Hide-and-seek, cat-and-mouse, lies! If you wish to break your principles, go ahead and satisfy your wild tendencies, but why abase yourself for my sake. Why these tricks to deceive me.'

Taking Hemangini's hand, I took her to my bedroom. I ran my hands over her face and body; she appeared to be beautiful, and not less than fourteen or fifteen years old.

'What are you doing?' Suddenly the girl laughed sweetly and loudly. 'Are you trying to exorcise me?'

The sound of her free, simple laughter dispelled the dark cloud between us in an instant. Putting my right arm around her neck, I said, 'I'm looking at you, my dear,' and ran my hand over her soft face once more.

'Looking at me?' she said, laughing again. 'Am I an eggplant or cauliflower from your kitchen garden that you're examining to see how well it's grown?'

It occurred to me suddenly that Hemangini did not know that I was blind. 'I am blind, you see,' I told her. She turned solemn for a few minutes at this. I could clearly make out that she examined my sightless eyes and expression with her own young and curious eyes before saying, 'Oh, is that why you've got Kaki here with you?'

'I didn't ask her to come,' I answered. 'Your aunt is here by her own choice.'

'As a favour?' The girl laughed again as she spoke. 'Then Lady Favour won't budge in a hurry. But why did my father send me here?'

My husband's aunt entered the room. She had been talking to my husband all this while. 'When are we going back home, Kaki?' Hemangini asked her as soon as she came in.

'But you just got here. Why do you want to leave so soon? Never seen a girl so restless.'

'I don't see any sign of your leaving soon, Kaki,' Hemangini said. 'But then these are your relatives, you can stay here as long as you like; but I shall leave, I'm warning you.' Taking my hand, she added, 'Don't you agree, my dear, you people are not my family, after all.' Without answering, I drew her to myself. I observed that no matter how formidable my husband's aunt might be, she was not capable of controlling this girl. Without openly displaying displeasure, my husband's aunt tried to be nice to her; the girl appeared to shake her off. Laughing off the entire thing as though a spoilt child were having a little fun, my husband's aunt was about to leave. But a thought struck her, and she returned to tell Hemangini, 'Come along Himu, it's time for your bath.' Coming up to me, Hemangini said, 'Let's go together, shall we.' My husband's aunt gave up reluctantly; she knew that insisting would only lead to Hemangini getting her way, and the conflict between them would be inappropriately revealed to me.

'Why don't you have any children?' Hemangini asked on our way to the tank at the back of the house. 'How would I know,' I said with a smile, 'God did not see it fit to give me any.' 'There must be something sinful about you then,' Hemangini responded. 'Only the almighty knows whether there is,' I replied. As proof, she said, 'Don't you see, Kaki is so twisted that she is unable to have children.' I neither understood the theories of good deeds and bad or joy and sorrow or reward and punishment myself, nor did I try to explain them to the girl; I only sighed and said to Him in my head, no one but you knows! Hemangini put her arms around me at once, saying, 'But you're sighing because of what I said! As if anyone bothers with what I say!'

I observed that my husband's medical practice was being disrupted. Attending to calls from distant places was out of the question, he even attended to nearby calls in a big hurry and returned swiftly. Earlier, when he worked at home, he came into the women's part of the house only for his meals and to sleep. Now my husband's aunt sent for him every now and then, he came often on his own too, asking after her. Whenever she called out, 'Get my paan, will you, Himu,' it was obvious that my husband was visiting her. Hemangini would take her the paan, or the hair-oil, or the sindoor, as directed, for the first two or three days. But thereafter, she simply refused to go when summoned, directing the maid to provide whatever her aunt had asked for.

'Hemangini, Himi, Himu,' her aunt would call—the girl would cling to me tightly as though overcome by compassion; anxiety and melancholy subsumed her. After that she did not refer to my husband even by mistake.

Meanwhile my brother came to visit me. I knew his eyes were sharp. It would be virtually impossible to conceal from him the way things were developing. My brother was a stern judge. He did not know how to forgive the slightest of transgressions. My biggest fear was that my husband would appear a sinner to none other than him. I kept everything hidden under a layer of extra good cheer. I talked incessantly, bustled about, and made elaborate arrangements—all to raise a covering dust-storm, as it were. But this was so uncharacteristic of me that it increased the chances of being caught out. However, my brother was unable to stay very long, for my husband began to express such impatience that it took the form of rudeness. He left. Before his departure, he placed a trembling, affectionate hand on my head, keeping it there for the longest time; I understood the blessings he heaped upon me with all his heart; his tears fell on my tear-stained cheeks.

I remember people were on their way back home in the evening on a market day in April. A rain-bearing storm was on its way from the distance, the smell of damp earth and moisture-laden wind was spreading across the sky; companions separated from one another were calling out loudly and desperately to each other in the darkened fields. As long as I was alone with my blinded eyes in my bedroom, the lamps were never lit, lest the flames sear my garments or some other accident take place. Sitting on the floor of my room in that desolate darkness I was praying to the emperor of my eternally blind world with folded hands, saying, 'When I cannot feel your compassion, Lord, when I cannot fathom your intentions, I hold on to the rudder of my orphaned broken heart with all my might; I bleed but I cannot contain the tempest within me; how many more tests will you subject me to, what power do I have in any case.' Tears welled in my eyes as I spoke, I sobbed with my head on the bed. I had to do household chores all day. Hemangini stayed by my side like my shadow, I had no opportunity to shed the tears that gathered in my heart; I was weeping that day after a long time. Suddenly I sensed the bed shake, there was a rustle of movement from someone, and a moment later Hemangini silently put her arms around me, wiping away my tears with the end of her sari. I had not even realized when and why she had lain down on my bed in the early part of the evening. She asked me no questions, nor did I say anything to her. She ran her cooling hand over my brow. I did not realize when the thunderstorm struck, accompanied by torrential rain; after a long time a pleasant sense of serenity brought peace to my fevered heart.

'If you don't come home with me now, Kaki,' Hemangini told my husband's aunt the next day, 'I'm going back by myself with Kaibarta-Dada, I'm warning you.' 'Don't do that,' my husband's aunt intervened, 'I'm going tomorrow, we can all go together. Here, Himu, take a look at the pearl ring my Avinash has got for you.' She handed over the ring proudly to Hemangini. 'See how good my aim is, Kaki,' said Hemangini, flinging the ring though the window at the middle of the tank at the back of the house. My husband's aunt bristled with rage and displeasure. Taking my hand, she told me repeatedly, 'You must not tell Avinash about this childishness, Bouma, my son will be very upset. Promise me you won't!' 'There's no need to entreat me over and over again, Pishima, I won't tell him a thing.'

'Don't forget me, Didi,' Hemangini told me the next day as she was about to leave. 'The blind never forget, my dear,' I told her, running my hands over her face repeatedly. 'I have no world, all I have is my own heart.' Breathing in the fragrance of her hair, I kissed her head. My tears streamed down on her tresses.

My world became arid with Hemangini's departure—when the fragrance, the beauty, the music, the lustre and the tender greenness she had brought into my heart had all dissipated, I stretched my arms out to my home, to my surroundings, to find out how things stood for me. 'Thank goodness they've left,' my husband said with extra good cheer, 'I can get down to work now.' Shame, shame on me. Why this sham on my account? Did I fear the truth? Had I ever feared turmoil? Didn't my husband know? Had I not accepted eternal darkness calmly when I gave up my eyes?

All this time my husband and I were only separated by

blindness, now another gulf was created. My husband never mentioned Hemangini to me, not even by mistake, as though she had been obliterated completely from the world related to him, as though she had never made the slightest impression on it. Yet I could easily discern that he kept himself informed through letters; just as the stalk of the lotus feels a tug as soon as the floodwater enters the lake, in the same way I could sense something in my heart when he became even a little more animated than usual. I was not unaware of the occasions on which he heard from her, nor of those when he did not. But I could not ask him about her. I used to yearn for some news of—or to talk about—the frenzied, tempestuous, dazzling star that had risen briefly in my darkened heart, but I did not have the right to mention her name even once to my husband. This silence, pregnant with words and with pain, reigned unwaveringly between us.

Around the end of April, the maid appeared to ask, 'The boat is being readied with great attention, Mathakrun, where is Babamoshai going?' I knew that some preparations were afoot; the oppressive silence that precedes a storm, followed by the scattered clouds signalling imminent destruction, had been gathering in my fate; I had realized that the divine destroyer Shiva had been silently amassing devastating forces of annihilation. 'I haven't heard anything,' I told the maid. She left with a sigh, not daring to ask any more questions.

Late that night my husband appeared to tell me, 'I have been called away somewhere, I have to leave early in the morning. It may be two or three days before I am back.'

'Why are you lying to me?' I asked, rising from my bed.

'Lying to you?' said my husband indistinctly, his voice trembling.

'You are going to get married,' I told him.

He remained silent. I stood without a word. There was no sound in the room for a long time. Eventually I said, 'Answer me. Say, yes, I am going to get married.'

'Yes, I am going to get married,' he repeated like an echo.

'No, you cannot go,' I told him. 'I shall protect you from this terrible danger, this terrible sin. What kind of a wife am I if I cannot do this, what are all those prayers worth?'

The room was silent again for a long time. Slumping to the

floor and clutching my husband's feet, I asked, 'What sin have I committed, where have I gone wrong, why do you need another wife? Tell me the truth, swear by me.'

'I am telling you the truth,' he answered gently, 'I am afraid of you. Your blindness has wrapped you in an impenetrable covering, I have no right of entry. You are my god, you are as fearsome as a god, I cannot live my life every day with you. I want an ordinary woman, someone I can scold, someone I can be angry with, someone I can love, someone for whom I can buy jewellery.'

'Carve my heart and look inside. I am an ordinary woman, deep inside I'm nothing but your young bride; I want to trust you, I want to depend on you, I want to worship you; do not raise me to a higher pedestal than yourself—you make me suffer intolerably when you humiliate yourself, let me languish at your feet all the time.'

Could I possibly remember all that I said? Can the agitated sea possibly hear itself roar? All I remember saying was, 'As God is my witness, if I have been a pious wife, you shall not violate your sacred vow in any circumstances. Before you can commit such a dreadful sin, either I shall be widowed, or Hemangini shall not live.' After that, I fainted to the floor.

When I recovered, the birds had not yet begun chirping at daybreak and my husband had left.

I sat down to pray behind the closed doors of my puja room. I did not leave the room all day. In the evening the house shook under the impact of a nor'wester. I did not say, 'My husband is on the river, protect him, o God.' All I kept saying with all my heart was, 'Let my fate bring what it may, but make my husband desist from sinning.' The entire night passed. I did not abandon my position even the day after. I do not know who gave me strength through my fasting, sleepless hours, but I sat like stone before the stone idol.

In the evening people began knocking on the door. When they finally broke it open, they found me unconscious on the floor.

The first word I heard when I regained consciousness was 'Didi!' I found myself lying with my head in Hemangini's lap. Her bridal dress rustled as she moved her head. So you have rejected my prayers, o God. My husband has fallen.

'I have come for your blessings, Didi,' Hemangini said softly, her head bowed.

As stiff as a block of wood for a moment, I sat up the very next instant, saying, 'Why should I not, my sister! You are not to blame.'

'Blame!' Hemangini laughed in her sweet, high voice. 'You are not to be blamed for getting married, but I am?'

Putting my arms around Hemangini, I laughed too. 'As if my prayers make the world go round,' I thought to myself. 'It's His will that's the last word, not mine. Let this attack assail me physically, but I shall not let it assail my heart, where my faith and my trust reside. I shall remain as I was.' Planting herself near my feet, Hemangini touched them with her hands and raised her hands to her brow. 'May you always have good fortune and eternal happiness,' I said.

'Your blessings alone won't do,' said Hemangini, 'you must escort your sister's husband and your sister in with your own chaste hands. You must not feel embarrassed to see him. I shall bring him in here if you will permit me.'

'Do,' I answered.

I heard fresh footsteps enter my room after a while. 'How are you, Kumu?' I heard someone ask lovingly.

'Dada!' I jumped out of bed hurriedly and touched his feet with my hands.

'What do you mean, Dada,' said Hemangini. 'Box his ears, he's your sister's husband.'

I understood everything then. I knew that my brother had vowed not to marry; with our mother dead, there was no one to coax him either. Now it was I who had arranged for him to be married. Tears streamed from my eyes, I simply could not staunch them. My brother ran his hand through my hair gently; Hemangini just put her arms around me and laughed.

I could not sleep that night; I awaited my husband's return anxiously. I could not imagine how he would conceal his disgrace and disappointment.

Extremely late at night, the door opened very slowly. I sat up in bed, startled. My husband's footsteps. My heart hammered in my breast.

'Your brother has saved me,' he said, coming to bed and taking my hand. 'I was about to succumb to temporary infatuation. The almighty alone knows the burden I was weighed down by when I climbed into the boat the other day; when the storm struck us in mid-river, I was afraid for my life, but I also wished that I could perish in the waves, for that would save me. When I reached Mathurganj, I heard that your brother had married Hemangini the previous day. I cannot explain with what humiliation and joy I returned to the boat. I have become convinced over these past few days that I shall never be happy if I am parted from you. You are my goddess.'

'No, I do not wish to be a goddess,' I smiled. 'I am the mistress of your house, I am merely an ordinary woman.'

'You must honour my request too,' my husband said. 'Do not embarrass me ever again by turning me into a god.'

The next day the neighbourhood was roused by the sound of ululation and conch shells. While he ate and while he slept, in the morning and at night, Hemangini began to mock my husband, there was no end to his travails; but no one made the slightest mention of where he had been and what had transpired.

Misplaced Hope

Arriving in Darjeeling, I found the town enveloped in mist and rain. I felt little inclination to go out, and even less of an inclination to stay indoors.

After breakfast at the hotel, I went out for a walk in thick boots, wrapped from head to foot in a mackintosh. It drizzled intermittently, and the curtain of dense fog everywhere made it appear that the Creator was intent on obliterating the canvas of the world with an eraser.

Pacing up and down in solitude on the deserted Calcutta Road, I mused on the unbearable nature of the featureless kingdom of fog, for my heart yearned for a mother earth whose wealth of sounds and textures and form I wished to grasp once again with each of my five senses.

Suddenly I heard a woman weeping pitifully. In a household wracked by illnesses, the sound of sobbing would hardly have been unexpected, I doubt whether I would even have turned a hair, but in this infinite realm of clouds, she seemed to be the only person weeping in the now-obliterated universe—I could not dismiss this as insignificant.

Following the sound, I went closer to its source to discover a woman in saffron, her golden yellow matted locks piled high on her head like a mountain peak, seated on a rock by the side of the road, weeping softly; she was not grieving for a recent loss; many years of silent, repressed fatigue and weariness had burst forth in a torrent today, under the weight of the foggy bleakness.

This is excellent, I thought to myself; it has started just like a homespun story. In all my life, I had never harboured the hope of actually setting eyes on a weeping woman ascetic on a mountainside.

I could not discern her origins. 'Who are you, what is the matter?' I asked compassionately in Hindi.

There was no answer at first, she only cast a tearful glance at me, her eyes glistening through the mist.

'You need not be afraid of me,' I continued. 'I am a gentleman.'

At this she laughed, saying in chaste Hindustani, 'It's been a long time since I've been afraid, nothing can embarrass me anymore. Once upon a time even my own brother had to seek permission to enter the ladies' chamber I lived in, babuji, but no curtain secludes me from the world today.'

I was irked; considering my deportment, entirely like a sahib's, why had this wretched woman unhesitatingly addressed me as babuji? I considered ending my novel this very instant and staging a swift, emphatic exit, emitting cigarette smoke like an English steam engine with its nose in the air. But curiosity triumphed eventually. Loftily I asked, tilting my head, 'May I be of help? Do you need anything?'

She looked steadily at me, then answered briefly after a few moments, 'I am the daughter of Nawab Ghulam Kader Khan of Badraon.'

What kingdom Badraon was located in, what kind of nawab Ghulam Kader Khan was, or what misery had forced his daughter to become a woman of religion and weep by the side of Calcutta Road in Darjeeling, was entirely beyond my knowledge or belief, but I decided not to ruin the atmosphere, for the story was turning out to be most fascinating.

Saluting her gravely at once, I said, 'Pardon me, Bibisahiba, I could not recognize you.'

There were a number of logical reasons for not recognizing her, primary among them being that I had never seen her in my life. Moreover, the dense fog made it difficult even to identify one's own limbs.

Bibisahiba took no offence, and gesturing with her right hand at an adjacent rock, she gave me permission in a satisfied tone. 'Please take a seat.'

I observed that the lady possessed the ability to issue orders. Receiving her approval for occupying the wet, moss-covered slab of rock, hard and uninviting, felt like an unexpected honour. The daughter of Ghulam Kader Khan of Badraon, Noor-un-neesa, aka Meher-un-neesa, aka Noor-Ulmulk had granted me the privilege of sitting on a low, slippery rock not far from herself. When I had left the hotel in my mackintosh, I had not even dreamed of such a sublime possibility.

The tale of a mysterious dialogue between a wayfaring couple amidst Himalayan peaks sounds like a freshly-completed poetic narrative hot off the author's pen. But although the sound of rushing torrents from distant, desolate mountain ranges and the exotic notes of music from Kalidasa's *Meghdootam* and *Kumarsambhava* might come alive in the reader's heart, we must all acknowledge that there are very few modern Bengalis in boots and mackintosh capable of retaining their full sense of self-importance while sharing a mud-spattered seat by the side of Calcutta Road with a Hindustani woman in rags. But the world was shrouded in a dense vapour that day, and there was nothing anywhere to cause the slightest embarrassment; in the unending realm of mist there remained only the daughter of Ghulam Kader Ali Khan, Nawab of Badraon, and I, a freshly-bloomed Bengali Englishman. Like two pieces of debris from the universe after the apocalypse, we sat on our respective slabs of stone, an incongruous juxtaposition whose extreme irony was visible to no one but destiny.

'Who has done this to you, Bibisahiba?' I asked.

The princess of Badraon smote herself on the forehead. 'What do I know of who is instrumental in such acts?' she declared. 'Who has cloaked these enormous Himalayan mountains behind a flimsy veil of mist?'

I accepted this without any philosophical argument. 'True,' I said. 'Who can claim to understand the mysteries of fate? We are mere insects.'

I would have debated the point without letting Bibisahiba off the hook so easily, but my linguistic skills would not have proved equal to the task. Whatever little Hindi I had mastered through interaction with doormen and bearers would have made it impossible for me to discuss destiny and free will cogently with the daughter of the Nawab of Badraon—or of any other place, for that matter—by the side of Calcutta Road.

'The astonishing saga of my life has drawn to a close this very day,' announced Bibisahiba. 'If you so command, I shall narrate it to you.'

'But of course,' I replied, flustered. 'Where's the question of commanding? If you deign to recount it, I shall be gratified to be your audience.'

Let no one imagine I used these precise words in Hindustani, for I had the desire but not the prowess. When Bibisahiba spoke, a sweet, temperate breeze seemed to waft over a soothing, verdant harvest with dew-soaked golden crests, such was the facile gentleness, the beauty, the untrammelled flow of her words. And I could only respond in terse, direct fragments, like a barbarian. I had never acquired the well-rounded, uninterrupted and natural grace of speech that she displayed; for the first time, while conversing with Bibisahiba, I sensed my shortcoming at every step.

She said, 'The blood of the emperors of Dilli coursed in my veins; it had become well-nigh impossible for my father to locate a suitable groom for my lineage to be preserved. A proposal had been sent by the Nawab of Lucknow, which my father was hesitating over, when a battle broke out between the sepoys and the British Raj over the business of biting bullets; Hindustan was darkened by the smoke from cannons.'

I had never heard Hindustani spoken in a woman's voice, especially in the voice of a lady of noble blood. Hearing it now made it obvious that this was the language of the aristocracy. The period to which this language belonged no longer existed; the railway, the telegraph, swarms of industrial workers, and the eclipse of the upper classes had made everything small and insignificant, without embellishments. No sooner did I hear the daughter of the nawab speak than a wonderful power made the imagined palace of the Mughal emperor materialise before my eyes through the impenetrable web of fog and mist there in the modern hill-station of Darjeeling built by the British. Large marble pillars soaring into the sky, long-tailed horses adorned with finely-woven fabric, canopies with golden fringes on the backs of elephants, citizens sporting multihued headgear dressed in diverse apparel of silk, wool and muslin, curved swords dangling at their waists, the tips of their embroidered shoes curling upwards. Long hours of leisure; long, flowing garments; and an abundance of courtesy.

'Our fort was situated by the Yamuna,' the nawab's daughter told me. 'The general of our troops was a Hindu Brahmin. His name was Kesharlal.'

The woman seemed to pour all the melody in her feminine voice at once into her pronunciation of the name. Placing my walking stick on the ground, I stirred and sat up.

'Kesharlal was an upright Hindu. Every morning at dawn I would observe through the window of the ladies' chamber how he immersed himself up to his neck in the waters of the Yamuna, pivoting on his heels as he offered his prayers to the newly-risen sun with raised arms, the palms joined. Later, he would sit down on the steps of the ghat in his sodden clothes and count his beads before returning home, all the while singing devotional songs in the Bhairav raga in his clear, pleasant voice.

'I was a Muslim girl, but I had never been instructed about my own religion, nor was I aware of the methods of worship that it demanded; the bonds of our faith among the men had been loosened at the time by debauchery, drinking and tyranny, nor were its tenets pursued actively in the pleasure chambers in the inner sanctum.

'Possibly the lord had given me a natural longing for a religious way of life. Or perhaps there was some other hidden reason, I cannot say. But at the sight of Kesharlal's prayers and rituals under the newly risen sun on the desolate ivory-coloured steps leading into the placid blue Yamuna every tranquil morning, my recently-awakened heart would be flooded with the indescribable sweetness of devotion.

'The Brahmin Kesharlal's regular, disciplined acts of self-cleansing made his fair, sprightly, ageless figure appear like a pure flame unsullied by smoke; the sacred aura of the Brahmin made the heart of this daughter of a Muslim defer to him with exquisite reverence.

'I had a Hindu maid, who would bow in respect to Kesharlal every day, touching his feet devotedly, a sight that aroused both joy and envy in me. On auspicious occasions and festivals she would serve a ritual feast to Brahmins to signal her faith. Helping her with money, I would ask her, "Are you not going to invite Kesharlal?" Biting her tongue to indicate the impropriety of such an act, she would answer, "Kesharlal thakur accepts neither hospitality nor alms."

'Thus unable to display any direct or indirect sign of my devotion to Kesharlal, my famished heart was discontented.

'One of our forefathers had forcibly married a Brahmin woman, it was her sacred blood that I sensed in my veins there in the ladies' chamber, and imagining a connection with Kesharlal by virtue of this lineage offered me a modicum of satisfaction.

'From my Hindu maid, I used to hear the details of every single Hindu ritual, each of the wonderful stories about their gods and goddesses, the glorious history of the Ramayana and the Mahabharata. Listening to them there in the corner of my sanctum unveiled a wondrous image of the Hindu world to my mind's eye. Idols and statues, the sonorous sound of conch-shells, the temples with their spires cased in gold, the smoke rising from the incense, the fragrance of flowers mixed with sandalwood and perfume, the miraculous powers of yogis and sages, the superhuman greatness of the Brahmin, and the wondrous play of the gods and goddesses masquerading as human beings all combined to put within my reach a vast, primordial, remote and supernatural world of illusion; like a tiny bird cut off from its nest, my heart seemed to flutter from room to room within an enormous, ancient palace at dusk. The Hindu world was like a charming fairytale to the soul of the young girl that I was.

'That was when the battle broke out between the British and the sepoys. A revolutionary wave swept our little fort in Badraon too.

'"It is time to banish the beef-eating British from the land of the Aryans and resume the game of dice between Hindus and Muslims for the right to rule Hindustan," declared Kesharlal.

'My father Ghulam Kader Khan was a cautious man; referring to the British in terms of unflattering kinship, he said, "They are capable of performing impossible tasks; the people of Hindustan cannot overcome them. I do not intend to lose my little fort for the sake of uncertain expectations; I shall not fight the British."

'At a time when the blood of all Hindus and Muslims in Hindustan was boiling, this mercantile prudence on my father's part elicited condemnation from us all. Even my mothers, the begums, grew agitated.

'An armed Kesharlal arrived with troops. "If you do not join us, Nawab Sahib, we will incarcerate you and I shall take command of your fort," he told my father.

'"You need not go to such trouble," answered my father, "I am on your side."

"You must give us some money from the treasury," said Kesharlal.

'My father did not offer very much, saying, "I shall provide it as needed."

'Tying up every single ornament I possessed, from head to toe, in a cloth bundle, I sent them to Kesharlal secretly through my Hindu maid. He accepted them. My unadorned limbs thrilled in delight at this.

'As Kesharlal prepared to scrub and clean the barrels of rusted guns and disused swords, one afternoon the commissioner of the district, accompanied by British redcoats, entered our fort in a cloud of dust.

'My father Ghulam Kader Khan had surreptitiously passed on information about the rebellion to him.

'Such was Kesharlal's magical influence over the troops of Badraon that they prepared to join battle with their damaged guns and blunt swords and die if needed.

'My treacherous father's house seemed like hell to me. My heart was breaking with rage and sorrow and hatred, but not a single teardrop escaped my eyes. Disguising myself in my cowardly brother's clothes I left the women's chambers; no one had the leisure to notice my departure.

'By then the cloud of dust and the gunpowder fumes, the cries of the soldiers and the sound of the guns had stopped, and the land and water and skies were in the grip of the terrible calm of death. The sun had set after painting the waters of the Yamuna a bloody red, a near full moon hung in the evening sky.

'The battlefield was strewn with grotesque scenes of death. At another time my heart would have ached in compassion, but that day I wandered about like a person in a dream, searching for Kesharlal's whereabouts. This was the only objective in my life; all else appeared unreal.

'In the course of my search I discovered under the bright moonlight, late at night, the corpses of Kesharlal and his devoted servant Devkinandan, in the shade of a mango orchard on the bank of the Yamuna, not far from the battlefield. I realized that, grievously injured, the master had borne the servant—or the servant the master—away from the battleground to the shelter of this spot and given him up into the arms of death.

'My very first act was to fulfil my pent-up desire for expressing my devotion. Throwing myself at Kesharlal's feet, and releasing my hair which flowed down to my hips, I repeatedly wiped the dust off those feet and held his ice-cold toes against my heated brow. As soon as I kissed his feet, the tears I had held back all this time welled up.

'Kesharlal's body stirred, and hearing a sudden, stifled groan emerge from his lips, I released his feet in shock. "Water," I heard him say, his eyes still closed and his voice parched.

'At once I soaked the scarf around my shoulder in the water of the Yamuna and ran back. Wringing the water out of the scarf, I poured it drop by drop into Kesharlal's parted lips, and bandaged the severe wound that had destroyed his left eye with the torn-off end of my sodden garment.

'After I had fetched water several times from the Yamuna in this way and sprinkled it on his face and eyes, he regained consciousness gradually. "Do you wish for some more water?" I enquired. "Who are you?" asked Kesharlal. Unable to restrain myself, I said, "Your servant is your devotee. I am Nawab Ghulam Kader Khan's daughter." I had assumed that, death being imminent, he would depart with the knowledge of his disciple's identity; no one would be able to deprive me of this joy.

'As soon as he discovered my identity, Kesharlal roared like a lion, "Daughter of a traitor! Heretic! You have cut me off from my faith by making me drink water offered by a Muslim at the hour of my death." With these words he struck a mighty blow on my face with his right hand. I almost fainted; a veil of darkness descended before my eyes.

'I was sixteen then, having emerged from the women's chamber for the first time in my life; the fiery and lascivious sun in the external sky had not yet robbed me of the glow on my tender cheeks. The instant I entered the world outside I received my first greeting from it, from the god of my universe.'

My cigarette had extinguished, I had been listening transfixed all this time. I did not know whether it was the story or the form of the music that I was listening to, but I hadn't said a word. Now I could hold myself back no longer. 'Beast!' I exclaimed suddenly.

'Who is the beast?' The nawab's daughter said. 'Can a beast in the throes of death refuse the water held to its lips?'

'That is true,' I replied, subdued. 'He was a god.'

'What sort of god!' responded the nawab's daugher. 'Can a god reject the follower's devoted offering?'

'That is also true,' I answered, and fell silent.

'At first I was shattered,' continued the nawab's daughter. 'I felt as though the universe had collapsed around me. Regaining consciousness in an instant, I offered my respects, from a distance, at the feet of the harsh, unbending, cruel, indifferent, pious Brahmin. To myself, I said, "You accept nothing, Brahmin—the humble man's service, another's hospitality, the rich man's gift, the maiden's youth and the woman's love—none of it. You are unique, you are solitary, you are detached, you are distant and I do not even have the right to surrender to you!"

'I cannot say what Kesharlal thought when he saw the daughter of the nawab offering her respects with her forehead touching the ground, but there was no surprise or change of expression in his face. He gave me a single serene glance, then got to his feet slowly. Startled, I extended by arm to offer support, which he rejected in silence, and went up to the bank of the Yamuna with great effort. A ferry boat was moored at the spot, but there was neither anyone to row him across, nor anyone to be ferried. Climbing into the boat, Kesharlal untied it from the stake. The boat drifted midstream and then disappeared gradually. On that hushed night I wished, with all the burden of my soul and of my youth, with all the unacknowledged devotion in my heart, to join my palms in reverence towards this invisible boat, and like a flower fallen prematurely from its stem, give up my failed life to the tranquil waters of the Yamuna, joyous under the moonlight.

'But I could not. The moon in the sky, the dense, black line of forest by the Yamuna, the deep blue unwavering waters of the river, the turrets of our fort shining in the moonlight beyond the mango orchard, all sang the symphony of death in silent harmony; on that night the three soundless worlds of land, air and water, studded with the stars and planets, ordered me in unison to die. Only a single invisible ramshackle boat floating along the tranquil Yamuna, with not a wave disturbing its surface, prised me away from the embracing arms of dignified, soothing, eternal and universally enchanting death to drag me along the path of life. Like one entranced by a dream I walked along the Yamuna, passing through reeds as well as sandy beaches, traversing land that was cleft and uneven in some places, and overgrown with trees, weeds and vines in others.'

The speaker stopped. I did not say a word, either.

After a long silence, the nawab's daughter continued. 'The events that unfolded thereafter were complex. I do not know how to explain them clearly. I was passing through a dense forest; I could no longer determine the path I had taken. How should I begin? Where should I end? What should I purge and what should I keep? How do I tell this tale clearly and directly so that nothing appears impossible or improbable or unnatural?

'But what I have learnt during my brief life is that nothing is impossible or beyond reach. To a girl brought up in the inner sanctum of the nawab's home, the world outside might seem inaccessible, but this is an imaginary notion; once you have stepped outside, there is always a road to take. It is not the royal path, but it is a path nevertheless; mankind has always taken this path—it is rocky and strange and unending, it branches out in different directions, it is made difficult by joys and sorrows and obstacles and hindrances, but it is a path.

'The details of the solitary nawab's daughter's journey along this path taken by everyday human beings will not make for pleasant hearing, nor do I feel any enthusiasm for recounting them. To put it briefly, many miseries and dangers and much humiliation had to be endured, but still life did not become unbearable. Like fireworks, the more I burnt, the more irresistible my pace became. All the time that I moved swiftly, I had no sensation of burning, but now that this flame of intense sorrow and extreme joy has been extinguished, depositing me in the dust on the roadside like an inanimate object, my journey is over, my story ends here.'

With these words, the nawab's daughter stopped. Mentally, I shook my head; by no means could the story end here. After a brief silence I said in broken Hindi, 'Pardon my insolence: if you could explain the end in greater detail, your servant would be relieved greatly of his anxiety.'

The nawab's daughter smiled. I realized that my broken Hindi had worked. Had I been able to conduct the conversation in chaste Hindi, her reserve would not have been lowered, but the fact that I knew very little of her mother tongue created a substantial gap, drawing a veil between us.

'I received news of Kesharlal frequently,' she resumed, 'although I was unable to meet him despite my best efforts. Having joined Tantia Tope's group, he would strike without warning like lightning under the revolutionary sky, sometimes in the east, sometimes in the west, sometimes in the northwest or the southeast, and disappear instantly.

'I had disguised myself as an ascetic in Kashi, where I addressed Swami Shivananda as my father and learnt Sanskrit from him. All the news from everywhere in India would gather at his feet; I would study Sanskrit devotedly and follow the news of the battles with dreadful anxiety.

'Gradually the British Raj ground out the flames of revolution in Hindustan under its feet. Suddenly, there was no more news of Kesharlal. The valiant figures from distant parts of the country who had become visible every now and then in the bloodied light of the apocalypse were eclipsed unexpectedly.

'I could hold myself back no longer. Abandoning the protection of my teacher, I became a wanderer again in the guise of a worshipper. I travelled through the roads, to places of pilgrimage, to temples and hermitages, but nowhere did I find any trace of Kesharlal. One or two people who were familiar with him said, "He has been killed, either in battle or by royal decree." My soul said, "Never, Kesharlal cannot die. This Brahmin, this flame that burns unbearably bright, has not yet found release; the fire in him is still blazing up to the skies in some remote spot readied for a holy fire ritual, awaiting my self-sacrifice."

'The Hindu scriptures say that knowledge and penance can turn a Shudra into a Brahmin, but they make no reference to whether a Muslim can become a Brahmin, the only reason being that there were no Muslims at the time. I knew that it would be a long while before I could be united with Kesharlal, for I would have to become a Brahmin first. One by one, thirty years passed. In my soul and in my appearance, in my behaviour and in my habits, I became a Brahmin in word and in deed; the blood of the Brahmin woman, my ancestor, flowed in my veins without impurity. Mentally establishing myself without reservation at the feet of the first Brahmin of my youth, the last Brahmin at the end of my life, the only Brahmin in my entire universe, I acquired a magnificent radiance.

'I had heard many accounts of Kesharlal's valour during the revolutionary battles, but none of them had been imprinted on my heart. The image I had seen of a solitary Kesharlal silently floating along in a tiny boat midstream on a placid Yamuna on a moonlit night was the one that had remained in my consciousness. Every day I would see the Brahmin rowing along the desolate currents day and night, towards an undefined mysterious destination, without a companion, without an attendant. He needed no one; a pure and self-absorbed man, he was complete in himself and the stars and moon and planets in the sky observed him in silence.

'Then I heard that Kesharlal had escaped from prison and taken shelter in Nepal. I went to Nepal too. After a long sojourn there, I was informed that he had left Nepal long ago. No one knew where he had gone.

'Since then I have been wandering around the mountains. This is not a land of Hindus—Bhutias, Lepchas and others are heathens, their daily acts follow no principles; their gods, their prayers, their rituals are all different. I began to worry about the possibility of the slightest defilement of the sacred purity that I had acquired after years of penance and devotion. With great effort I proceeded to protect myself from all manner of impure contact. I knew that my boat was close to the shore now; the ultimate holy destination of my life was at hand.

'What more is there to say? The final chapter is brief. When the lamp goes out it needs only a single puff of breath. How do I elaborate on this?

'Thirty-eight years later, here in Darjeeling, I found Kesharlal this morning.'

When the speaker stopped here, I asked, bursting with curiosity, 'What did you see?'

The nawab's daughter said, 'I saw an aged Kesharlal living amidst the Bhutias with a Bhutia wife and the grandchildren she has engendered, harvesting corn in tattered clothes in their soiled courtyard.'

The story had ended; I thought it imperative to offer some consolation. 'How can someone who has had to live thirty-eight years in fear for his life in the company of people of other faiths possibly adhere to prescribed behaviour?'

'I understand that,' said the nawab's daughter. 'But what about the illusion under which I had been living all these years? I did not know that the Brahminism which had conquered my adolescent heart was nothing but habit, nothing but practice. I had thought of it as dharma, as eternal, without beginning or end. If that were not so, why had I accepted the unbearable humiliation I had suffered from the Brahmin's right hand on that moonlit night in return for the adoration which resonated within my blossoming mind, body and soul? Why had I thought of it as a rite of initiation from my mentor and acknowledged it with bowed head and redoubled devotion? Ah, Brahmin, you have exchanged one set of practices for another; but how will I get my youth, my life back in exchange for another?'

With these words, the woman rose to her feet, saying, 'Namaste, babuji.'

The very next moment she said, as though correcting herself, 'Salaam, Babu Sahib!' With this Muslim form of address, she seemed to bid her final farewell to the decayed, ruined Brahminism lying in the dust. Before I could say a word, she disappeared like a cloud in the grey fog gathered over the Himalayan peaks.

For a few brief moments I closed my eyes to see all these events taking place before my mind's eye. I saw the sixteen-year-old girl comfortably seated on her fabric cushion at the window by the bank of the river, I saw the intent figure of the female ascetic brimming over with devotion during the evening prayers at the temple, and then I saw, too, the form of the woman of advancing years, weighed down by her broken heart and her misery, shrouded in fog here on Calcutta Road in Darjeeling. The wondrous, ardent music rising from the conflicting flow of Muslim and Hindu blood within the veins of a tender young woman melted into the self-contained beauty of the Urdu language to reverberate in my mind.

Opening my eyes, I discovered that the clouds had lifted suddenly, with the unsullied sky glittering in the pleasant sunlight. Englishwomen in carriages and Englishmen on horseback were out for some fresh air, interspersed by one or two Bengalis casting amused glances at me from faces wrapped in mufflers.

I rose to my feet quickly. At the sight of this uncovered world lit up by the sun, the story wrapped in layers of fog no longer seemed real. I believe I must have mixed the fog over the mountains with the smoke from my cigarette to spin an imaginary tale. The Muslim Brahmin woman, the revolutionary, the fort by the Yamuna—perhaps none of them had ever existed.

Dead or Alive

1

The widowed daughter-in-law of Sharadashankar, the zamindar of Ranihat, had no family of her own on her father's side; one by one, all of them had died. She had no one to speak of on her husband's side either—neither husband, nor son. Her elder brother-in-law's youngest son was the apple of her eye. His mother had been severely ill for a long time after giving birth to him, which was why his widowed aunt Kadambini—whom he addressed as Kakima—had brought him up. Rearing someone else's child seems to strengthen the bond, for one has no right over the child; there are no social demands, only the demands of love—but unalloyed love cannot cite any documentary evidence to establish its right, nor does it wish to. It only adores the uncertain object of its affection twice as fervently.

After she had showered all the suppressed love of the widow on the little boy, Kadambini died unexpectedly one monsoon night. For some unknown reason her heart stopped beating suddenly, everything else in the world continued to function as before, but only the spring in her tiny, tender heart—ever thirsty for love—stopped working forever.

To avoid the unwelcome intrusion of the police, four Brahmin employees of the zamindar proceeded to cremate the body without any delay.

The crematorium in Ranighat was a long way from habitation. The enormous burning ground was completely bare, other than a hut next to the lake and, close by, a huge banyan tree. A river used to flow here in the past, but it had completely dried up now. A section of the dried riverbed had been dug up to create the lake.

People hereabouts considered the lake a representative of the river in full flow.

Placing the corpse inside the hut, the four of them awaited the arrival of the wood for the pyre. It was taking so long that Nitai and Gurucharan went off to enquire about the delay, while Bidhu and Banamali stayed back to guard the corpse.

It was a dark monsoon night. The sky was overcast, not a star was visible; the pair waited in silence in the darkness of the hut. One of them had a box of matches and a lamp. But despite all their efforts, the dampness prevented the matches from being lit—the lantern they had brought had died long ago.

After a long silence, one of them said, 'I'm dying for a smoke. We came away in such a hurry that I forgot to bring any along.'

'I can get some at once,' offered his companion.

Sensing Banamali's desire to flee, Bidhu exclaimed, 'Really! And I suppose I'm expected to wait here alone, am I?'

The conversation ended. Every minute seemed like an hour. The pair that had stayed back cursed the one that had supposedly gone off in search of wood—every passing moment deepened their suspicion that the other two were having a cosy smoke and chat somewhere.

There were no sounds to be heard besides the constant chirping of crickets and the croaking of frogs from the lake. Suddenly the bed appeared to shake, as though the corpse was turning over on its side.

Bidhu and Banamali began to tremble and muttered prayers. A sigh was heard inside the hut. Bidhu and Banamali leapt out of the room in an instant and raced off towards their village.

Nearly three miles away, they ran into the rest of their party, who were returning with lanterns. They had in fact stopped for a smoke, and had no idea about the wood. Still, they informed the other two that the wood was being chopped and would be despatched shortly. Whereupon Bidhu and Banamali proceeded to describe all that had taken place in the hut. Dismissing their account in disbelief, Nitai and Gurucharan reproached them angrily.

Without further ado, all four of them returned to the hut at the burning ground. Entering, they discovered the bed empty and the corpse missing.

Stories

They exchanged glances. What if a jackal had dragged the corpse away? But even the sheet covering her was missing. Investigating, they spotted a woman's small footprints, fresh in the mud gathered outside the door.

Sharadashankar was not an easy man to deal with, and telling him this ghost story was unlikely to yield dividends. After prolonged discussions, the quartet concluded that it would be best to inform the zamindar that the cremation had been completed.

Those who finally brought the wood for the pyre at dawn were told that because of the delay the body had been burnt already, using some wood kept in the hut. No one was likely to be suspicious about this—a corpse was not a valuable object for anyone to steal.

2

As everyone knows, even when there are no signs of life in a person, sometimes life still persists, and the body resumes its normal functioning at the appropriate time. Kadambini had not died either, only her vital signs had stopped for some reason.

When she regained her senses, she found herself enveloped in darkness. It seemed this was not the place where she normally slept. 'Didi,' she called out, but no one answered in the dark room. Sitting up in fear, she recollected her experience of dying. The sudden pain in her chest, the inability to breathe. Her sister-in-law was warming the milk for Khoka—her son—on a fire; unable to stay on her feet anymore, Kadambini had tumbled on to the bed and in a choked voice she said, 'Didi, ask Khoka to come to me, I am dying.' Then everything grew dark, like a bottle of ink overturned on a sheet of paper covered in writing, and Kadambini's entire memory and consciousness, every letter in the book of the world, dissipated in an instant. The widow could not remember whether Khoka had addressed her as Kakima one last time in his endearing voice, could not recollect whether she had succeeded in collecting a final allowance of love for her eternal, alien journey of death from this ever-familiar world.

At first she thought that hell was eternally desolate and eternally dark, just like this—that there was nothing to see there, nothing to hear, nothing to do, that she would only have to stay awake like this till eternity.

But when a cold gust of moisture-laden wind blew in through the door and she heard the croaking of the frogs, all the memories of the rains that she had amassed since childhood in her brief life condensed in her mind in a single moment, enabling her to feel the touch of the real world. There was a flash of lightning; the lake, the banyan tree, the huge burning ground and a distant row of trees became visible for a moment. She recalled bathing in this lake on auspicious dates, and how horrifying death had seemed at the sight of corpses here.

Her first thought was to go back home. But, she reflected the very next moment, why will they take me back since I am not alive anymore. It will be bad luck for them. I have been exiled from the kingdom of the living, after all. I am my own dead spirit.

If that were not so, how could she have arrived here at this desolate crematorium from Sharadashankar's well-protected ladies' chambers? If she had not been cremated yet, where were the people who had come to cremate her body? Her last memory was of the final moments of her death in Sharadashankar's well-lit residence. Discovering herself alone the very next moment in this distant, barren, dark burning ground, she realized, I am no longer a member of the human tribe on this planet; I am dangerous, a harbinger of ill fortune, I am my dead spirit.

As soon as she was struck by this thought, the rules that bound her to the world seemed to melt away. She felt possessed by extraordinary power, infinite freedom—as though she could go where she liked, do as she pleased. Driven into a frenzy by this unprecedented new ability, she swept out of the room like a sudden gust of wind and walked across the burning ground without a trace of diffidence, fear or concern in her heart.

As she marched on, her footsteps faltered, her body weakened. The fields and meadows just wouldn't end—they were interspersed by paddy fields, some of them knee-deep in water. When the first light of dawn became visible, a bird or two was heard from a bamboo grove located near a cluster of houses not too far away.

Now she felt a kind of trepidation. She did not know where her relationship with the world and the people who inhabited it stood. As long as she had been at the crematorium, in the fields, in the darkness of the monsoon night, she had been unafraid, as though in her own world. In daylight, the settlement seemed a treacherous place. Humans fear ghosts, ghosts fear humans too, they occupy opposite banks of the river of death.

3

Her mud-spattered clothes, the strange state of her mind, and the unhinged demeanour brought on by a sleepless night had transformed Kadambini's appearance to one that would have made people afraid and young boys pelt stones at her from a distance. Fortunately, the first person to see her in this state was a gentleman travelling on that road.

'You seem to be from a genteel family,' he said to her. 'Where are you going in this condition all by yourself?'

At first Kadambini looked at him without responding. She could not summon an answer quickly. That she was still in this world, that she looked like a gentlewoman, that a passer-by on the village road was asking her a question, seemed unbelievable.

'Let me take you home,' the passer-by said to her again. 'Tell me where you live.'

Kadambini considered what her reply should be. She could not entertain thoughts of returning to her in-laws' home, and she had no home of her own—suddenly she remembered a childhood friend of hers.

Although they had been separated as children, her friend Jogomaya and she still wrote to each other now and then. At times this escalated into a full-fledged war of love. Kadambini attempted to convey that hers was the stronger emotion, while Jogomaya insinuated that Kadambini did not reciprocate her sentiments adequately. Neither of them harboured the slightest doubt that, if only some miracle were to bring them together, they would be unable to let each other out of their sights even for an instant.

'I want to go to Sripaticharan-babu's house in Nishchindapur,' Kadambini told the gentleman.

The traveller was on his way to Calcutta; although it was not near, Nishchindapur was on the way. He personally escorted Kadambini to Sripaticharan-babu's house.

The friends were reunited. It took a few moments for them to recognize each other, but the resemblance to their respective childhood selves soon became obvious to both.

'How fortunate I am,' exclaimed Jogomaya. 'I had never expected to set eyes on you in my lifetime. But how did you happen to visit me, my dear? How did your in-laws let you go!'

After a pause, Kadambini said, 'Do not ask me about my in-laws, my dear. Let me live like a maid in one corner of your house, I will perform all your household tasks.'

'What do you mean?' responded Jogomaya. 'Why should you live like a maid? You are my friend, you are my . . .' etcetera.

Sripati entered. After a brief gaze at him, Kadambini left slowly—neither covering her head with the end of her sari in a show of respect, nor displaying any sign of diffidence or uncertainty.

Jogomaya quickly began to explain to Sripati, lest he think badly of her friend. But so few explanations were required, and Sripati approved of every one of her proposals so easily, that Jogomaya was not particularly satisfied.

Kadambini had come to her friend's house, but she could not mingle with her friend—death was a gulf between them. Constant self-awareness and doubts about oneself made socializing impossible. Kadambini would gaze at Jogomaya, her thoughts drifting; she felt as though her friend occupied a distant planet with her husband and household. With all her love and tenderness and responsibilities, she is an inhabitant of the world, while I am nothing but an empty shadow. She is in the realm of existence and I, in the universe of the infinite.

Jogomaya, too, found all this strange, but she could fathom none of it. Womankind cannot tolerate mystery—for you can make poetry with uncertainty, you can be valorous with it, but you cannot live in a household with it. That is why women either eliminate the very existence of what they cannot understand, maintaining no relationship with it, or else they convert it with their own hands into a new form where they can put it to some use. If they can do neither, they become exceedingly angry with it.

The more obscure Kadambini's behaviour seemed to become, the angrier Jogomaya got with her. What kind of menace is this that has descended on me, she reflected.

There was another problem. Kadambini was afraid of herself. She simply could not run away from herself. Those who are afraid of ghosts fear their own backs—they are terrified of whatever they cannot keep an eye on. But Kadambini's biggest fear lay within herself, she was not afraid of the external world.

That was why she would scream sometimes alone in her room in the middle of the afternoon. In the evening, she would tremble on spotting her own shadow in the lamplight.

Her fear made everyone in the house afraid too. The maids, the servants and even Jogomaya herself began to see ghosts everywhere, at all hours.

One night, Kadambini ran sobbing from her own room all the way to Jogomaya's, saying, 'I beg of you, Didi, don't let me be alone.'

Jogomaya was as angry as she was scared. She felt an impulse to throw Kadambini out of her home at once. A compassionate Sripati calmed her down with a great deal of effort and let Kadambini occupy the room next to theirs.

The next day, Sripati was summoned to the ladies' chambers at an unusual hour. Turning on him unexpectedly, Jogomaya said, 'What kind of man are you! A woman leaves her own in-laws' home and ensconces herself in yours, a month goes by and she shows no sign of budging, and I don't hear a word of protest from you! Please explain what you have in mind. All you men are the same.'

Men indeed have a natural bias in favour of women, and women hold them responsible for this. Even if Sripati had been willing to swear on Jogomaya's head that his compassion for the helpless yet beautiful Kadambini was not inappropriately high, his behaviour would have proved otherwise.

'Her in-laws must have tortured the childless widow,' he mused, 'unable to stand it anymore, Kadambini must have arrived here to seek shelter from me. Since she has no parents, how can I abandon her.' With this thought he had desisted from making any kind of enquiry; nor did he have the inclination to cause Kadambini any pain by asking her questions on this unpleasant subject.

Thereupon his wife proceeded to assault his numbed sense of responsibility. He realized that sending word to Kadambini's in-laws had become absolutely crucial to maintain domestic harmony. Finally he decided that the outcome of an unexpected letter might not be favourable, and that he would make enquiries personally at Ranighat before deciding on a course of action.

While Sripati went off, Jogomaya went to Kadambini to tell her, 'It isn't proper for you to stay here anymore, my dear. What will people say?'

Looking gravely at Jogomaya Kadambini said, 'What do I have to do with people?'

Jogomaya was astonished at this response. 'You may not, but we do,' she said in a fit of rage. 'How can we hold on to the daughter-in-law of another family?'

'What family am I the daughter-in-law of?' Kadambini responded.

Oh my god, thought Jogomaya to herself. What does the woman think she's saying?

'Do you think I really am one of you?' Kadambini continued slowly. 'Do you think I belong to this world? You people laugh, you love, you cry, you live with your own families, I can only watch. You are people, and I am a shadow. I cannot fathom why God has chosen to keep me amongst all of you. You are afraid too, lest I bring misery to your happy lives, and I cannot understand either what relationship I have with all of you. But since the Almighty has not earmarked a place for me, although the ties have been snapped I continue to haunt your lives.'

Because of the way she kept speaking, Jogomaya made some sense of it without grasping the real meaning, but she could neither respond, nor repeat her question. Bowed down with concern, she left.

4

It was almost ten at night when Sripati returned from Ranighat. The world was flooding under torrential rain. The continuous sound suggested that neither the downpour nor the night would end.

'What did you learn?' Jogomaya asked.

'A great deal,' answered Sripati. 'We'll talk about it later.' He changed his clothes, ate his dinner, had his late night smoke and went to bed. He looked rather disturbed.

Having suppressed her curiosity for a long time, Jogomaya asked as soon as she got into bed, 'What did you hear?'

'You must have made a mistake,' Sripati responded.

Jogomaya was enraged at this. Women never made mistakes, and even if they did, the duty of wise men was not to refer to them, but to accept them as their own. 'Such as?' retorted Jogomaya a little hotly.

'The woman you have given shelter to in your household is not Kadambini,' declared Sripati.

Such a statement could easily evoke anger especially when it comes from one's own husband. 'So I don't know my own friend, I have to consult you to identify her—what a thing to say!'

Sripati explained that they could not argue over the nature of his statement, for they had to consider the evidence. There was no doubt that Jogomaya's childhood friend Kadambini was dead.

'Listen to you,' countered Jogomaya. 'You must have made some mistake. There's no telling where you've really been, what you've really heard. Who asked you to go yourself, a letter would have clarified everything.'

Extremely disappointed with his wife's lack of faith in his efficiency, Sripati proceeded to present detailed evidence—with no effect. Their arguments ran on into the middle of the night.

Although there was no difference of opinion between husband and wife over throwing Kadambini out of their home this instant, for Sripati was convinced that their guest had deceived his wife all this time under a false identity, while Jogomaya believed that she had abandoned her family, neither of them was willing to concede the current argument.

Their voices became progressively louder; they forgot that Kadambini was in the very next room.

'What a predicament,' said the one. 'I heard it with my own ears.'

'Why should I believe you?' said the other with conviction, 'I can see her with my own eyes.'

Finally Jogomaya said, 'Very well, tell me when Kadambini is supposed to have died.'

She assumed that she would be able to find an inconsistency between his date and one of Kadambini's letters, thus proving her point.

The date that Sripati mentioned turned out, when they had both calculated backwards, to be that of the day before the one on which Kadambini had arrived at their house in the evening. Jogomaya's heart trembled at this and Sripati began to get an eerie feeling too.

Their door opened suddenly, a gust of rain-laden wind snuffing out the lamp. The darkness rushed in instantly, filling every inch of space. Kadambini appeared in the middle of the room. It was past two-thirty in the morning, and it was raining incessantly outside.

'I am the same Kadambini, my dear,' said Kadambini, 'but I am not alive anymore. I am dead now.'

Jogomaya screamed in terror; Sripati couldn't utter a word.

'But what crime have I committed other than dying? If there is no room for me in this world or in the next, where should I go then, tell me.' Her plaintive cry seemed to awaken the Creator, asleep at this hour on this monsoon night, as she asked, 'Where should I go then, tell me?'

With these words, Kadambini left the couple unconscious in their room to seek her place in the world.

5

It is difficult to explain how Kadambini returned to Ranighat. But she did not show herself to anyone at first, spending the day without food in a ruined temple.

When the monsoon evening descended early, and villagers anxiously took shelter in their own homes in anticipation of the imminent deluge, Kadambini went out on the road. At the threshold of her in-laws' house she felt a moment of panic, but when she entered, her face covered by the end of her sari, the doormen mistook her for a maid and did not block her way. The rain intensified at this moment, and the wind picked up.

The lady of the house, Sharadashankar's wife, was playing cards with her husband's widowed sister. The maid was in the kitchen and an ill Khoka, who had a fever, was sleeping in the bedroom. Evading everyone's eyes, Kadambini arrived in the bedroom. She did not know herself what impulse had brought her to her in-laws' house, but she did know that she wanted to set her eyes on the little boy one more time. She had not thought of where she would go, or what would happen thereafter.

In the light of the lamp she saw the sickly little boy sleeping with his hands clenched tightly. The sight made her agitated heart yearn—how could she live without clasping the sick child to her bosom once. She pondered, now that I am gone, who will look after him here? His mother enjoys company, enjoys chatting with people, a game of cards, she was happy all this while entrusting the responsibility for the child to me, she had never had to bear the burden of bringing him up. Who will take care of this boy now?

The little boy turned on his side, saying in his sleep, 'Water, Kakima.' Oh my! You haven't forgotten your Kakima, my darling! Quickly pouring out a glass of water from the pitcher kept in the corner, Kadambini took the child in her arms and gave him his water.

As long as he was under the influence of sleep, the boy was not the least surprised to have his aunt giving him his glass of water. When she had fulfilled her long cherished desire and tucked him back into bed after kissing him, he woke up. Putting his arms around her, he said, 'Did you die, Kakima?'

'Yes, Khoka,' she replied.

'You've come back to Khoka now? You won't die again?'

Before she could answer there was a commotion. About to enter the room with a bowl of food for the boy, the maid dropped it with a clatter and collapsed on the floor, exclaiming 'Oh!'

The lady of the house came running at the sound, her cards forgotten, turning to a block of wood the moment she entered, unable to speak or to make her escape.

All this scared the little boy, who sobbed loudly, saying, 'Go away, Kakima.'

After a long time, Kadambini was feeling today as though she had not died—the familiar house, the boy, her love for him, all of it was as alive as they had ever been, she could sense no gap, no gulf. At her friend's house she had felt that her childhood friend had died but in the boy's room she realized that nothing of his aunt had died.

'Why are you afraid of me, Didi?' she pleaded. 'Look at me, I'm just as I always was.'

The lady of the house could stay on her feet no longer, she fainted in a heap on the floor.

Informed by his sister, Sharadashankar-babu appeared personally in the ladies' chambers. His palms joined in supplication, he said, 'Is this fair, Chhotobouma? Satish is my only male heir, why must you cast your eye on him? Are we not your family? Ever since you went he has been wasting away, his illness won't leave him, he calls for you all the time. Since you have left the world, you must cut the strings now. We will perform your last rites suitably.'

Kadambini could take it no longer, she cried out frantically, 'But I am not dead, I am not dead. How do I convince all of you I am not dead? Look, I am alive.'

Seizing the metal bowl from the floor, she struck herself on the forehead with it, her forehead began to bleed immediately.

'Look, I am alive,' she declared.

Sharadashankar was transfixed, like a statue. The little boy called out to him in fear. The two women who had fainted remained on the floor.

Shouting, 'I am not dead, I am not dead, not dead,' Kadambini left the room, climbed down the stairs and plunged into the pond behind the ladies' chambers. Sharadashankar heard a splash from the room upstairs.

It rained incessantly all night, the next morning the rain did not let up in the afternoon either. Kadambari died to prove that she had not died.

A Letter from a Wife

A submission at your lotus feet,
    We have been married for fifteen years now, but I have never written you a letter. I've been at hand for you always—you have heard me say much, and so have I; there has never been room for a letter.
    Today I am on a pilgrimage to Puri, and you are busy at office. Your relationship with Calcutta is as the snail's to its shell; it is fastened to your body and your soul. So you did not apply for leave of absence. That is what the almighty had intended; he has approved my application for leave.
    I am what they call the mejobou of your family. The second-eldest son's wife. As I stand here on the edge of the ocean, I have finally learnt after fifteen years that I also have another relationship with my world and its creator. Which is why I have mustered the courage to write you this letter—it is not a letter from your family's mejobou.
    In my infancy, when the possibility of my future relationship with your family could have been known only by the one who had destined it, my brother and I fell victim to typhoid at the same time. My brother died, but I survived. All the women among the neighbours said, 'Mrinal survived because she's a girl, she'd never have pulled through had she been a boy.' Yama is a master thief, he has his eye only on the valuable.
    Death does not await me. It is to explain this fact that I am writing to you.
    I was twelve when a distant relative of yours came home with your friend Nirad to inspect the prospective bride. We lived in a remote village, where jackals howled even by day. People had to

travel fourteen miles in a buggy and walk another six along an unpaved road from the station to reach the village. It was such a struggle for them that day. On top of which, there was our east Bengal cooking—your uncle has still not forgotten the farce.

Your mother was absolutely adamant on using her second son's wife to compensate for the fact that her eldest son's wife was not pretty. Why else would your family have taken so much trouble to visit our village? No one has to go looking for jaundice, hepatitits, heartburn or brides in Bengal—they take possession uninvited, and never leave.

My father's heart thumped, my mother prayed incessantly. How was the village priest to please the city gods? They were depending on their daughter's beauty, but the daughter took no pride in her loveliness—her price was no higher than whatever was offered. That is why a woman can never cast off her uncertainty, no matter how exquisitely beautiful she is.

The apprehension of the entire family, the entire neighbourhood, weighed me down. All the light in the sky and all the forces in the world that day had combined to ensure that a village girl of twelve was exposed remorselessly to the two pairs of eyes belonging to the two examiners. I had nowhere to hide.

The flute made the skies weep—I moved to your house. Even after examining my flaws closely, the squad of housewives all admitted that, on the whole, I was beautiful. My sister-in-law's expression turned grim. But I wonder why it was necessary for me to be beautiful. If an old-fashioned artist had created this thing called beauty with a lump of clay, it might have been held in some regard; but since the lord had made it only to please his own fancy, it had no value whatsoever in your righteous household.

It didn't take you long to forget that I am beautiful. But each of you had to be reminded at every step that I am intelligent. This is a quality so intrinsic to me that it has survived all the years I have spent in your household. Your uncle was rather worried about this intelligence, for it is a hindrance for women. Someone who must live her life within prescribed limits will always be thwarted if she tries to follow her intelligence instead. But what can I do? The almighty was careless enough to endow me with more intelligence than is necessary for a woman in your family—

whom do I return the excess to? Your family heaped abuse on me all the time for being a precocious daughter-in-law. Only the weak resort to insults; I forgive all of you.

There was something else I did, beyond managing the household, which none of you knows about. I wrote poetry in secret. However bad it may have been, the walls of your ladies' chambers did not come up around it. That was my freedom, that was where I was me. You and your family neither appreciated, nor recognized the things about me that lay outside my existence as the mejoubou of your family. Not even in these fifteen years have you found out that I am a poet.

The first memory of your house that is strongest in my mind is of the cowshed. Your cows live in a space just to the left of the stairs leading to the inner chambers. They have nowhere to go except the front yard. In one corner of the yard is the wooden basin in which their fodder is kept. The manservant has many other tasks every morning: by then the starving cows lick and bite the sides of the basin out of hunger. My heart wept for them. I'm a village girl. When I arrived at your house for the first time, of all the people in the city it was those two cows and their three calves that seemed to be my dearest ones. As long as I was the new bride, I'd pass my food to them; when I grew older, those in the family who had the privilege of ridiculing me expressed doubts about my caste after noticing my affection for the cows.

My daughter died soon after her birth. She tried to take me along with her. Had she been alive, she would have brought me all that is noble, all that is true in my life; from a daughter-in-law I would have become a mother. You see, a mother belongs to the world even if she is part of only one family. I experienced the pain of motherhood but not its emancipation.

I remember the English doctor's surprise when he saw our inner chambers. He berated us angrily when he saw the labour room. Your house has a small garden in front. The rooms are beautifully done up with furniture and decorations, but the inner chambers are like the reverse side of silk; no modesty, no grace, no adornment. The lights glow dimly; the breeze steals in like a thief; the rubbish in the yard refuses to budge; every blemish on the floor and the walls flourishes in immortality. But the doctor made a mistake in assuming that these conditions were a constant source of unhappiness for us. Actually, it was just the opposite—neglect is like a heap of ashes; it may nurture the fire within itself, but it doesn't allow the heat of the flames to be felt. When self-respect is eroded, such neglect no longer seems unfair. That is why it causes no pain. That is why women are embarrassed even to feel unhappiness. So I say, if you have arranged things in a way that ensures unhappiness for women, then it's best to neglect her. Caring for a woman will only increase her pain when she suffers.

But in whatever condition you keep us, it had never occurred to me to even consider the possibility of unhappiness. Death stood near my door in the labour room, but I felt no fear. After all, does life mean anything important enough for us to fear death? Only those whose lives have been strengthened by love and attention are afraid to die. Had Yama tugged at my hand that day, I would have been uprooted as effortlessly as a loose clod of grass from the earth. Bengali women can die at will. But what glory to such a death? It's embarrassing to die, it's so easy for us.

Like an evening star, my daughter rose in the sky only to sink soon afterwards. I went back to my daily chores and the cows. Life would have passed the same way till the very end; I would have had no reason to write this letter to you today. But the wind can blow in an insignificant seed and force a banyan sapling to spring up through a marble floor; this small beginning can ultimately break the ribs of brick and mortar. A tiny speck of life flew in from somewhere into the paved setting of my daily life; and the crack appeared at once.

When Bindu appeared in our house to take shelter with her elder cousin—my sister-in-law—to save herself from the tyranny of her cousins after her father's death, all of you wondered what kind of nuisance she would prove to be. And my accursed nature, how do I change it? As soon as I saw all of you annoyed, my heart seemed to leap to the aid of the homeless girl. To have to take sanctuary in someone else's house against their will—how great a humiliation it is. How could I possibly ignore someone forced to accept such mortification?

And then I saw the state my sister-in-law was in. She had brought her cousin over out of sheer compassion, but when she saw how reluctant her husband was, she began to behave as though this was a terrible burden for her, one she would be relieved to get rid of. She did not dare open her heart to her orphaned cousin. She was devoted to her husband.

Her dilemma caused me more pain. When I saw how my sister-in-law made markedly frugal arrangements for her cousin's food and clothing, and how she engaged her in all kinds of menial tasks around the house, specifically for the benefit of the family, I was not just unhappy but also embarrassed. She was desperate to prove that Bindu had been engaged in the household at a very low cost, which was a triumph. She did a great deal of work, but proved cheap in terms of expenses.

The only asset that my sister-in-law's father had was the family line—he could offer neither riches nor a beautiful daughter. You know all the details of how she was married into your family after her father pleaded with my father-in-law. She has always considered her marriage a heinous crime towards your family, shrinking herself as much as possible in every respect, occupying a very small space in your family.

But her admirable example has made things very difficult for the rest of us. I cannot be so impossibly self-effacing in everything. I will never accept something as bad for someone else's sake when I know that it is good—you have had plenty of proof of this.

I drew Bindu into my own room. 'Mejobou is going to spoil this girl who is used to life in a poor family,' declared my sister-in-law. She complained to everyone, as though I was tempting fate. But I am sure she was secretly relieved. The blame would not be hers to shoulder. Her heart was lightened as she had induced me to shower the affection on her cousin that she herself had not been able to provide. My sister-in-law would try to take a few years off Bindu's age. But there was no harm in admitting in private that the girl was at least fourteen. As you know, she was so plain to look at that if she were to slip and hit her head on the floor, it was the floor that people would be worried for. So, in the absence of her parents, there was no one to arrange a marriage for her; and how many men would have the determination to marry her anyway?

Bindu came up to me very apprehensively, as though she were

contaminated. She perpetually sidestepped people, avoiding their eye, as if she was not supposed to have been born at all. In her father's house, her uncle's sons were not willing to grant her even a corner reserved for unwanted objects. Unwanted refuse easily finds space for itself around the room, for people ignore it, but an unwanted woman who is not only unwanted but also difficult to ignore is not accommodated even on the rubbish heap. And yet, it cannot exactly be claimed that Bindu's uncle's sons are highly prized objects in this world. But they are thriving.

So when I called Bindu in, she was trembling. I was saddened to see her so afraid. I conveyed to her with great affection that there would always be a little corner for her in my room.

But my room doesn't belong to me alone. Therefore it did not prove easy. Within a few days of her moving in, red marks appeared on her skin. Perhaps they weren't rashes but something else. Your family would call it smallpox. For it was Bindu, after all. An amateur doctor from the neighbourhood said he couldn't be sure till another day or two had passed. But who was going to wait? Bindu could have died of embarrassment at her illness. I said, never mind if it's pox, I'll stay with her in the labour room, no one else needs to be involved. Just as all of you were ready to beat me up in anger, and even Bindu's cousin pretended annoyance and proposed sending the wretched girl to hospital, the red marks disappeared. All of you grew even more anxious. The pox must have settled in, you said. For it was Bindu, you see.

One of the greatest benefits of being brought up in neglect is that it makes the body immune, immortal. Illness is virtually impossible, the front doors to death are all bolted tight. So the sickness mocked at her, but could do nothing more. But it became very clear that the most insignificant people in the world are the most difficult to give shelter to. Their need for sanctuary is not as great as the obstacles to it.

When Bindu finally lost her fear for me, she entered another phase. She began to love me so intensely that it made me afraid. I had never seen love in this form before. I had read about it, true, but that was between a man and a woman. For the longest time I had had no reason to remember I was beautiful; now this ugly girl became preoccupied with my beauty. She could never have enough of gazing at me. 'No one but me has seen this face of yours, Didi,' she would tell me. She was very upset when I did my hair myself. She used to love playing with my masses of hair. I did not have to dress up unless I was going out to honour an invitation. But Bindu would exasperate me, forcing me to dress up in some special way every day. The girl grew obsessed with me.

There isn't a bit of land at the back of your house. An ebony tree had somehow sprung up next to a drain running past the northern wall. When I saw the fresh leaves on the tree turning to a fiery orange, I knew spring had indeed arrived in the world. When this unloved girl's soul also turned a fiery orange in my household, I realized that a spring breeze blows in the world of the heart too—it comes, not from the end of the lane, but from an unknown heaven.

The irresistible force of Bindu's love disturbed me. I admit to feeling irked with her at times, but through her love I saw myself in a way that I had never seen before in my life. This was my free, real self.

Meanwhile, everyone in your family found my care for Bindu excessive. The objections and bickering over this were endless. When my bracelet was stolen from my room, none of you hesitated to suggest that Bindu had had a hand in the theft. When houses began to be searched as a result of the freedom movement, all of you immediately suspected Bindu of being a spy employed by the police. There was no proof of any of this except one: she was Bindu.

The maids in your house refused to do anything for her—if I instructed any of them, even the girl would stiffen with embarrassment. Because of all this my expenses for her increased. I engaged a maid specially for her. None of you approved. All of you were so angry that I gave Bindu saris to wear that you stopped my pocket money. The next day onwards, I began to dress in coarse mill dhotis costing a rupee and a quarter. And when the maid came to take away the plate I had eaten out of, I stopped her, washing the plate myself under the tap in the yard and feeding the leftovers to the calf. You weren't particularly pleased at the sight. I have not yet acquired the wisdom that tells I must please all of you irrespective of whether any of you make any effort to please me or not.

Meanwhile, just like the rage within all of you, Bindu's age was rising too. All of you grew unnaturally perturbed about this natural development. The one thing that surprises me when I think about it is why your family didn't throw Bindu out. I understand clearly that all of you are actually frightened of me. You cannot help admiring the intelligence that god has endowed me with.

Unable to get rid of Bindu with your own efforts, your family finally resorted to marriage. A match was arranged for her. 'Thank god,' said my sister-in-law, 'the family's honour will be protected.'

I didn't know what kind of a groom he was. You said he was suitable in every way. Bindu clasped my feet and began to cry. 'Why do you want me to get married?' she asked.

'Don't be frightened, Bindu,' I consoled her. 'I've been told he's very suitable.'

'If he's so suitable,' said Bindu, 'why would he like me?'

The groom's family showed no signs of visiting to take a look at her. My sister-in-law was extremely relieved.

But, morning or night, Bindu wouldn't stop weeping. I knew what she was unhappy about. I had fought a great deal for her with your family, but I did not dare suggest that her wedding be called off. With what conviction could I have said it? What would happen to her if I were to die? First, she was a woman, and a darkskinned one at that—it was no use wondering what kind of family she was being married into, or what would happen to her.

'Five days to the wedding,' Bindu told me. 'Is there no hope of my dying before that?'

I scolded her soundly, but the almighty knows how relieved I would have been had Bindu had a natural death.

On the day before the wedding, Bindu told her cousin, 'I'll just live in the cowshed, I'll do whatever you ask me to, just don't throw me out this way.'

My sister-in-law had been weeping in secret for some time now, she wept today too. But then it wasn't just a question of the heart, but also the scriptures. 'You know, Bindu,' she said, 'a woman's freedom and salvation all come through her husband. If fate holds sorrows for you, no one can stop it.'

The fact was that there was no alternative, Bindu had no choice but to get married, whatever the outcome might be.

I had wanted the wedding to take place in our house, but your family said that it must be held at the groom's house—such was their tradition.

I concluded that your resident deity would not tolerate any expenditure on Bindu's wedding. So I had to remain silent. But there's something none of you knows. I had wanted to inform my sister-in-law but I didn't, for she would have died of fright. I had secretly dressed up Bindu in some of my ornaments. My sister-in-law may have noticed, but she pretended not to. Forgive her for this, I beg of you.

Before leaving Bindu put her arms around me, saying, 'So you really are forsaking me, Didi?'

'No Bindu,' I told her. 'No matter what happens, I will not abandon you till the end.'

Three days passed. The subjects of your taluk had given you a lamb to slaughter, but I had saved it from your raging appetite and given it shelter in one corner of the coal shed. I would feed him grains myself first thing in the morning; when I left it to your servants, I found them more interested in eating him than in feeding him.

That morning I found Bindu crouching in one corner of the shed. She flung herself at my feet when she saw me and began to weep silently.

Bindu's husband was mad.

'Really, Bindu?'

'Could I possibly tell you such a big lie, Didi? He is mad. My father-in-law was not in favour of this marriage—but he is terrified of my mother-in-law. He left for Kashi before the wedding. My mother-in-law insisted on her son's marriage.'

I sat down heavily on the heap of coal. Women do not spare other women. 'She's nothing but a woman, after all,' they say. 'So what if my son is mad, he is a man at least.'

It wasn't always obvious that Bindu's husband was mad, but his condition deteriorated so much sometimes that he had to be locked up. He was stable on the wedding night, but staying up all night and various other demands had turned him unstable the next day. When Bindu was having her lunch in a brass plate in the afternoon, her husband had suddenly snatched the plate from her and flung it out on the yard. He had imagined that she was actually a queen, whose servant had stolen her plate of gold and served her food on his own plate instead. He was infuriated. Bindu had nearly died of fright. When her mother-in-law had asked her to sleep in her husband's room on the third night, her heart had shrunk in fear. Her mother-in-law had a wild temper—she was mad too, and all the more dangerous because she was not entirely insane. Bindu had had no choice but to enter her husband's room. He had been calm that night, but a terrified Bindu had turned to ice. Late in the night, when her husband was asleep, she had managed to escape, using a method that does not need detailing here.

I began to burn with hatred. 'Marriage through such subterfuge is no marriage at all,' I said. 'Just go on living with me as you did, Bindu, let me see who dares take you away.'

'Bindu is lying,' your family said.

'She has never lied,' I said.

'How do you know?' your family asked.

'I'm sure,' I replied.

'We'll be in trouble if Bindu's in-laws file a police case,' your family warned me.

'Won't the judge listen when we say they tricked her into a marrying a mad man?' I argued.

'Does that mean we have to go to court over this?' your family asked. 'How is this our responsibility?'

'I shall sell my jewellery and do what I can,' I declared.

'Do you plan to consult a lawyer?' your family said.

I could not answer. I could smite my forehead, but there was little more I could do.

Meanwhile, Bindu's husband's elder brother arrived. Creating a scene, he threatened to inform the police.

I do not know what strength I summoned—but I could not accept that the cow which had escaped the butcher and taken shelter with me out of fear for its life would now be persecuted. 'Let them inform the police,' I said bravely.

I thought it best to take Bindu into my bedroom and lock the door. When I looked for her, she was gone. While I was arguing with all of you, Bindu had surrendered to her brother-in-law. She had realized that she would get me in deep trouble if she stayed on in this house.

Bindu made things worse for herself with her brief escape. Her mother-in-law's point of view was that her son was not going to eat Bindu up. There was no dearth of examples of bad husbands, her son was a model husband in comparison.

My sister-in-law said, 'What's the use of our sighing over her wretched luck? Mad or bad, he's her husband after all.'

All of you reminded me of the example of the pure wife who carried her leprous husband to a whore. You men have never felt the slightest hesitation in spreading this story of the basest form of cowardice in the world, which was why all of you human beings could be angry about Bindu's behaviour—you felt no shame. My heart broke for Bindu, but I was ashamed of all of you. I was a village girl who had slipped into your house accidentally, but how did god give me such ideas? I simply couldn't stand your family's righteousness.

I was certain Bindu would die before she came back to this house, but I had assured her on the day before her wedding that I would never forsake her. My younger brother was at college in Calcutta; as you know, he was so enthusiastic about volunteering or killing rats that cause plague or running off to help when the Damodar flooded over that he was not the least bit put out despite failing his FA examinations twice. Sending for him, I said, 'You have to get me news of Bindu, Sarat. She will not dare write to me, and even if she does, I will not get the letter.'

He would have been happier had I asked him to kidnap Bindu or break her mad husband's head instead.

You entered during my discussion with Sarat to ask, 'Now what trouble are you brewing?'

'The same one that I had brewed right at the beginning,' I told you, 'when I came to your house. But that was your family's doing.'

'Have you brought Bindu again and hidden her somewhere?' you asked.

'Had Bindu come I would certainly have hidden her,' I replied. 'But don't worry, she won't come.'

You became suspicious when you saw Sarat. I knew that none

of you liked the idea of him visiting me. You were apprehensive. The police had their eyes on him, and if he were to be implicated in a political case, all of you would be drawn in. This was why I didn't invite him even for the bhaiphonta rituals, performing them through a messenger instead.

From your family I heard that Bindu had run away again, and that her brother-in-law had come to check whether she was here. I felt an arrow pierce my heart. I realized how terribly the poor girl was suffering, but there was nothing I could do.

Sarat rushed off to make enquiries. Returning in the evening, he told me that Bindu had turned to her uncle's sons for help, but they had flared up in rage and taken her back to her husband's home. The trouble that they went through, and the money they had to spend on transportation, still rankled.

Your aunt arrived at your house on her way to a pilgrimage at Puri. 'I want to go, too,' I told all of you.

Your family was so happy at my sudden religious turn that they offered no objections. They also felt that if I stayed in Calcutta, I might spark a fresh crisis involving Bindu. I was such a problem.

We were to leave on Wednesday. All the arrangements were made on Sunday. I sent for Sarat and told him, 'You have to get Bindu on Wednesday's train to Puri somehow.'

Sarat looked elated. 'Don't worry, Didi,' he told me. 'I will get her on the train and go all the way to Puri with her. A chance for me to visit the Jagannath temple.'

Sarat returned that evening. My heart sank. 'What is it, Sarat?' I asked. 'Didn't it work?'

'No,' he replied.

'You couldn't persuade her?' I asked.

'No need,' he answered. 'She set herself on fire last night and burnt to death. I heard from the nephew I'd made friends with. She left a letter for you, but they have destroyed it.'

Peace at last.

People were furious. 'This is a new fashion,' they said, 'women setting themselves on fire and burning to death.'

'Drama, all of it,' your family said. Probably. But it's worth considering why the brunt of the comedy is always borne by Bengali women, and not by the crinkled dhotis of Bengal's valorous men.

Bindu's luck was wretched indeed. As long as she was alive, she received no praise for beauty or accomplishments and when it came to death, too, her fate did not allow her to invent a new way to die, one that men could applaud appreciatively. She only enraged everyone.

My sister-in-law wept secretly in her room. But her tears held a consolation. Whatever may have happened, a crisis had been averted. She had died, that was all. Just imagine the things that could have happened if she had been alive.

I am on pilgrimage. Bindu did not need to come, after all, but I did.

In your family I have never experienced what people refer to as suffering. You are affluent, and however dubious your brother's morals may be, there is no flaw in your character that I can blame god for. If you had been like your brother, my days might on the whole have passed this way, and like my purest of pure sister-in-law, I might have blamed the creator instead of my husband. I do not wish to level accusations against any of you; that is not the intention of this letter.

But I shall not return to No. 27, Makhan Baral Lane anymore. I have seen Bindu's life, and I have come to know the place of the woman in a family. I do not need it.

I found that although she was a woman, god did not forsake her. You people could force her into many things, but within limits. She was greater than her ill-fated life as a human. You are not powerful enough to grind her life forever under your feet according to your own wishes and customs. Death is stronger than you. And in that death she transcended everything—here Bindu is not merely a woman in a Bengali family, not just a cousin to the males in her generation, not just the deceived wife of an insane stranger. In death she is eternal.

I was stricken when the broken-hearted girl sang of death by the river flowing through my life. I questioned the almighty, why is the most insignificant thing in the world the hardest to accomplish? Why is this fragile bubble of walled unhappiness in this lane such a fearsome impediment? When your world beckons alluringly to me with its nectar of six seasons, why can't I cross the threshold even momentarily? Why must I die agonisingly behind this flimsy brick barricade in a world that you have given us? How petty this daily routine is, how trite all its predetermined rules, predetermined practices, predetermined declarations, all its predetermined losses—will it ultimately be the coils of deprivation that triumph, while the joyful world you have created is vanquished?

But death played its flute, and where then was the mason's wall, where the barbed wire of your domestic rules? With what sorrows and humiliation could they keep human beings imprisoned anymore? There, the victorious flag of life is fluttering in the hands of death. Are you not afraid, mejobou! It won't take a moment for this skin of daughter-in-law to be shed.

I am no longer intimidated by your lane. The blue sea stretches before me today, and monsoon clouds, over my head.

The darkness of your customs kept me covered. Bindu got a fleeting glimpse through a hole in the shroud. With her death, she ripped the shroud completely. Now that I have emerged outside, I see no room for my glory. The beautiful one, to whom my unappreciated beauty was a joy, gazes at me now with all the sky. Mejobou's dead.

You may think I am about to kill myself. Don't worry, I shall not play such an ancient joke on you. Meerabai too was a woman like me—her chains were no less heavy, but she did not have to die in order to live. In her song she said, 'Let my father abandon me, my mother too, let everyone forsake me, but Meera will not give up, my lord, whatever the consequences.' Not giving up is to stay alive. I too will live. I am saved.

No longer seeking shelter at your feet,
Mrinal

The Laboratory

1

Nandakishore was an engineer with a degree from London University. He was what is formally referred to as a brilliant student; a first-class horseman at every examination gate from school onwards.

His intelligence was formidable, and his needs, generous, but his finances were strained.

He had succeeded in insinuating himself into the construction of two large railway bridges. Costs fluctuate frequently in such projects, but he didn't set a good example. As long as both his hands were busy accepting payments, he found nothing to grumble about. Apparently all transactions in such projects were connected to an abstract entity named the company, which meant that personal accounts of profit or loss did not have to be disturbed.

His superiors used to refer to him as a genius in his own line of work—he had a perfect head for accounting. He was not recompensed suitably simply because he was a Bengali. He did not enjoy being thumped on the back by a lowly Englishman who would take a hand out of his pocket for the purpose, and say with his feet planted wide, 'Hello, Mr Mullick.' Especially since they always turned to him when it came to work, but to themselves when it was a matter of salary and fame. As a result, he had a personal estimate of how much money he should actually have been earning and he knew very well how to bridge the gap.

Nandakishore had never been profligate with his honestly and otherwise earned money. He used to live in a one-and-a-half storeyed building in Sikdarpara Lane, and did not even have the time to change his clothes, which still carried the stamp of the mill. If anyone laughed at this, he said, 'My attire carries the mark of the king of labourers.'

But he had built a big house specifically for his scientific collections and experiments. He was so absorbed in his passion that he could not hear the question everyone murmured: where was the Aladdin's lamp that had made such a huge edifice possible?

Sometimes an individual is so consumed by an interest that it turns into an addiction and they no longer heed public suspicion. The man was eccentric, and science was his madness. As he leafed through the catalogue, his hands gripped the arms of his chair in excitement. He imported expensive equipment from Germany and America, not to be found even in India's biggest universities. This is every scholar's regret. The leftovers from feasts of knowledge are used to serve cheap meals in this accursed country. It is because of the lack of opportunity to use modern equipment—unlike in foreign countries—that our students here rummage amidst scraps in their dry textbooks. Our ability is in our brains, Nandakishore would announce loudly, and our inability in our pockets. He had vowed to open up an avenue to science for students—a wide, open avenue.

The more he collected priceless equipment, the more his colleagues grew righteous. Finally the burra sahib saved him from imminent danger. He had reposed considerable faith in Nandakishore's abilities. Besides, he was aware of examples of fistfuls of money being siphoned off from railway projects.

The job had to be given up. Cashing in on the sahib's munificence, Nandakishore bought cheap iron scrap and set up a factory. The first war in Europe was generating high demand. The man was so skilful that a flood of profits cascaded his way through ever-new channels.

Now a new passion took over.

Nandakishore's business had taken him to Punjab at one point. There he found a companion. He was sipping his tea in the veranda one morning when a young woman of twenty appeared, without any reserve in her behaviour, her skirt swirling. Her eyes were bright, and a smile hung on her lips like a honed dagger. Sitting down close to his feet, she said, 'I've been watching you morning and night for a few days, babuji. You've astonished me.'

'Why, don't you have a zoo here?' smiled Nandakishore.

'There's no need for one,' she told him. 'Those who should be inside are roaming about at large. So I'm looking for a man.'

'Found one?'

'Here,' she said, pointing to Nandakishore.

'What qualities have you observed?' he asked with a smile.

'All the big traders here, with gold chains round their necks and diamond rings on their fingers, were circling you—a Bengali from a distant land who doesn't understand business. A juicy prey. But none of their tricks worked. Instead, you trapped all of them. They don't know it yet, but I do.'

Nandakishore was astounded. She was turning out to be unusual, not an ordinary girl at all.

'I'll tell you about myself,' she told him, 'better remember the details. There's a powerful astrologer in our neighbourhood. When he scanned my horoscope, he said I would be famous one day. The devil has his eye on my birthplace, he had said.'

'Really?' exclaimed Nandakishore. 'The devil himself?'

'You know, babuji, the most famous man in the world is the devil,' the girl said. 'Let people criticise him, but he's genuine. Our lord Bholanath is perpetually inebriated. He's not capable of running the universe. See for yourself, the British have grabbed the world on the strength of the devil, not of Christianity. But because they're sincere, they've managed to preserve their kingdom. The day they go back on their word, they will perish at the hands of the same devil.'

Nandakishore was amazed.

'Don't be angry, babu,' said the girl, 'but you have the devil's mantra in you. Which is why you'll win. I have bewitched many men, but for the first time I've come across a man who can go one better than me. Don't leave me, babu, the loss will be yours.'

'What must I do?' asked Nandakishore, smiling.

'My grandmother's property is being sold to pay off her debts. You must pay it off for her.'

'How much is your debt?'

'Seven thousand.'

Nandakishore was stunned at the audacity of her demand. 'Very well, I shall. Then what?'

'Then I will never leave you.'

'What will you do?'

'I'll make sure no one can cheat you except me.'

Laughing, Nandakishore said, 'Very well, you have my word. Here's my ring.'

His mind held a touchstone, on which a precious metal seemed to have left a mark. He could see the girl's spirit glittering within her; it was clear that she knew her own worth. 'I shall pay,' Nandakishore declared unhesitatingly, handing over seven thousand rupees to the aged grandmother.

Everyone called her Sohini. She was austere and beautiful, in a western mould. But Nandakishore was not one to be swayed by physical beauty. He had no time to gamble with his heart in the marketplace of youth.

The conditions from which Nandakishore extricated her lacked both cleanliness and privacy. But this obstinate, single-minded individual did not care to collect sufficient information or apply conventional yardsticks. Have you married her, his friends would ask. The reply they would get: Not deeply, just as much as is tolerable. People would laugh because he was devoted heart and soul to nurturing his wife in his own scholarly mould. 'Is she going to be a professor?' they would ask her. Nanda would say, 'No, she has to be a Nandakishore, which is beyond the average woman's reach.' He would add, 'I am not in favour of mixed marriages.'

'What do you mean?'

'The laws of man forbid that a husband should be an engineer while the wife is a cook. In every family I see two different classes bound by marriage. I want to ensure that the classes match. If you want a wife to be devoted to her husband, first make sure they are both devoted to the same thing.'

2

Nandakishore died in old age of an accident connected to an audacious scientific experiment.

Sohini shut the business down. Dealers intent on cheating widows materialised from every direction. Those with the slimmest of family connections laid traps of litigation. Sohini mastered all the intricacies of the law herself. And, sensing an opportunity, she spread a net of feminine mystique over the community of lawyers. She was not the least diffident in exercising this skill, without a hint of orthodoxy. She won all the cases one by one, and a distant cousin of her husband's even went to jail for forging documents.

They had a daughter, who had been named Neelima. The girl had changed it herself to Nila. Let no one imagine that the parents had responded to a dark-skinned daughter by concealing the disapproval under a silken name. The girl had a complexion of peaches and cream. Her mother used to say that their ancestors were from Kashmir, which is why the glow of the ivory lotus of that region was evident in the girl's body, while her eyes held a hint of the blue lotus, and her hair gleamed with shades of gold.

There was no question of considering caste or creed when it came to thinking about her marriage. The only course available was to win her heart, the magic of which leapfrogged over tradition. A young Marwari man, whose wealth was inherited and whose education was modern was suddenly caught in Cupid's lurking trap. Nila was waiting for the car one day at the entrance to her school, which was when the young man had chanced to catch a glimpse. Since then he had stood on the same road often, taking in the air. On the strength of her natural womanly instincts, the girl would take up her position at the gate well before it was time for the car to arrive. Not just the Marwari young man, but a few others, from diverse communities, also walked up and down unnecessarily at that very spot. But it was the original young man who took the plunge into her web. He did not return. They had a civil marriage, beyond the frontiers of society. But not for a very long time. Fate had held the advent of a wife, but then typhoid inserted a full-stop in his conjugal life, followed by release.

The turmoil continued, with reason and madness built into it. The mother could see the daughter's restlessness. She was reminded how explosive her own volcano was in her early youth. Anxiety assailed her. She tried to fence her daughter in closely with education. Instead of appointing a male tutor, she engaged an accomplished woman. Nila's youth seared Sohini too, stoking her with the hot vapours of indeterminable desire. A swarm of admirers crowded around. But the doors were locked. Other girls attempting to strike up a friendship with Nila sent invitations to tea and tennis and the cinema, but the invitations did not reach her. Hundreds of greedy young men kept returning to the honey-scented sky, but not one of the hapless beggars could earn Sohini's approval. Meanwhile, the impatient young woman was found to be eager to step into unsuitable territory given half a chance. The books she read were not those endorsed by the textbook committee; secretly she procured pictures that made a mockery of a well-rounded education. She even managed to distract her accomplished tutoress. A young man with unkempt hair and a barely visible moustache dropped a letter into her carriage when she was on her way back from Diocesan School. Her blood tingled. She hid the letter in her dress, only to be caught by her mother. She had to spend the day locked in her room without food.

Sohini had been looking for a groom amongst the talented students whom her husband had granted scholarships to. Almost all of them cast sidelong glances at her wealth. One of them even dedicated his thesis to her. 'Oh dear,' she said, 'how you've embarrassed me. I was told your postgraduate days are ending, but here you're worshipping the wrong goddess entirely. How will you make progress if you offer your devotion without suitable calculations?' Sohini had had her eyes on one particular young man for some time. His name was Rebati Bhattacharya. He had acquired a doctorate in science already. One or two of his publications had even been reviewed in the West.

3

Sohini was extremely adept at social skills. Manmatha Chowdhury was one of Rebati's professors in his younger days. She bewitched Manmatha. After feeding him toast, omelettes and, now and then, the fried roe of Hilsa, along with tea for several days, she brought the subject up. 'Maybe you're wondering why I invite you to tea so frequently,' she said.

'I can tell you, Mrs Mullick, that it's the least of my worries.'

'People think we make friends with an ulterior motive,' said Sohini.

'Look, Mrs Mullick, I think whatever the motive might be, the friendship is the real gain. Moreover, it would be no small matter if a professor like me could actually help someone realize their objective. The wits of this particular class have been dulled because they cannot breathe outside textbooks. I see I amuse you. Look, even if I'm a teacher, I'm capable of a joke. It's best you know that before inviting me to tea again.'

'I'll keep it in mind—I'm relieved. I've met many professors. You need a doctor to extract a smile out of them.'

'Superb, I see we're like-minded. Then let us get to the point.'

'As you probably know, the only joy in my husband's life was his laboratory. I have no son, so I'm looking for one to settle in the laboratory. I've heard of Rebati Bhattacharya.'

'A suitable boy indeed,' said the professor. 'In his line of research he will need resources to keep making progress.'

'My accumulated money is rusting,' said Sohini. 'Widows of my age pay commissions to the agents for the gods in order to open the door to the afterlife. You may be upset to hear this, but I don't believe in any of this.'

His eyes bulging, Chowdhury asked, 'What do you believe in, then?'

'If I can discover a true human being, I will give him all his dues, as far as I can afford to. That is my religion, my ritual.'

'Hurray!' exclaimed Chowdhury. 'The stone floats. I see it is possible to stumble upon signs of intelligence even among women. I have an idiot with a BSc degree—the other day I discovered her turning reverse somersaults holding on to her godman's feet. Her intelligence was draining out of her brain like from an exploded pod of cotton. So you want to install him in the laboratory in your own home? Can't you do it somewhere else?'

'Make no mistake, Chowdhury-moshai, I'm still a woman. My husband's mission was here in this laboratory. If I can find a worthy person to keep the flame burning there beneath his altar, he will be pleased, wherever he is.'

'By jove, at last I hear a woman's voice,' said Chowdhury. 'Not bad at all. But remember, if you do want to help Rebati all the way, it will take even more than a lakh.'

'Even if it does, I'll have some small change left over.'

'But the one from the afterworld whom you want to please will not be upset, will he? I'm told they can cling to our shoulders and bump us about if they want to.'

'You read the newspapers, don't you? As soon as someone dies, their praises are sung in every paragraph. There's nothing wrong in depending on the generosity of a dead man. Anyone who has accumulated wealth has accumulated sins too alongside. What are we here for if we cannot empty the sack out to mitigate our husbands' sins? Let the money go, I don't need it.'

'What more can I say?' said the professor animatedly. 'The gold that's excavated from a mine is pure gold, even if impurities are mixed into it. You're a nugget of gold in disguise. Now that I know who you are, tell me what I have to do.'

'Get the boy to agree.'

'I'll try, but it won't be easy. Anyone else would have accepted your gift with alacrity.'

'What's getting in the way?'

'A female planet has monopolized his horoscope since his childhood. An unshakeable lack of common sense stands in the way.'

'Really! A man . . .'

'Look, Mrs Mullick, whom will you be angry with? Do you know what a matriarchal society is? It is a society where women are superior to men. Once upon a time the waves of this Dravidian society used to wash over Bengal.'

'Those happy days are over,' said Sohini. 'Maybe the waves still play underneath, confusing us, but the steering wheel is in the hands of men. They pour advice into our ears, and then rip those same ears off to punish us.'

'You do know how to talk. If we had an age of women like you, in this matriarchal society I would immediately make a laundry list only for women's clothes, and I would send our college principal off to slice vegetables. Psychology says matriarchy in Bengal is not external, it exists in our hearts. Have you heard the men of any other land moo their mothers' names all the time? Let me inform you, it's a woman who's perched on Rebati's brain.'

'Does he love someone?'

'That would have suggested there's a heart beating in his veins.

This is the age at which to lose your head for a woman. But he has turned into a bead in the hands of a bead-counting female instead. Nothing can save him—not youth, not intelligence, not science.'

'Do you you think I could invite him to tea? Will he deign to have a cup of tea with untouchables like us?'

'Untouchables! If he refuses I'll thrash him till he turns so amenable that not even a sign of that woman will remain in his blood. Let me ask you something—apparently you have a daughter?'

'I do. The wretched girl is beautiful too. What can I do?'

'No, don't misunderstand me. As for me, I prefer beautiful women. You could call it an affliction. But his relations are so colourless that they will be afraid.'

'They needn't. I have decided to marry my daughter only to someone of our own caste.'

This was complete fiction.

'But you married out of your caste.'

'And I've paid for it too. I had to fight so many cases over the property. How I won doesn't bear retelling.'

'I've heard some of it. There was a rumour about you and the articled clerk of your opponents. You disappeared after winning your case, but that poor man almost killed himself!'

'How do you think women have survived through the ages? It takes a lot of tricks to deceive, no less than preparations for war, but then you need to add some honey too. This is the traditional way for the feminine personality to wage war.'

'There, you've misunderstood me again. We're scientists, not judges—we observe the play of human nature dispassionately. The game goes on to its inevitable outcome. The result was quite predictable in your case. I said then that you're an admirable woman. I even thought that I was fortunate to be a professor and not an articled clerk at the time. Mercury is saved from the sun by the slight distance at which it orbits. It's a matter of mathematics, beyond good or evil. You have probably learnt all this.'

'Indeed I have. The planets are both attracted and repelled, this is certainly a principle to be learnt.'

'I have another confession. I have been making calculations in my head all this time while talking to you. This too is a mathematical computation. Just imagine the trouble we could have been in had

I been ten years younger. We barely averted a collision. But still my heart is steaming up. Think about it—creation is nothing but a game of mathematics.'

Slapping his knees, Chowdhury burst into laughter. The one thing that he had not realized was that Sohini had spent two hours before his arrival changing her age so effectively with make-up that she had fooled the creator entirely.

4

When the professor arrived the next day, he discovered Sohini bathing and towelling a mangy, gaunt dog.

'Why such regard for this bad omen?' asked Chowdhury.

'Because I saved him. He was run over by a car and broke his leg, I bandaged him and ensured his recovery. Now I own shares in his life.'

'Isn't the sight of this wretched animal every day going to depress you?'

'He isn't here by virtue of his looks. I like the fact that he survived after being on the brink of death. When I can meet this creature's need to stay alive every single day, I don't need to perform my religious duties by putting a rope around the neck of a goat and leading it to the goddess. I've decided to start a hospital for the lame and blind rabbits and dogs in your biology laboratory.'

'The more I see you the more you astonish me, Mrs Mullick.'

'If you see even more of me the effect will be diminished. You had promised to tell me more about Rebati-babu—start now.'

'I have a distant connection with them, which is why I know the family history. Rebati's mother died immediately after he was born. He has been brought up by his aunt—his father's sister. Her adherence to rituals is flawless. She turned the household upside down whenever she spotted the slightest deviance. There was no one in the family who wasn't frightened of her. Rebati's manhood was pulverised in her care. Five minutes' delay in returning from school required twenty-five minutes of explanations.'

'I always believed that men should discipline and women indulge,' said Sohini. 'That keeps things balanced.'

The professor said, 'It's not in the nature of graceful women to remain balanced. They will always lean this way or that. Don't mind, Mrs Mullick, but even among them you do accidentally get one or two who keep their heads erect and walk straight. For instance . . .'

'No need to say anything more. But my roots are in womanhood too. Can't you see my new fancy? My get-a-man fancy. Would I have bothered you otherwise?'

'Listen, don't keep saying that. For your information, I have come over to meet you instead of preparing my class lecture. That's how much I'm enjoying neglecting my work.'

'You are probably kind to all women.'

'Not impossible at all. But still there are distinctions to be made. But never mind, we can talk about that later.'

'We needn't even talk about it,' smiled Sohini. 'Please finish what we *are* talking about now. What lies behind Rebati-babu's ascent?'

'It is nothing compared to what it could have been. He needed to go to the mountains for some research, and had planned to go to Badrikashram. Oh my god! His aunt also had an aunt once, and, of all places, the hag had chosen to die on the road to Badri. So his aunt said, "No mountains as long as I'm alive." I should not utter what I have been fervently praying for since then. Never mind all that.'

'But why blame the aunts alone? Aren't the nephews—those apples of their mothers' eyes—ever going to resist?'

'I've answered that already. Matriarchy brings the cow out in all males, the poor dears are bewildered. This was just the first of many hindrances. The next time, when Rebati decided to accept a government scholarship to Cambridge, the same aunt began to wail and beat her breast. She was convinced he was going to marry an Englishwoman. Let him marry one, I said. It was an ill-conceived statement. Speculation turned to certainty. The aunt said, "If he goes to England I'll hang myself." Being an atheist, I didn't know which god to pray to in order to ensure that the rope was within reach, and so no rope materialised. I heaped abuse on Rebati, using choice epithets like stupid, dunce and imbecile. That was it. Rebu is now squeezing oil out of an Indian press.'

An impatient Sohini said, 'I wish I could break my head

against the wall and die. One woman has sunk Rebati, but I vow that it will be another woman who will draw him back to land.'

'Let me tell you clearly, madam. You're adept at grabbing the beasts by their horns and drowning them, but you haven't yet developed the skill of pulling them up by the tail. You might as well start now. But let me ask you something—how did you get so interested in science?'

'My husband was engaged with all the sciences. His addiction was to Burmese cigars and to his laboratory. He got me addicted to the cigars too and almost turned me into a Burmese woman. But I gave them up, because men looked askance. He transferred another of his passions to me. Men win women over by fooling them, but he won me over with his erudition. Look, Chowdhurymoshai, a husband's weaknesses are never hidden to his wife, but I saw no deficiency in him. When I was near him, he appeared great; now that I am at a distance, he appears greater still.'

'Where did his greatness lie?' asked Chowdhury.

'Should I tell you? Not because he was learned, but because he was dispassionately devoted to knowledge. He breathed the air of his worship, he lived by the light of his worship. We women cannot worship something that cannot be touched or seen. His laboratory has become the god I worship. Sometimes I am inclined to light incense sticks here and blow the ritual conchshell, but I fear my husband's loathing. When he conducted his rituals every day, college students would gather around these instruments, learning from him, and I'd be present too.'

'Could the boys still concentrate on science?'

'Those who could were the ones to be selected. I've seen boys who were genuinely detached. And then there were others who would use the pretext of taking notes to practise their literary skills through letters.'

'How did it feel?'

'The truth? Not bad at all. My husband would be busy, while the imaginative souls hovered about.'

'Please don't mind my asking, I study psychology, you see. Did they get anything for their effort?'

'I don't really want to say this, but I am bad. I did come to know three or four who still make my heart twist when I think about them.'

'Three or four?'

'The heart is greedy, you see. It buries the covert flames of desire beneath its flesh and blood, but the flames flare up when stoked. I disgraced myself at the outset, so I have no hesitation in telling the truth. We are not lifelong ascetics. Women are dying from keeping up pretences. The Draupadis and Kuntis have to disguise themselves as Sitas and Savitris. Let me tell you something, Chowdhury-moshai, remember this—I had no clear sense of right and wrong since childhood. No teacher taught me. So I plunged into the wrong easily, and overcame it easily too. It left a stain on my body but did not leave a mark on my heart. None of it clung to me. Anyway, as he was leaving, he set my desires to fire on his funeral pyre—all my accumulated sins are going up in flames. The sacrificial fires are burning in this very laboratory.'

'Bravo! You're not afraid to tell the truth.'

'It's easy when there's someone who makes me tell the truth. You are straightforward, you are the truth, you see.'

'Those boys who wrote letters to earn your favours—do they still visit you?'

'That is how they have wiped away the stains in my heart. I saw they were clustering round me with an eye on my chequebook. They had imagined that women are always vulnerable to attention, and that they could tunnel in with love to reach the safe in which my money is kept. They did not know that I am not soft. I have a dry, Punjabi heart. I can sweep away the rules of society for my physical desires, but I will die before I am treacherous. They could not take a penny away from my laboratory. My life force is like a giant rock weighing down the trapdoor leading to my god's treasures. They don't have the power melt the rock down. The person who chose me didn't make a mistake.'

'I offer my homage to him, and I'd box the ears of those young men if I could get my hands on them.'

Before the professor left he took a tour of the laboratory with Sohini. 'Feminine guile has been distilled here, the sediment of the evil spirit has been left behind, only the pure version has been decanted.'

'Say what you will, but my fear persists,' said Sohini. 'Feminine guile is god's original creation. It lurks behind the bushes as long as a woman is young and strong-willed. But once the hot blood of youth cools, the traditional aunt emerges from within her. I'd rather die before that happens.'

'Don't worry,' said the professor, 'I am sure you will die in your senses.'

5

Putting on a white sari, Sohini sprinkled talcum powder on her greying hair and summoned a pious, abstemious glow to her face. Accompanied by her daughter, she arrived at the Botanical Garden in a motor launch. She had dressed her daughter in a blue-green Benaras sari, with an orange blouse visible underneath. Nila's brow was adorned with a vermilion dot, her eyes lined with kohl, her hair cascading down to her shoulder, her feet in black leather sandals embroidered with red velvet.

Having forearmed herself with information, Sohini discovered Rebati beneath the tall margosa tree where he spent his Sundays. She greeted him by touching his feet with her forehead. Rebati was flustered.

'Please don't mind, son,' said Sohini. 'You're the son of a Brahmin, and I'm the daughter of a Chhatri. Chowdhury-moshai may have told you about me.'

'He has. But how do I find a seat for you here?'

'Is there a better seat anywhere than this green grass? You must be wondering what I'm doing here. I have come to fulfil my vow. I won't find another Brahmin like you, after all.'

'A Brahmin like me?' asked Rebati in surprise.

'Of course. My guru says that the one who has the best hold on knowledge is the finest Brahmin today.'

Unprepared for this, Rebati said, 'My father was the priest, I know no chants.'

'What do you mean! The incantations that you know have brought the universe under the control of human beings. You may be wondering how a woman has learnt to speak this way. I have learnt from a man who was a real man—my husband. Promise me, son, that you will visit the temple to which he dedicated himself.'

'I am free tomorrow morning, I shall go.'

'I see you're fond of plants and trees. I'm very happy. My husband went to Burma in search of plants, and I never left his side.'

She didn't, but not for the pursuit of science. She could not but assume that her husband had the same weaknesses in his character that she did. Suspicion was inherent to her nature. Once, when Nandakishore was seriously ill, he told his wife, 'The only joy of dying is that you will not be able to follow me and bring me back.'

'I can come along,' said Sohini.

'What a disaster that would be!' laughed Nandakishore.

Sohini told Rebati, 'I brought the seeds of a special plant from Burma. The Burmese call it ji xue teng. Such a lovely array of flowers but they didn't survive.'

Sohini had rummaged through her husband's library that morning to get this name. She had never even seen the plant in her life, she only wanted to cast a net of knowledge to catch the scholar.

Rebati was surprised. 'Do you know its Latin name?' he asked.

'Milettia,' answered Sohini casually.

'My husband was not a believer,' she added, 'but he did believe blindly that if a woman in a particular condition directed her attention to all that is beautiful in nature—flowers or fruits—the child is certain to be beautiful. Do you believe this too?'

Needless to say, this was not Nandakishore's opinion.

Scratching his head, Rebati said, 'There isn't sufficient proof yet.'

'I have found at least one piece of evidence in my own home. How did my daughter become so extraordinarily beautiful? Like all the flowers of spring . . . never mind, you'll know for yourself when you see her.'

Rebati grew eager for a glimpse. All the props for the drama were in place. Sohini had dressed up her cook as a priest. He was wearing a scarf with a sacred mark on his forehead, flowers tied to his tuft, and a thick sacred thread. Calling out to him, Sohini said, 'It's time, thakur, fetch Nilu now.'

Nila's mother had made her wait on the launch. She was

supposed to have stepped off it holding a basket, offering a prolonged view in the light and shade of the morning.

Meanwhile, Sohini scanned Rebati closely. His complexion was smooth and dark, though a little sallow. His brow was wide, with the hair having been finger-brushed off the forehead. His eyes were not big, but the clear light of vision shone in them—they were the most prominent feature on his face. The lower half of his face was as silken as a woman's. Of all the information that Sohini had gathered about Rebati, one fact had caught her attention. He harboured a sentimental love, replete with tears, for his childhood friends. The vulnerability in his face had the ability to charm boys' hearts.

Sohini felt a misgiving. She believed that men did not have to be remotely good-looking to grip women's hearts like an anchor. Intelligence and education were secondary too. The real requirement was male magnetism. It was like a radio signal sent out by the nerves, expressing itself as the unstated arrogance of desire.

Sohini recollected her own early years of wild longing. The person she had drawn to herself—or perhaps he had drawn her—was not in possession of either good looks, education or family glory. But he seemed to exude an invisible heat whose influence had made her perceive him keenly as a man with her entire body and soul. She was constantly beset by worries about the same inevitable upheavals in Nila's life too. The last stage of youth is the most dangerous one—relentless pursuit of science had kept Sohini largely distracted in this period. But as it happened, her mind was naturally fertile. However, not every woman could be attracted to impersonal knowledge.

Gradually Nila became visible at the steps leading out of the river. The sunlight slanted down on her brow and hair, the zari lines on her Benaras sari sparkling. Rebati's eyes took in her entire form in an instant, lowering his eyes the very next moment. This was how he had been trained since childhood. The beautiful woman representing the enchanting game of nature was usually hidden from his view by his aunt's wagging finger. When he got the opportunity, therefore, he had to gulp down the nectar quickly with his eyes.

Reproving Rebati in her head, Sohini said, 'Just look at her, will you?'

Startled, Rebati raised his eyes and looked.

'Look for yourself, doctor of science, how beautifully the colour of her sari matches the colour of the leaves.'

'Beautiful,' said Rebati bashfully.

'Impossible,' said Sohini to herself. 'There's orange peeping beneath the greenish-blue,' she continued. 'Can you tell me which flower she resembles?'

Encouraged, Rebati looked closely. 'I am reminded of a particular flower, but its outer layer is not exactly blue, it's brown.'

'Which flower is that?'

'Melina,' answered Rebati.

'Oh, of course. Five petals, one of them bright yellow, the others dark.'

Rebati was astonished. 'How do you know so much about flowers?' he asked.

'It isn't right to, son,' Sohini smiled. 'I think of any flowers except those meant for worshipping the gods as other men.'

Nila approached slowly with the basket. 'Don't just stand there,' said her mother. 'Go touch his feet.'

'Oh no,' said Rebati in unease. Since he was sitting with his legs tucked beneath his body, Nila had to grope for his feet. Rebati shivered. The basket contained a sprig of rare orchids, along with badam takti, pesta barfi, chandrapuli, kheer, malai barfi and squares of steamed doi.

'Nila has made all of this herself,' said Sohini.

A complete lie. Nila had neither the skill nor the inclination for such things.

'You must taste a little, son, it's all been made for you at home,' said Sohini.

The entire spread had been ordered at a shop in Burrabazar that they knew well.

Gesturing apologetically, Rebati protested, 'I don't normally eat at this hour. If you permit, I'd rather take it home.'

'That might be better,' responded Sohini. 'My husband's rulebook did not allow force-feeding. Humans aren't anacondas, he would say.'

Sohini transferred all the food into the different layers of a tiffin-carrier. 'Place the flowers on the tray,' she told her daughter. 'Don't mix them up. And spread that silk handkerchief you've tied your hair with over the flowers.'

The universal curiosity in the scientist's eyes turned to eagerness. This was beyond the objects of the natural world that could be weighed and measured. Amidst the different hues of the petals, Nila's shapely fingers made different movements to the rhythm of flower-arrangement—Rebati could not tear his eyes away. He threw intermittent glances at Nila's face, whose edges were defined at one end by a rainbow—a single strand of rubies, pearls and emeralds wound around her hair—and at the other by the prominent flaming border of her orange blouse. Sohini was stacking the sweets, but she seemed to have a third eye. The enchantment in progress did not escape her attention.

Going by her husband's experience, Sohini used to believe that the fenced-in field of knowledge was not for all kinds of cattle to graze in. Today she sensed that the fence was not equally strong for everyone. The realization did not please her.

6

Sohini sent for the professor the next day. 'I disturb you unnecessarily for my own needs, perhaps I even harm your work,' she said.

'Call me over more often, I beg of you. If there's a reason, wonderful. If not, even more so.'

'You know that my husband recklessly indulged his passion for collecting expensive equipment. He cheated his masters with this Platonic desire of his. Like him, I was also consumed by the determination that Asia should not have another laboratory such as this one. It was this determination that has kept me alive, else my alcoholic blood would have fermented and frothed by now. Look, Chowdhury-moshai, you're the one friend to whom I can unreservedly confess my bad traits. The mind breathes a sigh of relief when it finds an open door to display its flaws.'

'There is no need to suppress the truth from those who can see everything,' said Chowdhury. 'Half-truths are embarrassing. We scientists are inclined to see the full picture.'

'My husband would say that humans are desperate to save their lives but lives cannot be saved. Which is why humans try to satiate their desire for life by searching for something beyond existence. For him this rare quest was in his laboratory. If I cannot keep it alive, I will be responsible for his ultimate end, the slayer of my husband. I am looking for someone to preserve it, and hence my search for Rebati.'

'Have you tried to get him?'

'I have. There's hope of quick results, but it won't last.'

'Why not?'

'As soon as Rebati's aunt gets to know, she will come running to snatch him away. She will assume I'm laying a trap to have my daughter married to him.'

'What's wrong with that—it would turn out well. But didn't you say you wouldn't allow your daughter to marry out of your caste?'

'I didn't know your mind, so I lied. I wanted it very much. But I have abandoned the idea.'

'Why?'

'I can tell she's a destructive woman. Whatever she gets hold of will be destroyed.'

'But she's your daughter.'

'Of course she is, which is why I've known her from the womb.'

'But how can you forget that women can inspire men?' asked the professor.

'I know that very well. Meat is fine for a man's plate, but once you serve wine, he's finished. My daughter is a brimming wineglass.'

'Then what would you like to do?'

'I want to donate my laboratory to the public.'

'Cutting your only daughter off?'

'My daughter? If I bequeath it to her I have no idea which hole it will vanish in. I will make Rebati the president of the trust for the property. His aunt cannot object to that, surely?'

'Why would I have been born a man if I could grasp the logic of women's refusal? But what I don't understand is why you want him as the president if you don't want him as your son-in-law.'

'What use is all this equipment alone? It needs a human being to breathe life into it. Another thing—not a single piece of new equipment has been added since my husband's death. Not because of a dearth of money. But there has to be an objective behind the purchase. I've been told that Rebati is working on magnetism. Let the collection be expanded for this purpose, no matter how much it costs.'

'What do I say?I If you'd been a man I'd have hoisted you on my shoulders. Your husband stole the railway company's money, and you stole his manly heart. I have never seen two intellects so well-matched. I am astonished you actually feel the need for advice from me.'

'That is because you are absolutely genuine, you know how to tell the truth.'

'Don't make me laugh. I'm not the kind of perfect idiot who will tell you a lie and be caught out. You'd better swing into action then—lists have to be drawn up, prices have to be compared, a top-class lawyer has to be engaged to assess your rights, the statutes have to be drawn up . . . there's lots to do.'

'You have to take the responsibility for all this.'

'Only nominally. You know very well that I will speak your words, perform your actions. The benefit for me will be meeting you twice a day. You have no idea how I have come to regard you.'

Springing up off her chair, Sohini put her arm around Chowdhury, kissing his cheek in a flash and moving away at once, resuming her seat innocently.

'And thus begins disaster.'

'I wouldn't have come anywhere near you if I'd been the least bit frightened of that. You will get these from time to time.'

'Are you sure?'

'I am. It costs me nothing, and you don't look like you expect more.'

'In other words, this is like a woodpecker pecking on dead wood. I'm off to the lawyer's.'

'Come by tomorrow.'

'Whatever for?'

'To wind up Rebati's heart.'

'And to lose mine.'

'You think you're the only one with a heart?'

'Is anything left of yours?'
'Plenty of leftovers.'
'Which will be used to make dogs jump through hoops.'

7

The next day Rebati arrived at the laboratory at least ten minutes before the appointed time. Sohini wasn't prepared. She was dressed in an ordinary sari. Rebati realized his gaffe. 'My watch is running a little fast,' he said.

'Certainly,' said Sohini briefly. Startled by a sound, Rebati looked at the door. Sukhan the bearer entered with the key to the glass case.

'May I get you a cup of tea?' asked Sohini.

Rebati thought he should accept the offer. 'Why not?' he replied.

The poor boy was not used to tea—at the first hint of a cold he was served warm water with boiled bel leaves. He was expecting Nila to bring him the tea.

'Do you like your tea strong?' asked Sohini.

'Yes,' he said impulsively.

He was under the impression that this was the appropriate answer. The tea arrived, undoubtedly strong. As black as ink, as bitter as neem. The Muslim cook had brought it in. This was also to test him. But he couldn't bring himself to protest. Sohini did not approve of such diffidence. 'Why don't you pour the tea, Mobarak,' she told the cook. 'It's getting cold.'

Rebati had not turned up twenty minutes early in the expectation of having his tea poured by the cook.

Only the almighty knew how he was suffering as he raised the cup to his mouth, and so did Sohini. She was a woman, after all. Sensing Rebati's predicament, she said, 'Never mind that cup. I'll pour you some milk. Have some fruit. Considering how early you came here, you probably haven't eaten breakfast.' This was true. Rebati had expected an encore of Botanical Gardens. Nothing remotely like that was offered, and only the bitter taste of the strong tea remained in his mouth, along with the bitter experience of broken hope in his head.

The professor entered; clapping Rebati on the back, 'What is it? You're a block of wood. Why are you gulping down milk like a little girl? Do you think these are toys for boys around you? Those who have discerning eyes know what all this is—the disciples of death perform their wild dances here.'

'Oh poor thing, why are you scolding him? He left before breakfast this morning. He looked so pale when he came.'

'And here comes aunt the second. One aunt slaps him on one cheek, the other one kisses him on the other. Caught in between, the young man turns into a lump of clay. The truth is that the goddess of wealth is ignored when she comes on her own; so she submits herself only to those who scour the world in search of her. If you don't want, you'll never get. Tell me, Mrs . . . no, to hell with Mrs, I *shall* call you Sohini, like it or not.'

'May I die, why shouldn't I like it? Call me Sohini—I'll be even happier if you call me Suhi.'

'I might as well tell you my secret. The Bengali word that rhymes with your name, mohini, is the pure truth—you *are* an enchantress. Every morning I chant those two words in rhythm in my head.'

'Your research in chemistry has accustomed you to finding similiarities, this is just a side-effect.'

'People even die in their quest for rhyme. Best not to mess with it—most inflammable.'

He laughed uproariously.

'But no, we mustn't discuss all this in this little boy's presence. He has not yet started his apprenticeship in the gunpowder factory. His aunt makes him hide behind the end of her sari and the sari is incombustible.'

Rebati's womanly face grew red.

'I was about to ask you whether you fed him opium this morning, Sohini. Why is he dozing?'

'If I have, I did it unknowingly.'

'Wake up, Rebu, wake up. You mustn't be so shy in the company of women. It only makes them more audacious. They keep probing for weaknesses in males, and the moment they find a chink they raise the temperature. I'm familiar with the subject, which is why I have to warn men. You can only learn from someone like me, who's been afflicted but has not succumbed. Please don't be offended, Rebu, my son. The ones who don't talk are the deadliest of the species. Come with me, let me take you on a round. Here, two galvanometers, the very latest of their kind. This is a high vacuum pump, and this, a microphotometer—these aren't smoke-and-mirror tricks to make students pass their examinations. If you can just establish yourself here, I'd love to see how that bald professor's face who I will not name, falls. Didn't I tell you when you started your education as my student that what they call "a future" is dangling in front of your nose? Don't neglect it. If my name can be written in tiny letters in one corner of the first chapter of your biography, that will be my greatest reward as your teacher.'

The scientist awoke in no time. His eyes blazed. His very appearance was transformed from within. An entranced Sohini said, 'Anyone who knows you expects big achievements from you—not everyday achievements, but eternal ones. But the greater the expectation, the greater the obstacles to it both within and without.'

The professor slapped Rebati on the back again with great enthusiasm. His spine jangled. In his baritone, Chowdhury said, 'Look, Rebu, the noble future should have been brought in by the divine elephant, but the miserly present has put it on a bullock-cart instead, miring it in a swamp. Are you listening, Sohini, Suhi? . . . No, don't be afraid, I won't slap you on the back, but tell me honestly whether I've explained it well.'

'Beautifully.'

'Write it down in your diary.'

'I shall.'

'Did you understand, Rebi?'

'I think so.'

'Remember, great talent has a great responsibility. It doesn't belong to any one person, it must justify itself to eternity. Are you listening, Suhi? Tell me whether I'm right or not.'

'Of course you are. In another era a king would have taken his necklace off and . . .'

'They're all dead, but . . .'

'That "but" hasn't died, I shall remember.'

'Don't worry, nothing can make me waver,' declared Rebati.

He tried to touch Sohini's feet in respect. She stopped him quickly.

'What have you done!' said Chowdhury. 'It's bad enough not to perform your own good deeds, but it's worse to prevent others from performing theirs.'

'If you must pay homage, do it there,' said Sohini, pointing to Nandakishore's photograph, with incense sticks burning and a plate heaped with flowers in front.

'I've read in the scriptures of sinners being rescued. I was rescued by this noble man here. He had to lower himself a long way down, but eventually he succeeded in lifting me from the depths to a place—I would be lying if I said it was by his side—at his feet. He indoctrinated me in the principle of saving humans with knowledge. "I have mined many precious stones," he told me, "don't cast them into a heap of ashes for the glory of our daughter and son-in-law. There's my salvation," he said, "and my country's salvation too."'

'I hope you heard that, Rebu,' the professor said. 'The laboratory will become the property of a trust, and you will be in charge.'

Alarmed, Rebati said, 'I am not worthy to be in charge. I cannot do it.'

'Cannot do it!' exclaimed Sohini. 'Shame, is this how a man speaks?'

'I have spent all my life studying,' said Rebati, 'I have never taken the responsibility for such a task.'

'The duck doesn't swim before the egg is hatched,' said Chowdhury. 'Your eggshell will crack today.'

'Don't worry,' said Sohini, 'I'll be there with you.'

Rebati left, reassured.

Sohini looked at the professor. Chowdhury said, 'There are many varieties of fools in the world, but the finest of them are male fools. Remember, though, that an aptitude for shouldering responsibility does not grow unless one is actually given the responsibility. Mankind became human because everyone had a pair of hands, but if they had been given a pair of hooves instead, a tail for wagging would have sprouted automatically. Have you observed hooves instead of hands on Rebati?'

'No, I'm not pleased. Those brought up by women alone never lose their milk teeth. It's destiny. Why did I have to think of anyone else when you were here?'

'I'm happy to hear that. Now explain my qualities to me.'

'You're not greedy at all.'

'What a low opinion you have of me! Do you suppose I'm not greedy about things that deserve greed? Of course I am . . .'

Stopping him in mid-sentence, Sohini kissed him on both cheeks and stepped back.

'What account do these accrue to, Sohini?'

'I will never be able to return what I have borrowed from you, this is just the interest.'

'One the first day, two today. Will the number keep rising?'

'Of course it will, following the principles of compound interest.'

8

'Did you *have* to appoint me the priest for your husband's last rites, Sohini?' said Chowdhury. 'My goodness, this is no small responsibility—pleasing the one whose existence cannot even be established. This isn't your everyday charitable act . . .'

'You're not an everyday priest either; your method will be established as the official process. I hope you've made the arrangements for the allocations.'

'That's all I've been doing these past few days. I've scoured the shops and everything's in the big room downstairs. There's no doubt that the living souls who will misappropriate them will be extremely pleased.'

Going downstairs with Chowdhury, Sohini discovered a range of instruments, models, expensive books, and microscope slides with biological specimens—all for the science students. Every item was labelled with the name and address of the recipient. Cheques had been made out to two hundred and fifty young men, covering a year's scholarship for each. No expense had been spared. The extent of money spent was much more than the amount splurged on Brahmins during the last rites of wealthy zamindars, yet the lavishness was not particularly visible.

'You haven't said what the priest's fees are.'

'That's up to you.'

'Along with which I have put aside this chronometer for you. My husband bought it in Germany—he had always used it for his research.'

'I don't have words for the thoughts in my head,' said Chowdhury. 'I don't want to say anything trite. My priest's duties have been fulfilled.'

'There's someone else whom I cannot forget today—our Manik's widow.'

'Who's Manik?'

'He was the chief technician at my husband's laboratory. Incredibly skilful. His hand wouldn't waver at all during the most delicate operations, and his grasp of the principles of machinery was flawless. My husband used to consider him a dear friend, taking him around in his car to show him how large factories worked. But he was a drunkard, and his assistants dismissed him as a wastrel. My husband would say, this man is so talented, talent like this cannot be acquired. My husband gave him all the respect he deserved. This will tell you why he held me in such high esteem till the end. He thought my worth was much higher than my blemishes. Not once did I betray the specific faith that he had reposed in a foundling like me. I honour that faith even today with all my heart and soul. No one gave him as much as I did. I did not attract his attention with my deficiencies—it was my good qualities for which he held me in regard. Can you imagine how I would have sunk without his attention? I am a bad woman, but I can claim that I am good, for he would never have tolerated me otherwise.'

'Look, Sohini, I can boast that I spotted your qualities right away. If these qualities had been the cheap sort, the stigma would never have been rubbed off.'

'Never mind, let people think what they will. The respect he gave me remains even now, and will remain till my last breath.'

'Let me tell you, Sohini, that the more I come to know you, the more I realize that you do not belong to the tribe of women who swoon when their husband is mentioned.'

'No, I do not. But I saw the power in him, from the very first day I knew that he was human—I didn't set out to be a devoted wife as the scriptures ordered. I can brag that the pearls within me are fit for a necklace that adorns his throat alone, no one else's.'

Nila entered. 'Please don't mind, professor, but I need to talk to Ma.'

'Not at all, my girl, I'm off to the laboratory. Let me find out whether Rebati is making progress.'

'You needn't worry,' said Nila. 'He's making good progress. I spot him sometimes through the window, writing away furiously, taking notes, lost in thought with his pen clamped between his teeth. I'm not allowed in, lest Sir Isaac's gravitation is shaken. Ma was telling someone the other day that he's working with magnetism, which is why the needle shakes every time someone walks past, especially a girl.'

Bursting into laughter, Chowdhury said, 'The laboratory is within us, my girl, where the research into magnetism is continuous. So one has to fear those who can make the needle shake. One loses one's way. I'm off.'

'How much longer will you keep me tied down?' Nila asked her mother. 'You won't succeed, and you'll only be hurt.'

'What do you want to do?'

'You know there's a higher study movement for women—you've made large contributions to the funds too. Why can't I work for it?'

'I'm worried—what if you make wrong choices?'

'Is closing all choices the right choice?'

'I know it isn't, that's why I worry.'

'Why don't you stop worrying and let me do it instead? I'm not a little girl anymore. You think the public places where people come and go are dangerous. But people will not stop going where they want to just for your sake. Nor are you armed with a law that can prevent me from meeting them.'

'I know, I know, fear cannot keep the cause of fear away. So you want to join the higher study circle?'

'I do.'

'Very well. I know you will send the male professors to hell one by one. But you must make one promise. You must not go anywhere near Rebati. And you must not enter his laboratory on any pretext whatsoever.'

'I don't know what you think of me, Ma. Do you think my taste runs towards that mini Sir Isaac Newton of yours? Over my dead body.'

Imitating the wriggle that Rebati subjected his body to when embarrassed, Nila said, 'A man with such mannerisms won't do for me. It's best to preserve him for women who like helping overgrown children become mature. He's not a worthy prey.'

'You're exaggerating, Nila, which makes me think you're not speaking from your heart. Still, whatever you may feel for him, it won't serve you well to reduce him to dust.'

'I don't understand your whims, Ma. You think I don't know that you dressed me up as a doll as a prelude to arranging my marriage with him? Is that why you don't want me to hover too close to him—lest familiarity mar the gloss?'

'Look, Nila, I'm telling you that you cannot marry him in any circumstances.'

'Then may I marry the prince of Motigarh?"

'If you like.'

'It would be convenient. He has three wives already, so my responsibility will be lightened. And he drinks and flirts at nightclubs. I'll have a lot of time to myself.'

'Very well. I shall not let you marry Rebati.'

'Why? Do you fear I will addle your Sir Isaac Newton's brains?'

'I won't get into an argument. Remember what I said.'

'What if he turns greedy?'

'Then he will have to leave this neighbourhood—you can support him. He won't get a penny from your father's funds.'

'Good god! Then goodbye, Sir Isaac.'

This was the end of the act that day.

9

'Everything else is going well, Chowdhury-moshai, but I cannot stop worrying for my daughter. I cannot determine whom she's training her sights on.'

'You also have to consider who might be training his sights on her,' remarked Chowdhury. 'The thing is, rumour has it that your husband has left behind unlimited coffers for the protection of the laboratory. And the amount keeps getting inflated by word of mouth. Now they're all rolling the dice to win the princess and the kingdom.'

'I am aware that the princess will go for a song, but the kingdom will not be sold cheaply as long as I'm alive.'

'But people have begun to flock around her. Just the other day I saw our Professor Majumdar come out of the cinema holding her hand. He looked away the moment he saw me. The young man delivers worthy lectures everywhere, he has the gift of the gab when it comes to talking about the welfare of the nation. But his averted gaze that day made me worry for my homeland.'

'The barriers have been broken, Chowdhury-moshai.'

'But of course they have. The poor people will have to look after themselves.'

'Let there be an epidemic amongst the Majumdars for all I care, it's Rebati I'm worried about.'

'Not at the moment,' said Chowdhury. 'He's engrossed and doing some very fine work.'

'Chowdhury-moshai, the danger is that no matter how much of an expert he might be at science, when it comes to what you call matriarchy, he's a rank amateur.'

'That's true. He hasn't been vaccinated even once. If the contagion hits it will be hard to save him.'

'You must examine him every day.'

'I hope he doesn't pick up an infection somewhere. What if I were to die at this age? Don't be afraid, I hope you get a joke even though you're a woman. I've traversed the epidemic zone already—I won't be contaminated even if I come into contact with it. But there's a problem. I have to go to Gujranwala the day after tomorrow.'

'Is this a joke too? Pity a poor woman.'

'It's not a joke. My colleague Amulya Addy was a doctor there, with a practice of twenty-five years. He had amassed some property too. But he has suddenly died of a heart attack, leaving behind his widow and children. I have to ensure that his debts are paid back, his property sold, and that his family returns. I don't know how long it will take.'

'Can't argue with that.'

'You cannot argue with anything in this world, Sohini. Say what you must fearlessly—whatever will be, will be. Those who believe in destiny are not wrong. We scientists also declare that the inevitable cannot be changed even slightly. As long as there's something you can do, do it. When you simply cannot do anything anymore, just say you're done.'

'All right.'

'The Majumdar I mentioned is not the most dangerous in the group. They include him so as not to humiliate him. If you consider some of the others I've heard of, even a distance of a hundred feet from them is, as Chanakya put it, hazardous. There's Bankubehari the attorney—taking his help and embracing an octopus are the same thing. These people adore hot-blooded widows. File this information away, and act upon it if you need to. And finally, remember my philosophy.'

'Never mind your philosophy, Chowdhury-moshai. I shan't care for your destiny, I shan't care for your unshakeable principles of cause and effect if anyone lays a finger on my laboratory. I'm a woman from Punjab, using the dagger comes naturally to me. I can murder anyone—whether it's my own daughter or her suitor.'

She had on a belt under her sari, from which she whipped out a dagger, allowing the light to flash on it. 'He chose me,' she said. 'I'm not a Bengali woman, I don't shed copious tears over love. I can lay down my life for love, or take someone's life. Between my laboratory and my heart lies this dagger.'

'I could write poetry once upon a time,' said Chowdhury. 'I feel like I might be able to, again.'

'Write all the poetry you want, but withdraw your philosophy. Till the last day I shan't accept what cannot be accepted. I'll fight alone. And I'll assert boldly that I *shall* win, I *shall* win, I *shall* win.'

'Bravo, I am withdrawing my philosophy. I shall beat the drums to your victory march from now on. I am saying goodbye for now, I won't be away long.'

Unexpectedly, Sohini's eyes filled with tears. 'Please don't mind,' she said. Putting her arms around Chowdhury's neck, she said, 'No bond in the world lasts, this too is momentary.'

Letting go at once, Sohini bent to touch the professor's feet in respect.

10

What the newspapers refer to as a 'situation' appears unexpectedly, and in multitudes. The story of life is slowed down by pains and pleasures. In the final chapter there is a sudden collision, and everything is destroyed, silenced. The almighty builds his tale slowly, but breaks it with a single stroke.

Sohini's grandmother lived in Ambala. She received a telegram, 'Come quickly if you want a last look.'

This grandmother was her only living relative. It was from her that Nandakishore had purchased Sohini.

'You come too,' Nila was told by her mother.

'That's impossible.'

'Why?'

'They're making arrangements to felicitate me.'

'Who are "they"?'

'Members of the Awakening Club. Don't worry, it's a very respectable club. You'll know once you see the list of members. Hand-picked.'

'What is your objective?'

'It's difficult to state it clearly. The objective is stated in the name. It holds all kinds of meanings deep within—spiritual, literary, artistic, everything. Nabakumar-babu gave a wonderful explanation. They've decided to approach you for a contribution.'

'I see they want all I have. You are in their hands entirely. But no further. They have got what I have disowned. They will get nothing more from me.'

'Why so angry, Ma? They want to work for the country selflessly.'

'Never mind this discussion. You must have heard from your friends by now that you are free.'

'Yes, I have.'

'The selfless must have informed you that you can use the money put aside for your husband in any manner you wish to.'

'Yes, they have.'

'I've been told you are preparing to obtain a probate on the will. It must be true.'

'Yes, it is. Banku-babu is my solicitor.'

'He must have offered you additional hope and advice.'

Nila was silent.

'I will straighten out your Banku-babu if he dares to set foot on my territory. By force if not by law. I shall visit Peshawar on my way back here. My laboratory will be guarded day and night by four Sikh sentries. And before I leave, let me show you something— I am a woman from Punjab.'

Whipping the dagger out of the belt, she said, 'This dagger recognizes neither my daughter, nor her solicitor. I'm leaving its memory in your care. When I'm back, I'll tot up the accounts if I have to.'

11

The laboratory was surrounded by open land on all sides, to ensure that vibrations or sounds did not disturb the work. The silence helped Rebati concentrate, which was why he often came here at night to work.

The clock downstairs struck two. For a moment Rebati looked at the sky though the window, pondering on his subject.

Suddenly a shadow fell on the wall. He discovered Nila in the room, dressed in her nightclothes—a thin silk gown. Startled, he was about to leap off his chair when Nila settled herself on his lap, wrapping her arms around him. Rebati's body began to tremble, his chest rising and falling rapidly. Overcome with emotion, he said, 'Go away, go away from here.'

'Why?' she asked.

'I cannot bear this,' said Rebati, 'why did you have to come here?'

Tightening her arms around him, Nila said, 'But don't you love me?'

'I do, I do, I do,' answered Rebati. 'But go away from this room.'

Suddenly one of the Punjabi guards barged in. 'This is shameful, madam,' he rebuked Nila in Hindi. 'Please leave.'

Rebati had pressed the electric bell unconsciously.

'Don't betray our trust, babuji,' the Punjabi guard told him.

Pushing Nila away, Rebati rose to his feet. 'Please leave the room,' the guard repeated to Nila, 'or else I shall be compelled to follow my mistress's orders.'

In other words, he would force her to leave in humiliation. As she left, Nila said, 'Can you hear me, Sir Isaac Newton? You're invited home to tea tomorrow, precisely at 4.45. Can't you hear? Have you fainted?' Nila turned back to look at him.

'I heard,' came the choked reply.

Nila's flawless body was visible though her nightclothes like a sculptor's figure—Rebati could not help staring in enchantment. Nila left. Rebati remained, his head slumped on the desk. He could not have imagined such an astonishing turn of events. An electrical storm seemed to be raging in his arteries, racing about as lines of fire. Clenching his fists, Rebati kept telling himself that he would not go to tea the next day. He tried to take a hard vow, but the words would not escape his lips. On the blotter he wrote, I shall not go, I shall not go, I shall not go. Suddenly he spotted a deep red handkerchief on his desk, with the name embroidered in the corner: Nila. He held the handkerchief to his face, its scent suffusing his brain. An intoxication seized his body.

Nila returned. 'I forgot something,' she said.

The guard tried to stop her. 'Don't worry,' Nila said, 'I'm not here to steal anything. I only need a signature. We want you to be the president of the Awakening Club—you're a famous man.'

Shrinking, Rebati said, 'I know nothing about your club.'

'You don't need to. All you need to know is that Brajendra-babu is one of our patrons.'

'But I don't know Brajendra-babu.'

'It's enough to know that he is a director of the Metropolitan Bank. Come on, darling, it's just a signature, that's all.' Encircling his shoulder with one arm, she took his hand with the other. 'Sign.'

He signed, hypnotised.

As Nila was folding the piece of paper, the guard said, 'I have to take a look.'

'You won't understand it,' said Nila.

'I don't need to,' said the guard, snatching it out of her hand and ripping it up. 'Make your deeds elsewhere, not in here,' he said.

Rebati breathed a mental sigh of relief. 'Now let me take you home,' the guard told Nila, escorting her out.

He came back a little later. 'I keep all the doors locked,' he said. 'You must have let her in.'

Such suspicions, such effrontery! 'I didn't let her in,' Rebati said repeatedly.

'Then how did she get in?'

True. The scientist proceeded to investigate all the rooms. Finally he discovered that during the day someone had unlocked a large window which was normally kept locked and that looked out on the road.

The guard did not hold Rebati in high enough esteem to attribute any cunning to him. A foolish scholar—that was the extent of his abilities. Finally he slapped his forehead, muttering, 'Women! They're devils by nature.'

Rebati told himself repeatedly during the few remaining hours of darkness that he would not accept the invitation to tea.

The birds began to chirp. Rebati went home.

12

Rebati arrived precisely at 4.45. He had expected an intimate tea for two. Incapable of dressing fashionably, he was in a shirt and a dhoti, freshly laundered, with a neatly folded shawl slung over a shoulder. When he arrived he discovered a large gathering in the garden—a crowd of stylish people, none of whom he knew. Disappointed, he wished he could hide himself somewhere. But when he tried to sit down in a corner, everyone rose to their feet. 'This way, Dr Bhattacharya, your seat is here.'

They seated him on a high-backed velvet chair in the centre of the gathering. He realized that he was the target of all eyes. Nila garlanded him, putting a sandalwood mark on his forehead. Brajendra-babu proposed his name as the president of the Awakening Club. Banku-babu seconded the motion, and applause broke out. The litterateur Haridas-babu held forth on his international fame. 'Our Awakening Club will use the wind in the sails of Rebati-babu's fame to visit every port on the western ocean.'

'None of the metaphors must be omitted from the report,' whispered the organizers in the reporters' ears.

As each of the speakers rose to aver that 'at last Dr Bhattacharya has put the victorious mark of science on the brow of mother India', Rebati's chest swelled with pride. He saw himself established at the zenith of the sky over civilization. In his mind he protested against all the slurs he had heard people heap on the Awakening Club. When Haridas-babu said, 'An amulet named Rebati Bhattacharya is now being placed around the throat of this gathering as a talisman of protection, this should confirm how exalted out ambitions are,' Rebati felt the glory and responsibility of his image most keenly. He cast off his shell of tentativeness. Lowering their cigarettes, the women leant over his chair, saying with the sweetest of smiles, 'I'm sorry to bother you, but you simply must give me an autograph.'

Rebati felt as though he had been living in a dream all this time, but now the chrysalis had been shed and the butterfly had emerged.

The guests left one by one. 'You mustn't leave yet,' Nila told Rebati, her hand on his arm.

Someone poured an agonising wine into his veins.

Daylight was dwindling, with the green glow of twilight spreading amongst the vines.

They sat down together on a bench. Taking Rebati's hand in hers, Nila said, 'Being a man, why are you so afraid of women, Dr Bhattacharya?'

'Afraid?' said Rebati recklessly. 'Never!'

'Are you not afraid of my mother?'

'Why should I be afraid? I respect her.'

'And me?'

'Certainly I fear you.'

'That's good news. Ma has said she will never allow me to marry you. I will kill myself.'

'I will brook no opposition—we *shall* be married.'

Putting her head on his shoulder, Nila said, 'You have no idea how much I want you.'

Drawing her closer, Rebati said, 'No power on earth can take you away from me.'

'Caste?'

'To hell with it.'

'Then we must give notice to the registrar tomorrow.'
'Of course I shall.'
Rebati had begun to display a manly spirit.
Events raced towards culmination.
Sohini's grandmother began to display symptoms of paralysis. Death was imminent. She refused to let Sohini go till she died. Nila seized the opportunity with both hands—her frenzied passions had been roused.

The weight of Rebati's punditry had dulled the taste of his manliness. Nila was not enamoured enough of him. But marrying him was safe, for he was too weak to stop her from leading a dissolute life after her marriage. That was not all. The riches associated with the laboratory were considerable. Rebati's well-wishers claimed there was no one worthier of taking charge of the laboratory; Sohini would not let him go in any circumstances, concluded Nila's discerning friends.

Meanwhile, ignoring the condemnation of his associates, Rebati announced his appointment as president of the Awakening Club in the newspapers. When Nila asked, 'Are you afraid?' he would respond, 'I don't care.' He was determined not to allow the slightest doubt to persist over his masculine resolve. 'I exchange correspondence with Eddington,' he said. 'I shall invite him to address the club.' 'We are blessed,' responded the members.

Rebati's real work had stopped. His line of thought had snapped. His heart only waited for Nila to appear, to cover his eyes from the back, to sit on the arm of his chair and put her arm around his neck. He assured himself that the interruption was temporary, and that the broken flow would be resumed as soon as he had settled down in his head. But there were no imminent signs of his settling down. There wasn't even an iota of anxiety in Nila's mind about the world's suffering because Rebati's work was suffering. She considered it all a farce.

The net was tightening by the day. The Awakening Club clustered around him, turning him into a virile male. He did not mouth obscenities yet, but he laughed at others' expletives. Dr Bhattacharya had turned into an object of amusement for them.

At times Rebati was stung by jealousy. Nila lit her cigar directly from the one clamped between the bank director's teeth. It was beyond Rebati to imitate him. He felt dizzy if he inhaled cigar smoke but the sight made him feel even more sick in body and mind. And he could not but object to all the nudging and tugging that went on. Nila said, 'We have no great enchantment about our bodies. What does it matter to us anyway? The rare thing is love, which we cannot scatter everywhere.' And she grasped Rebati's hand. Whereupon Rebati considered the rest of them unworthy, for they were happy with the shell, without getting to the kernel.

The laboratory remained under watch day and night, while the interrupted work languished within. No one was to be seen inside.

13

Nila was sitting with her feet up on the drawing-room sofa, leaning against the cushions, while Rebati sat near her feet, holding a sheaf of foolscap paper covered in writing.

Shaking his head, Rebati said, 'The language is far too ornamental. I'll be embarrassed to read such extravagant prose.'

'As if you are a great connoisseur of language. This isn't your chemistry formula, so stop fussing and memorise it. Do you know it's been written by the novelist Pramadaranjan-babu?'

'It will be very difficult to memorise those long sentences and bombastic phrases.'

'As if they're very difficult. I've read them out to you so many times that even I have memorised them: "At this, the finest, most auspicious moment of my life, the Awakening Club has chosen to honour me with a wreath of the flowers embodying the wisdom of Amravati . . . " How grand! Don't worry, I'll be by your side, I'll prompt you.'

'I do not understand Bengali literature very well, but this entire thing seems to mock me. How much easier it would have been to say it my way, in English. Dear friends, allow me to offer you my heartiest thanks for the honour you have conferred upon me on the behalf the Awakening Club . . . etc. A couple of such sentences and . . .'

'You haven't a hope. Your Bengali will sound so entertaining— you know where it says "o ye young of Bengal, o pilots of the chariot of self-rule, o vanguard on the road of broken shackles" . . . Say what you will, none of this can work in any other language. Young Bengal will dance like charmed snakes when they hear such words from a scholar of science. There's plenty of time, I'll help you.'

Carrying his long, heavy body upstairs noisily, Brajendra Haldar, the bank manager dressed in western clothes, entered the room with crisp footsteps. 'No, this is intolerable,' he declared. 'Whenever I'm here I find you've appropriated Nila. You're like the barbed wire that keeps Nili apart from us, come rain, come shine.'

Intimidated, Rebati said, 'I had some special business today, so . . .'

'Of course you do, I've come with that very hope; you've invited the members to dinner tonight, so I dropped by with half an hour to spare before going on to office. And now I find your business has bound you to this very place. How strange! When he has no other work, he spends his leisure here, but when he does have work, it's with you. How do we working people compete with such limpets? Is it fair, Nili?'

'Dr Bhattacharya's problem is that he cannot state the truth,' said Nila. 'It is a lie that he is here on business. He is here because he cannot stay away—that is what you should be hearing and that is the truth. He has occupied all my hours with sheer insistence. That is his manliness. All of you have had to admit defeat to this yokel.'

'Very well, we shall have to flaunt our masculinity too in that case. The members of the Awakening Club will practise abduction of women from now on. The ancient ages will come back to life.'

'Very interesting,' observed Nila. 'Abducting a woman sounds much better than seeking her hand. But what is the method?'

'I can demonstrate,' said Haldar.

'Now?'

'Yes, now.'

He lifted Nila bodily from the sofa.

Shrieking with laughter, Nila wrapped her arms around his neck.

Rebati's face darkened. His problem was that he was not physically strong enough to either protest or follow suit. He was especially angry with Nila for indulging these uncivilized brutes.

'The car is waiting,' said Haldar. 'I'm taking you to Diamond Harbour. I shall return you to the evening dinner. I had work at the bank, but to hell with it. This will be my good deed—giving Dr Bhattacharya the opportunity to work in peace and quiet. It is best to take away a disturbing element like you. He will thank me for it.'

Rebati observed that Nila offered no resistance, making no attempt to extricate herself. On the contrary, she remained in Haldar's arms quite comfortably, keeping her arms wrapped around his neck in quite a besotted manner. As she left, she said, 'Don't worry, Mr Scientist, this is merely a rehearsal of abduction. I am not going to Lanka, I shall be back at your feast.'

Rebati ripped up the speech. His pride in his own erudition proved puny in comparison to Haldar's forearm and forthright assertion of his rights.

The dinner that night was at a renowned restaurant. The host was Rebati Bhattacharya himself, with Nila as his honoured companion. A famous performer from the cinema was to sing. Bankubihari rose to his feet to propose a toast, with praises being sung to Rebati and, by extension, to Nila. The young women smoked furiously to prove that they weren't entirely feminine. The middle-aged ones donned masks of youth and engaged in a frenzied race to outdo their younger counterparts with signals and gestures and laughter and nudges.

Suddenly, Sohini entered. The entire room fell silent. Turning to Rebati, Sohini said, 'I don't recognize you. Dr Bhattacharya, isn't it? You asked for money to meet expenses, which I sent last Friday—now I can clearly see you haven't run short. You'd better come with me now. I shall reconcile the laboratory equipment with the list tonight.'

'You don't trust me?'

'I did until now. But if you have any sense of shame, don't mention trust again.'

Rebati made to rise, but Nila tugged at his shirt and made him sit down again. 'He has invited his friends tonight. He will join you once everyone has left.'

There was a cruel blow in there. Sir Isaac was her mother's favourite. There was no one more trustworthy, which was why he had been chosen over everyone else to take charge of the laboratory. To deepen the cut, she said, 'Do you know, Ma? There are sixty-five guests tonight—not all of them could fit in here, there's another group in the next room. Can't you hear them laughing? Twenty-five rupees per head, and you have to pay for drinks whether everyone drinks or not. The fine for empty glasses isn't a small one. Anyone else would have been deflated but the bank manager is astonished by his generosity. Do you know how much the cinema singer is charging? Four hundred rupees for one night.'

Rebati's heart fluttered like a headless chicken; he sat in wan silence.

'What are the celebrations for?' asked Sohini.

'Don't you know? Associated Press has put it out already. He has become the president of the Awakening Club, this feast is in commemoration. He will pay the life membership fee of six hundred rupees later at his convenience.'

'It may not be convenient soon.'

A steamroller ran through Rebati's head.

'So you cannot leave now?' Sohini asked him.

Rebati looked at Nila. Her sly barb aroused his male ego. 'How can I, with the invitees all . . .'

'Very well, I shall wait here till then,' declared Sohini. 'Man the door, Nasirulla.'

'That's impossible, Ma,' said Nila. 'We have something confidential to discuss, it would be best for you not to be present.'

'Look, Nila, you've barely begun to play your game of cunning, you cannot beat me at it yet. Do you think I do not know what you have to discuss? Let me tell you that I am the one who must be present at those discussions.'

'What have you heard?' asked Nila. 'From whom?'

'There are ways to ferret out information from a sack of money like a snake from its hole. You want to examine the documents with a team of three lawyers to find out whether there are chinks in the armour around the laboratory funds. Isn't that right, Nilu?'

'I don't mind admitting the truth,' said Nila. 'It would be unnatural for a daughter not to get a share of her father's wealth. That's why everyone suspects . . .'

Sohini stood up. 'There's a deeper reason for doubt. Who is your father? Whose wealth do you seek a share of? Aren't you ashamed to claim you are the daughter of a man like him?'

Nila leapt up. 'What are you saying, Ma?'

'The truth. Nothing was hidden from him, he knew everything. He got all that he had to from me, and he will get it today too. He didn't care for anything else.'

'Your claim is not proof,' said Barrister Ghosh.

'He knew that. He has disclosed everything in a registered document.'

'It's getting late, Banku. Let's go.'

The sixty-five guests left following the declaration by the woman lately returned from Peshawar.

Chowdhury arrived, suitcase in hand. 'Your telegram brought me back,' he said. 'What is it, Rebi my baby, why is your face so pale? Where's the boy's feeding bottle?'

Pointing at Nila, Sohini said, 'There's the one who will provide it.'

'Are you starting a milk business, my girl?'

'She has started a business to snare milkmen, there's her prey.'

'What, our Rebi?'

'This time my daughter has saved the laboratory. I didn't recognize his true colours, but my daughter concluded correctly that I had set up a cowshed in the laboratory—the whole thing would have been buried in a heap of dung.'

'Since you have discovered this creature, my girl, you must take charge of him. He has everything besides intelligence, but if you stay by his side the absence won't be obvious. It's easier to make foolish men jump through the hoops.'

'Well, my dear Sir Isaac Newton, would you like to withdraw the notice from the registry office?'

'Over my dead body,' declared Rebati boldly.

'It will be an inauspicious marriage then.'

'Certainly.'

'But stay away from the laboratory,' said Sohini.

'Nilu, my girl, he is foolish but not incapable,' said the professor. 'Once he has regained his senses, you will not have to worry about his livelihood.'

'You must get yourself some decent clothes then, Sir Isaac, or else I'll have to hide my face in your presence.'

Suddenly another shadow fell on the wall. Rebati's aunt had appeared. 'Come along, Rebi,' she said.

Rebati followed his aunt out meekly, without a single backward glance.

STAY WITH ME, MY FRIEND, STAY

বন্ধু রহো রহো সঙ্গে

Stay with me, my friend, stay
On this grey morning of rain
Were you in my dreams
That friendless night?
The hours go waste, my friend
Through this rain
In this plaintive wind
Talk to my heart
Put your hand in mine
Stay with me
My friend, stay

Chandalika

চণ্ডালিকা

A PLAY

Introduction

The story of this one-act play has been taken from the brief account of Shardulakarna Avadana in *Buddhist Literature of Nepal*, edited by Rajendra Mitra.

The story is set in Sravasti. Lord Buddha was living abroad in Anathpinda's garden. His favourite disciple Ananda, on his way back after a meal at a citizen's home, felt thirsty. Spotting the daughter of a Chandala, whose name was Prakriti, drawing water from a well, he asked her for some water, which she gave him. The young woman was mesmerized by his beauty. Having no other way of getting him as her own, she turned to her mother for help. Her mother knew magic. Smearing cowdung on the courtyard, Prakriti's mother prepared an altar, lit a fire in it and, chanting her spell, cast 108 flowers into the flames, one by one. Ananda could not resist the effect of this magic. He arrived at the house at night. When he took a seat on the altar, Prakriti proceeded to prepare a bed for him. But Ananda was struck by remorse. Seeking deliverance from god, he began to weep.

Learning of his disciple's plight through supernatural means, the Buddha uttered a chant. The Chandala woman's hypnotic powers were weakened and Ananda returned to his monastery.

ACT ONE, SCENE ONE

MOTHER: Prakriti! Prakriti! Where *is* she? I wonder what's happened to the girl. She's hardly ever home.

PRAKRITI: Here I am, Ma, right here.

MOTHER: Where?

PRAKRITI: Here, by the well.

MOTHER: You astonish me. It's past noon, just look at the scorching sun, the earth's roasting, you can't set foot on the ground. We drew water long ago in the morning. The neighbourhood women have all gone home with their pitchers. There, see the crows are gasping on the amloki branches. And here you are, soaking in the sun at the height of summer without rhyme or reason. I've heard from the Puranas that Uma chose to leave home so that she could burn under the sun and pray. You too?

PRAKRITI: Yes, Ma, I am indeed praying.

MOTHER: Really? For whom?

PRAKRITI: *For the one who called me out*
The one who called, the one who called
Who made this mute girl speak
The one who knows my name
Let his name stay in my heart

MOTHER: Call? What call?

PRAKRITI: He has sung in my heart, 'Give me water'.

MOTHER: Accursed fate! So he told you, 'Give me water.' Who was it? Someone from our caste?

PRAKRITI: That is what he said, he is from our own caste.

MOTHER: You didn't hide anything, did you? You did tell him you're a Chandala's daughter?

PRAKRITI: I did. That's a lie, he said. What if you were to name the dark monsoon clouds Chandala? That wouldn't change their caste, that wouldn't make their water any less precious, he said. Don't debase yourself, he said. Demeaning oneself is a sin, even more than killing oneself is.

MOTHER: What's all this you're saying? Is this something you remember from your previous life?

PRAKRITI: This is something from my new life.

MOTHER: You make me laugh. A new life! When exactly did you get one?

PRAKRITI: The clock at the palace had just struck two that day, the sun was blinding. I was bathing the motherless calf at the well. Suddenly a Buddhist monk appeared in front of me in his yellow robe. Give me water, he said. My heart leapt into my mouth. Trembling, I greeted him from a distance. He seemed to be made of the light at dawn. I am the daughter of a Chandala, I told him, the water in this well is impure. He said, I am a human being, just as you are; any water is holy water if it cools the one who is burning, comforts the one who is parched. I was hearing this for the first time. Cupping my hands, I gave him water, a man whose feet I was terrified of touching.

MOTHER: Such impudence, you foolish girl. You will have to pay for this madness. Are you not aware of the caste you have been born into?

PRAKRITI: He took only a single drink of water from my hands, but it became infinite. The seven oceans merged into the water, my caste was drowned, my birth was washed away.

MOTHER: Even your words have changed. You talk under a spell. Do you even understand what you are saying?

PRAKRITI: Was there no water anywhere else in Sravastinagar, Ma? Why did he have to visit this particular well? This is what I call the turn of a new life. He came to bestow on me the mantle of one who quenches thirst. It was this very act of virtue that he was seeking to perform. The water that fulfilled his mission could not have been found anywhere else, not in any holy place. He said Janki had bathed in this same water at the onset of her exile in the forest. Guhak the Chandala had drawn the water. My heart has been dancing since then. I hear his deep voice constantly—give me water, give me water.

> Give me water, give me water,
> Do I have the means?
> Seeing the lowering clouds
> The bird came flying
> Parched, overwhelmed
>
> Give me water, give me water
>
> Lost underground
> The water source
> Imprisoned
> In the dark
> Whose deep voice
> Struck a hole in
> The black paved floor?
>
> Give me water, give me water

MOTHER: I don't know, my dear, I don't like all this. I don't understand the spells they weave, and today I don't understand what you say. Tomorrow I may not even recognize you. This black magic of theirs gives people a new life.

PRAKRITI: You did not recognize me all this time. The one who did will help you now. That is why I wait. The clock strikes the afternoon hours at the palace gates, the women draw water and take it home, the hawk circles alone in the distant sky, I wait with my pitcher by the well.

MOTHER: For whom?

PRAKRITI: For the traveller.

MOTHER: Which traveller do you think will ever come to you, mad girl?

PRAKRITI: Just the one traveller, Ma, just that one. In him lives every traveller on every path in the world. The days keep passing, but he has not returned. He said nothing, but still he gave his word, why did he not keep it? My heart has turned into a desert, a blistering wind blows through it, and it cannot draw water anymore. No one has come to ask for water.

Thirsty my eyes
And thirst in my heart
I am a rainless summer day
The heat burns my soul
A storm in the fiery wind
Sends my heart far away
The veil flies off
The flower that lit up the garden
Is now dry and blackened
Who dammed the waterfall,
Trapped by the blazing heat
At suffering's peak?

MOTHER: I cannot understand a word of what you're saying today, I wish I knew what trance you're in. What do you want, tell me plainly.

PRAKRITI: I want him. He arrived from nowhere to tell me that what I offer is also acceptable in the world that god has created—it was such a wonder. I too can serve—picking this truth out of the dust, he clasped it to his breast, clasped this thorny flower.

MOTHER: Remember, Prakriti, what they say is only for the ears, not for practical use. No iron pick in the world can break through the barriers of sludge around the caste that you were born into because of ill-fate. You are impure, don't spread your impurity anywhere, stay just where you are, be cautious. You are a mistake anywhere outside this space.

PRAKRITI: *The flower says I'm blessed on earth*
My god, I live to serve you
Please let me forget
I was born in the dirt
For my heart is clean
Lower your eyes
My petals tremble
Let me feel your feet
Turn the dust to divine wealth
I bow to the earth
For your sake

MOTHER: I understand some of the things you're saying, my dear.

You are a woman, to serve is worship for you, to serve is to rule. Only women can overcome their caste in an instant. If only fate drew the curtain aside, they would all be revealed as queens. You did get the opportunity when the prince had appeared by this very well when he was out hunting. Do you remember?

PRAKRITI: Yes, I do.

MOTHER: Why did you not go to the palace? Your beauty made him forget everything.

PRAKRITI: Of course he forgot. He forgot that I am a human. He was out hunting beasts, what he saw was a beast whom he wanted to bind with golden chains.

MOTHER: But still he noticed your appearance, even if you were a quarry. But the monk, did he identify you as a woman?

PRAKRITI: You don't understand. You'll never understand. He's the first one to have identified me after all these years. It is a miracle.

> Through your eyes I see the truth
> You made me what I am
> I bow to you, I bow to you
> I bow to you again
> I am a young sunbeam
> I am a ray of pure light
> I am the first benedictory rain
> From dark and tender clouds
> I bow to you, I bow to you
> I bow to you again

I want him, Ma. I want him so much. I want to lay at his feet all the worshipping I shall do in this life. He will not be discomfited. Let people see my daring. I want to say proudly, I shall serve you, for the alternative is to languish as a maid in chains at the feet of everyone else in the world.

MOTHER: Do not be angry without reason, my dear. You have been born a slave. Who can change god's will?

PRAKRITI: Shame on you, Ma. I am telling you again, don't forget, don't heap such calumny on yourself—it is a sin, a sin.

Slaves are born in royal families in every house. I am no slave. Chandalas are born to Brahmins in every land, I am no Chandala.

MOTHER: I do not have the words to argue with you. Very well, I shall go to him myself. I shall plead with him—since you accept food from everyone, come to my house for nothing but a drink of water.

PRAKRITI: *I shan't call you where the world can hear*
If I can I'll call you in your heart
Deep down in my breast I ache to give
But I cannot find the one who will take
Who will unite these two?
Will my pain never merge with his?
Won't the Ganga flow into the black Yamuna?
The music plays on its own
It comes without being asked
It leaves with a word of hope

When the earth is cracked from the drought, what use is a single pot of water, Ma? Will the clouds not come along the sky on their own?

MOTHER: Why say all this? The clouds will either come on their own, or not at all. They don't care whether the earth has turned arid. All we can do is gaze at the sky.

PRAKRITI: Impossible. I shall not sit here waiting. You know magic, use it so that I can draw him into my arms.

MOTHER: Do you know what you're saying, you witch! You're getting more and more brazen! Playing with fire. Do you think these are ordinary people? How can I work my magic on them? My heart trembles at the thought.

PRAKRITI: But you dared to think of casting a spell on the prince.

MOTHER: I am not afraid of the king, he can have me executed. But these people do nothing to retaliate.

PRAKRITI: I don't fear anything other than falling again, forgetting myself again, entering the dark cell again. It's a fate worse than death. Is it not wondrous that I dare to insist on his return? It is he who has wrought this miracle. Will more miracles not take place? Will he not come to me and sit by my side?

MOTHER: I may be able to get him here, but can you pay the price? You will have nothing left.

PRAKRITI: Yes, I shall have nothing left. None of my debts from all my lifetimes shall remain—I shall pay them all back at once and be saved. That is why I want him. I shall have nothing left. My vigil over all my existences over the ages will be fulfilled in this single lifetime—my heart tells me this incessantly. I shall be fulfilled. That is why I heard those wonderful words—give me water. Today I learnt that I too can give. People had forced me to forget this. I shall give, I shall, it is to give everything that I wait for him.

MOTHER: Don't you believe in dharma?

PRAKRITI: How can I say? I believe in the one who believes in me. The dharma that humiliates is a lie. People have blindfolded me, gagged me, to make me submit to this dharma. But now I am forbidden from following it. I am not afraid anymore. Weave your magic, bring the monk to the Chandala's daughter. I shall honour him—the kind of honour that no one else can give him.

> I know him and him alone
> The one who makes me his
> I only claim a gift from him
> Who stakes a claim to me
> He knows me for who I am
> And thus he makes me know him
> The same lamp lights the path
> To his heart and to mine
> Some do hide in their inner darkness
> I lose myself in them
> Touched by the magic wand
> The shroud of sleep is cast aside
> My eyes are racing towards
> His face which lights the world

MOTHER: Do you not fear being cursed?

PRAKRITI: I have been cursed since birth. The poison of one curse will neutralize the venom of another. I shan't listen to any objections, Ma, I shan't. Begin your magic. I cannot bear to wait.

MOTHER: Very well, tell me his name.

PRAKRITI: His name is Ananda.

MOTHER: Ananda? The Buddha's disciple?

PRAKRITI: Yes, that very same monk.

MOTHER: You're the jewel of my heart, the apple of my eyes. It's only for you that I am sinning so grievously.

PRAKRITI: What sin! What's wrong with bringing me the one who draws everyone to himself?

MOTHER: They draw people to themselves with their piety. We do it with magic, the technique we use to trap animals. We churn the earth and bring up slime.

PRAKRITI: Good, for there can be no purification without this.

MOTHER: My lord, you are a saint, your power to forgive is far greater than my power to sin. I am about to dishonour you, my lord, but accept my reverence still.

PRAKRITI: What are you afraid of, Ma? The magic is mine, you are the instrument. If my pain draws him here, and if that is a crime, then I *shall* commit a crime, I shall. I reject a verdict that offers only punishment and no comfort.

> *Blame me if you will, blame me*
> *Let the faded blossom in the dust*
> *Be ground beneath your feet*
> *Empty out the basket of sins*
> *With your hands, and then*
> *Fill it to the brim again*
> *With your compassion*
> *You are noble, I am base*
> *I shall trap you*
> *With my sin*
> *Your greatness*
> *Will cleanse my taint*
> *Thread my flaws with your forgiveness*
> *And wear them round your neck*

MOTHER: You have great courage, Prakriti.

Chandalika

PRAKRITI: My courage! Think of the power of his courage. How easily he said to me what no one else could—give me water. Such a short statement but so spirited. It lit up my entire existence. It pushed away the heavy weight that has always burdened my heart. It allowed my feelings to surge. Your fears are misplaced, for you haven't seen him, you know. He begged for alms all morning at Sravastinagar; then he came across the fields and the scorched earth, along the river, with a searing sun overhead. For what? Just to tell a girl no better than me—give me water. I shall die. From where did such compassion, such love, rain on me? On the coward who is the most unworthy of them all? What else have I to fear? Give me water. The same water that is now overflowing my life, I must give it if I am to survive. Give me water. In an instant I knew I have water to give, an unending supply but whom shall I tell this? And so I call out to him all the time. No matter if he cannot hear, cast your spell. He can bear it, he can.

MOTHER: Who are those people in yellow robes walking along the path beyond the field, Prakriti?

PRAKRITI: You're right, they're monks from the Buddhist monastery. Can't you hear them chanting?

MONKS: *The Buddha is an ocean of compassion*
Perfect, purest, the eye of knowledge
Slayer of human sin and defilement
I adore him with the greatest devotion

PRAKRITI: There he is, Ma, leading them. He didn't even glance at this well. He could have said once more, give me water. I had assumed he would not be able to forsake me, am I not his own creation, after all. (Slumping to the ground and knocking her forehead on it.) This earth, this earth, only this earth is yours. Wretched girl, who made you bloom in the light for a moment? Can this be called compassion? I had to return to this same earth and this is where I must remain all my life, beneath the feet of everyone who walks along this road.

MOTHER: Forget this, my dear, forget all this. They're shattering your short-lived dream—let them, let them. If it cannot last, the sooner it goes the better.

PRAKRITI: This constant wanting, this continuous humiliation, this bird that thrashes about and dies in the cage in my heart, is this what a dream is? This feeling that grips every artery, every vein, unrelentingly, is this a dream? And those people there, who have no bonds, no joys or sorrows, no worldly burden—floating away like autumn clouds—are they the only ones who are awake, who are not in a dream?

MOTHER: I cannot bear to see you suffer, Prakriti. Get up. I *shall* bring him with my magic. Along this same dusty path. I shall break the pride with which he says, 'I want nothing.' He will be forced to come here in desperation, saying, 'I want, I want.'

PRAKRITI: Your magic goes back to the ancient times when the first creatures appeared. Their magic is undeveloped, it was created just the other day. They cannot contend with you. Your incantations will unravel theirs. He has no choice but to lose. He must love.

MOTHER: Where are they going?

PRAKRITI: All I know is that they go, but they don't go anywhere. The rains will come in a while, and then their four months of rituals will follow. They will be on the move again, I don't know where. This is what they call wakefulness.

MOTHER: Then what magic are you talking of, you mad girl? They're going so far away, how will I bring him back from such a distance?

PRAKRITI: You must get him back from wherever he goes, your magic knows no distance.

> *Let him go to the sea if he must*
> *Let him return, return, return to me*
> *I shall keep a seat for him*
> *In my heart and*
> *Moisten his road of dirt with my tears*
> *Let him go to the mountain if he must*
> *Let him return, return to me*
> *I shall hide in a cave*
> *And call out to him*
> *My dream will envelop his wakefulness*

If he is not compassionate with me, I shall not show him pity. Cast your cruellest spell—let it coil itself around his heart. Where can he escape from me, how can he get away?

MOTHER: Don't fret. It's not beyond me. I will give you the mirror of illusions. Dance with it in your hand. His reflection will appear in it. In that mirror you will see what has become of him, how far he has travelled in your direction.

PRAKRITI: There, the clouds are gathering in the west, storm clouds. Your spell will work, Ma, it will. Their austere endeavours will be blown away like dry leaves. The lights will go out. The way forward will be hidden. Like the bird which appears in the darkened courtyard, its nest destroyed by the hurricane of the night, he too will wander around to eventually arrive at my door. My heart is beating faster, lightning is flashing in my head, I cannot see the shore of the sea where the waves are foaming.

MOTHER: There's still time to think it over. You won't stop in fear midway? Will you be patient? When the spell is at its height, I will find it next to impossible to contain it. Everything that's combustible will be burnt to ashes before the fire goes out, remember that.

PRAKRITI: Whom do you fear for? Do you think he is a mere mortal? Nothing can affect him—let him come all the way, let him walk though the flames. In my mind's eyes I can see the apocalyptic night, the storm of consummation, the joy of destruction.

> *Tattoo of drumbeats in the heart*
> *Dense clouds with furrowed brows*
> *The forests are enthralled*
> *Trees swaying in their passion*
> *Who is this in my dream of a tryst?*
> *Resounding with incessant rain*
> *The night terrified by thunder*
> *Jasmine creepers shake the leaves*
> *With a plaintive rustle*
> *The groves fear the crickets' buzz*

SCENE TWO

PRAKRITI: My heart will break. I shall not look in the mirror, I cannot. Such a tempest of sorrow. Will the giant tree crumple to the ground and roll in the dust? Will its glory, once reaching for the stars, be destroyed?

MOTHER: Even now I can try to withdraw my spell if you tell me to. Let my guts be wrenched apart, let my life end, even that is all right if it means saving this noble soul.

PRAKRITI: That's best then, Ma, let your magic be. No need. No no no no ... How long can the distance be, after all. Let him come, let him come all the way, here to my breast. I shall take away all his sorrows by giving him every last thing in my world. The traveller will arrive late at night, I shall light a lamp for him with all the agony in my heart. All that is sweet flows deep within me, he will be cleansed in those waters. He, who is exhausted, burning, wounded. Once more he will say, give me water—the water of the ocean in my heart. This day will come. Let your magic go on, let it go on.

> With my sorrows I shall erase yours
> Bathe you in the deep waters of pain
> I shall set my world on fire
> Cleanse the stains of infatuation
> Lay my gift of death at your feet

MOTHER: I didn't realize it would take so much time, my dear. My spell is about to end. My heart is in my mouth.

PRAKRITI: Don't be afraid, Ma, bear it a little longer. Just a little. It won't be long now.

MOTHER: The rains are here, their four-month period is beginning.

PRAKRITI: They have gone to the Goshir monastery in Vaishali.

MOTHER: How cruel you are. That is so far away.

PRAKRITI: Not all that far. Seven days from here. A fortnight has passed. Finally it seems that the throne is tottering, that he is coming, what lies in the remote distance, across hundreds of thousands of miles, beyond the sun and the moon, as far from my grasp as infinity itself, is coming to me. He is coming, and my heart is quaking.

MOTHER: I have completed my incantation. It is powerful enough to have summoned the king of the gods but still he is not here. This is a battle unto death. What did you see in the mirror?

PRAKRITI: At first I saw the sky covered in fog, like the waxen face of a god fatigued by his battle against the demon. Flames were visible through gaps in the fog. And then the mist was shred like a bouquet of flowers coming apart—the sky turned red like a swollen pustule about to burst. The day passed. The next day I saw a background of thick black clouds and forked lightning, while he stood in front, a fire raging around him. My blood ran cold. I was about to run to you and ask for the spell to be turned off. I found you sunk in a trance, turned to stone, breathing heavily, lost to the world. It seemed there was a fire within you too. The flames with which he had shielded himself were being attacked by the snorting serpent of fire inside you, a duel was underway. When I looked in the mirror later, I found that the light had been put out—all I saw was darkness, nothing but darkness, the form of endless darkness.

MOTHER: How did these sights not kill you? This is what struck at my heart too. I thought I would be able to bear it no longer.

PRAKRITI: The suffering I saw was not his alone, it was mine too. It was ours. A fiery heat had melted the copper and the gold into a single mass.

MOTHER: Did you not feel any fear?

PRAKRITI: What I felt was so much greater than fear. I thought I had discovered that the god of creation is more dreadful than the god of destruction. He was whipping the fire to bend it to his will, and the flames kept roaring and snarling. What was that at his feet in the container made of seven metals—was it life or was it death? A joy began to rise within me. What do I call it? The immense, dispassionate sensation of creating something new. No fear, no worry, no compassion, no suffering; only destruction, burning, melting, sparks flying everywhere. I could not stay still, my body and my heart began to dance like the flames themselves.

> *Shiva, destroyer, dreaded one,*
> *God of the apocalypse*
> *Let your locks spew fire*
> *Let the animate and inanimate world*
> *Be stricken by your stinging*
> *Draw your bow*

MOTHER: And what did your monk look like?

PRAKRITI: I saw his steadfast eyes gazing into the distance, like stars in the twilight sky. I wished I could go away from myself, go a million miles away.

MOTHER: Could he see you while you danced in front of the mirror?

PRAKRITI: Oh shame, how mortified I was. His eyes reddened with anger every now and then, as though he was about to curse me. The next moment he ground out the embers of rage beneath his feet. Eventually I saw his fury return, shaking and striking at the core.

MOTHER: And you could bear all this?

PRAKRITI: I was astounded. Here I am, this girl, your daughter, no one knows who she is and yet his suffering and her suffering are the same today. Which fire of creation can enable this? Who would have thought it possible?

MOTHER: When will this turmoil cease?

PRAKRITI: Not till my suffering is quelled. I *shall* make him suffer until then. How will he be released if I am not?

MOTHER: When did you last look in your mirror?

PRAKRITI: Last evening. He emerged from the main gate of Vaishali a few days ago, in the dead of night. Possibly in secret, without telling the other monks. After that I caught glimpses of him. Sometimes crossing the river on the ferry; on a remote mountain; traversing the fields alone in the evening. I saw him in the darkness too, late at night, on a forest trail. With every passing day the trance he is in grows stronger, he is on his way without regard for obstacles, having ended all conflict with himself. He looks overwhelmed, there is a languor in his body, as though his eyes alight on nothing. There is no truth, there are no lies; only a blind objective, devoid of thought, meaningless.

MOTHER: Can you surmise where he is today?

PRAKRITI: Last evening I saw him in the village of Paatol by the river Upli. The currents are raging under fresh rains, an ancient peepal tree stands near the steps leading into the water, fireflies are flickering on the branches, the paved bed beneath the tree is moss-ridden—that is where he came to an abrupt halt. It is a familiar spot; I've been told that the Buddha had advised King Suprabhas here once. He sat down, covering his face with his hands, perhaps the trance was broken. I threw the mirror away at once, for I was afraid of what I might see. An entire day has passed since then, I have not tried to find out, I live in hope, I give up hope . . . that is how I wait. Now the night is closing in. The sentry is calling out on the road, the first hour of darkness has passed. There is no more time, no more time, Ma, don't fail me tonight. Pour all your power into your spell.

MOTHER: I cannot do anymore, my dear. My spell is weakening, my heart and body are numb.

PRAKRITI: You must not be weak now. Maybe he is looking back the way he came, about to retrace his steps. It is the final pull—the rope may not hold. Perhaps he will leave the world I occupy in this life, he will never be within my reach again. It will be my turn to be in a trance then, taking up once more the illusory form of the Chandala girl. I shan't be able to bear this lie. I beg of you, Ma, make one last attempt with all your power. Begin your earth magic now, shake the gratified heaven of the pious.

I am a daughter of your soil
Mother earth
Then why deprive me
Of human life
You are pure, I know

> My sacred birthplace
> A daughter am I, blessed
> The piety of life is in me
> For which heaven's sake
> Do they demean you?
> On your breast I'll stay
> I am still yours
> Close to you
> Give me your power to bewitch
> To steal the heart

MOTHER: Have you made all the preparations as I asked you to?

PRAKRITI: I have. It was the second night in the fortnight of the full moon yesterday, I bathed in the holy river. Here, you can see the circles I have drawn in the courtyard with rice grains and pomegranate flowers and vermilion and seven precious stones. I have planted yellow flags, arranged the garlands and sandalwood paste on the plate, lit the lamps. I have dressed in garments the colour of paddy seeds, my scarf is the colour of the magnolia. On a seat on the eastern side I have meditated all night on his form. On my left hand I have put on a rakhi made of sixteen strands of sixteen golden threads.

MOTHER: Very well. Then perform your welcome dance in a circle. I shall chant my spell near the altar beneath the tree.

PRAKRITI: Come to my unopened blossoms
        With the scent of nectar
        Come to my unknown darkness
        On a glorious night
        My shell is of no value
        Be my freedom in a pearl
        Come as music
        To all my muted strings
        Come as a call to the rising sun
        Come as the end to eternal night
        Come as a smiling evening star
        Come as flowing tears of dew
        Mark the dawn with the vermilion
        Of your beams

MOTHER: Now look in your mirror, Prakriti. Can you see a dark shadow on the altar? My heart is breaking, I cannot do this anymore. Check the mirror—how much longer?

PRAKRITI: No, I shan't look, I shan't. I shall listen, inside my heart, within my meditation. And then I will look up, in case he shows himself. Bear this a little longer, Ma. He will show himself, surely he will. Here comes the storm, the storm signalling his arrival, the earth is trembling beneath his footsteps, the heart is quaking.

MOTHER: It heralds a curse on you, wretched girl. I'm about to die, my veins are bursting.

PRAKRITI: Not a curse, not a curse, it is my transformation that it heralds. The front gates of death are opening under the hammering of the thunder. The doors have been shattered, the walls have been demolished, all the lies in this life of mine have been destroyed. My mind trembles in fear, my heart sways in happiness. Oh my destruction, oh my everything, you are here. I shall place you at the pinnacle of all my humiliation, I shall craft a throne for you with my shame, with my fear, with my joy.

MOTHER: My final hour is at hand. I cannot go on. Look in your mirror quickly.

PRAKRITI: I am afraid, Ma. His journey is about to end but after that? What lies ahead? Only me, nothing else. Will the cruel suffering of all this time be mitigated by so little? Just me? What was this long, arduous journey for? Where does it end? Only with me.

> *Where does the road end, where?*
> *What lies there?*
> *Where do desire and worship meet?*
> *Waves of tears rise and fall*
> *Deep darkness ahead*
> *Where is the shore?*
> *I tell myself today*
> *Thirst cannot be quenched*
> *By the search for the mirage*
> *Fear strikes at my heart*
> *Rudderless, its sails ripped,*
> *Pain floats into the unknown*

MOTHER: Have pity on me, my heartless daughter, I cannot endure anymore. Look in the mirror at once.

PRAKRITI: (looking into the mirror and flinging it away) Oh, Ma, stop stop stop stop, take your spell back. Now, this instant! What have you done, you demoness, what have you done, why didn't you die! What was this I saw! Where is my bright, radiant, pure and unsullied light from a distant heaven? How dull, how tired, what an enormous burden of defeat has arrived at my door. I hang my head in shame. Clear all this, clear everything. (Smashing the apparatus for the magic spell with her feet.) If you are not the daughter of a Chandala, do not insult the hero. Hail, hail to him.

(Ananda enters)

You have come to rescue me, my lord, that is why you suffered so, forgive me, forgive me. Destroy all this pain with a single blow from your feet. I have dragged you down to earth, for how else will you raise me to your holy realm? There is grime on your feet, pure one, but it shall not go waste. My unreal shroud will fall at your feet and wipe off all the dust. Hail, hail to you, hail to you.

MOTHER: Hail, my lord. I lay both my sins and my life at your feet, my days end here on the shore of your compassion.

(Dies)

ANANDA: *The Buddha is an ocean of compassion*
Perfect, purest, the eye of knowledge
Slayer of human sin and defilement
I adore him with the greatest devotion

DO YOU MEAN WE'LL FORGET THOSE OLD DAYS
ভুলবে সেই দিনের কথা

Do you mean we'll forget those old days
When our eyes met, when our hearts did talk
Come back now into my heart, my friend
We'll talk of joys and sorrows, calm our souls
We picked flowers at dawn, shared a swing
Played our pipes and sang beneath the trees
Thrown apart, we lost each other, but now
We've met again, so join my heart, my friend